INTRODUCING DISCWORLD

The Discworld series is a continuous history of a world not totally unlike our own, except that it is a flat disc carried on the backs of four elephants astride a giant turtle floating through space, and that it is peopled by, among others, wizards, dwarves, policemen, thieves, beggars, vampires and witches. Within the history of Discworld there are many individual stories, which can be read in any order, but reading them in sequence can increase your enjoyment through the accumulation of all the fine detail that contributes to the teeming imaginative complexity of this brilliantly conceived world.

BOOKS BY TERRY PRATCHETT

The Discworld® series

——————— **Other books about Discworld** ———————

TURTLE RECALL: THE DISCWORLD COMPANION ... SO FAR
(with Stephen Briggs)

NANNY OGG'S COOKBOOK
(with Stephen Briggs, Tina Hannan and Paul Kidby)

THE PRATCHETT PORTFOLIO
(with Paul Kidby)

THE DISCWORLD ALMANAK
(with Bernard Pearson)

THE UNSEEN UNIVERSITY CUT-OUT BOOK
(with Alan Batley and Bernard Pearson)

WHERE'S MY COW?
(illustrated by Melvyn Grant)

THE ART OF DISCWORLD
(with Paul Kidby)

THE WIT AND WISDOM OF DISCWORLD
(compiled by Stephen Briggs)

THE FOLKLORE OF DISCWORLD
(with Jacqueline Simpson)

THE WORLD OF POO
(with the Discworld Emporium)

MRS BRADSHAW'S HANDBOOK
(with the Discworld Emporium)

THE COMPLEAT ANKH-MORPORK
(with the Discworld Emporium)

THE STREETS OF ANKH-MORPORK
(with Stephen Briggs, painted by Stephen Player)

THE DISCWORLD MAPP
(with Stephen Briggs, painted by Stephen Player)

A TOURIST GUIDE TO LANCRE – A DISCWORLD MAPP
(with Stephen Briggs, illustrated by Paul Kidby)

DEATH'S DOMAIN (with Paul Kidby)

THE DISCWORLD ATLAS
(with the Discworld Emporium)

A complete list of Terry Pratchett ebooks and audio books as well as other books based on the Discworld series – illustrated screenplays, graphic novels, comics and plays – can be found on
www.terrypratchett.co.uk

Non-Discworld books

THE DARK SIDE OF THE SUN

STRATA

THE UNADULTERATED CAT (illustrated by Gray Jolliffe)

GOOD OMENS (with Neil Gaiman)

Shorter Writing

A BLINK OF THE SCREEN

A SLIP OF THE KEYBOARD

SHAKING HANDS WITH DEATH

With Stephen Baxter

THE LONG EARTH

THE LONG WAR

THE LONG MARS

THE LONG UTOPIA

Non-Discworld novels for young adults

THE CARPET PEOPLE

TRUCKERS

DIGGERS

WINGS

ONLY YOU CAN SAVE MANKIND

JOHNNY AND THE DEAD

JOHNNY AND THE BOMB

NATION

DODGER

JACK DODGER'S GUIDE TO LONDON

DRAGONS AT CRUMBLING CASTLE

MONSTROUS
REGIMENT

Terry Pratchett

CORGI BOOKS

TRANSWORLD PUBLISHERS
61-63 Uxbridge Road, London W5 5SA
A Random House Group Company
www.transworldbooks.co.uk

MONSTROUS REGIMENT
A CORGI BOOK : 9780552167673

First published in Great Britain
in 2003 by Doubleday
an imprint of Transworld Publishers
Corgi edition published 2004
Corgi edition reissued 2011
Corgi edition reissued 2014

Addresses for Random House Group Ltd companies outside the UK
can be found at: www.randomhouse.co.uk
The Random House Group Ltd Reg. No. 954009.

Penguin Random House is committed to a sustainable future for
our business, our readers and our planet. This book is made from
Forest Stewardship Council® certified paper.

Typeset in 12/14.5pt Minion by Falcon Oast Graphic Art Ltd.
Printed and bound in Great Britain by Clays Ltd, St Ives plc

6 8 10 9 7 5

MONSTROUS REGIMENT

Polly cut off her hair in front of the mirror, feeling slightly guilty about not feeling very guilty about doing so. It was supposed to be her crowning glory, and everyone said it was beautiful, but she generally wore it in a net when she was working. She'd always told herself it was wasted on her. But she was careful to see that the long golden coils all landed on the small sheet spread out for the purpose.

If she would *admit* to any strong emotion at all at this time, it was sheer annoyance that a haircut was all she needed to pass for a young man. She didn't even need to bind up her bosom, which she'd heard was the normal practice. Nature had seen to it that she had barely any problems in this area.

The effect that the scissors had was . . . erratic, but it was no worse than other male haircuts here. It'd do. She did feel cold on the back of her neck, but that was only partly because of the loss of her long hair. It was also because of the Stare.

The Duchess watched her from above the bed.

It was a poor woodcut, hand-coloured mostly in blue and red. It was of a plain, middle-aged woman whose sagging chin and slightly bulging eyes gave the

cynical the feeling that someone had put a large fish in a dress, but the artist had managed to capture something extra in that strange, blank expression. Some pictures had eyes that followed you around the room; this one looked right through you. It was a face you found in every home. In Borogravia, you grew up with the Duchess watching you.

Polly knew her parents had one of the pictures in their room, and knew also that when her mother was alive she used to curtsy to it every night. She reached up and turned this picture round so that it faced the wall. A thought in her head said *No*. It was overruled. She'd made up her mind.

Then she dressed herself in her brother's clothes, tipped the contents of the sheet into a small bag which went into the bottom of her pack along with the spare clothes, put the note on her bed, picked up the pack and climbed out of the window. At least, Polly climbed out of the window, but it was Oliver's feet that landed lightly on the ground.

Dawn was just turning the dark world into monochrome when she slipped across the inn's yard. The Duchess watched her from the inn sign, too. Her father had been a great loyalist, at least up to the death of her mother. The sign hadn't been repainted this year, and a random bird-dropping had given the Duchess a squint.

Polly checked that the recruiting sergeant's cart was still in front of the bar, its bright banners now drab and heavy with last night's rain. By the look of that big fat sergeant, it would be hours before it was on the

road again. She had plenty of time. He looked like a slow breakfaster.

She let herself out of the door in the back wall and headed uphill. At the top, she turned back and looked at the waking town. Smoke was rising from a few chimneys, but since Polly was always the first to wake, and had to yell the maids out of their beds, the inn was still sleeping. She knew that the Widow Clambers had stayed overnight (it had been 'raining too hard for her to go home', according to Polly's father) and, personally, she hoped for his sake that she'd stay every night. The town had no shortage of widows, and Eva Clambers was a warm-hearted lady who baked like a champion. His wife's long illness and Paul's long absence had taken a lot out of her father. Polly was glad some of it was being put back. The old ladies who spent their days glowering from their windows might spy and peeve and mumble, but they had been doing that for too long. No one listened any more.

She raised her gaze. Smoke and steam was already rising from the laundry of the Girls' Working School. It hung over one end of the town like a threat, big and grey with tall, thin windows. It was always silent. When she was small, she'd been told that that was where the Bad Girls went. The nature of 'badness' was not explained, and at the age of five Polly had received the vague idea that it consisted of not going to bed when you were told. At the age of eight she'd learned it was where you were lucky not to go for buying your brother a paint box. She turned her back and set off between the trees, which were full of birdsong.

Forget you were ever Polly. *Think* young male, that was the thing. Fart loudly and with self-satisfaction at a job well done, move like a puppet that'd had a couple of random strings cut, never hug anyone and, if you meet a friend, punch them. A few years working in the bar had provided plenty of observational material. No problem about not swinging her hips, at least. Nature had been pretty sparing there, too.

And then there was the young male walk to master. At least women swung only their *hips*. Young men swung *everything*, from the shoulders down. You have to try to occupy a lot of space, she thought. It makes you look bigger, like a tomcat fluffing his tail. She'd seen it a lot in the inn. The boys tried to walk big in self-defence against all those other big boys out there. I'm bad, I'm fierce, I'm cool, I'd like a pint of shandy and me mam wants me home by nine . . .

Let's see, now . . . arms out from the body as though holding a couple of bags of flour . . . check. Shoulders swaying as though she was elbowing her way through a crowd . . . check. Hands slightly bunched and making rhythmical circling motions as though turning two independent handles attached to the waist . . . check. Legs moving forward loosely and ape-like . . . check . . .

It worked fine for a few yards until she got something wrong and the resultant muscular confusion somersaulted her into a holly bush. After that, she gave up.

The thunderstorm came back as she hurried along the trail; sometimes one would hang around the

mountains for days. But at least up here the path wasn't a river of mud, and the trees still had enough leaves to give her some protection. There was no time to wait out the weather, anyway. She had a long way to go. The recruiting party would cross at the ferry, but Polly was known to all the ferrymen by sight and the guard would want to see her permit to travel, which Oliver Perks certainly didn't have. So that meant a long diversion all the way to the troll bridge at Tübz. To the trolls all humans looked alike and any piece of paper would do as a permit, since they didn't read. Then she could walk down through the pine forests to Plün. The cart would have to stop there for the night, but the place was one of those nowhere villages that existed only in order to avoid the embarrassment of having large empty spaces on the map. No one knew her in Plün. No one ever went there. It was a dump.

It was, in fact, just the place she needed. The recruiting party would stop there, and she could enlist. She was pretty certain the big fat sergeant and his greasy little corporal wouldn't notice the girl who'd served them last night. She was not, as they said, conventionally beautiful. The corporal *had* tried to pinch her bottom, but probably out of habit, like swatting a fly, and there was not enough for a big pinch, at that.

She sat on the hill above the ferry and had a late breakfast of cold potato and sausage while she watched the cart cross over. No one was marching behind it. No lads had been recruited back in Munz this time. People had kept away. Too many young men

had left over the last few years, and not enough had come back. And, of the ones who'd come back, sometimes not enough of each man had come back. The corporal could bang his big drum all he liked. Munz was running out of sons almost as fast as it accumulated widows.

The afternoon hung heavy and humid, and a yellow pine warbler followed her from bush to bush. Last night's mud was steaming when Polly reached the troll bridge, which crossed the river in a narrow gorge. It was a thin, graceful affair, put together, it was said, with no mortar at all. And it was said that the weight of the bridge anchored it ever more deeply into the rock on either side. It was said to be a wonder of the world, except that very few people around here ever wondered much about anything and were barely aware of the world. It cost one penny to cross, or one hundred gold pieces if you had a billygoat.* Halfway across Polly peered over the parapet and saw the cart far, far below, working its way along the narrow road just above the white water.

The afternoon's journey was downhill all the way, through dark pines on this side of the gorge. She didn't hurry and, towards sunset, she spotted the inn. The cart had already arrived, but by the looks of it the recruiting sergeant had not even bothered to make an effort. There was no drumbanging like there had been last night, no cries of 'Roll

* Trolls might not be quick thinkers but they don't forget in a hurry, either.

up, my young shavers! It's a great life in the Ins-and-Outs!'

There was always a war. Usually it was a border dispute, the national equivalent of complaining that the neighbour was letting his hedge grow too long. Sometimes it was bigger. Borogravia was a peace-loving country in the midst of treacherous, devious, warlike enemies. They had to be treacherous, devious and warlike, otherwise we wouldn't be fighting them, eh? There was always a war.

Polly's father had been in the army before he took over The Duchess from Polly's grandfather. He didn't talk about it much. He'd brought his sword back with him, but instead of hanging it over the fireplace he used it to poke the fire. Sometimes old friends would turn up and, when the bars were shut for the night, they'd gather round the fire and drink and sing. The young Polly found excuses to stay up and listen to the songs they sang, but that had stopped when she'd got into trouble for using one of the more interesting words in front of her mother; now she was older, and served the beer, it was presumably assumed that she knew the words or would find out what they meant soon enough. Besides, her mother had gone where bad words would no longer offend and, in theory, never got said.

The songs had been part of her childhood. She knew all the words of 'The World Turned Upside Down' and 'The Devil Shall Be My Sergeant' and 'Johnny Has Gone For A Soldier' and 'The Girl I Left

Behind Me' and, after the drink had been flowing for a while, she'd memorized 'Colonel Crapski' and 'I Wish I'd Never Kissed Her'.

And then, of course, there had been 'Sweet Polly Oliver'. Her father used to sing it when she was small and fretful or sad, and she'd laughed to hear it simply because it had her name in it. She was word perfect on the words before she'd known what most of them meant. And now . . .

. . . Polly pushed open the door. The recruiting sergeant and his corporal looked up from the stained table where they were sitting, beer mugs halfway to their lips. She took a deep breath, marched over, and made an attempt at saluting.

'What do you want, kid?' growled the corporal.

'Want to join up, sir!'

The sergeant turned to Polly and grinned, which made his scars move oddly and caused a tremor to shake all his chins. The word 'fat' could not honestly be applied to him, not when the word 'gross' was lumbering forward to catch your attention. He was one of those people who didn't have a waist. He had an equator. He had gravity. If he fell over, in any direction, he would rock. Sun and drink had burned his face red. Small dark eyes twinkled in the redness like the sparkle on the edge of a knife. Beside him, on the table, were a couple of old-fashioned cutlasses, weapons that had more in common with a meat cleaver than a sword.

'Just like that?' he said.

'Yessir!'

'Really?'

'Yessir!'

'You don't want us to get you stinking drunk first? It's traditional, you know.'

'Nosir!'

'I haven't told you about the wonderful opportunities for advancement and good fortune, have I?'

'Nosir!'

'Did I mention how the spanking red uniform will mean you'll have to beat the girls off with a stick?'

'Don't think so, sir!'

'Or the grub? Every meal's a banquet when you march along with us!' The sergeant smacked his belly, which caused tremors in outlying regions. 'I'm the living proof!'

'Yes, sir. No, sir. I just want to join up to fight for my country and the honour of the Duchess, sir!'

'You do?' said the corporal incredulously, but the sergeant appeared not to hear this. He looked Polly up and down, and Polly got the definite impression that the man was neither as drunk nor as stupid as he looked.

'Upon my oath, Corporal Strappi, it seems that what we've got ourselves here is nothin' less than a good, old-fashioned *patriot*,' he said, his eyes searching Polly's face. 'Well, you've come to the right place, my lad!' He pulled a sheaf of papers towards him with an air of bustle. 'You know who we are?'

'The Tenth Foot, sir. Light infantry, sir. Known as the "Ins-and-Outs", sir,' said Polly, relief bubbling through her. She'd clearly passed some sort of test.

'Right, lad. The jolly old Cheesemongers. Finest regiment there is, in the finest army in the world. Keen to join, then, are yer?'

'Keen as mustard, sir!' said Polly, aware of the corporal's suspicious eyes on her.

'Good lad!'

The sergeant unscrewed the top from a bottle of ink and dipped a nib pen in it. His hand hovered over the paperwork. 'Name, lad?' he said.

'Oliver, sir. Oliver Perks,' said Polly.

'Age?'

'Seventeen come Sunday, sir.'

'Yeah, right,' said the sergeant. 'You're seventeen and I'm the Grand Duchess Annagovia. What're you running away from, eh? Got a young lady in the family way?'

''e'd 'ave 'ad to 'ave 'elp,' said the corporal, grinning. 'He squeaks like a little lad.'

Polly realized she was starting to blush. But then, young Oliver would blush too, wouldn't he? It was very easy to make a boy blush. Polly could do it just by staring.

'Don't matter anyway,' said the sergeant. 'You make your mark on this here document and kiss the Duchess and you're *my* little lad, you understand? My name is Sergeant Jackrum. I will be your mother and your father and Corporal Strappi here will be just like your big brother. And life will be steak and bacon every day, and anyone who wants to drag you away'll have to drag me away too, because I'll be holding on to your collar. And you might well be thinking there's

no one that can drag that much, Mr Perks.' A thick thumb jabbed at the paper. 'Just there, right?'

Polly picked up the pen and signed.

'What's that?' said the corporal.

'My signature,' said Polly.

She heard the door open behind her, and spun round. Several young men— she corrected herself, several *other* young men had clattered into the bar, and were looking around warily.

'You can read and write, too?' said the sergeant, glancing up at them and then back to her. 'Yeah, I see. A nice round hand, as well. Officer material, you are. Give him the shilling, corporal. And the picture, of course.'

'Right, sergeant,' said Corporal Strappi, holding up a picture frame on a handle, like a looking-glass. ' 'Pucker up, Private Parts.'

'It's Perks, sir,' said Polly.

'Yeah, right. Now kiss the Duchess.'

It was not a good copy of the famous picture. The painting behind the glass was faded and something, some kind of moss or something, was growing on the inside of the cracked glass itself. Polly let her lips brush it while holding her breath.

'Huh,' said Strappi, and pressed something into her hand.

'What's this?' said Polly, looking at the small square of paper.

'An IOU. Bit short of shillings right now,' said the sergeant, while Strappi smirked. 'But the innkeeper'll stand you a pint of ale, courtesy of her grace.'

He turned and looked up at the newcomers. 'Well, it never rains but it pours. You boys here to join up too? My word, and we didn't even have to bang the drum. It must be Corporal Strappi's amazin' charisma. Step up, don't be shy. Who's the next likely lad?'

Polly looked at the next recruit with horror that she hoped she was concealing. She hadn't really noticed him in the gloom, because he was wearing black – not cool, styled black, but a dusty black, the kind of suit people got buried in. By the look of it, that person had been him. There were cobwebs all over it. The boy himself had stitches across his forehead.

'Your name, lad?' said Jackrum.

'Igor, thur.'

Jackrum counted the stitches.

'You know, I had a feeling it was going to be,' he said. 'And I see you're eighteen.'

'*Awake!*'

'Oh, gods . . .' Commander Samuel Vimes put his hands over his eyes.

'I beg your pardon, your grace?' said the Ankh-Morpork consul to Zlobenia. 'Are you ill, your grace?'

'What's your name again, young man?' said Vimes. 'I'm sorry, but I've been travelling for two weeks and not getting a lot of sleep and I've spent all day being introduced to people with difficult names. That's bad for the brain.'

'It's Clarence, your grace. Clarence Chinny.'

'Chinny?' said Vimes, and Clarence read everything in his expression.

'I'm afraid so, sir,' he said.

'Were you a good fighter at school?' said Vimes.

'No, your grace, but no one could beat me over the one-hundred-yard dash.'

Vimes laughed. 'Well, Clarence, any national anthem that starts "Awake!" is going to lead to trouble. They didn't teach you this in the Patrician's office?'

'Er . . . no, your grace,' said Chinny.

'Well, you'll find out. Carry on, then.'

'Yes, sir.' Chinny cleared his throat. 'The Borogravian National Anthem,' he announced, for the second time.

> 'Awake *sorry, your grace*, ye sons of the
> Motherland!
> Taste no more the wine of the sour apples
> Woodsmen, grasp your choppers!
> Farmers, slaughter with the tool formerly
> used for lifting beets the foe!
> Frustrate the endless wiles of our enemies
> We into the darkness march singing
> Against the whole world in arms coming
> But see the golden light upon the mountain
> tops!
> The new day is a great big fish!'

'Er . . .' Vimes said. 'That last bit . . .?'

'That is a literal translation, your grace,' said Clarence nervously. 'It means something like "an

amazing opportunity" or "a glittering prize", your grace.'

'When we're not in public, Clarence, "sir" will do. "Your grace" is just to impress the natives.' Vimes slumped back in his uncomfortable chair, chin in his hand, and then winced.

'Two thousand three hundred miles,' he said, shifting his position. 'And it's freezing on a broomstick, however low they fly. And then the barge, and then the coach . . .' He winced again. 'I read your report. Do you think it's possible for an entire nation to be insane?'

Clarence swallowed. He'd been told that he was talking to the second most powerful man in Ankh-Morpork, even if the man himself acted as though he was ignorant of the fact. His desk in this chilly tower room was rickety; it had belonged to the head janitor of the Kneck garrison until yesterday. Paperwork cluttered its scarred surface and was stacked in piles behind Vimes's chair.

Vimes himself did not look, to Clarence, like a duke. He looked like a watchman which, in fact, Clarence understood, he was. This offended Clarence Chinny. People at the top should look as though they belonged there.

'That's a very . . . interesting question, sir,' he said. 'You mean the people—'

'Not the people, the nation,' said Vimes. 'Borogravia looks off its head, to me, from what I've read. I expect the people just do the best they can and get on with raising their kids which, I might say, I'd

rather be doing right now, too. Look, you know what I mean. You take a bunch of people who don't seem any different from you and me, but when you add them all together you get this sort of huge raving maniac with national borders and an anthem.'

'It's a fascinating idea, sir,' said Clarence diplomatically.

Vimes looked round the room. The walls were bare stone. The windows were narrow. It was damn cold, even on a sunny day. All that bad food, and that bumping about and sleeping on bad beds . . . and all that travelling in the dark, too, on dwarf barges in their secret canals under the mountains – the gods alone knew what intricate diplomacy Lord Vetinari had pulled off to get *that*, although the Low King owed Vimes a few favours . . .

. . . all of that for this cold castle over this cold river between these stupid countries, with their stupid war. He knew what he wanted to do. If they'd been people, scuffling in the gutter, he'd have known what to do. He'd have banged their heads together and maybe shoved them in the cells overnight. You couldn't bang countries together.

Vimes picked up some paperwork, fiddled with it, and threw it down again. 'To hell with this,' he said. 'What's happening out there?'

'I understand there are a few pockets of resistance in some of the more inaccessible areas of the keep, but they are being dealt with. For all practical purposes the keep is in our hands. That was a clever ruse of yours, your gr— sir.'

Vimes sighed. 'No, Clarence, it was a dull old ruse. It should not be possible to get men into a fortress dressed as washerwomen. Three of them had moustaches, for goodness' sake!'

'The Borogravians are rather ... old-fashioned about things like that, sir. On that subject, we appear to have zombies in the lower crypts. Dreadful things. A lot of high-ranking Borogravian military men were interred down there over the centuries, apparently.'

'Really? What are they doing now?'

Clarence raised his eyebrows. 'Lurching, sir, I think. Groaning. Zombie things. Something seems to have stirred them up.'

'Us, probably,' said Vimes. He got up, strode across the room, and pulled open the big heavy door. 'Reg!' he yelled.

After a moment another watchman appeared, and saluted. He was grey-faced, and Clarence couldn't help noticing when the man saluted that the hand and fingers were held together with stitching.

'Have you met Constable Shoe, Clarence?' said Vimes cheerfully. 'One of my staff. Been dead for more than thirty years, and loves every minute of it, eh, Reg?'

'Right, Mister Vimes,' said Reg, grinning and revealing a lot of brown teeth.

'Some fellow countrymen of yours down in the cellar, Reg.'

'Oh, dear. Lurching, are they?'

' 'fraid so, Reg.'

'I shall go and have a word with them,' said Reg. He

saluted again and marched out, with a hint of lurch.

'He's, er, from here?' said Chinny, who had gone quite pale.

'Oh, no. The *undiscovered* country,' said Vimes. 'He's dead. However, credit where it's due, he hasn't let that stop him. You didn't know we have a zombie in the Watch, Clarence?'

'Er . . . no, sir. I've haven't been back to the city in five years.' He swallowed. 'I gather things have changed.'

Horribly so, in Clarence Chinny's opinion. Being consul to Zlobenia had been an easy job, which left him a lot of time to get on with his business. And then the big semaphore towers marched through, all along the valley, and suddenly Ankh-Morpork was an hour away. Before the clacks, a letter from Ankh-Morpork would take more than a two weeks to get to him, and so no one worried if he took a day or two to answer it. Now people expected a reply overnight. He'd been quite glad when Borogravia had destroyed several of those wretched towers. And then all hell had been let loose.

'We've got all sorts in the Watch,' said Vimes. 'And we bloody well need 'em now, Clarence, with Zlobenians and Borogravians scrapping in the streets over some damn quarrel that began a thousand years ago. It's worse than dwarfs and trolls! All because someone's great-to-the-power-of-umpteen-grandmother slapped the face of someone's great-ditto-uncle! Borogravia and Zlobenia can't even agree a border. They chose the river, and that changes

course every spring. Suddenly the clacks towers are now on Borogravian soil – or mud, anyway – so the idiots burn them down for religious reasons.'

'Er, there is more to it than that, sir,' said Chinny.

'Yes, I know. I read the history. The annual scrap with Zlobenia is just the local derby. Borogravia fights everybody. Why?'

'National pride, sir.'

'What in? There's nothing there! There's some tallow mines, and they're not bad farmers, but there's no great architecture, no big libraries, no famous composers, no very high mountains, no wonderful views. All you can say about the place is that it isn't anywhere else. What's so special about Borogravia?'

'I suppose it's special because it's theirs. And of course there's Nuggan, sir. Their god. I've brought you a copy of the *Book of Nuggan*.'

'I looked through one back in the city, Chinny,' said Vimes. 'Seemed pretty stu—'

'That wouldn't have been a recent edition, sir. And I suspect it wouldn't be, er, very current that far from here. This one is more up to date,' said Chinny, putting a small but thick book on the desk.

'Up to date? What do you mean, up to date?' said Vimes, looking puzzled. 'Holy writ gets ... written. Do this, don't do that, no coveting your neighbour's ox ...'

'Um ... Nuggan doesn't just leave it at that, sir. He, er ... updates things. Mostly the Abominations, to be frank.'

Vimes took the new copy. It was noticeably thicker than the one he'd brought with him.

'It's what they call a Living Testament,' Chinny explained. 'They – well, I suppose you could say they "die" if they're taken out of Borogravia. They no longer . . . get added to. The latest Abominations are at the end, sir,' said Chinny helpfully.

'This is a holy book with an appendix?'

'Exactly, sir.'

'In a *ring binder*?'

'Quite so, sir. People put blank pages in and the Abominations . . . turn up.'

'You mean magically?'

'I suppose I mean religiously, sir.'

Vimes opened a page at random. 'Chocolate?' he said. 'He doesn't like chocolate?'

'Yes, sir. That's an Abomination.'

'Garlic? Well, I don't much like that, so fair enough . . . cats?'

'Oh, yes. He really doesn't like cats, sir.'

'*Dwarfs?* It says here "The dwarfish race which worships Gold is an Abomination unto Nuggan"! He must be mad. What happened there?'

'Oh, the dwarfs that were here sealed their mines and vanished, your grace.'

'I bet they did. They know trouble when they see it,' said Vimes. He let 'your grace' pass this time; Chinny clearly derived some satisfaction from talking to a duke.

He leafed through the pages, and stopped. '*The colour blue?*'

'Correct, sir.'

'What's abominable about the colour blue? It's just a colour! The *sky* is blue!'

'Yes, sir. Devout Nugganites try not to look at it these days. Um . . .' Chinny had been trained as a diplomat. Some things he didn't like to say directly. 'Nuggan, sir . . . um . . . is rather . . . tetchy,' he managed.

'Tetchy?' said Vimes. 'A *tetchy* god? What, he complains about the noise their kids make? Objects to loud music after nine p.m.?'

'Um . . . we get the *Ankh-Morpork Times* here, sir, eventually, and, er, I'd say, er, that Nuggan is very much like, er, the kind of people who write to its letter column. You know, sir. The kind who sign their letters "Disgusted of Ankh-Morpork" . . .'

'Oh, you mean he really *is* mad,' said Vimes.

'Oh, I'd never mean anything like that, sir,' said Chinny hurriedly.

'What do the priests do about this?'

'Not a lot, sir. I think they quietly ignore some of the more, er, extreme Abominations.'

'You mean Nuggan objects to dwarfs, cats and the colour blue and there're more insane commandments?'

Chinny coughed politely.

'All right, then,' growled Vimes. 'More *extreme* commandments?'

'Oysters, sir. He doesn't like them. But that's not a problem because no one there has ever seen an oyster. Oh, and babies. He Abominated them, too.'

'I take it people still make them here?'

'Oh, yes, your gr— I'm sorry. Yes, sir. But they feel guilty about it. Barking dogs, that was another one. Shirts with six buttons, too. And cheese. Er . . . people just sort of, er, *avoid* the trickier ones. Even the priests seem to have given up trying to explain them.'

'Yes, I think I can see why. So what we have here is a country that tries to run itself on the commandments of a god who, the people feel, may be wearing his underpants on his head. Has he Abominated underpants?'

'No, sir,' Chinny sighed. 'But it's probably only a matter of time.'

'So how do they manage?'

'These days, people mostly pray to the Duchess Annagovia. You see icons of her in every house. They call her the Little Mother.'

'Ah, yes, the Duchess. Can I get to see her?'

'Oh, no one sees her, sir. No one except her servants has seen her for more than thirty years. To be honest, sir, she's probably dead.'

'Only probably?'

'No one really knows. The official story is that she's in mourning. It's rather sad, sir. The young Duke died a week after they got married. Gored by a wild pig during a hunt, I believe. She went into mourning at the old castle at PrinceMarmadukePiotreAlbertHans JosephBernhardtWilhelmsberg and hasn't appeared in public since. The official portrait was painted when she was about forty, I believe.'

'No children?'

'No, sir. On her death, the line is extinct.'

'And they pray to her? Like a god?'

Chinny sighed. 'I *did* put this in my briefing notes, sir. The royal family in Borogravia have always had a quasi-religious status, you see. They're the head of the church and the peasants, at least, pray to them in the hope that they'll put in a good word with Nuggan. They're like . . . living saints. Celestial intermediaries. To be honest, that's how these countries work in any case. If you want something done, you have to know the right people. And I suppose it's easier to pray to someone in a picture than to a god you can't see.'

Vimes sat looking at the consul for some time. When he next spoke, he frightened the man to his boots.

'Who'd inherit?' he said.

'Sir?'

'Just following the monarchy, Mr Chinny. If the Duchess isn't on the throne, who should be?'

'Um, it's incredibly complex, sir, because of the intermarriages and the various legal systems, which for example—'

'Who's the smart money on, Mr Chinny?'

'Um, Prince Heinrich of Zlobenia.'

To Chinny's astonishment Vimes laughed. 'And he's wondering how auntie's gettin' on, I expect. I met him this morning, didn't I? Can't say I took to him.'

'But he is a friend of Ankh-Morpork,' said Chinny reproachfully. 'That was in my report. Educated. Very interested in the clacks. Got great plans for his country. They used to be Nugganatic in Zlobenia, but

he's banned the religion and, frankly, hardly anyone objected. He wants Zlobenia to move forward. He admires Ankh-Morpork very much.'

'Yes, I know. He sounds almost as insane as Nuggan,' said Vimes. 'Okay, so what we've probably got is an elaborate charade to keep Heinrich out. How's this place governed?'

'There isn't much. A bit of tax collecting, and that's about all. We think some of the senior court officials just drift on as if the Duchess was alive. The only thing that really works is the army.'

'All right, how about coppers? Everyone needs coppers. At least they have their feet on the ground.'

'I believe informal citizens' committees enforce Nugganatic law,' said Chinny.

'Oh, gods. Prodnoses, curtain-twitchers and vigilantes,' said Vimes. He stood up and peered out through the narrow window at the plain below. It was night-time. Cooking-fires in the enemy camp made demonic constellations in the darkness.

'Did they tell you why I've been sent here, Clarence?' he said.

'No, sir. My instructions were that you would, um, oversee things. Prince Heinrich is not very happy about it.'

'Oh, well, the interests of Ankh-Morpork are the interests of all money-lov— oops, sorry, all *freedom*-loving people everywhere,' said Vimes. 'We can't have a country that turns back our mail coaches and keeps cutting down the clacks towers. That's *expensive*. They're cutting the continent in half, they're the pinch

in the hourglass. I'm to bring things to a "satisfactory" conclusion. And frankly, Clarence, I'm wondering if it's even worth attacking Borogravia. It'll be cheaper to sit here and wait for it to explode. Although I notice . . . where was that report . . . ah, yes . . . it will starve first.'

'Regrettably so, sir.'

Igor stood mutely in front of the recruiting table.

'Don't often see you people these days,' said Jackrum.

'Yeah, run out of fresh brains, 'ave yer?' said the corporal nastily.

'Now then, corporal, no call for that,' said the sergeant, leaning back in his creaking chair. 'There's plenty of lads out there walking around on legs they wouldn't still have if there hadn't been a friendly Igor around, eh, Igor?'

'Yeah? Well, *I* heard about people waking up and findin' their friendly Igor had whipped out their brains in the middle of the night and buggered off to flog 'em,' said the corporal, glaring at Igor.

'I promith you your brain ith entirely thafe from me, corporal,' said Igor. Polly started to laugh, and stopped when she realized absolutely no one else was doing so.

'Yeah, well, I met a sergeant who said an Igor put a man's legs on *backwards*,' said Corporal Strappi. 'What good's that to a soldier, eh?'

'Could advance and retreat at the thame time?' said Igor levelly. 'Thargent, I know all the thtorieth, and

they are nothing but vile calumnieth. I theek only to therve my country. I do not want trouble.'

'Right,' said the sergeant. 'Nor do we. Make your mark, and you've got to promise not to mess about with Corporal Strappi's brain, right? *Another* signature? My word, I can see we've got ourselves a bleedin' *college* of recruits today. Give him his cardboard shilling, corporal.'

'Thank you,' said Igor. 'And I would like to give the picture a wipe, if it'th all the thame to you.' He produced a small cloth.

'Wipe it?' said Strappi. 'Is that allowed, sergeant?'

'What do you want to wipe it for, mister?' said Jackrum.

'To remove the invithible demonth,' said Igor.

'I can't see any invis—' Strappi began, and stopped.

'Just let him, all right?' said Jackrum. 'It's one of their funny little ways.'

'Dun't seem right,' muttered Strappi. 'Practically treason . . .'

'Can't see why it'd be wrong just to give the old girl a wash,' said the sergeant shortly. 'Next. Oh . . .'

Igor, after carefully wiping the stained picture and giving it a perfunctory peck, came and stood next to Polly, giving her a sheepish grin. But she was watching the next recruit.

He was short and quite slim, which was fairly usual in a country where it was rare to get enough food to make you fat. But he was dressed in black and expensively, like an aristocrat; he even had a sword. The sergeant was, therefore, looking worried. Clearly

a man could get into trouble talking wrong to a nob who might have important friends.

'You sure you've come to the right place, sir?' he said.

'Yes, sergeant. I wish to enlist.'

Sergeant Jackrum shifted uneasily. 'Yes, sir, but I'm not sure a gentleman like you—'

'Are you going to enlist me or not, sergeant?'

'Not usual for a *gentleman* to enlist as a common soldier, sir,' mumbled the sergeant.

'What you mean, sergeant, is: is anyone after me? Is there a price on my head? And the answer is no.'

'How about a mob with pitchforks?' said Corporal Strappi. 'He's a bloody *vampire*, sarge! Anyone can see that! He's a Black Ribboner! Look, he's got the badge!'

'Which says "Not One Drop",' said the young man calmly. 'Not one drop of human blood, sergeant. A prohibition I have accepted for almost two years, thanks to the League of Temperance. Of course, if you have a personal objection, sergeant, you only need to give it to me in writing.'

Which was quite a clever thing to say, Polly thought. Those clothes cost serious money. Most of the vampire families were highly nobby. You never knew who was connected to who ... not just connected to who, in fact, but to whom. Whoms were likely to be far more trouble than your common everyday who. The sergeant was looking down a mile of rough road.

'Got to move with the times, corporal,' he said,

deciding not to go there. 'And we certainly need the men.'

'Yeah, but s'posin' he wants to suck all my blood out in the middle of the night?' said Strappi.

'Well, he'll just have to wait until Private Igor's finished looking for your brain, won't he?' snapped the sergeant. 'Sign here, mister.'

The pen scratched on the paper. After a minute or two the vampire turned the paper over and continued writing on the other side. Vampires had long names.

'But you can call me Maladict,' he said, dropping the pen back in the inkwell.

'Thank you very much, I must say, si— private. Give him the shilling, corporal. Good job it's not a silver one, eh? Haha!'

'Yes,' said Maladict. 'It is.'

'Next!' said the sergeant. Polly watched as a farm boy, breeches held up with string, shuffled in front of the table and looked at the quill pen with the resentful perplexity of those confronted with new technology.

She turned back to the bar. The landlord glared at her in the manner of bad landlords everywhere. As her father always said, if you kept an inn you either liked people or went mad. Oddly enough, some of the mad ones were the best at looking after their beer. But by the smell of the place, this wasn't one of those.

She leaned on the bar. 'Pint, please,' she said, and watched glumly as the man gave a scowl of acknowledgement and turned to the big barrels. It'd be sour, she knew, with the slop bucket under the tap tipped

back in every night, and the spigot not put back, and
. . . yes, it was going to be served in a leather tankard
that had probably never been washed.

A couple of new recruits were already knocking
back their pints, though, with every audible sign of
enjoyment. But this was Plün, after all. Anything that
made you forget you were there was probably worth
drinking.

One of them said, 'Lovely pint, this, eh?' and the
boy next to him belched and said, 'Best I've tasted,
yeah.'

Polly sniffed at the tankard. The contents smelled
like something she wouldn't feed to pigs. She took a
sip, and completely changed her opinion. She *would*
feed it to pigs. Those lads have never tasted beer
before, she told herself. It's like dad said. Out in the
country there's lads who'd join up for an uninhabited
pair of breeches. And they'll drink this muck
and pretend to enjoy it like men, hey up, we
supped some stuff last night, eh, lads? And then next
thing—

Oh, lor' . . . that reminded her. What'd the privy be
like here? The men's one out in the yard back at home
was bad enough. Polly sloshed two big pails of water
into it every morning while trying not to breathe.
There was weird green moss growing on the slate
floor. And The Duchess was a good inn. It had
customers who took their boots off before going to
bed.

She narrowed her eyes. This stupid fool in front of
her, a man making one long eyebrow do the work

of two, was serving them slops and foul vinegar just before they marched off to war—

'Thith beer,' said Igor, on her right, 'tathteth of horthe pith.'

Polly stood back. Even in a bar like this, that was killing talk.

'Oh, you'd know, would you?' said the barman, looming over the boy. 'Drunk horse piss, have you?'

'Yeth,' said Igor.

The barman stuck a fist in front of Igor's face. 'Now you listen to me, you lisping little—'

A slim black arm appeared with amazing speed and a pale hand caught the man's wrist. The one eyebrow contorted in sudden agony.

'Now, it's like this,' said Maladict calmly. 'We're soldiers of the Duchess, agreed? Just say "aargh".'

He must have squeezed. The man groaned.

'Thank you. And you're serving up as beer a liquid best described as foul water,' Maladict went on in the same level, conversational tone. 'I, of course, don't drink . . . horse piss, but I have a highly developed sense of smell, and really would prefer not to list aloud the things I can smell in this murk, so we'll just say "rat droppings" and leave it at that, shall we? Just whimper. Good man.' At the end of the bar, one of the new recruits threw up. The barman's fingers had gone white. Maladict nodded with satisfaction.

'Incapacitating a soldier of her grace in wartime is a treasonable offence,' he said. He leaned forward. 'Punishable, of course, by . . . death.' Maladict pronounced the word with a certain delight. '*However*, if

there happened to be another barrel of beer around the place, you know, good stuff, the stuff you'd keep for your friends if you had any friends, then I'm sure we can forget this little incident. Now, I'm going to let go of your wrist. I can tell by your eyebrow that you are a thinker, and if you're thinking of rushing back in here with a big stick, I'd like you to think about *this* instead: I'd like you to think about this black ribbon I'm wearing. Know what it means, do you?'

The barman winced, and mumbled: 'Temp'rance League . . .'

'Right! Well done!' said Maladict. 'And one more thought for you, if you've got room. I've only taken a pledge not to drink human blood. It doesn't mean I can't kick you in the fork so hard you suddenly go deaf.'

He released his grip. The barman slowly straightened up. Under the bar he *would* have a short wooden club, Polly knew. Every bar had one. Even her father had one. It was a great help, he said, in times of worry and confusion. She saw the fingers of the usable hand twitch.

'Don't,' she said. 'I think he means it.'

The barman relaxed. 'Bit of a misunderstanding there, gents,' he mumbled. 'Got the wrong barrel in. No offence meant.' He shuffled off, his hand almost visibly throbbing.

'I only thaid it wath horthe pith,' said Igor.

'He won't cause trouble,' said Polly to Maladict. 'He'll be your friend from now on. He's worked out he can't beat you so he's going to be your best mate.'

Maladict subjected her to a thoughtful stare. '*I* know that,' he said. 'How do you?'

'I used to work in an inn,' said Polly, feeling her heart begin to beat faster, as it always did when the lies lined up. 'You learn to read people.'

'What did you do in the inn?'

'Barman.'

'There's another inn in this hole, is there?'

'Oh no, I'm not from round here.'

Polly groaned at the sound of her own voice, and waited for the question: 'Then why come here to join up?' It didn't come. Instead, Maladict just shrugged and said, 'I shouldn't think anyone is from round here.'

A couple more new recruits arrived at the bar. They had the same look – sheepish, a bit defiant, in clothes that didn't fit well. Eyebrow reappeared with a small keg, which he laid reverentially on a stand and gently tapped. He pulled a genuine pewter tankard from under the bar, filled it, and timorously proffered it to Maladict.

'Igor?' said the vampire, waving it away.

'I'll thtick with the horthe pith, if it'th all the thame to you,' said Igor. He looked around in the sudden silence. 'Look, I never thaid I didn't *like* it,' said Igor. He pushed his mug across the sticky bar. 'Thame again?'

Polly took the new tankard and sniffed at it. Then she took a sip. 'Not bad,' she said. 'At least it tastes like it's—'

The door pushed open, letting in the sounds of the

storm. About two-thirds of a troll eased its way inside, and then managed to get the rest of itself through.

Polly was okay about trolls. She met them up in the woods sometimes, sitting amongst the trees or purposefully lumbering along the tracks on the way to whatever it was trolls did. They weren't friendly, they were . . . resigned. The world's got humans in it, live with it. They're not worth the indigestion. You can't kill 'em all. Step around 'em. Stepping on 'em doesn't work in the long term.

Occasionally a farmer would hire one to do some heavy work. Sometimes they turned up, sometimes they didn't. Sometimes they'd turn up, lumber around a field pulling out tree stumps as if they were carrots, and then wander off without waiting to be paid. A lot of things humans did mystified trolls, and vice versa. Generally, they avoided one another.

But she didn't often see trolls as . . . trollish as this one. It looked like a boulder that had spent centuries in the damp pine forests. Lichen covered it. Stringy grey moss hung in curtains from its head and its chin. It had a bird's nest in one ear. It had a genuine troll club, made from an uprooted sapling. It was almost a joke troll, except that no one would laugh.

The root end of the sapling bumped across the floor as the troll, watched by the recruits and a horrified Corporal Strappi, trudged to the table.

'Gonna En List,' it said. 'Gonna do my bit. Gimme shillin'.'

'You're a troll!' Strappi burst out.

'Now, now, none of that, corporal,' said Sergeant Jackrum. 'Don't ask, don't tell.'

'Don't ask? Don't *ask*? It's a troll, sarge! It's got crags! There's grass growing under its fingernails! It's a troll!'

'Right,' said the sergeant. 'Enlist him.'

'You want to fight with us?' Strappi squeaked. Trolls had no sense of personal space, and a ton of what was, for practical purposes, a kind of rock was looming right over the table.

The troll analysed the question. The recruits stood in silence, mugs halfway to mouths.

'No,' said the troll at last. 'Gonna fight wi' En Army. Gods save the . . .' The troll paused, and looked at the ceiling. Whatever it was seeking there didn't appear to be visible. Then it looked at its feet, which had grass growing on them. Then it looked at its free hand and moved its fingers as if counting something. '. . . Duchess,' it said. It had been a long wait. The table creaked as the troll laid a hand on it, palm upwards. 'Gimme shillin'.'

'We've only got the bits of pape—' Corporal Strappi began. Sergeant Jackrum jabbed an elbow into his ribs.

'Upon my oath, are you mad?' he hissed. 'There's a ten-man bounty for enlisting a troll!' With his other hand he reached into his jacket pocket, pulled out a real silver shilling, and placed it delicately in the huge hand. 'Welcome to your new life, friend! I'll just write your name down, shall I? What is it?'

The troll looked at ceiling, feet, sergeant, wall and

table. Polly saw its lips move. 'Carborundum?' it volunteered.

'Yeah, probably,' said the sergeant. 'Er, how'd you like to shav— to cut off some of that hai— moss? We've got a, a sort of a . . . regulation . . .'

Wall, floor, ceiling, table, fingers, sergeant. 'No,' said Carborundum.

'Right. Right. Right,' said the sergeant quickly. 'It's not a regulation as per such, actually, it's more of an advisory. Silly one, too, eh? I've always thought so. Glad to have you with us,' he added fervently.

The troll licked the coin, which gleamed like a diamond in its hand. It actually did have grass growing under its fingernails too, Polly noticed. Then Carborundum trudged to the bar. The crowd parted instantly, because trolls *never* had to stand at the back of the press of bodies, waving money and trying to catch the barman's eye.

He broke the coin in two and dropped both halves on the bar top. Eyebrow swallowed. He looked as though he would have said 'Are you sure?' except that this was not a question barmen addressed to people weighing over half a ton. Carborundum thought for a while, and then said: 'Gimme drink.'

Eyebrow nodded, disappeared briefly into the room behind the bar, and came back holding a double-handled mug. Maladict sneezed. Polly's eyes watered. It was the kind of smell you sense with your teeth. The pub might make foul beer as a matter of course, but *this* was eye-stinging vinegar.

Eyebrow dropped one half of the silver coin into it,

and then took a copper penny out of the money drawer and held it over the fuming mug. The troll nodded. With just a hint of ceremony, like a cocktail waiter dropping the little umbrella into a Double Entendre, Eyebrow let the copper fall.

More bubbles welled up. Igor watched with interest. Carborundum picked the mug up in two fingers of each shovel-like hand, and swallowed the contents in one gulp. He stood stock still for a moment, then carefully put the mug back on the bar.

'You gentlemen might like to move back a bit,' murmured Eyebrow.

'What's going to happen?' said Polly.

'It takes 'em all differently,' said Eyebrow. 'Looks like this one's – no, there he goes . . .'

With considerable style, Carborundum went over backwards. There was no sagging at the knees, no girly attempt to soften the fall. He just went from standing up, one hand out, to lying down, one hand up. He even rocked gently for some time after hitting the floor.

'Got no head for his drink,' said Eyebrow. 'Typical of the young bucks. Wants to play the big troll, comes in here, orders an Electrick Floorbanger, doesn't know how to handle it.'

'Is he going to come round?' said Maladict.

'No, that's it until dawn, I reckon,' said Eyebrow. 'Brain stops working.'

'Shouldn't affect *him* too much, then,' said Corporal Strappi, stepping up. 'Right, you miserable

lot. You're sleeping in the shed out the back, understand? Practically waterproof, hardly any rats. We're out of here at dawn! You're in the army now!'

Polly lay in the dark, on a bed of musty straw. There was no question of anyone's getting undressed. The rain hammered on the roof and the wind blew through a crack under the door, despite Igor's attempt to stuff it with straw. There was some desultory conversation, during which Polly found that she was sharing the dank shed with 'Tonker' Halter, 'Shufti' Manickle, 'Wazzer' Goom and 'Lofty' Tewt. Maladict and Igor didn't seem to have acquired repeatable nicknames. She'd become Ozzer by general agreement.

Slightly to Polly's surprise the boy now known as Wazzer had taken a small picture of the Duchess out of his pack and had nervously hung it on an old nail. No one else said anything as he prayed to it. It was what you were supposed to do.

They said the Duchess was dead . . .

Polly had been washing up when she'd heard the men talking late one night, and it's a poor woman who can't eavesdrop while making a noise at the same time.

Dead, they said, but the people up at PrinceMarmadukePiotreAlbertHansJoseph-BernhardtWilhelmsberg weren't admitting it. That was 'cos what with there being no children, and with royalty marrying one another's cousins and grannies

all the time, the ducal throne would go to Prince Heinrich of Zlobenia! There! Can you believe that? That's why we never see her, right? And there hasn't been a new picture all these years? Makes you think, eh? Oh, they *say* she's been in mourning 'cos of the young Duke, but that was more'n seventy years ago! They *say* she was buried in secret and—

At which point her father had stopped the speaker dead. There are some conversations where you don't even want people to remember you were in the same room.

Dead or alive, the Duchess watched over you.

The recruits tried to sleep.

Occasionally, someone belched or expelled wind noisily, and Polly responded with a few fake eructations of her own. That seemed to inspire greater effort on the part of the other sleepers, to the point where the roof rattled and dust fell down, before everyone subsided. Once or twice she heard people stagger out into the windy darkness, in theory for the privy but probably, given male impatience in these matters, to aim much closer to home. Once, coasting in and out of a troubled dream, she thought she heard someone sobbing.

Taking care not to rustle too much, Polly pulled out the much-folded, much-read, much-stained last letter from her brother, and read it by the light of the solitary, guttering candle. It had been opened and heavily mangled by the censors, and bore the stamp of the Duchy. It read:

Dear all,

We are in ████████ which is ████████ with a ████big thing
with knobs. On████we will ████████ which is just as well
because ████out of. I am keeping well. The food is ████████
████ we'll ████ at the ████ but my mate ████er says not
to worry, it'll be all over by ████████ and we shall all have
medals.

Chins up!
Paul

It was in a careful hand, the excessively clear and
well-shaped writing of someone who has to think
about every letter. She slowly folded it up again. Paul
had wanted medals, because they were shiny. That'd
been almost a year ago, when any recruiting party that
came past went away with the best part of a battalion,
and there had been people waving them off with flags
and music. Sometimes, now, smaller parties of men
came back. The lucky ones were missing only one arm
or one leg. There were no flags.

She unfolded another piece of paper. It was a
pamphlet. It was headed 'From the Mothers of
Borogravia!' The mothers of Borogravia were very
definite about wanting to send their sons off to war
against the Zlobenian Aggressor and used a great
many exclamation marks to say so. And this was odd,
because the mothers in Munz had not seemed keen
on the idea of their sons going off to war, and
positively tried to drag them back. Several copies of
the pamphlet seemed to have reached every home,

even so. It was very patriotic. That is, it talked about killing foreigners.

Polly had learned to read and write after a fashion because the inn was big and it was a business and things had to be tallied and recorded. Her mother had taught her to read, which was acceptable to Nuggan, and her father made sure that she learned how to write, which was not. A woman who could write was an Abomination unto Nuggan, according to Father Jupe; anything she wrote would by definition be a lie.

But Polly had learned anyway because Paul hadn't, at least to the standard needed to run an inn as busy as The Duchess. He could read if he could run his finger slowly along the lines, and he wrote letters at a snail's pace, with a lot of care and heavy breathing, like a man assembling a piece of jewellery. He was big and kind and slow and could lift beer kegs as though they were toys, but he wasn't a man at home with paperwork. Their father had hinted to Polly, very gently but very often, that Polly would need to be right behind him when the time came for him to run The Duchess. Left to himself, with no one to tell him what to do next, her brother just stood and watched birds.

At Paul's insistence, she'd read the whole of 'From the Mothers of Borogravia!' to him, including the bits about heroes and there being no greater good than to die for your country. She wished, now, she hadn't done that. Paul did what he was told. Unfortunately, he believed what he was told, too.

Polly put the papers away and dozed again, until

her bladder woke her up. Oh, well, at least at this time of the morning she'd have a clear run. She reached out for her pack and stepped as softly as she could out into the rain.

It was mostly just coming off the trees now, which were roaring in the wind that blew up the valley. The moon was hidden in the clouds, but there was just enough light to make out the inn's buildings. A certain greyness suggested that what passed for dawn in Plün was on the way. She located the men's privy which, indeed, stank of inaccuracy.

A lot of planning and practice had gone into this moment. She was helped by the design of the breeches, which were the old-fashioned kind with generous buttoned trapdoors, and also by the experiments she'd made very early in the mornings when she was doing the cleaning. In short, with care and attention to detail, she'd found that a woman could pee standing up. It certainly worked back home in the inn's privy, which had been designed and built in the certain expectation of the aimlessness of the customers.

The wind shook the dank building. In the dark she thought of Auntie Hattie, who'd gone a bit strange round her sixtieth birthday and persistently accused passing young men of looking up her dress. She was even worse after a glass of wine, and she had one joke: 'What does a man stand up to do, a woman sit down to do and a dog lift its leg to do?' And then, when everyone was too embarrassed to answer, she'd triumphantly shriek, 'Shake hands!' and fall over.

Auntie Hattie was an Abomination all by herself.

Polly buttoned up the breeches with a sense of exhilaration. She felt she'd crossed a bridge, a sensation that was helped by the realization that she'd kept her feet dry.

Someone said, 'Psst!'

It was just as well she'd already taken a leak. Panic instantly squeezed every muscle. Where were they hiding? This was just a rotten old shed! Oh, there were a few cubicles, but the smell alone suggested very strongly that the woods outside would be a much better proposition. Even on a wild night. Even with extra wolves.

'Yes?' she quavered, and then cleared her throat and demanded, with a little more gruffness: '*Yes?*'

'You'll need these,' whispered the voice. In the fetid gloom she made out something rising over the top of a cubicle. She reached up nervously and touched softness. It was a bundle of wool. Her fingers explored it.

'A pair of *socks*?' she said.

'Right. Wear 'em,' said the mystery voice hoarsely.

'Thank you, but I've brought several pairs . . .' Polly began.

There was a faint sigh. 'No. Not on your feet. Shove 'em down the front of your trousers.'

'What do you mean?'

'Look,' said the whisperer patiently, 'you don't bulge where you shouldn't bulge. That's good. But you don't bulge where you should bulge, either. You know? Lower down?'

'Oh! Er . . . I . . . but . . . I didn't think people

noticed . . .' said Polly, glowing with embarrassment. She'd been spotted! But there was no hue and cry, no angry quotations from the *Book of Nuggan*. Someone was *helping*. Someone who had *seen* her . . .

'It's a funny thing,' said the voice, 'but they notice what's missing more than they notice what's there. Just one pair, mark you. Don't get ambitious.'

Polly hesitated. 'Um . . . is it obvious?' she said.

'No. That's why I gave you the socks.'

'I *meant* that . . . that I'm not . . . that I'm . . .'

'Not really,' said the voice in the dark. 'You're pretty good. You come over as a frightened young lad trying to look big and brave. You might pick your nose a bit more often. Just a tip. Few things interest a young man more than the contents of his nostrils. Now I've got a favour to ask you in return.'

I didn't *ask* you for one, Polly thought, quite annoyed at being taken for being a frightened young lad when she was sure she'd come over as quite a cool, non-ruffled young lad. But she said calmly: 'What is it?'

'Got any paper?'

Wordlessly, Polly pulled 'From the Mothers of Borogravia!' out of her shirt and handed it up. She heard the sound of a match striking, and a sulphurous smell which only improved the general conditions.

'Why, is this the escutcheon of her grace the Duchess I see in front of me?' said the whisperer. 'Well, it won't be in front of me for long. Beat it . . . boy.'

Polly hurried out into the night, shocked, dazed,

confused and almost asphyxiated, and made it to the shed door. But she'd barely shut it behind her and was still blinking in the blackness when it was thrust open again, to let in the wind, rain and Corporal Strappi.

'All right, all right! Hands off ... well, you lot wouldn't be able to find 'em ... and on with socks! Hup hup hi ho hup hup ...'

Bodies were suddenly springing up or falling over all round Polly. Their muscles must have been obeying the voice directly, because no brain could have got into gear that quickly. Corporal Strappi, in obedience to the law of non-commissioned officers, responded by making the confusion more confusing.

'Good grief, a lot of old women could shift better'n you!' he shouted with satisfaction as people flailed around looking for coats and boots. 'Fall in! Get shaved! Every man in the regiment to be clean shaven, by order! Get dressed! Wazzer, I've got my eye on you! Move! Move! Breakfast in five minutes! Last one there doesn't get a sausage! Oh deary me, what a bloody *shower*!'

The four lesser horsemen of Panic, Bewilderment, Ignorance and Shouting took control of the room, to Corporal Strappi's obscene glee. Polly, though, ducked out of the door, pulled a small tin mug out of her pack, dipped it into a water butt, balanced it on an old barrel behind the inn, and started to shave.

She'd practised this, too. The secret was in the old cut-throat razor that she'd carefully blunted. After that, it was all in the shaving brush and soap. Get a lot of lather on, shave a lot of lather off, and you'd had a

shave, hadn't you? Must have done, sir, feel how smooth the skin is . . .

She was halfway through when a voice by her ear screamed: 'What d'you think you're doing, Private Parts?'

It was just as well the blade *was* blunt.

'Perks, sir!' she said, rubbing her nose. 'I'm shaving, sir! It's Perks, sir!'

'Sir? *Sir?* I'm not a sir, Parts, I'm a bloody *corporal*, Parts. That means you calls me "corporal", Parts. And you are shaving in an official regimental mug, Parts, what you have not been issued with, right? You a deserter, Parts?'

'No, s— corporal!'

'A thief, then?'

'No, corporal!'

'Then how come you got a bloody mug, Parts?'

'Got it off a dead man, sir— corporal!'

Strappi's voice, pitched to a scream in any case, became a screech of rage. 'You're a *looter?*'

'No, corporal! The soldier . . .'

. . . had died almost in her arms, on the floor of the inn.

There had been half a dozen men in that party of returning heroes. They must have been trekking with grey-faced patience for days, making their way back to little villages in the mountains. Polly counted nine arms and ten legs between them, and ten eyes.

But it was the apparently whole who were worse, in a way. They kept their stinking coats buttoned tight, in lieu of bandages, over whatever unspeakable mess

lay beneath, and they had the smell of death about them. The inn's regulars made space for them, and talked quietly, like people in a sacred place. Her father, not usually a man given to sentiment, quietly put a generous tot of brandy into each mug of ale, and refused all payment. Then it turned out that they were carrying letters from soldiers still fighting, and one of them had brought the letter from Paul. He pushed it across the table to Polly as she served them stew and then, with very little fuss, he died.

The rest of the men moved unsteadily on later that day, taking with them, to give to his parents, the pot-metal medal that had been in the soldier's coat pocket and the official commendation from the Duchy that went with it. Polly had taken a look at it. It was printed, including the Duchess's signature, and the man's name had been filled in, rather cramped, because it was longer than average. The last few letters were rammed up tight together.

It's little details like that which get remembered, as undirected white-hot rage fills the mind. Apart from the letter and the medal, all the man left behind was a tin mug and, on the floor, a stain which wouldn't scrub out.

Corporal Strappi listened impatiently to a slightly adjusted version. Polly could see his mind working. The mug had belonged to a soldier; now it belonged to another soldier. Those were the facts of the matter, and there wasn't much he could do about it. He resorted, instead, to the safer ground of general abuse.

'So you think you're smart, Parts?' he said.

'No, corporal.'

'Oh? So you're stupid, are you?'

'Well, I did enlist, corporal,' said Polly meekly. Somewhere behind Strappi, someone sniggered.

'I've got my eye on you, Parts,' growled Strappi, temporarily defeated. 'Just you put a foot wrong, that's all.' He strode off.

'Um . . .' said a voice beside Polly. She turned to see another youth, wearing secondhand clothes and an air of nervousness that didn't quite conceal some bubbling anger. He was big and red-haired, but it was cut so close that it was just head fuzz.

'You're Tonker, right?' she said.

'Yeah, and, er . . . could I have a borrow of your shaving gear, right?'

Polly looked at a chin as free of hair as a billiard ball. The boy blushed.

'Got to start sometime, right?' he said defiantly.

'The razor'll need sharpening,' said Polly.

'That's all right, I know how to do that,' said Tonker.

Polly wordlessly handed over the mug and razor, and took the opportunity to duck into the privy while everyone else was occupied. It was the work of a moment to put the socks in place. Anchoring them was a problem, which she solved by unwinding part of one sock and tucking it up under her belt. They felt odd, and strangely heavy for a little package of wool. Walking a little awkwardly, Polly went in to see what horrors breakfast would bring.

It brought stale horse-bread and sausage and very weak beer. She grabbed a sausage and a slab of bread and sat down.

You had to concentrate to eat horse-bread. There was a lot more about these days, a bread made from flour ground up with dried pease and beans and vegetable scrapings. It used to be made just for horses, to put them in fine condition. Now you hardly ever saw anything else on the table, and there tended to be less and less of it, too. You needed time and good teeth to work your way through a slice of horse-bread, just as you needed a complete lack of imagination to eat a modern sausage. Polly sat and concentrated on chewing.

The only other area of calm was around Private Maladict, who was drinking coffee like a young man relaxing in a pavement café, with the air of someone who has life thoroughly worked out. He nodded at Polly.

Was that him in the privy? she wondered. I got back in just as Strappi started yelling and everyone started running around and rushing in and out. It could have been *anyone*. Do vampires use the privy? Well, do they? Has anyone ever dared ask?

'Sleep well?' he asked.

'Yeah. Did you?' said Polly.

'I couldn't stand that shed, but Mr Eyebrow *kindly* allowed me to use his cellar,' said Maladict. 'Old habits die hard, you know? At least,' he added, 'old *acceptable* habits. I've never felt happy not hanging down.'

'And you got *coffee*?'

'I carry my own supply,' said Maladict, indicating an exquisite little silver and gilt coffee-making engine on the table by his cup, 'and Mr Eyebrow kindly boiled some water for me.' He grinned, showing two long canine teeth. 'It's amazing what you can achieve with a smile, Oliver.'

Polly nodded. 'Er . . . is Igor a friend of yours?' she said. At the next table Igor had obtained a sausage, presumably raw, from the kitchen, and was watching it intently. A couple of wires ran from the sausage to a mug of the horrible vinegary beer, which was bubbling.

'Never seen him before in my life,' said the vampire. 'Of course, if you've met one you have in a sense met them all. We had an Igor at home. Wonderful workers. Very reliable. Very trustworthy. And, of course, so good at stitching things together, if you know what I mean.'

'Those stitches round his head don't look very professional,' said Polly, who was beginning to object to Maladict's permanent expression of effortless superiority.

'Oh, that? It's an Igor thing,' said Maladict. 'It's a Look. Like . . . tribal markings, you know? They like them to show. Ha, we had a servant once who had stitches all the way round his neck, and he was *extremely* proud of them.'

'Really?' said Polly weakly.

'Yes, and the droll part of it all was that it wasn't even *his* head!'

Now Igor had a syringe in his hand, and was watching the sausage with an air of satisfaction. For a moment, Polly thought that the sausage moved . . .

'All right, all right, time's up, you horrible lot!' barked Corporal Strappi, strutting into the room. 'Fall in! That means line up, you shower! That means you too, Parts! And you, Mr Vampire, sir, will you be joining us for a morning's light soldiering? On your feet! And where's that bloody Igor?'

'Here, thur,' said Igor, from three inches behind Strappi's backbone. The corporal spun round.

'How did you get there?' he bellowed.

'It'th a gift, thur,' said Igor.

'Don't you *ever* get behind me again! Fall in with the rest of them! Now . . . Attention!' Strappi sighed theatrically. 'That means "stand up straight". Got it? Once more with feeling! Attention! Ah, I see the problem! You've got trousers that are permanently at ease! I think I shall have to write to the Duchess and tell her she should ask for her money back! What are you smiling about, Mr Vampire sir?' Strappi positioned himself in front of Maladict, who stood faultlessly to attention.

'Happy to be in the regiment, corporal!'

'Yeah, right,' mumbled Strappi. 'Well, you won't be so—'

'*Everything all right, corporal?*' asked Sergeant Jackrum, appearing in the doorway.

'Best we could expect, sergeant,' sighed the corporal. 'We ought to throw 'em back, oh dear me, yes. Useless, useless, useless . . .'

'Okay, lads. Stand easy,' said Jackrum, glancing at Strappi in a less than friendly way. 'Today we're heading on down towards Plotz, where we'll meet up with the other recruiting parties and you'll be issued with your uniforms and weapons, you lucky lads. Any of you ever used a weapon? You *have*, Perks?'

Polly lowered her hand. 'A bit, sarge. My brother taught me a bit when he was home on leave, and some of the old men in the bar where I worked gave me some, er, tips.' They had, too. It was funny to watch a girl waving a sword around, and they'd been kind enough when they weren't laughing. She was a quick learner, but she'd made a point of staying clumsy long after she'd got the feel for the blade, because using a sword was also 'the work of an Man' and a woman doing it was an Abomination unto Nuggan. Old soldiers, on the whole, were on the easy-going side when it came to Abominations. She'd be funny just as long as she was useless, and safe as long as she was funny.

'Expert, are yer?' said Strappi, grinning nastily. 'A real fencin' genius, are yer?'

'No, corporal,' said Polly meekly.

'All right,' said Jackrum. 'Anyone else—'

'Hang on, sarge, I reckon we'd *all* like a bit of instruction from swordmeister Parts,' said Strappi. 'Ain't that right, lads?' There was a general murmuring and shrugging from the squad, who recognized a right little bullying bastard when they saw one but, treacherously, were glad he hadn't picked on them.

Strappi drew his own sword. 'Lend him one of

yours, sarge,' he said. 'Go on. Just a little bit of fun, eh?'

Jackrum hesitated, and glanced at Polly. 'How about it, lad? You don't have to,' he said.

I'll have to sooner or later, Polly thought. The world was full of Strappies. If you backed away from them, they only kept on coming. You had to stop them at the start. She sighed. 'Okay, sarge.'

Jackrum pulled one of his cutlasses out of his sash and handed it to Polly. It looked amazingly sharp.

'He won't hurt you, Perks,' he said, while looking at the smirking Strappi.

'I'll try not to hurt him either, sir,' said Polly, and then cursed herself for the idiot bravado. It must have been the socks talking.

'Oh, *good*,' said Strappi, stepping back. 'We'll just see what you're made of, Parts.'

Flesh, thought Polly. Blood. Easily cut things. Oh, well . . .

Strappi waved his sabre like the old boys had done, down low, in case she was one of those people who thought the whole idea was to hit the other man's sword. She ignored it, and watched his eyes, which was no great treat. He wouldn't stick her, not mortally, not with Jackrum watching. He'd try for something that'd hurt and make everyone laugh at her. That was the Strappi type through and through. Every inn counted one or two amongst its regulars.

The corporal tested her more aggressively a couple of times, and twice, by luck, she managed to knock the blade out of the way. Luck would run out, though, and if she looked like putting up a decent show

Strappi *would* sort her out good and proper. Then she remembered the cackled advice of old Gummy Abbens, a retired sergeant who'd lost his left arm to a broadsword and all his teeth to cider: 'A good swordsman 'ates comin' up against a newbie, gel! The reason bein', he don't know what the bugger's gonna do!'

She swung the cutlass wildly. Strappi had to block it, and for a moment the swords locked.

'That the best you can do, Parts?' the corporal jeered.

Polly reached out and grabbed his shirt. 'No, corporal,' she said, 'but *this* is.' She pulled hard and lowered her head.

The collision hurt more than she'd hoped, but she heard something crunch and it didn't belong to her. She stepped back quickly, slightly dizzy, with the cutlass at the ready.

Strappi had sunk to his knees, blood gushing from his nose. When he got up, *someone* was going to die . . .

Panting, Polly appealed wordlessly to Sergeant Jackrum, who had folded his arms and was looking innocently at the ceiling.

'I bet you didn't learn *that* from your brother, Perks,' he said.

'No, sarge. Got that from Gummy Abbens, sarge.'

Jackrum suddenly looked down at her, grinning. 'What, old Sergeant Abbens?'

'Yes, sarge!'

'There's a name from the past! He's still alive? How is the evil old sot?'

'Er . . . well preserved, sarge,' said Polly, still trying to get her breath.

Jackrum laughed. 'Yeah, I'll bet. Did his best fighting in bars, he did. And I'll bet that's not the only trick he told you about, eh?'

'No, sir.' And the other men had scolded the old boy for telling her, and Gummy had chuckled into his cider mug, and anyway it had taken Polly a long time to find out what 'family jewels' meant.

'Hear that, Strappi?' said the sergeant to the cursing man dribbling blood on to the floor. 'Looks like you was lucky. But there's no prizes for fighting fair in a mêlée, lads, as you will learn. All right, fun over. Go and put some cold water on that, corporal. It always looks worse than it is. And *that's an end of it*, the pair of you. That is an *order*. A word to the wise. Understood?'

'Yes, sarge,' said Polly meekly. Strappi grunted.

Jackrum looked at the rest of the recruits. 'Okay. Any of the rest of you boys ever held a stick? Right. I can see we're going to have to start slow and work up . . .'

There was another grunt from Strappi. You had to admire the man. On his knees, with blood bubbling through the hand cupping his injured nose, he could find time to make life difficult for someone in some small way.

'Private Bloodfnucker hnas a fnord, fnargeant,' he said accusingly.

'Any good with it?' said the sergeant to Maladict.

'Not really, sir,' said Maladict. 'Never had training. I carry it for protection, sir.'

'How can you protect yourself by carrying a sword if you don't know how to use it?'

'Not me, sir. Other people. They see the sword and don't attack me,' said Maladict patiently.

'Yes, but if they did, lad, you wouldn't be any good with it,' said the sergeant.

'No, sir. I'd probably settle for just ripping their heads off, sir. That's what I mean by protection, sir. Theirs, not mine. And I'd get hell from the League if I did that, sir.'

The sergeant stared at him for a while. 'Well thought out,' he mumbled.

There was a thud behind them and a table over-turned. Carborundum the troll sat up, groaned, and crashed back down again. At the second attempt, he managed to stay upright, both hands clutching his head.

Corporal Strappi, now on his feet, must have been made fearless by fury. He headed for the troll in a high-speed strut and stood in front of him, vibrating with rage and still oozing blood in sticky strings.

'You 'orrible little man!' he screamed. 'You—'

Carborundum reached down and, with care and no apparent effort, picked the corporal up by his head. He brought him to one crusted eye and turned him this way and that.

'Did I join th' army?' he rumbled. 'Oh, coprolite . . .'

'This is affnault on a fnuperior officer!' screamed the muffled voice of the corporal.

'Put Corporal Strappi down, please,' said Sergeant

Jackrum. The troll grunted, and lowered the man to the floor.

'Sorry about dat,' he said. 'Thought you was a dwarf.'

'I dnemand this man is affrested for—' Strappi began.

'No you don't, corporal, no you don't,' said the sergeant. 'This is not the time. On your feet, Carborundum, and get in line. Upon my oath, you try that little trick one more time and there will be trouble, understand?'

'Yes, sergeant,' growled the troll, and knuckled himself to his feet.

'Right, then,' said the sergeant, stepping back. 'Now today, my lucky lads, we're goin' to learn about something we call marching . . .'

They left Plün to the wind and rain. About an hour after they'd vanished round a bend in the valley, the shed they'd slept in mysteriously burned down.

There have been better attempts at marching, and they have been made by penguins. Sergeant Jackrum brought up the rear in the cart, shouting instructions, but the recruits moved as if they'd never before had to get from place to place. The sergeant yelled the swagger out of their steps, stopped the cart and for a few of them held an impromptu lesson in the concepts of 'right' and 'left' and, by degrees, they left the mountains.

Polly remembered those first days with mixed feelings. All they did was march, but she was used to long

walks and her boots were good. The trousers ceased to chafe. A watery sun took the trouble to shine. It wasn't cold. It would have been fine, if it hadn't been for the corporal.

She'd wondered how Strappi, whose nose was now about the same colour as a plum, was going to handle the situation between them. It turned out that he intended to deal with it by pretending it hadn't happened, and also by having as little as possible to do with Polly.

He didn't spare the others, although he was selective. Maladict was left strictly alone, as was Carborundum; whatever else Strappi was, he wasn't suicidal. And he was bewildered by Igor. The little man did whatever stupid chore Strappi found for him, and he did it quickly, competently, and giving every impression of someone happy in his work, and that left the corporal completely mystified.

He'd pick on the others for no reason at all, harangue them until they made some trivial mistake, and then bawl them out. His target of choice was Private Goom, better known as Wazzer, who was stick-thin and round-eyed and nervous and said grace loudly before meals. By the end of the first day, Strappi could make him throw up just by shouting. And then he'd laugh.

Only he never really *laughed*, Polly noted. What you got instead was a sort of harsh gargling of spit at the back of the throat, a noise like *ghnssssh*.

The presence of the man cast a damper on everything. Jackrum seldom interfered. He often watched

Strappi, though, and once when Polly caught his eye, he winked.

On the first night a tent was shouted off the cart by Strappi and shouted up and, after a supper of stale bread and sausage, they were shouted in front of a blackboard to be shouted at. Across the top of the board Strappi had written WHAT WE ARE FIGHTING FOR and down the side he had written 1, 2, 3.

'Right, pay attention!' he said, slapping the board with a stick. 'There's some who think that you boys ought to know *why* we are fighting this war, okay? Well, here it comes. Point One, remember the town of Lipz? It was viciously attacked by Zlobenian troops a year ago! They—'

'Sorry, but I thought *we* attacked Lipz, didn't we, corporal? Last year they said—' said Shufti.

'Are you trying to be smart, Private Manickle?' Strappi demanded, naming the biggest sin in his personal list.

'Just want to know, corporal,' said Shufti. He was stocky, running to plump, and one of those people who bustle about being helpful in a mildly annoying way, taking over small jobs that you wouldn't have minded doing for yourself. There was something odd about him, although you had to bear in mind he was currently sitting next to Wazzer, who had enough odd for everybody and was probably contagious . . .

. . . and had caught Strappi's eye. There was no fun in having a go at Shufti, but Wazzer, now, Wazzer was always worth a shout.

'Are you *listening*, Private Goom?' he screamed.

Wazzer, who had been sitting and looking up with his eyes closed, jerked awake. 'Corporal?' he quavered, as Strappi advanced.

'I *said*, are you listening, Goom?'

'Yes, corporal!'

'*Really?* And what did you hear, may I ask?' said Strappi, in a voice of treacle and acid.

'Nothing, corporal. She's not speaking.'

Strappi took a deep, delighted breath of evil air. 'You are a useless, worthless pile of—'

There was a sound. It was a small, nondescript sound, one that you heard every day, a noise that did its job but never expected to be, for example, whistled or part of an interesting sonata. It was simply the sound of stone scraping on metal.

On the other side of the fire Jackrum lowered his cutlass. He had a sharpening stone in his other hand. He returned their group gaze.

'What? Oh. Just maintaining the edge,' he said innocently. 'Sorry if I interrupted your flow there, corporal. Carry on.'

A basic animal survival instinct came to the corporal's aid. He left the trembling Wazzer alone, and turned back to Shufti.

'Yes, yes, we attacked Lipz, too—' said Strappi.

'Was that before the Zlobenians did?' said Maladict.

'Will you listen?' Strappi demanded. 'We valiantly attacked Lipz to reclaim what is Borogravian territory! And *then* the treacherous swede-eaters stole it back . . .'

Polly tuned out a little at this point, now that there was no immediate prospect of seeing Strappi decapitated. She knew about Lipz. Half the old men who came and drank with her father had attacked the place. But no one had expected them to *want* to do it. Someone had just shouted, 'Attack!'

The trouble was the Kneck River. It wandered across the wide, rich, silty plain like a piece of dropped string, but sometimes a flash flood or even a big fallen tree would cause it to crack like a whip, throwing coils of river round areas of land miles from its previous bed. And the river was the international border . . .

She surfaced to hear: '. . . but this time *everyone's* on their side, the bastards! And you know why? It's 'cos of Ankh-Morpork! Because we stopped the mail coaches going over our country and tore down their clacks towers, which are an Abomination unto Nuggan. Ankh-Morpork is a godless city—'

'I thought it had more than three hundred places of worship?' said Maladict.

Strappi stared at him in a rage that was incoherent until he managed to touch bottom again. 'Ankh-Morpork is a *godawful* city,' he recovered. 'Poisonous, just like its river. Barely fit for humans now. They let everything in – zombies, werewolves, dwarfs, vampires, trolls . . .' He remembered his audience, faltered and recovered. '. . . which *in some cases* can be a good thing, of course. But it is a foul, lewd, lawless, overcrowded mess of a place, which is why Prince Heinrich loves it so much! He's been taken over by it,

bought by cheap toys, because that's the way Ankh-Morpork plays it, men. They *buy* you, they *will you stop interrupting!* What's the good of me trying to teach you stuff if you're going to keep on asking questions?'

'I was just wondering why it's so crowded, corp,' said Tonker. 'If it's so bad, I mean.'

'That's because they are a degraded people, private! And they've sent a regiment up here to help Heinrich take over our beloved Motherland. He has turned aside from the ways of Nuggan and embraced Ankh-Morpork's godlessn— godawfulness.' Strappi looked pleased at having spotted that one, and went on, 'Point Two: in addition to its soldiers, Ankh-Morpork has sent Vimes the Butcher, the most evil man in that evil city. They are bent on nothing less than our destruction!'

'I heard that Ankh-Morpork was just angry that we cut the clacks towers down,' said Polly.

'They were on our sovereign territory!'

'Well, it was Zlobenian until—' Polly began.

Strappi waved an angry finger at her. 'You listen to me, Parts! You can't get to be a great country like Borogravia without making enemies! Which leads me on to Point Three, Parts, who's sitting there thinking he's so smart. You all are. I can see it. Well, be smart about this: you might not like everything about your country, eh? It might not be the perfect place, but it's ours. You might think we don't have the best laws, but they're ours. The mountains might not be the prettiest ones or the tallest ones, but they're ours.

We're fighting for what's ours, men!' Strappi slammed his hand over his heart.

> 'Awake, ye sons of the Motherland!
> Taste no more the wine of the sour
> apples . . .'

They joined in, at various levels of drone. You had to. Even if you just opened and shut your mouth, you had to. Even if you just went 'ner, ner, ner', you had to. Polly, who was exactly the kind of person who looks around surreptitiously at times like these, saw that Shufti was singing it word-perfectly and Strappi actually did have tears in his eyes. Wazzer wasn't singing at all. He was praying. That was a good wheeze, said one of the more treacherous areas at the back of Polly's mind.

To the bewilderment of all, Strappi continued – alone – all through the second verse, which nobody ever remembered, and then gave them a smug, I'm-more-patriotic-than-you smile.

Afterwards, they tried to sleep on as much softness as two blankets could provide. They lay there in silence for some time. Jackrum and Strappi had tents of their own, but instinctively they knew that Strappi at least would be a sneaker and a listener at tent flaps.

After about an hour, when rain was drumming on the canvas, Carborundum said: 'Okay, den, I fink I've worked it out. If people are groophar stupid, then we'll fight for groophar stupidity, 'cos it's *our* stupidity. And dat's good, yeah?'

Several of the squad sat up in the darkness, amazed at this.

'I realize I ought to know these things, but what does "groophar" mean?' said the voice of Maladict in the damp darkness.

'Ah, well . . . when, right, a daddy troll an' a mummy troll—'

'Good, right, yes, I think I've got it, thank you,' said Maladict. 'And what *you've* got there, my friend, is patriotism. My country, right or wrong.'

'You *should* love your country,' said Shufti.

'Okay, what part?' the voice of Tonker demanded, from the far corner of the tent. 'The morning sunlight on the mountains? The horrible food? The damn mad Abominations? All of my country except whatever bit Strappi is standing on?'

'But we are at war!'

'Yes, that's where they've got you,' sighed Polly.

'Well, I'm not buying into it. It's all trickery. They keep you down and when they piss off some other country, *you* have to fight for them! It's only *your* country when they want you to get killed!' said Tonker.

'All the good bits in this country are in this tent,' said the voice of Wazzer.

Embarrassed silence descended.

The rain settled in. After a while, the tent began to leak. Eventually someone said, 'What happens, um, if you join up but then you decide you don't want to?'

That was Shufti.

'I think it's called deserting and they cut your head

off,' said the voice of Maladict. 'In my case that would be a drawback but you, dear Shufti, would find it puts a crimp in your social life.'

'I never kissed their damn picture,' said Tonker. 'I swivelled it round when Strappi wasn't looking and kissed it on the back!'

'They'll still say you kissed the Duchess, though,' said Maladict.

'You k-kissed the D-Duchess on the b-bottom?' said Wazzer, horrified.

'It was the back of the picture, okay?' said Tonker. 'It wasn't her real backside. Huh, wouldn't have kissed it if it was!' There was some unidentified sniggering from various corners and just a hint of giggle.

'That was w-wicked!' hissed Wazzer. 'Nuggan in heaven saw you d-do that!'

'It was just a picture, all right?' muttered Tonker. 'Anyway, what's the difference? Front or back, we're all here together and I don't see any steak and bacon!'

Something rumbled overhead. 'I joined t' see exciting forrin places and meet erotic people,' said Carborundum.

That caused a moment's thought. 'I think you mean exotic?' said Igor.

'Yeah, that kind of stuff,' agreed the troll.

'But they always lie,' said someone, and then Polly realized it was her. 'They lie all the time. About everything.'

'Amen to that,' said Tonker. 'We fight for liars.'

'Ah, they may be liars,' snapped Polly, in a passable imitation of Strappi's yap, 'but they're *our* liars!'

'Now, now, children,' said Maladict. 'Let's try to get some sleep, shall we? But here's a happy little dream from your Uncle Maladict. Dream that when we go into battle, Corporal Strappi is *leading* us. Wouldn't that be fun?'

After a while, Tonker said: 'In front of us, you mean?'

'Oh, yes. I can see you're with me, Tonk. Right in front of you. On the noisy, frantic, *confusing* battle-field, where oh so much can go wrong.'

'And we'll have weapons?' said Shufti wistfully.

'Of course you'll have weapons. You're soldiers. And there's the enemy, right in front of you . . .'

'That's a good dream, Mal.'

'Sleep on it, kid.'

Polly turned over, and tried to make herself comfortable. It's all lies, she thought muzzily. Some of them are just prettier than others, that's all. People see what they think is there. Even I'm a lie. But I'm getting away with it.

A warm autumnal wind was blowing leaves off the rowan trees as the recruits marched among the foothills. It was the morning of the next day, and the mountains were behind them. Polly passed the time identifying the birds in the hedgerows. It was a habit. She knew most of them.

She hadn't set out to be an ornithologist. But birds brought Paul alive. All the . . . slowness in the rest of his thinking became a flash of lightning in the presence of birds. Suddenly he knew their names, habits and

habitats, could whistle their songs and, after Polly had saved up for a box of paints off a traveller at the inn, had painted a picture of a wren so real you could hear it.

Their mother had been alive then. The row had gone on for days. Pictures of living creatures were an Abomination in the Eyes of Nuggan. Polly had asked why there were pictures of the Duchess everywhere, and had been thrashed for it. The picture had been burned, the paints thrown away.

It was a terrible thing. Her mother had been a kind woman, or as kind as a devout woman could be who tried to keep up with the whims of Nuggan, and she'd died slowly amidst pictures of the Duchess and amongst the echoes of unanswered prayers, but that was the memory that crawled treacherously into Polly's mind every time: the fury and the scolding, while the little bird seemed to flutter in the flames.

In the fields women and old men were getting in the spoilt wheat after last night's rain, hoping to save what they could. There weren't any young men visible. Polly saw some of the other recruits steal a glance at the scavenging parties, and wondered if they were thinking the same thing.

They saw no one else on the road until midday, when the party was marching through a landscape of low hills; the sun had boiled away some of the clouds and, for a moment at least, summer was back – moist and sticky and mildly unpleasant, like a party guest who won't go home.

A red blob in the distance became a rather larger blob and resolved itself into a loose knot of men. Polly

knew what to expect as soon as she saw it. By the reaction of some of the others, they did not. There was a moment of collision and confusion as people walked into one another, and then the party stopped, and stared.

It took the wounded men some time to draw level, and some time to pass. Two able-bodied men, as far as Polly could tell, were trundling a handcart on which a third man lay. Others were limping on crutches, or had arms in slings, or wore red jackets with an empty sleeve. Perhaps worse were the ones like the man in the inn, grey-faced, staring straight ahead, jackets buttoned tight despite the heat.

One or two of the injured glanced at the recruits as they lurched past, but there was no expression in their eyes beyond a terrible determination.

Jackrum reined in the horse.

'All right, twenty minutes' breather,' he muttered.

Igor turned, nodded to the party of wounded heading grimly onward, and said, 'Permithion to thee if I can do anything for them, tharge?'

'You'll get your chance soon enough, lad,' said the sergeant.

'Tharge?' said Igor, looking hurt.

'Oh, all right. If you must. D'you want someone to give you a hand?'

There was a nasty laugh from Corporal Strappi.

'Some athithtance would be a help, yeth, thargeant,' said Igor, with dignity.

The sergeant looked at the squad, and nodded.

'Private Halter, step forward! Know anything about doctorin'?'

The red-headed Tonker stepped forward smartly. 'I've butchered pigs for me mam, sarge,' he said.

'Capital! Better than an army surgeon, upon my oath. Off you go. Twenty minutes, remember!'

'And don't let Igor bring back any souvenirs!' said Strappi, and laughed his scraping laugh again.

The rest of the boys sat down on the grass by the road, and one or two of them disappeared into the bushes. Polly went on the same errand, but pushed in a lot further, and took the opportunity to make a little sock adjustment. They had a tendency to creep if she wasn't careful.

She froze at a rustling behind her, and then relaxed. She'd been careful. No one would have seen anything. So what if someone else was taking a leak? She'd just push her way back to the road and take no notice—

Lofty sprang up as Polly parted the bushes, breeches round one ankle, face red as a beetroot.

Polly couldn't help herself. Maybe it was the socks. Maybe it was the pleading expression on Lofty's face. When someone's broadcasting 'Don't look!' the eyes have a mind of their own, and go where they're not wanted. Lofty jumped up, dragging at her clothes.

'No, look, it's all right—' Polly began, but it was too late. The girl had gone.

Polly stared at the bushes, and thought: Blast! There's *two* of us! But what would I have said next? 'It's okay, I'm a girl too. You can trust me. We could be friends. Oh, and here's a good tip about socks'?

* * *

Igor and Tonker arrived back late, without a word. Sergeant Jackrum said nothing. The squad moved off.

Polly marched at the back, with Carborundum. This meant she could keep a wary eye on Lofty, whoever she was. For the first time, Polly really looked at her. She was easy to miss, because she was always, as it were, in Tonker's shadow. She was short, although now Polly knew she was female the word 'petite' could be decently used, dark and dark-haired and had a strange, self-absorbed look, and she was always marching with Tonker. Come to think of it, she always slept close to him, too.

Ah, so that was it. She's following her boy, Polly thought. It was kind of romantic, and very, very dumb. Now she knew to look beyond the clothes and haircut, she could see all the little clues that Lofty was a girl, and a girl who hadn't planned enough. She saw Lofty whisper something to Tonker, who half turned and gave Polly a look of instant hatred and a hint of threat.

I *can't* tell her, she thought. She *would* tell him. I can't *afford* to let them know. I've put too much into this. I didn't just cut my hair and wear trousers. I *planned* . . .

Ah, yes . . . the plans.

It had *begun* as a sudden strange fancy, but it had continued as a plan. First, Polly had started to watch boys closely. This had been reciprocated hopefully by a few of them, to their subsequent disappointment. She observed how they moved, she listened to the

rhythm of what passed, among boys, for conversation, she'd noted how they punched one another in greeting. It was a new world.

She already had good muscles for a girl, because running a large inn was all about moving heavy things, and she took over a number of the grittier chores, which coarsened her hands nicely. She'd even worn a pair of her brother's old breeches under her long skirt, to get the feel of them.

A woman could be beaten for that sort of thing. Men dressed like men and women like women; doing it the other way round was 'a blasphemous Abomination unto Nuggan', according to Father Jupe.

And that was probably the secret of her success so far, she thought, as she trudged through a puddle. People didn't *look* for a woman in trousers. To the casual observer, men's clothes and short hair and a bit of swagger were what it took to be a man. Oh, and a second pair of socks.

That had been gnawing at her, too. Someone knew about her, just as she knew about Lofty. *And he hadn't given her away.* She'd suspected it was Eyebrow, but doubted it; he'd have told the sergeant about her, he was that sort. Right now she was guessing it was Maladict, but perhaps that was just because he seemed so *knowing* all the time.

Carbor— no, he'd been out cold, and in any case . . . no, not the troll. And Igor lisped. Tonker? After all, he'd know about Lofty so maybe . . . No, because why would he want to help Polly? No, there was nothing

but danger in owning up to Lofty. The best she could do was try to see to it that the girl didn't give both of them away.

She could hear Tonker whispering to his girl. '... had just died so he cut off one of his legs and an arm and sewed 'em on men who needed 'em, just like I'd darn a tear! You should've seen it! You couldn't see his fingers move! And he has all these ointments that just ...' Tonker's voice died away. Strappi was haranguing Wazzer again.

'Dat Strappi really gets on my crags,' muttered Carborundum. 'You want I should pull the head off'f him? I c'd make it look like a accident.'

'Better not,' said Polly, but she did entertain the thought for a moment.

They'd reached a junction, where the road down from the mountains joined what passed for a main highway. It was crowded. There were carts and wheel-barrows, people driving herds of cows, grandmothers carrying all the household possessions on their backs, a general excitement of pigs and children ... and it was all heading one way.

It was the opposite way to the way the squad was going. The people and animals flowed around it like a stream around an inconvenient rock. The recruits bunched up. It was that or be separated by cows.

Sergeant Jackrum stood up in the cart. 'Private Carborundum!'

'Yes, sergeant?' rumbled the troll.

'To the front!'

That helped. The stream still flowed, but at least the crowds parted some distance further ahead and gave the squad a wide berth. No one wants to barge up against even a slow-moving troll.

But faces stared as the people hurried by. An old lady darted out for a moment, pressed a loaf of stale bread into Tonker's hands, and said, 'You poor boys!' before being swept away in the throng.

'What's this all about, sarge?' said Maladict. 'These look like refugees!'

'Talk like that spreads Alarm and Despondency!' shouted Corporal Strappi.

'Oh, you mean they're just people getting away early for the holidays to avoid the rush?' said Maladict. 'Sorry, I got confused. It must be that woman carrying a whole haystack we just passed.'

'D'you know what can happen to you for cheeking a superior officer?' screamed Strappi.

'No! Tell me, is it worse than whatever it is these people are running away from?'

'You signed up, Mr Bloodsucker! You obey orders!'

'Right! But I don't remember anyone ordering me not to think!'

'Enough of that!' snapped Jackrum. 'Less shouting down there! Move on! Carborundum, you give people a push if they don't make way, y'hear?'

They moved on. After a while the press of people abated a little, so that what had been a torrent became a trickle. Occasionally there would be a family group, or just one hurrying woman, burdened with bags. One old man was struggling with a wheelbarrow full of turnips.

They're even taking the crops out of the fields, Polly noted. And everyone moved at a kind of half-run, as if things would be a little better when they'd caught up with the mass of people ahead. Or merely passed the squad, perhaps.

They made way for an old woman bent double under the weight of a black and white pig. And then there was just the road, rutted and muddy. An afternoon mist was rising from the fields on either side, quiet and clammy. After the noise of the refugees, the silence of the low countryside was suddenly oppressive. The only sound was the trudge and splash of the recruits' boots.

'Permission to speak, sarge?' said Polly.

'Yes, private?' said Jackrum.

'How far is it to Plotz?'

'You don't have to tell 'em, sarge!' said Strappi.

'About five miles,' said Sergeant Jackrum. 'You'll get your uniforms and weapons at the depot there.'

'That's a milit'ry secret, sarge,' Strappi whined.

'We could shut our eyes so's we don't see what we're wearing, how about that?' said Maladict.

'Stop that, Private Maladict,' said Jackrum. 'Just keep moving, and guard that tongue.'

They plodded on. The road grew muddier. A breeze sprang up, but instead of carrying the mist away it merely streamed it across the damp fields in twisty, clammy, unpleasant shapes. The sun became an orange ball.

Polly saw something large and white flutter across the field, blown by the wind. At first she thought it

was a migratory lesser egret that had left things a little late, but it was clearly being blown by the wind. It flopped down once or twice and then, as a gust caught it, blew across the road and wrapped itself across Corporal Strappi's face.

He screamed. Lofty grabbed at the fluttering thing, which was damp. It tore in his— *her* hands, and most of it dropped away from the struggling corporal.

'It's just a bit of paper,' she said.

Strappi flailed at it. 'I *knew* that,' he said. 'I never asked you!'

Polly picked up one of the torn scraps. The paper was thin, and stained with mud, although she recognized the word Ankh-Morpork. The godawful city. And the genius of Strappi was that anything he was against automatically sounded attractive.

'*Ankh-Morpork Times . . .*' she read aloud, before the corporal snatched it out of her hand.

'You can't just read *anything* you see, Parts!' he shouted. 'You don't know who wrote it!' He dropped the damp scrap pages on to the mud and stamped on them. 'Now let's move on!' he said.

They moved on. When the squad were more or less in rhythm, and staring at nothing more than their boots or the mist ahead of them, Polly raised her right hand to chest height and carefully turned it palm up so that she could see the fragment of paper that had soggily stayed behind when the rest had been pulled away.

'No Surrender' to Alliance says Duchess (97)

From William de Worde
Valley of the Kneck, Sektober 7

Borogrovian troops assisted by Lord V
Light Infantry took Kneck Keep this mo
after fierce hand-to-hand fig
I write its armaments which
are being turned on the remn
Borogravian forces acr
 His Grace Commander Sir S
told the *Times* that
surrender had been rej
view the enemy commande
load of stiff-necked fools, don'
in the paper.'
 It is understoo
desperate situ
-spread fami
across t
No altern
invas

They *were* winning, weren't they? So where did the word 'surrender' come from? And what was the Alliance?

And then there was the problem of Strappi, which had been growing on her. She could see he got on Jackrum's nerves as well, and he had a struttiness about him, a certain – er ... sockiness, as if he was really the one in charge. Perhaps it was

just general unpleasantness, but . . .

'Corporal?' she said.

'Yes, Parts?' said Strappi. His nose was still very red.

'We are winning this war, aren't we?' said Polly. She'd given up correcting him.

Suddenly, every ear in the squad was listening.

'Don't you bother yourself about that, Parts!' snapped the corporal. 'Your job is to fight!'

'Right, corp. So . . . I'll be fighting on the winning side, will I?'

'Oho, we've got someone who asks too many questions here, sarge!' said Strappi.

'Yeah, don't ask questions, Perks,' said Jackrum, absent-mindedly.

'So we're losing, then?' said Tonker. Strappi turned on him.

'That's spreading Alarm and Despondency again, that is!' he shrieked. 'That's aiding the enemy!'

'Yeah, knock it off, Private Halter,' said Jackrum. 'Okay? Now get a—'

'Halter, I'm placing you under arrest for—'

'*Corporal Strappi, a word in your shell-like ear, please? You men, you stop here!*' growled the sergeant, clambering down from the cart.

Jackrum walked back down the road about fifty feet. Glaring round at the squad, the corporal strutted after him.

'Are we in trouble?' said Tonker.

'You guess,' said Maladict.

'Bound to be,' said Shufti. 'Strappi can always get you for *something*.'

'They're having an argument,' said Maladict. 'Which is odd, don't you think? A sergeant is supposed to give *orders* to a corporal.'

'We *are* winning, aren't we?' said Shufti. 'I mean, I know there's a war, but ... I mean, we get weapons, don't we, and we'll ... well, they've got to train us, right? It'll probably be all over by then, right? Everyone says we're winning.'

'I will ask the Duchess in my prayers tonight,' said Wazzer.

The rest of the squad looked at one another with a shared expression.

'Yeah, right, Wazz,' said Tonker kindly. 'You do that.'

The sun was setting fast, half hidden in the mist. Here, on the muddy road between damp fields, it suddenly felt as cold as it could be.

'No one says we're winning, except maybe Strappi,' said Polly. 'They just say that everyone says we're winning.'

'The men Igor ... repaired didn't even say that,' said Tonker. 'They said "you poor bastards, you'll leg it if you've any sense." '

'Thank you for sharing,' said Maladict.

'It looks as though everyone's feeling sorry for us,' said Polly.

'Yeah, well, so am I, and I *am* uth,' said Igor. 'Thome of thothe men—'

'All right, all right, stop lollygagging, you lot!' shouted Strappi, marching up.

'Corporal?' said the sergeant quietly, hauling himself back on to the cart. Strappi paused, and then in a

voice dripping with syrup and sarcasm went on: 'Excuse *me*. The sergeant and myself would be *obleejed* if you brave heroes to be would join us in a little light marching? Jolly good! And there will be embroidery later on. Best foot forward, ladies!'

Polly heard Tonker gasp. Strappi turned, eyes glinting with sinister anticipation. 'Oh, someone doesn't like being called a *lady*, eh?' he said. 'Dear me, Private Halter, you've got a lot to learn, haven't you? You're a sissy little *lady* until we make a man of you, right? And I dread to think how long that's going to take. Move!'

I know, thought Polly, as they set off. It takes about ten seconds, and a pair of socks. One sock, and you could make Strappi.

Plotz turned out to be like Plün, but it was worse because it was bigger. The rain started again as they marched into the cobbled square. It looked as though it always rained here. The buildings were grey, and mud-spattered near the ground. Roof gutters over-flowed, pouring rain on to the cobbles and sending a spray over the recruits. There was no one about. Polly saw open doors banging in the wind, and bits of debris in the streets, and remembered the lines of hurrying people on the road. There was no one here.

Sergeant Jackrum climbed down from the cart as Strappi bawled them into line. Then the sergeant took over, leaving the corporal to glower from the sidelines.

'This is wonderful Plotz!' he said. 'Have a look round, so that if you is killed and goes to hell, it won't come as a shock! You'll be bivvying in that barracks

over there, what is milit'ry property!' He waved a hand towards a crumbling stone building that looked about as military as a barn. 'You will be issued with your equipment. And tomorrow it's a nice long march to Crotz, where you will arrive as boys and leave as men *did I just say something funny, Perks?* No, I thought so, too! Attention! That means stand up straight!'

'That's *straight!*' yelled Strappi.

A young man was riding across the square on a tired, skinny brown horse, which was quite suitable because he was a tired, skinny man. The skinniness was helped by the fact that he wore a tunic which had clearly been made for someone a couple of sizes larger. The same applied to his helmet. He must have padded it, Polly thought. One cough and it'll be over his eyes.

Sergeant Jackrum snapped off a salute as the officer approached. 'Jackrum, sir. You'll be Lieutenant Blouse, sir?'

'Well done, sergeant.'

'These are the recruits from upriver, sir. Fine body of men, sir.'

The rider peered at the squad. He actually leaned forward over the horse's neck, causing rain to pour off his helmet.

'This is *all*, sergeant?'

'Yessir.'

'Most of them look very young,' said the lieutenant, who didn't look very old.

'Yessir.'

'And isn't that one a troll?'

'Yessir. Well spotted, sir.'

'And the one with stitches all round his head?'

'He's an Igor, sir. Sort of like a special clan up in the mountains, sir.'

'Do they fight?'

'Can take a man apart very quickly, sir, as I understand it,' said Jackrum, his expression not changing.

The young lieutenant sighed. 'Well, I'm sure they're all good fellows,' he said. 'Now then, er . . . men, I—'

'Pay attention and listen to what the lieutenant has to say!' bawled Strappi.

The lieutenant shuddered. '—thank you, corporal,' he said. 'Men, I have good news,' he added, but in the voice of one who hasn't. 'You were probably expecting a week or two in the training camp in Crotz, yes? But I'm glad to be able to tell you that the . . . the war is progressing so . . . so . . . so *well* that you are to go directly to the front.'

Polly heard one or two gasps, and a snigger from Corporal Strappi.

'*All* of you are to go to the lines,' said the lieutenant. 'That includes you too, corporal. Your time for action has come at last!'

The snigger stopped. 'Sorry, sir?' said Strappi. 'The front? But you know that I'm— well, you know about the special duties—'

'My orders said all able-bodied men, corporal,' said Blouse. 'I expect that you'll be itching for the fray after all these years, eh, a young man like you?'

Strappi said nothing.

'However,' said the lieutenant, fumbling under his soaking cloak, 'I do have a package here for *you*, Sergeant Jackrum. A very welcome one, I've no doubt.'

Jackrum took the packet gingerly. 'Thank you, sir, I'll look at this later on—' he began.

'On the contrary, Sergeant Jackrum!' said Blouse. 'Your last recruits should see this, since you are both a soldier and, as it were, a "father of soldiers"! And so it's only right that they see a fine soldier get his reward: *an honourable discharge, sergeant!*' Blouse spoke the words as if they had cream and a little cherry on top.

Apart from the rain, the only sound now was Jackrum's pudgy finger slowly ripping open the package.

'Oh,' he said, like a man in shock. 'Good. A picture of the Duchess. That's *eighteen* I have now. Oh, and, oo, a piece of paper saying it's a medal, so it looks like we've even run out of pot metal now. Oh, and my discharge with a printing of the Duchess's very own signature itself!' He turned the packet over and shook it. 'Not my three months' back pay, though.'

'Three loud hurrahs for Sergeant Jackrum!' said the lieutenant to the rain and wind. 'Hip-hip—'

'But I thought we needed every man, sir!' said Jackrum.

'Judging by all the notes pinned on that packet, it has been following you around for years, sergeant,' said Blouse. 'You know the military. That is your

official discharge, I am afraid. I cannot rescind it. I am sorry.'

'But—' Jackrum began.

'It bears the Duchess's signature, sergeant. Will you argue with that? I said I am sorry. In any case, what would you do? We will not be sending out any more recruiting parties.'

'What? But we always need men, sir!' Jackrum protested. 'And I'm fit and well again, got the stamina of a horse—'

'You were the only man to return with recruits, sergeant. That is how the matter is.'

The sergeant hesitated for a moment, and then saluted. 'Yessir! Very good, sir! Will see the new lads settled in, sir! Pleasure to have served, sir!'

'Can I ask something?' said Maladict.

'You do not address an officer directly, private,' snapped Jackrum.

'No, let the man speak, sergeant,' said the lieutenant. 'These are . . . unusual times, after all. Yes, my man?'

'Did I hear you say we're going into battle without training, sir?'

'Oh, well, most of you will almost certainly be pikemen, haha,' said the lieutenant nervously. 'Not a lot of training there, eh? You just need to know which end is which, haha.' He looked as though he wanted to die.

'Pikemen?' said Maladict, looking puzzled.

'You heard the lieutenant, Private Maladict,' snapped the sergeant.

'Yes, sir. Thank you, sir,' said Maladict, stepping back into the ranks.

'Are there any more questions?' said Blouse, looking along the line. 'Jolly good, then. We leave by the last boat, at midnight. Carry on, sergeant . . . for now. What was the other thing . . . oh, yes. And I shall need a batman.'

'Volunteers to be the lieutenant's batman step forward! *Not you, Private Maladict!*' snapped the sergeant.

No one moved.

'Oh, come now,' said the lieutenant.

Polly slowly raised a hand. 'What's a batman, sir?'

The sergeant grinned mirthlessly. 'Fair question,' he said. 'A batman is, like, a personal servant who takes care of the officer. Fetches his meals to him, sees he's smartly turned out, that style of thing. So's he is free to perform his duties more adequatelier.'

Igor stepped forward. 'Igorth are uthed to thervice, thargeant,' he said.

Using the amazing powers of deafness and restricted vision sometimes available even to the most nervous officers, the lieutenant appeared not to notice him. He looked fixedly at Polly.

'What about you, private?' he said.

'Private Perks used to work in a bar, sir,' the sergeant volunteered.

'Capital. Report to my quarters in the inn at six, Private Perks. Carry on, sergeant.'

As the skinny horse staggered away, Sergeant Jackrum directed his glare at the squad, but there was

no real fire to it. He appeared to be operating on automatic, with his mind elsewhere. 'Don't just stand there trying to look pretty! There's uniforms and weapons inside! Get kitted up! If you want grub, cook it yerself! At the double! Disssssss*miss*!'

The squad dashed for the barracks, propelled by sheer volume. But Polly hesitated. Corporal Strappi hadn't moved since the snigger had been cut short. He was staring blankly at the ground.

'You all right, corporal?' she said.

'You go away, Parts,' said the corporal, in a low voice that was much worse than his normal petulant shout. 'Just go away, all right?'

She shrugged, and followed the others. But she had noticed the steaming dampness round the corporal's feet.

There was chaos inside. The barracks was really just one large room which did duty as mess, assembly room and kitchen, with big bunk rooms beyond it. It was empty, and well on the way to decay. The roof leaked, the high windows were broken, dead leaves had blown in and lay around on the floor, among the rat droppings. There were no pickets, no sentries, no people. There was a big pot boiling on the sooty hearth, though, and its hiss and seethe were the only liveliness in the place. At some point part of the room had been set up as a kind of quartermaster's store, but most of the shelves were empty. Polly had expected some sort of queue, some kind of order, possibly someone handing out little piles of clothes.

What there was, instead, was a rummage stall. Very much like a rummage stall, in fact, because nothing on it appeared to be new and little on it appeared to be worth having. The rest of the squad were already pawing through what might have been called merchandise if there were any possibility that anyone could be persuaded to buy it.

'*What's this? One Size, Doesn't Fit Anyone?*'

'*This tunic's got blood on it!* Blood!'

'*Well, it is one of the thtubborn thtainth, it's alwayth very hard to get it out without—*'

'*Where's the proper armour?*'

'*Oh, no! There's an arrow hole in this one!*'

'*What dis? Nuffin fits a troll!*'

A small, leathery old man was at bay behind the table, cowering under the ferocity of Maladict's glare. He wore a red uniform jacket, done up badly, with a corporal's stripes, stained and faded, on the sleeve. The left breast was covered in medals.

One arm ended in a hook. One eye was covered by a patch.

'We're going to be pikemen, the lieutenant said!' said the vampire. 'That means a sword and pike per man, right? And a shield if there's an arrow storm, right? And a heavy helmet, right?'

'Wrong! You can't yell at me like that!' said the man. 'See these medals? I'm a—'

A hand descended from above and lifted him over the table. Carborundum held the man close to his face and nodded.

'Yah, can see 'em, mister,' he rumbled. 'And . . . ?'

The recruits had fallen silent.

'Put him down, Carborundum,' said Polly. 'Gently.'

'Why?'

'He's got no legs.'

The troll focused. Then, with exaggerated care, he lowered the old soldier to the ground. There were a couple of little tapping sounds as the two wooden peg-legs touched the planking.

'Sorry about dat,' he said.

The little man steadied himself against the table and shuffled his arms round a couple of crutches.

'All right,' he said gruffly. 'No harm done. But watch it, another time!'

'But this is ridiculous!' said Maladict, turning to Polly and waving a hand at the heap of rags and bent metal. 'You couldn't equip three men out of this mess. There's not even any decent boots!'

Polly looked along the length of the table. 'We're supposed to be well equipped,' she said to the one-eyed man. 'We're supposed to be the finest army in the world. That's what we're told. And aren't we winning?'

The man looked at her. Inside, she stared at herself. She hadn't meant to speak out like that.

'So they say,' he said, in a blank kind of way.

'And w-what do *you* say?' said Wazzer. He'd picked up one of the few swords. It was stained and notched.

The corporal glanced up at Carborundum, and then at Maladict.

'I'm not s-stupid, you know!' Wazzer went on, red in the face and trembling. 'All this stuff is off d-dead men!'

'Well, it's a shame to waste good boots—' the man began.

'We're the last o-ones, aren't we?' said Wazzer. 'The last r-recruits!'

The peg-legged corporal eyed the distant doorway, and saw no relief heading in his direction.

'We've got to stay here all night,' said Maladict. 'Night!' he went on, causing the old corporal to wobble on his crutches. 'When who knows what evil flits through the shadows, dealing death on silent wings, seeking a hapless victim who—'

'Yeah, all right, all right, I *did* see your ribbon,' said the corporal. 'Look, I'm closing up after you've gone. I just run the stores, that's all. That's all I do, honest! I'm on one-tenth pay, me, on account of the leg situation, and I don't want trouble!'

'And this is all you've got?' said Maladict. 'Don't you have a little something . . . put by . . .'

'Are you saying I'm dishonest?' said the corporal hotly.

'Let's say I'm open to the idea that you might not be,' said the vampire. 'C'mon, corporal, you said we're the last to go. What are you saving up? What've you got?'

The corporal sighed, and swung with surprising speed over to a door, which he unlocked. 'You'd better come and look,' he said. 'But it's not good . . .'

It was worse. They found a few more breastplates, but one was sliced in half and another was one big dent. A shield was in two pieces, too. There were bent

swords and crushed helmets, battered hats and torn shirts.

'I done what I can,' sighed the corporal. 'I hammered stuff out and washed out the clothes but it's been weeks since I had any coal for the forge and you can't do nothin' about the swords without a forge. It's been months since I got any new weapons and, let me tell you, since the dwarfs buggered off the steel we've been getting is crap anyway.' He rubbed his nose. 'I know you think quartermasters are a thieving bunch and I won't say we might not skim a bit off the top when things are going well, but this stuff? A beetle couldn't make a living off this.' He sniffed again. 'Ain't been paid in three months, neither. I guess one-tenth of nothing is not as bad as nothing, but I was never that good at philosophy.'

Then he brightened up. 'Got plenty to eat, at least,' he said. 'If you like horse, that is. Personally I prefer rat, but there's no accounting for taste.'

'I can't eat horse!' said Shufti.

'Ah, you'd be a rat man?' said the corporal, leading the way out into the big room.

'No!'

'You'll learn to be one. You'll *all* learn,' said the little one-tenth corporal, with an evil grin. 'Ever eaten scubbo? No? Nothing like a bowl of scubbo when you're hungry. You can put *anything* in scubbo. Pork, beef, mutton, rabbit, chicken, duck . . . anything. Even rats, if you've got 'em. It's food for the marching man, scubbo. Got some on the boil out there right now. You can have some of that, if you like.'

The squad brightened up.

'Thoundth good,' said Igor. 'What'th in it?'

'Boiling water,' said the corporal. 'It's what we call "blind scubbo". But there's going to be old horse in a minute unless you've got something better. Could do with some seasonings, at least. Who's looking after the rupert?'

They looked at one another.

The corporal sighed. 'The officer,' he explained. 'They're all called Rupert or Rodney or Tristram or something. They get better grub than you do. You could try scrounging something at the inn.'

'Scrounge?' said Polly.

The old man rolled his one eye.

'Yeah. Scrounge. Scrounge, nick, have a lend of, borrow, thieve, lift, acquire, purrrr-loin. That's what you'll learn, if you're gonna survive this war. Which they say we're winnin', o' course. Always remember that.' He spat vaguely in the direction of the fire, possibly missing the cooking pot only by accident. 'Yeah, an' all the lads I see coming back down the road walking hand in hand with Death, they probably overdid the celebrating, eh? So easy to take your hand right off if you open a bottle of cham-pag-nee the wrong way, eh? I see you've got an Igor with you, you lucky devils. Wish we'd had one when I went off to battle. I wouldn't be kept awake by woodworm if we had.'

'We have to *steal* our food?' said Maladict.

'No, you can starve if that takes your fancy,' said the corporal. 'I've starved a few times. There's no future in

it. Ate a man's leg when we were snowed up in the Ibblestarn campaign but, fair's fair, he ate mine.' He looked at their faces. 'Well, it's not on, is it, eating your own leg? You'd probably go blind.'

'You *swapped* legs?' said Polly, horrified.

'Yeah, me an' Sergeant Hausegerda. It was his idea. Sensible man, the sergeant. That kept us alive for the week and by then the relief had got through. We were certainly relieved about *that*. Oh, dear. Where's my manners? How d'yer do, lads, my name's Corporal Scallot. They call me Threeparts.' He held out his hook.

'But that's cannibalism!' said Tonker, backing away.

'No it's not, not officially, not unless you eat a whole person,' said Threeparts Scallot levelly. 'Milit'ry rules.'

All eyes turned to the big pot bubbling on the fire.

'Horse,' said Scallot. 'Ain't got nothing *but* horse. I *told* you. I wouldn't lie to you, boys. Now kit yerselves up with the best yer can find. What's your name, stone man?'

'Carborundum,' said the troll.

'Got a wee bit o' decent snacking anthracite saved up out the back, then, and some official red paint for you 'cos I never met a troll yet that wanted to wear a jacket. The rest of you, mark what I'm telling yer: fill up with grub. Fill yer pack with grub. Fill yer shako with grub. Fill yer boots with soup. If any of you run across a pot of mustard, you hang on to it – it's amazin' what mustard'll help down. And look after your mates. And keep out of the way of officers, 'cos

they ain't healthy. That's what you learn in the army. The enemy dun't really *want* to fight you, 'cos the enemy is mostly blokes like you who want to go home with all their bits still on. But officers'll get you killed.' Scallot looked round at them. 'There. I've said it. And if there's a political amongst you: mister, you can go an' tell tales and to hell with you.'

After a few moments of embarrassed silence Polly said: 'What's a political?'

'Like a spy, only on your own side,' said Maladict.

'That's right,' said Scallot. 'There's one in every battalion these days, snitching on their mates. Get promotion that way, see? Don't want dissent in the ranks, eh? Don't want loose talk about losing battles, right? Which is a load of bloody cludgies, 'cos the infantry grumbles all the time. Moaning is part of *bein'* a soldier.' He sighed. 'Anyway, there's a bunkhouse out the back. I beats the pallyarses regular so there's probably not too many fleas.' Once again he looked at blank faces. 'That's straw mattresses to you. Go on, help yourselves. Take what you like. I'm closing up after you've gone, anyway. We *must* be winning now you rattling lads are joining, right?'

The clouds had broken when Polly stepped out into the night, and a half-moon filled the world with cold silver and black. The inn opposite was another rubbishy alehouse for selling bad beer to soldiers. It stank of ancient slops, even before she opened the door. The sign was flaked and unrecognizable, but she could read the name: The World Turned Upside

Down. She pushed open the door. The smell got worse. There were no customers and no sign of Strappi or Jackrum, but Polly did see a servant methodically spreading the inn's dirt evenly across the floor with a mop.

'Excuse m—' she began, and then remembered the socks, raised her voice and tried to sound angry. 'Hey, where's the lieutenant?'

The servant looked at her and gestured up the stairs with a thumb. There was only one candle alight up there, and she knocked on the nearest door.

'Enter.'

She entered. Lieutenant Blouse was standing in the middle of the floor in his breeches and shirtsleeves, holding a sabre. Polly was no expert in these matters, but she thought she recognized the stylish, flamboyant pose as the one beginners tend to use just before they're stabbed through the heart by a more experienced fighter.

'Ah, Perks, isn't it?' he said, lowering the blade. 'Just, er, limbering up.'

'Yes, sir.'

'There's some laundry in the bag over there. I expect someone in the inn will do it. What's for supper?'

'I'll check, sir.'

'What are the men having?'

'Scubbo, sir,' said Polly. 'Possibly with hor—'

'Then bring me some, will you? We are at war, after all, and I must show an example to my men,' said

Blouse, sheathing the sword at the third attempt. 'That would be good for morale.'

Polly glanced at the table. A book lay open on top of a pile of others. It looked like a manual of swordsmanship, and the page it was open at was page five. Beside it was a thick-lensed pair of spectacles.

'Are you a reading man, Perks?' said Blouse, closing the book.

Polly hesitated. But, then, what did Ozzer care? 'A bit, sir,' she admitted.

'I suspect I shall have to leave most of these behind,' he said. 'Do take one if you want it.' He waved a hand at the books. Polly read the titles. *The Craft of War. Principles of Engagement. Battle Studies. Tactical Defence.*

'All a bit heavy for me, sir,' she said. 'Thanks all the same.'

'Tell me, Perks,' said Blouse, 'are the recruits in, er, good spirits?'

He gave her a look of apparently genuine concern. He really did have no chin, she noticed. His face just eased its way into his neck without much to disturb it on the way, but his Adam's apple, now, that was a champion. It went up and down his neck like a ball on a spring.

Polly had been soldiering for only a couple of days, but already an instinct had developed. In summary, it was this: lie to officers. 'Yes, sir,' she said.

'Getting everything they need?'

The aforesaid instinct weighed the chances of their getting anything more than they'd got already

as a result of a complaint, and Polly said, 'Yes, sir.'

'Of course, it is not up to us to question our orders,' said Blouse.

'Wasn't doing so, sir,' said Polly, momentarily perplexed.

'Even though at times we might feel—' the lieutenant began, and started again. 'Obviously warfare is a very volatile thing, and the tide of battle can change in a moment.'

'Yessir,' said Polly, still staring. The man had a small spot where his spectacles had rubbed on his nose.

The lieutenant seemed to have something on his mind, too. 'Why did you join up, Perks?' he said, groping on the table and finding his spectacles at the third attempt. He had woollen gloves on, with the fingers cut out.

'Patriotic duty, sir!' said Polly promptly.

'You lied about your age?'

'Nosir!'

'*Just* patriotic duty, Perks?'

There were lies, and then there were lies. Polly shifted awkwardly. 'Would quite like to find out what's happened to my brother Paul, sir,' she said.

'Ah, yes.' Lieutenant Blouse's face, not a picture of happiness to begin with, suddenly bore a hunted look.

'Paul Perks, sir,' Polly prompted.

'I'm, er, not really in a position to know, Perks,' said Blouse. 'I was working as a . . . I was, er, in charge of, er, I was engaged in special work back at headquarters, er . . . obviously I don't know all the soldiers, Perks. Older brother, w— is he?'

'Yessir. Joined the Ins-and-Outs last year, sir.'

'And, er, have you any younger brothers?' said the lieutenant.

'No, sir.'

'Ah, well. That's something to be thankful for, at any rate,' said Blouse. It was a strange thing to say. Polly's brow wrinkled in puzzlement.

'Sir?' she said.

And then she felt an unpleasant sensation of movement. Something was slipping slowly down the inside of her thigh.

'Anything the matter, Perks?' said the lieutenant, catching her expression.

'Nosir! Just a . . . a bit of cramp, sir! All the marching, sir!' She clamped both hands around one knee and edged backwards towards the door. 'I'll just go and . . . go and see to your supper, sir!'

'Yes, yes,' said Blouse, staring at her leg. 'Yes . . . please . . .'

Polly paused outside the door to pull her socks up, retucked the end of one under her belt as an anchor, and hurried down to the inn's kitchens. A look told her all she wanted to know. Food hygiene here consisted of making a half-hearted effort not to gob in the stew.

'I want onions, salt, pepper—' she began.

The maid who was stirring the soot-black pot on the soot-black stove glanced up, realized she had been addressed by a man, and hastily pushed her damp hair out of her eyes.

'It's stoo, sir,' she announced.

'I don't want any. I just want the stuff,' said Polly. 'For the officer,' she added.

The kitchen maid pointed a soot-blackened thumb to a nearby door and gave Polly what she probably thought was a saucy grin.

'I'm sure you can have anything that takes your fancy, sir,' she said.

Polly glanced at the two shelves that had been dignified by the name of pantry, and grabbed a couple of large onions, one in each hand.

'May I?' she said.

'Oh, sir!' giggled the maid. 'I do hope you're not one of them *coarse* soldiers who'd take advantage of a helpless maiden, sir!'

'No, er . . . no. I'm not one of them,' said Polly.

'Oh.' This didn't seem to be the right answer. The maid put her head on one side. 'Have you had *much* to do with young women, sir?' she asked.

'Er . . . yes. Quite a lot,' said Polly. 'Er . . . lots, really.'

'Really?' The maid drew closer. She smelled mostly of sweat, tinged with soot. Polly raised the onions as a kind of barrier.

'I'm sure there's things you'd like to learn,' the maid purred.

'I'm sure there's something you wouldn't!' said Polly, and turned and ran.

As she made it out into the cold night air, a plaintive voice behind her called out, 'I'm off at eight o'clock!'

* * *

Ten minutes later, Corporal Scallot was impressed. Polly got the feeling this did not happen often. Shufti had wedged an old breastplate beside the fire, had hammered some slabs of horsemeat until they were tender, dipped them in some flour, and was frying them. The sliced onions sizzled next to them.

'I always just boil 'em,' said Scallot, watching him with interest.

'You just lose all the flavour if you do that,' said Shufti.

'Hey, lad, the stuff I've ate, you wouldn't want to *taste* it!'

'Sauté stuff first, especially the onions,' Shufti went on. 'Improves the flavour. Anyway, when you boil you ought to boil slow. That's what me mam always says. Roast fast, boil slow, okay? This isn't bad meat, for horse. Shame to boil it.'

'Amazin',' said Scallot. 'We could've done with you in Ibblestarn. The sarge was a good man but a bit, you know, tough in the leg?'

'A marinade would probably have helped,' said Shufti absently, flipping over a slice of meat with a broken sword. He turned to Polly. 'Was there any more stuff in the larder, Ozz? I can make up some stock for tomorrow if we can—'

'I'm not going in that kitchen again!' said Polly.

'Ah, that'd be Roundheels Molly?' said Corporal Scallot, looking up and grinning. 'She's sent many a lad on his way rejoicing.' He dipped a ladle in the boiling scubbo pot next to the pan. Disintegrated grey meat seethed in a few inches of water.

'That'll do for the rupert,' he said, and picked up a stained bowl.

'Well, he did say he wanted to eat what the men eat,' said Polly.

'Oh, *that* kind of officer,' said Scallot uncharitably. 'Yeah, some young ones try that stuff, if 'n they've been readin' the wrong books. Some of 'em tries to be *friends*, the bastards.' He spat expertly between the two pans. 'Wait 'til he *tries* what the men eat.'

'But if we're having steak and onions—'

'No thanks to the likes o' him,' said the corporal, ladling the slurry into the bowl. 'The Zlobenian troops get one pound of beef and a pound of flour a day minimum, plus fat pork or butter and half a pound of pease. A pint o' molasses sometimes, too. *We* get stale horse-bread and what we scrounge. He'll have scubbo and like it.'

'No fresh vegetables, no fruit,' said Shufti. 'That's a very binding diet, corp.'

'Yeah, well, once battle commences I reckon you'll find constipation's the last thing on your mind,' said Scallot. He reached up, pushed some rags aside, and pulled down a dusty bottle from a shelf.

'Rupert's not having none o' this, neither,' he said. 'Got it off 'f the baggage of the last officer that went through, but I'll share it with you, 'cos you's good lads.' He casually knocked the top of the bottle off against the edge of the chimney. ''s only sherry, but it'll make you drunk.'

'Thanks, corp,' said Shufti, and took the bottle. He sloshed a lot over the sizzling meat.

'Hey, that's good drink you're wastin'!' said Scallot, making a grab for it.

'No, it'll spice up the meat a fair treat,' said Shufti, trying to hang on to the bottle. 'It'll— *sugar!*'

Half the liquid had gone on the fire as the two hands fought for it, but that wasn't what had felt like a small steel rod shooting through Polly's head. She looked round at the rest of the squad, who didn't appear to have—

Maladict winked at her and made a tiny gesture with his head towards the other end of the room, and strolled in that direction. Polly followed.

Maladict always found something to lounge against. He relaxed in the shadows, looked up at the rafters, and said: 'Now, I say a man who knows how to cook is no less of a man for that. But a man who says "sugar" when he swears? Have you *ever* heard a man say that? You haven't. I can tell.'

So it *was* you who gave me the socks, thought Polly. You know about me, I can tell you do, but do you know about Lofty? And maybe Shufti was very politely brought up . . . but one look at Maladict's knowing smile made her decide not to try that road. Besides, the moment you looked at Shufti with the idea that maybe he was a girl, you *saw* that he was. No man would say 'Sugar!' Three girls now . . .

'And I'm pretty sure about Lofty, too,' said Maladict.

'What're you going to do about . . . them?' she said.

'Do? Why should I do anything about anyone?' said Maladict. 'I'm a vampire officially pretending not to

be one, right? I'm the last person who'll say anyone has to play the hand they were dealt. So good luck to . . . him, say I. But you might like to take him aside later on and have a word with him. You know . . . man to man.'

Polly nodded. Was there a knowingness to that comment? 'I'd better go and take the lieutenant his scubbo,' she said. 'And . . . blast it, I forgot about his laundry.'

'Oh, I wouldn't worry about that, old chap,' said Maladict, and flashed a little smile. 'The way things are going around here, Igor's probably a washer-woman in disguise.'

Polly did the laundry, in the end. She wasn't sure that she'd be able to dodge Molly a second time, and there wasn't that much of it. Afterwards she hung it in front of the fire, which was roaring.

The horse had been surprisingly good, but not as surprising as Blouse's reaction to the scubbo. He had sat there in his evening dress uniform – wearing special clothes just to sit down and eat all by yourself was a new one on Polly – and had yummed it up and sent her back with the bowl for more. The meat had been boiled white and there was scum on the top. The squad wondered what kind of life an officer could have led that inclined him to like scubbo.

'Dun't know much about him,' said Scallot, upon questioning. 'He's been here two weeks, frettin' to get to the war. Brought a whole cartload of books with

him, I heard. Looks like a typical rupert to me. They were all behind the door when the chins were handed out. A sergeant who went through said he's not really a soldier at all, just some wonk from headquarters that's good at sums.'

'Oh, great,' said Maladict, who was brewing his coffee by the fire. The little engine gurgled and hissed.

'I don't think he can see very well without his glasses,' said Polly. 'But he's very, er, polite.'

'Not been a rupert for long, then,' said Scallot. 'They're more "Hey there! You! Damn your eyes, fwah fwah fwah!" I seen your sergeant before, though, old Jackrum. Been everywhere, he has. Everyone knows old Jackrum. He was with us in the snow up at Ibblestarn.'

'How many people did *he* eat?' said Maladict, to general laughter. The dinner had been good, and there had still been enough sherry for a glass each.

'Let's just say I heard he didn't come down much thinner than when he went up,' said Scallot.

'And Corporal Strappi?' said Polly.

'Never seen him before, either,' said Scallot. 'Cross-grained little bugger. Political, I'd say. Why's he gone and left you here? Got a nice cushy bed in the inn, has he?'

'I hope *he's* not g-going to be our sergeant,' said Wazzer.

'Him? Why?' said Scallot.

Polly volunteered the events of earlier in the evening. To her surprise, Scallot laughed.

'They're trying to get rid of the old bugger again,

are they?' he said. 'That's a laugh! Bless you, it'll take more'n a bunch of gawains and rodneys to lever Jackrum out of his own army. Why, he's been court-martialled twice. He got off both times. And d'you know he once saved General Froc's life? He's been everywhere, got the goods on everyone, knows more strings than me and I know a good few, mark my words. If he wants to march with you tomorrow he will, and no skinny little rupert'll get in his way.'

'So what was a man like that doing as a recruiting officer?' said Maladict sharply.

''cos he got his leg cut open in Zlobenia and bit the sawbones who tried to look at it when the wound went bad, clever dick,' retorted Scallot. 'Cleaned it out himself with maggots and honey, then drank a pint of brandy and sewed himself up and lay on his bed with a fever for a week. But the general got him, I heard, came and visited him while he was too weak to protest and told him he was going on the drumming for a year and no argument. Not even Froc hisself would hand him his papers, not after Jackrum'd carried him on his back for fourteen miles through enemy lines—'

The door swung open and Sergeant Jackrum walked in, tucking his hands into his belt.

'Don't bother to salute, lads,' he said, as they turned guiltily. 'Evening, Threeparts. Nice to see nearly all of you again, you artful ol' god-dodger. Where's Corporal Strappi?'

'Haven't seen him all evening, sarge,' said Maladict.

'Didn't he come in here with you?'

'No, sarge. We thought he was with you.'

Not a muscle moved on Jackrum's face. 'I see,' he said. 'Well, you heard the lieutenant. The boat leaves at midnight. We should be well down the Kneck by Wednesday's dawn. Get a few hours' sleep if you can. Tomorrow's going to be a long day, if you're lucky.'

And with that, he turned and went out again. Wind howled outside, and was cut off when the door shut. *We'll* be well down the Kneck, Polly noted. Well done, Threeparts.

'Missing a corporal?' said Scallot. 'Now there's a thing. Usually it's a recruit that goes ay-wole. Well, you heard the sergeant, boys. Time to wash up and turn in.'

There was a washroom and latrine, in a rough and ready fashion. Polly found a moment when she and Shufti were in it alone. She'd racked her brains about how best to raise the subject, but as it turned out just a look was all it took.

'It was when I volunteered to do the supper, wasn't it?' Shufti mumbled, staring into the stone sink, which had moss growing in it.

'That was a clue, yes,' said Polly.

'A lot of men cook, you know!' said Shufti hotly.

'Yes, but not soldiers, and not enthusiastically,' said Polly. 'They don't do marinades.'

'Have you told anybody?' mumbled Shufti, red in the face.

'No,' said Polly, which was, after all, strictly true. 'Look, you were good, you had me fooled right up until "sugar".'

'Yes, yes, I know,' Shufti whispered. 'I can do the belching and the walking stupidly and even the nose-picking, but I wasn't brought up to swear like you men!'

Us men, thought Polly. Oh, boy.

'We're the coarse and licentious soldiery. I'm afraid it's shit or bust,' she said. 'Er . . . *why* are you doing this?'

Shufti stared into the dank stone sink as if strange green slime was really interesting, and mumbled something.

'Sorry, what was that?' said Polly.

'Going to find my husband,' said Shufti, only a little bit louder.

'Oh, dear. How long had you been married?' said Polly, without thinking.

'. . . not married yet . . .' said Shufti, in a voice as tall as an ant.

Polly glanced down at the plumpness of Shufti. Oh, dear. Oh, dear. She tried to sound reasonable. 'Don't you think that you should—'

'Don't you tell me to go home!' said Shufti, rounding on her. 'There's nothing for me back home except disgrace! I'm not going home! I'm going to the war and I'm going to find him! No one's going to tell me not to, Ozzer! No one! This has happened before, anyway! And it ended right! There's a song about it and everything!'

'Oh, *that*,' said Polly. 'Yes. I know.' Folk singers should be *shot*. 'What I was *going* to say was that you might find this helps the disguise . . .' She produced a

soft cylinder of woolly socks from her pack and word-lessly handed it over. It was a dangerous thing to do, she knew, but now she was feeling a kind of responsi-bility to those whose sudden strange fancy hadn't been followed by a plan.

On the way back to her palliasse she caught sight of Wazzer hanging his little picture of the Duchess on a handy hook in the crumbling wall above his mattress. He looked around furtively, failed to spot Polly in the shadows of the doorway, and bobbed a very quick curtsy to the picture. A curtsy, not a bow.

Polly frowned. Four. She was barely surprised, now. And she had one pair of clean socks left. This was soon going to be a barefoot army.

Polly could tell the time by the fire. You got a feel for how long a fire burned, and the logs on this one were grey with ash over the glow beneath. It was gone eleven, she decided.

By the sound of it, no one was getting any sleep. She'd got up after an hour or two of lying on the crackling straw mattress, staring at darkness and listening to things move about underneath her; she'd have stayed on it for longer, but something in the straw seemed to want to push her leg out of the way. Besides, she didn't have any dry blankets. There *were* blankets in the barracks, but Threeparts had advised against them on account of their carrying, as he put it, 'the Itch'.

The corporal had left a candle alight. Polly had read Paul's letter again, and taken another look at the piece

of printed paper rescued from the muddy road. The words were fractured and she wasn't sure about all of them, but she didn't like the sound of any of them. 'Invas' had a particularly unpleasant ring to it.

And then there was the *third* piece of paper. She couldn't help that. It had been a complete accident. She'd done Blouse's laundry and *of course* you went through the pockets before you washed things, because anyone who'd ever tried to unroll a soggy, bleached sausage that'd once been a banknote didn't want to do it twice. And there had been this folded piece of paper. Admittedly, she needn't have unfolded it and, having unfolded it, needn't have read it. But there are some things that you just do.

It was a letter. Presumably Blouse had shoved it in a pocket and forgotten about it when he'd changed his shirt. She needn't read it again but, by candlelight, she did.

My Dearest Emmeline,

Fame and Fortune await! After only eight years as a 2nd Lieutenant I have now been promoted and am to have a command! Of course this will mean that there will be no officer left in the Adjutant-General's Blankets, Bedding and Horse Fodder Department, but I have explained my new filing system to Cpl Drebb and I believe he is Sound.

You know I cannot go into matters of detail, but I believe this will be a very exciting prospect and I am anxious to be 'at the Foe'. I am bold enough to hope that the name of Blouse will go down in military history. In the meantime, I am

brushing up my sword drill and it is definitely all 'coming back' to me. Of course, the promotion brings with it no less than One Shilling extra 'per Diem', plus Three Pence fodder allowance. To this end I have purchased a 'charger' from Mr 'Honest' Jack Slacker, a most entertaining gentleman, although I fear that his description of my steed's 'prowess' may have been prone to some exaggeration. Nevertheless, I am 'moving up' at last and if Fate smiles on me this will hurry forward the day when I can

And that was it, fortunately. After some thought, Polly went and carefully damped the letter, then dried it quickly over the remains of the fire and slipped it into the pocket of the washed shirt. Blouse might scold her for not removing it before washing, but she doubted it.

A blanket-counter with a new filing system. An ensign for eight years, in a war where promotion could be rather fast. A man who put inverted commas round any word or phrase he thought of as even slightly 'racy'. Brushing up on his 'sword drill'. And so short-sighted he'd bought a horse from Jack Slacker, who went around all the horse fairs' bargain bins and sold winded old screws that dropped a leg before you'd got home.

Our leader.

They were losing the war. Everyone knew that, but nobody would say it. It was as if they felt that if the words weren't said out loud then it wasn't really happening. They were losing the war and this squad,

untrained and untried, fighting in dead men's boots, could only help them lose it faster. Half of them were girls! Because of some bloody stupid song, Shufti was wandering off into a war to look for the father of her child, and that was a desperate errand for a girl even in peacetime. And Lofty was trailing after her boy, which would probably be romantic right up until five minutes into a battle. And she . . .

. . . well, yes. She'd heard the song, too. So what? Paul was her brother. She'd always kept an eye on him, even when she was small. Mother was always busy, *everyone* was always busy at The Duchess, so Polly had become a big sister to a brother fifteen months older than her. She'd taught him to blow his nose, taught him how to form letters, went and found him when crueller boys had got him lost in the woods. Running after Paul was a duty that had become a habit.

And then . . . well, it wasn't the only reason. When her father died The Duchess would be lost to her side of the family if there was no male to inherit. That was the law, plain and simple. Nugganatic law said that men could inherit 'the Things of Men ' such as land, buildings, money and all domestic animals except cats. Women could inherit 'the Things of Women', which were mostly small items of personal jewellery and spinning wheels passed from mothers to daughters. They certainly couldn't inherit a large, famous tavern.

So The Duchess would go to Paul if he was alive, or if he was dead it was allowable for it to go to Polly's husband if she was married. And since Polly saw no

prospect of that, she *needed* a brother. Paul could happily carry barrels around for the rest of his life; she would run The Duchess. But if she was left alone, a woman with no man, then at best all she'd get was maybe the chance to go on living there while the deeds went to cousin Vlopo, who was a drunkard.

Of course, all that wasn't *the* reason. Certainly not. But it was a reason, all the same. *The* reason was, simply, Paul. She'd always found him and brought him home.

She looked at the shako in her hands. There had been helmets, but since they all had arrow holes or gaping rips in them the squad had wordlessly gone for the softer hats. You'd die anyway, and at least you wouldn't have a headache. The shako's badge showed the regimental symbol of a flaming cheese. Maybe one day she'd find out why. Polly put it on, picked up her pack and the small bag of laundry, and stepped out into the night. The moon was gone, the clouds had come back. She was drenched by the time she'd crossed the square; the rain was coming horizontally.

She shoved open the inn door and saw, by the light of one guttering candle ... chaos. Clothing was strewn across the flagstones, cupboards were hanging open. Jackrum was coming down the stairs, cutlass in one hand, lantern in the other.

'Oh, it's you, Perks,' he said. 'They've cleaned the place out and buggered off. Even Molly. I heard 'em go. Pushing a cart, by the sound of it. What're you doing here?'

'Batman, sarge,' said Polly, shaking water off her hat.

'Oh, yeah. Right. Go and wake him up, then. He's snoring like a sawmill. I hope to hell the boat's still there.'

'Why'd they bug— scarper, sarge?' said Polly and thought: Sugar! If it comes to it, *I* don't swear, either! But the sergeant didn't appear to notice.

He gave her what is known as an old-fashioned look; this one had dinosaurs in it. 'Got wind of something, I don't doubt,' he said. 'Of course, we're winning the war, you know.'

'Ah. Oh. And we're not going to be invaded at all, I expect,' said Polly, with equally exaggerated care.

'Quite right. I detest those treacherous devils who'd have us believe that a vast army is about to sweep right across the country any day now,' said Jackrum.

'Er . . . no sign of Corporal Strappi, sarge?'

'No, but I haven't turned over every stone yet— ssh!'

Polly froze, and strained to listen. There were hoof-beats, getting louder as they approached, and changing from thuds into the ringing sound of horse-shoes on cobbles.

'Cavalry patrol,' Jackrum whispered, putting the lantern down on the bar. 'Six or seven horses.'

'Ours?'

'I bleedin' doubt it.'

The clattering slowed, and came to a stop outside.

'Keep 'em talking,' said Jackrum, reaching down

and sliding the door's bolt across. He turned and headed towards the rear of the inn.

'What? *What about?*' whispered Polly. 'Sarge?'

Jackrum had vanished. Polly heard murmuring outside the door, followed by a couple of sharp knocks.

She threw off her jacket. She wrenched the shako off her head and tossed it behind the bar. Now she wasn't a soldier, at least. And, as the door was shaken against the bolt, she saw something white lying in the debris. It was a terrible temptation . . .

The door burst open at the second blow, but the soldiers didn't immediately enter. Lying under the bar, struggling to put the petticoat on over rolled-up trousers, Polly tried to make sense of the sounds. As far as she could tell from the rustles and thuds, any-one waiting inside the doorway with ambush in mind would have been briefly and terminally sorry. She tried to count the invaders; it sounded as though there were at least three. In the tense silence, the sound of a voice speaking in normal tones came as a shock.

'We heard the bolt slide across. That means you're in here somewhere. Make it easy on yourself. We don't want to have to come and find you.'

I don't want you to either, Polly thought. I'm not a soldier! Go away! And then the next thought was: *What do you mean, you're not a soldier? You took the shilling and kissed the picture, didn't you?* And suddenly an arm had reached under the bar and grabbed her. At least she didn't have to act.

'No! Please, sir! Don't hurt me! I just got frightened! Please!'

But inside there was a certain . . . sock-ness that felt ashamed, and wanted to kick out.

'Ye gods, what are you?' said the cavalryman, pulling her upright and looking at her as if she was some kind of exhibit.

'Polly, sir! Barmaid, sir! Only they cleared out and left me!'

'Keep the noise down, girl!'

Polly nodded. The last thing she needed now was for Blouse to run down the stairs with his sabre and *Fencing for Beginners*.

'Yes, sir,' she squeaked.

'Barmaid, eh? Three pints of what you'd probably call your finest ale, then.'

That at least could happen on automatic. She'd seen the mugs under the bar, and the barrels were behind her. The beer was thin and sharp but probably wouldn't dissolve a penny.

The cavalryman watched her closely as she filled the mugs. 'What happened to your hair?' he said.

Polly had been ready for this. 'Oh, sir, they cut it off, sir! 'cos I smiled at a Zlobenian trooper, sir!'

'Here?'

'In Drok, sir.' It was a town much nearer the border. 'And me mam said it was shaming to the family and I got sent here, sir!'

Her hands shook as she put the mugs on the bar, and she was hardly exaggerating. Hardly . . .

but a bit, nevertheless. *You're acting like a girl,* she thought. *Keep it up!*

Now she could take stock of the invaders. They wore dark-blue uniforms, and big boots, and heavy cavalry helmets. One of them was standing by the shuttered windows. The other two were watching her. One had a sergeant's stripes and an expression of deep suspicion. The one who'd grabbed her was a captain.

'This is terrible beer, girl,' he said, sniffing the mug.

'Yes, sir, I know, sir,' Polly gabbled. 'They wouldn't listen to me, sir, and said you have to put a damp sheet over the barrels in this thundery weather, sir, and Molly never cleans the spigot and—'

'This town's empty, you know that?'

'They all scarpered, sir,' said Polly earnestly. 'Gonna be an invasion, sir. Everyone says. They're frightened of you, sir.'

'Except you, eh?' said the sergeant.

'What's your name, girl who smiles at Zlobenian troopers?' said the captain, smiling.

'Polly, sir,' said Polly. Her questing hand found what it was seeking under the bar. It was the barman's friend. There always was one.

'And are *you* frightened of me, Polly?' said the captain. There was a snigger from the soldier by the window.

The captain had a well-trimmed moustache which had been waxed to points, and was over six feet tall, Polly reckoned. He had a pretty smile, too, which was somehow improved by the scar on his face. A circle of

glass covered one eye. Her hand gripped the hidden cudgel.

'No, sir,' she said, looking back into one eye and one glass. 'Er . . . what's that glass for, sir?'

'It's a monocle,' said the captain. 'It helps me see you, for which I am eternally grateful. I always say that if I had two I'd make a spectacle of myself.'

That got a dutiful laugh from the sergeant. Polly looked blank.

'And are you going to tell me where the recruits are?' said the captain.

She forced her expression not to change. 'No.'

The captain smiled. He had good teeth, but there was, now, no warmth in his eyes.

'You are in no position to be ignorant,' he said. 'We won't hurt them, I assure you.'

There was a scream in the distance.

'Much,' said the sergeant, with more satisfaction than was necessary. There was another yell. The captain nodded to the man by the door, who slipped out. Polly pulled the shako out from under the bar and put it on.

'One of them gave you his cap, did he?' said the sergeant, and his teeth were nowhere near as good as the officer's. 'Well, I like a girl who'll smile at a soldier—'

The cudgel hit him along the head. It was old blackthorn, and he went down like a tree. The captain backed away as Polly came out from behind the bar with the club readied again. But he hadn't drawn his sword, and he was *laughing*.

'Now, girl, if you want—' He caught her arm as she swung, dragged her towards him in a tight grip, still laughing, and folded up almost silently as her knee connected with his sock drawer. Thank you, Gummy. As he sagged she stepped back and brought the cudgel down on his helmet, making it ring.

She was shaking. She felt sick. Her stomach was a small, red-hot lump. What else could she have done? Was she supposed to think *We have met the enemy and he is nice?* Anyway, he wasn't. He was smug.

She tugged a sabre from a scabbard and crept out into the night. It was still raining, and waist-deep mist was drifting up from the river. Half a dozen or so horses were outside, but not tied up. A trooper was waiting with them. Faintly, against the rustle of the rain, she heard him making soothing noises to comfort one of them. She wished she hadn't heard that. Well, she'd taken the shilling. Polly gripped the cudgel.

She'd gone a step when the mist between her and the man fountained up slowly as something rose out of it. The horses shifted uneasily. The man turned, a shadow moved, the man fell . . .

'Oi!' whispered Polly.

The shadow turned. 'Ozzer? It's me, Maladict,' it said. 'Sarge sent me to see if you needed help.'

'Bloody Jackrum left me surrounded by armed men!' Polly hissed.

'And?'

'Well, I . . . knocked two of them out,' she said, feeling as she said it that this rather spoilt her case as a victim. 'One went over the road, though.'

'I think we got that one,' said Maladict. 'Well, I say "got" . . . Tonker nearly gutted him. There's a girl with what I'd call unresolved issues.' He turned round. 'Let's see . . . seven horses, seven men. Yep.'

'*Tonker?*' said Polly.

'Oh, yes. Hadn't you spotted her? She went mad when the man charged at Lofty. Now, let's have a look at your gentlemen, shall we?' said Maladict, heading for the inn door.

'But Lofty and Tonker . . .' Polly began, running to keep up. 'I mean, the way they act, they . . . I thought she was his girl . . . but I thought Tonker . . . I mean, I know Lofty is a gi—'

Even in the dark, Maladict's teeth gleamed as he smiled. 'The world's certainly unfolding itself for you, eh? *Ozzer?* Every day, something new. Cross-dressing now, I see.'

'What?'

'You are wearing a *petticoat*, Ozzer,' said Maladict, stepping into the bar. Polly looked down guiltily and started to tug it off, and then thought: hang on a moment . . .

The sergeant had managed to pull himself up against the bar, where he was being sick. The captain was groaning on the floor.

'Good evening, gentlemen!' said the vampire. 'Please pay attention. I am a *reformed* vampire, which is to say, I am a bundle of suppressed instincts held together with spit and coffee. It would be wrong to say that violent, tearing carnage does not come easily to me. It's *not* tearing your throats out that doesn't

come easily to me. Please don't make it any harder.'

The sergeant pushed himself away from the bar top and took a muzzy swing at Maladict. Almost absent-mindedly, Maladict leaned away from it and then returned a roundhouse blow that knocked him over.

'The captain looks bad,' he said. 'What did he try to do to poor little you?'

'Patronize me,' said Polly, glaring at Maladict.

'Ah,' said the vampire.

Maladict knocked softly on the barracks door. It opened a fraction, and then all the way. Carborundum lowered his club. Wordlessly, Polly and Maladict dragged the two cavalrymen inside. Sergeant Jackrum was sitting on a stool by the fire, drinking a mug of beer.

'Well done, lads,' he said. 'Put 'em with the others.' He waved the mug vaguely towards the far wall, where four of the soldiers were hunched sullenly under the gaze of Tonker. They had been manacled together. The last soldier was lying on a table, with Igor at work on him with a needle and thread.

'How's he coming along, private?' said Jackrum.

'He'll be fine, tharge,' said Igor. 'It looked worthe than it wath, really. Jutht ath well, because until we get to the battlefield I won't get any thpareth.'

'Got a couple of legs for ol' Threeparts?' said Jackrum.

'Now then, sarge, none of that,' said Scallot evenly. He was sitting on the other side of the fireplace. 'You just leave me their horses and saddles.

Your lads could do with their sabres, I've no doubt.'

'They were looking for *us*, sarge,' said Polly. 'We're just a bunch of untrained recruits and they were *looking* for us. I could've been *killed*, sarge!'

'No, I know talent when I sees it,' said Jackrum. 'Well done, lad. Had to piss off myself, on account of a big man in full enemy uniform isn't easy to miss. Besides, you lads needed to be woke up. That's *milit'ry thinking*, that is.'

'But if I hadn't . . .' Polly hesitated. 'If I hadn't tricked them, they might've killed the lieutenant!'

'See? There's always a positive side, any way you look at it,' said Scallot.

The sergeant stood up, wiped his mouth on the back of his hand and hitched up his belt. He ambled over to the captain, reached down, and lifted him up by his jacket.

'Why were you looking for these boys, sir?' he enquired.

The captain opened his eye and focused on the fat man.

'I am an officer and a gentleman, sergeant,' he muttered. 'There are *rules*.'

'Not many gentlemen around here at this moment, sir,' said the sergeant.

'Damn right,' whispered Maladict. Polly, feeling drunk with relief and released tension, had to put her hand over her mouth to stop giggling.

'Oh, yeah. The rules. Prisoners of war and that,' Jackrum went on. 'That means you even have to eat

the same things as us, you poor devils. So you're not going to talk to me?'

'I am ... Captain Horentz of the First Heavy Dragoons. I'll say nothing more.' And something about the way he said it elbowed Polly in the brain. *He's lying.*

Jackrum stared at him blankly for a moment, and then said: 'Well, now ... it looks like what we have here is an embuggerance which, my lads of the Cheesemongers, is defined as an obstruction in the way of progress. I propose to deal with it in this wise!' He let go of the man's jacket and the captain fell back.

Sergeant Jackrum removed his hat. Then he removed his jacket, too, revealing a stained shirt and bright red braces. He was still almost spherical; from his neck, folds of skin lapped their way down to the tropical regions. The belt must have been there just to conform to regulations, Polly thought.

He reached up and undid a piece of string from around his neck. It was looped through a hole in a tarnished coin.

'Corporal Scallot!' he said.

'Yes, sarge!' said Scallot, saluting.

'You will note I am divestering myself of my insignia and am handing you my official shilling, which means, since last time I signed up it was for twelve years and that was sixteen years ago, I am now fully and legally a damn civilian!'

'Yes, Mister Jackrum,' said Scallot cheerfully. Among the prisoners, heads jerked up at the sound of the name.

'And that being the case, and since you, captain, are invading our country by night under the cover of darkness, and I am a humble civilian, I think there's no rule to stop me beating seven kinds of crap out of you until you tell me why you came here and when the rest of your mates are going to arrive. And that may take me some time, sir, because up until now I've only ever discovered five types of crap.' He rolled up his sleeves, hauled up the captain again and drew back a fist—

'We just had to take the recruits into custody,' said a voice. 'We weren't going to hurt them! Now put him down, Jackrum, damn you! He's still seeing stars!'

It was the sergeant from the inn. Polly looked at the other prisoners. Even with Carborundum and Maladict watching them, and Tonker glowering at them, there was a definite sense that the first blow landed on the captain was going to start a riot. And Polly thought: they *are* very protective, aren't they . . .

Jackrum must have picked it up, too. 'Ah, now we're talking,' he said, lowering the captain gently but still holding his coat. 'Your men speak up for you well, captain.'

'That's because we're not slaves, you bloody beeteater,' growled one of the troopers.

'Slaves? All my lads joined up of their own free will, turniphead.'

'Maybe they *thought* they did,' said the sergeant. 'You just lied to 'em. Lied to 'em for years. They're all gonna die because of your stupid lies! Lies and your raddled, rotting, lying old whore of a duchess!'

'*Private Goom, as you were! That is an order! As you were, I said! Private Maladict, take that sword off'f Private Goom! That is another order! Sergeant, order your men to ease back slowly! Slowly! Do it now! Upon my oath I am not a violent man, but any man, any man who disobeys me, bigod, that man is lookin' at a broken rib!*'

Jackrum screamed all that in one long explosion of sound without taking his eyes off the captain.

Reaction, order and breathless stillness had taken just a few seconds. Polly stared at the sudden tableau as her muscles untensed.

The Zlobenian troopers were settling back. Carborundum's raised club began to lower itself gently. Little Wazzer was held off the ground by Maladict, who'd wrenched a sword from her hand; possibly only a vampire could have moved faster than Wazzer as she'd charged the prisoners.

'Custody,' said Jackrum, in a quiet voice. 'That's a funny word. Look at my little lads, will you? Not a whisker between them yet, save for the troll, and lichen don't count. Still wet behind the ears, they are. What's dangerous about a harmless bunch of farm boys that'd concern a fine bunch of horse-wallopers like yourselves?'

'Can thomeone pleathe come and put their finger on thith knot?' said Igor, from his makeshift operating table. 'I've jutht about done.'

'*Harmless?*' said the sergeant, staring at the struggling Wazzer. 'They're a bunch of bloody madmen!'

'I want to speak to your officer, damn you,' said the captain, who looked a little less unfocused now. 'You do have an officer, don't you?'

'Yeah, we've got one somewhere, as I recall,' said Jackrum. 'Perks, go and fetch the rupert, will you? Best if you take that dress off first, too. You never know, with ruperts.' He carefully lowered the captain on to a bench, and straightened up.

'Carborundum, Maladict, chop something off any prisoner who moves, and any man who tries to attack a prisoner!' he said. 'Now then . . . oh, yes. Threeparts Scallot, I wish to enlist in your wonderful army, with its many opportunities for a young man willing to apply himself.'

'Any previous soldierin'?' said Scallot, grinning.

'Forty years fighting every bleeder within a hundred miles of Borogravia, corporal.'

'Special skills?'

'Stayin' alive, corporal, come what may.'

'Then allow me to present you with one shilling and immediate acceleration to the rank of sergeant,' said Scallot, handing back the coat and the shilling. 'Want to Osculate the Doxie?'

'Not at my time o' life,' said Jackrum, putting on his jacket again. 'There,' he said. 'All smart, all neat, all legal. Go on, Perks, I gave you an order.'

Blouse was snoring. His candle had burned down. A book was open on his blanket. Polly gently pulled it out from under his fingers. The title, almost invisible on the stained cover, was: *Tacticus: The Campaigns.*

'Sir?' she whispered.

Blouse opened his eyes, saw her, and then turned and frantically scrabbled by the bed.

'Here they are, sir,' said Polly, handing him his spectacles.

'Ah, Perks, thank you,' said the lieutenant, sitting up. 'Midnight, is it?'

'A bit after, sir.'

'Oh, dear! Then we must hurry! Quick, pass me my breeches! Have the men had a good night?'

'We were attacked by Zlobenian troops, sir. First Heavy Dragoons. We took them prisoner, sir. No casualties, sir.' . . . because they didn't expect us to fight. They wanted to take us alive. And they walked in on Carborundum and Maladict and . . . me.

It had been hard, very hard, to force herself to swing that cudgel. But once she had done it, it had been easy. And then she'd felt embarrassed about being caught in a petticoat, even though she had her breeches on underneath. She'd gone from boy to girl just by thinking it, and it had been so . . . easy. She needed some time to consider this. She needed time to think about a lot of things. She suspected that time was going to be in short supply.

Blouse was still sitting there with his breeches half on, staring at her.

'Run that past me again one more time, will you, Perks?' he said. 'You have *captured* some of the enemy?'

'Not just me, sir, I only got two of 'em,' said Polly. 'We all, er, piled in, sir.'

'*Heavy Dragoons?*'

'Yessir.'

'That's the Prince's personal regiment! They've invaded?'

'I think it was more of a patrol, sir. Seven men.'

'And none of you are hurt?'

'Nosir.'

'Pass me my shirt! Oh, blast!'

It was then that Polly noticed the bandage around his right hand. It was red with blood. He saw her expression.

'Bit of a self-inflicted wound, Perks,' he said nervously. ' "Brushing up" on my sword drill after supper. Nothing serious. Just a bit "rusty", you know. Can't quite manage buttons. If you would be so good . . .'

Polly helped the lieutenant struggle into the rest of his clothes, and threw his few other possessions in a bag. It took a special kind of man, she reflected, to cut his sword hand with his own sword.

'I should pay my bill . . .' the lieutenant muttered, as they hurried down the darkened stairs.

'Can't, sir. Everyone's fled, sir.'

'Perhaps I should leave them a note, do you think? I wouldn't like them to think that I had "done a runner" without—'

'They've all *gone*, sir!' said Polly, pushing him towards the front door. She stopped outside the barracks, straightened his coat and stared at his face. 'Did you wash last night, sir?'

'There was no—' Blouse began.

The response was automatic. Even though she was fifteen months younger, she'd been mothering Paul for too long.

'Handkerchief!' she demanded. And, since some things get programmed into the brain at an early age, one was obediently produced.

'Spit!' Polly commanded. Then she used the damp hanky to wipe a mark off Blouse's face and realized, as she was doing it, that she was doing it. There was no going back. The only way out was ahead.

'All right,' she said brusquely. 'Have you got everything?'

'Yes, Perks.'

'Have you been to the privy this morning?' her mouth went on, while her brain cowered in fear of a court martial. I'm in shock, she thought, and so's he. So you cling to what you know. And you can't stop . . .

'No, Perks,' said the lieutenant.

'Then you must go properly before we get on the boat, all right?'

'Yes, Perks.'

'In you go, then, there's a good lieutenant.'

She leaned against the wall and got her breath back in a few hurried gulps as Blouse stepped into the barracks, then slipped in after him.

'Officer present!' Jackrum barked. The squad, already lined up, stood to varying degrees of attention. The sergeant jerked a salute in front of Blouse, causing the young man to sway backwards.

'Apprehended enemy scouting party, sir! Dangerous business all round, sir! In view of the

emergency nature of the emergency sir, and seeing as how you have no NCO what with Corporal Strappi having scarpered, and seeing as how I'm an old soldier in good standing, you are allowed to conscript me as an auxiliary under Duchess's Regulations, Rule 796, Section 3 [a], Paragraph ii, sir, thank you, sir!'

'What?' said Blouse, staring around blearily and becoming aware that in a world of sudden turmoil there was a big red coat that seemed to know what it was doing. 'Oh. Yes. Fine. Rule 796, you say? Absolutely. Well done. Carry on, sergeant.'

'Are you in command here?' barked Horentz, standing.

'Indeed I am, captain,' said Blouse.

Horentz looked him up and down. '*You?*' he said, disdain oozing from the word.

'Indeed, sir,' said Blouse, his eyes narrowing.

'Oh well, we shall have to do what we can. That fat bastard,' said Horentz, pointing a threatening finger at Jackrum, 'that bastard offered me violence! As a prisoner! In *chains*! And that . . . *boy*,' the captain added, spitting the word towards Polly, 'kicked me in the privates and almost clubbed me to death! I *demand* that you let us go!'

Blouse turned to Polly. 'Did you kick Captain Horentz in the "privates", Parts?'

'Er . . . yessir. Kneed, actually. And it's Perks actually, sir, although I can see why you made the mistake.'

'What was he doing at the time?'

'Er . . . embracing me, sir.' Polly saw Blouse's eyebrows rise, and plunged on. 'I was temporarily

disguised as a girl, sir, in order to allay suspicion.'

'And then you . . . clubbed him?'

'Yessir. Once, sir.'

'What in the world possessed you to stop at once?' said Blouse.

'Sir?' said Polly, as Horentz gasped. Blouse turned with an almost seraphic look of pleasure on his face.

'And you, sergeant,' he went on, 'did you in fact lay a hand on the captain?'

Jackrum took a step forward and saluted smartly. 'Not as in fact per se and such, sir, no,' he said, keeping his eyes fixed on a point some twelve feet high on the far wall. 'I just considered, since he had invaded our country to capture our lads, sir, that it wouldn't hurt if he experienced temporary feelings of shock and awe, sir. On my oath, sir, I am not a violent man.'

'Of course not, sergeant,' said Blouse. And now, while he still smiled, it was edged with a kind of malevolent glee.

'For heaven's sake, you fool, you can't believe these ignorant yokels, they're the dregs of—' Horentz began.

'I do believe them, indeed I do,' said Blouse, shaking with nervous defiance. 'I would believe their testimony against yours, sir, if they told me the sky was green. And it would appear that untrained as they are, they have bested some of Zlobenia's finest soldiers by wit and daring. I have every confidence that they have further surprises in store for us—'

'*Dropping your drawers would do it,*' whispered Maladict.

'*Shutup!*' hissed Polly, and then had to cram a fist into her mouth again.

'I know you, Captain Horentz,' said Blouse, and just for a moment the captain looked worried. 'I mean I know your sort. I've had to put up with them all my life. Big jovial bullies, with their brains in their breeches. You *dare* to come riding into our country and think we're going to be frightened of you? You think you can appeal to me over the heads of my men? You *demand*? On the soil of my country?'

'Captain?' murmured the cavalry sergeant, as Horentz stared open-mouthed at the lieutenant, 'they'll be here soon . . .'

'Ah,' said Horentz uncertainly. Then he seemed, with some effort, to regain his composure. 'Reinforcements are coming,' he snapped. 'Free us now, you idiot, and I might just put this down to native stupidity. Otherwise I shall see to it that things go very, very badly for you and your . . . ha . . . men.'

'Seven cavalrymen were considered not enough to deal with farm boys?' said Blouse. 'You're sweating, captain. You are *worried*. And yet you have reinforcements coming?'

'Permission to speak, sir!' barked Jackrum, and went straight on to: '*Cheesemongers! Get bleedin' armed again right now! Maladict, you give Private Goom his sword back an' wish him luck! Carborundum, you grab a handful of them twelve-foot pikes! The rest of—*'

'There's these as well, sarge,' said Maladict. 'Lots of them. I got them off our friends' saddles.' He held up

what looked to Polly like a couple of large pistol cross-bows, steely and sleek.

'Horsebows?' said Jackrum, like a child opening a wonderful Hogswatch present. 'That's what you gets for leading an honest and sober life, my lads. Dreadful little engines they are. Let's have two each!'

'I don't want unnecessary violence, sergeant,' said Blouse.

'Right you are, sir!' said the sergeant. 'Carborundum! First man comes through that door runnin', I want him nailed to the wall!' He caught the lieutenant's eye, and added: 'But not too hard!'

. . . and someone did knock at the door.

Maladict levelled two bows at it. Carborundum lifted a couple of pikes in either hand. Polly raised her cudgel, a weapon she at least knew how to use. The other boys, and girls, raised whatever weapon Threeparts Scallot had been able to procure. There was silence. Polly looked around.

'Come in?' she suggested.

'Yeah, right, that should do it,' said Jackrum, rolling his eyes.

The door was pushed open and a small, dapper man stepped through carefully. In build, colouring and hairstyle he looked rather like Mala—

'A vampire?' said Polly softly.

'Oh, damn,' said Maladict.

The newcomer's clothing, however, was unusual. It was an old-fashioned evening dress coat with the sleeves removed and many, many pockets sewn all over it. In front of him, slung around his neck, was a

large black box. Against all common sense, he beamed at the sight of a dozen weapons poised to deliver perforated death.

'Vonderful!' he said, lifting up the box and unfolding three legs to form a tripod for it. 'But . . . could zer troll move a little to his left please?'

'Huh?' said Carborundum. The squad looked at one another.

'Yes, and if the sergeant vould be so kind as to move into the centre more, and raise those swords a little bit higher?' the vampire went on. 'Great! And you, sir, if you could give me a grrrrh . . . ?'

'Grrrrh?' said Blouse.

'Very good! Really fierce now . . .'

There was a blinding flash and a brief cry of 'Oh, sh—', followed by the tinkle of breaking glass.

Where the vampire had been standing was a little cone of dust. Blinking, Polly watched it fountain up into a human shape which coalesced once more into the vampire.

'Oh dear, I really thought ze new filter vould do it,' he said. 'Oh vell, ve live und learn.' He gave them a bright smile and added, 'Now – vhich vun of you is Captain Horentz, please?'

Half an hour had passed. Polly was still bewildered. The trouble was not that she didn't understand what was going on. The problem was that before she could understand that, she had to understand a lot of other things. One of them was the concept of a 'newspaper'.

Blouse was looking proud and worried by turns,

but nervous all the time. Polly watched him carefully, not least because he was talking to the man who had come in behind the iconographer. He was wearing a big leather coat and jodhpurs, and spent most of the time writing things down in a notebook, with occasional puzzled glances at the squad. Finally, Maladict, who had good hearing, sauntered over to the recruits from his lounging spot by the wall.

'Okay,' he said, lowering his voice. 'It's all a bit complicated, but ... do any of you know about newspapers?'

'Yeth, my thecond couthin Igor in Ankh-Morpork told me about them,' said Igor. 'They're like a kind of government announthement.'

'Um ... sort of. Except they're not written by the government. They're written by ordinary people who write things down,' said Maladict.

'Like a diary?' said Tonker.

'Um ... no ...'

Maladict tried to explain. The squad tried to understand. It still made no sense. It sounded to Polly like some kind of Punch and Judy show. Anyway, why would you trust anything written down? She certainly didn't trust 'Mothers of Borogravia!' and that was from the *government*. And if you couldn't trust the government, who *could* you trust?

Very nearly everyone, come to think of it ...

'Mr de Worde works for a newspaper in Ankh-Morpork,' said Maladict. 'He says we're losing. He says casualties are mounting and troops are deserting

and all the civilians are heading for the mountains.'

'W-why should we believe him?' Wazzer demanded.

'Well, we've seen a lot of casualties and refugees and Corporal Strappi hasn't been around since he heard he was going to the front,' said Maladict. 'Sorry, but it's true. We've all seen it.'

'Yeah, but he's just some man from a foreign country. Why w-would the Duchess lie to us? I mean, why would she send us out just to die?' said Wazzer. 'She w-watches over us!'

'Everyone says we're winning,' said Tonker, doubtfully, after that moment of embarrassment. Tears were running down Wazzer's face.

'No, they don't,' said Polly. 'I don't think we are, either.'

'Does *anyone* think we are?' said Maladict. Polly looked from face to face.

'But saying so . . . it's like treachery against the Duchess, isn't it?' said Wazzer. 'It's spreading Alarm and Despondency, isn't it?'

'Maybe we ought to be alarmed,' said Maladict. 'Do you know how he came to be here? He travels around writing down things about the war for his paper of news. He met these cavalry just up the road. In *our* country! And they told him they'd just heard that the very last recruits from Borogravia were here and they were nothing but, er, "a wet little bunch of squeaking boys". They said they'd capture us for our own good and he could get a picture of us for his paper. He could show everybody how dreadful things were, they

said, because we were scraping the bottom of the barrel.'

'Yeah, but we beat 'em so that's foxed him!' said Tonker, grinning nastily. 'Nothing for him to write down now, eh?'

'Um . . . not really. He says that this is even better!'

'Better? Whose side is *he* on?'

'Bit of a puzzler, really. He *comes* from Ankh-Morpork, but he's not exactly on their side. Er . . . Otto Chriek, who makes the pictures for him—'

'The vampire? He crumbled to dust when the light flashed!' said Polly. 'Then he . . . came back!'

'Well, I was standing behind Carborundum at the time,' said Maladict, 'but I know the technique. He probably had a thin glass vial of b . . . bl . . . blur . . . no, wait, I can say this . . . *blood*.' He sighed. 'There! *No* problem. A thin vial of . . . what I said . . . which smashed on the ground and pulled the dust back together again. It's a great idea.' Maladict gave them a wan smile. 'I think he really cares a lot about what he does, you know. Anyway, he told me de Worde just tries to find out the truth. And then he writes it down and sells it to anyone who wants it.'

'And people *let* him do that?' said Polly.

'Apparently. Otto says he makes Commander Vimes livid with rage about once a week, but nothing ever happens.'

'Vimes? The Butcher?' said Polly.

'He's a duke, Otto says. But not like ours. Otto says he's never seen him butcher anybody. Otto's a Black Ribboner, like me. He wouldn't lie to a fellow

Ribboner. And he says that picture he took is going on the clacks from the nearest tower tonight. It will be in the paper of news tomorrow! *And* they print a copy here!'

'How can you send a picture on the clacks?' said Polly. 'I know people who've seen them. It's just a lot of boxes on a tower that go clack-clack!'

'Ah, Otto explained that to me, too,' said Maladict. 'It's very ingenious.'

'How does it work, then?'

'Oh, I didn't *understand* what he said. It was all about . . . numbers. But it certainly sounded very clever. Anyway, de Worde just told the lieu— the rupert that news about a bunch of boys beating up experienced soldiers would certainly make people sit up and take notice!'

The squad looked at one another sheepishly.

'It was a bit of a fluke, and anyway we had Carborundum,' said Tonker.

'And I used trickery,' said Polly. 'I mean, I couldn't do it twice.'

'So what?' said Maladict. 'We did it. The squad did it! Next time we'll do it differently!'

'Yeah!' said Tonker. And there was a shared moment of exhilaration in which they were capable of anything. It lasted all of . . . a moment.

'But it won't work,' said Shufti. 'We've just been lucky. You know it won't work, Maladict. You *all* know it won't work, right?'

'Well, I'm not saying we could, you know, take on a regiment all at once,' said Maladict. 'And the lieu—

rupert might be a bit wet. But we could help make a difference. Old Jackrum knows what he's doing—'

'Upon my oath I am not a violent man . . . whack!' sniggered Tonker, and there were a few . . . yes, giggles, they *were* giggles, Polly knew, from the squad.

'No, you're not,' said Shufti flatly. 'None of us are, right? Because we're girls.'

There was a dead silence.

'Well, not Carborundum and Ozzer, okay,' Shufti went on, as if the silence was sucking unwilling words out of her. 'And I'm not sure about Maladict and Igor. But I *know* the rest of us are, right? I've got eyes, I've got ears, I've got a *brain*. Right?'

In the silence there was the slow rumble that preceded a pronouncement from Carborundum.

'If it any help,' she said, in a voice suddenly more sandy than gravelly, 'my real name's Jade.'

Polly felt questing eyes boring into her. She was embarrassed, of course. But not for the obvious reason. It was for the other one, the little lesson that life sometimes rams home with a stick: you are not the only one watching the world. Other people are people; while you watch them they watch you, and they think about you while you think about them. *The world isn't just about you.*

There was going to be no possibility of getting out of this. And, in a way, it was a relief.

'Polly,' she said, almost in a whisper.

She looked questioningly at Maladict, who smiled in a distinctly non-committal way. 'Is this the time?' he said.

'*All right, you lot, what're you standing about for?*' bawled Jackrum, six inches from the back of Maladict's head. No one saw him arrive there; he moved with an NCO's stealth, which sometimes mystifies even Igors.

Maladict's smile didn't change. 'Why, we're awaiting your orders, sergeant,' he said, turning round.

'D'you think you're clever, Maladict?'

'Um . . . yes, sarge. Quite clever,' the vampire conceded.

There wasn't a lot of humour in Jackrum's smile. 'Good. Glad to hear it. Don't want another stupid corporal. Yeah, I know you ain't even a proper private yet, but glory be, you're a corporal now, 'cos I need one and you're the snappiest dresser. Get some stripes from Threeparts. The rest of you . . . this isn't a bleedin' mothers' meeting, we're leaving in five minutes. Move!'

'But the prisoners, sarge—' Polly began, still trying to digest the revelation.

'We're goin' to drag 'em over to the inn an' leave 'em tied up in the nood, and shackled together,' said Jackrum. 'Vicious little devil when he's roused, our rupert, eh? And Threeparts is having their boots and horses. They won't be going too far for a while, not in the nood.'

'Won't the writing man let them out?' said Tonker.

'Don't care,' said Jackrum. 'He could probably cut the ropes, but I'm dropping the shackle key in the privy, and that'll take a bit of fishing out.'

'Whose *side* is he on, sarge?' said Polly.

'Dunno. I don't trust 'em. Ignore 'em. Don't talk to 'em. Never talk to people who writes things down. Milit'ry rule. Now, I know I just gave you lot an order 'cos I heard the bleedin' echo! Get on with it! We are *leaving*!'

'Road to perdition, lad, promotion,' said Scallot to Maladict, swinging up with two stripes hanging from his hook. He grinned. 'That's three pence extra a day you're due now, only you won't get it 'cos they ain't payin' us, but to look on the bright side, you won't get stoppages, and they're a devil for stoppages. The way I see it, march backwards and yer pockets'll overflow!'

The rain had stopped. Most of the squad were parading outside the barracks where there was, now, a small covered wagon belonging to the writer of the paper of news. A large flag hung from a pole attached to it, but Polly couldn't make out the design by moonlight. Beside the wagon, Maladict was deep in conversation with Otto.

The centre of attention, though, was the line of cavalry horses. One had been offered to Blouse, but he'd waved it away with a look of alarm, muttering something about 'being loyal to his steed', which to Polly's eye looked like a self-propelled toast-rack with a bad attitude. But he'd probably made the right decision, at that, because they were big beasts, broad, battle-hardened and bright-eyed; sitting astride one of them would have strained the crotch in Blouse's trousers and an attempt at reining one of them in would have pulled his arms off at the shoulder. Now

each horse had a pair of boots hanging from its saddle, except for the leading horse, a truly magnificent beast upon which Corporal Scallot sat like an afterthought.

'I'm no donkey-walloper as you know, Threeparts,' said Jackrum, as he finished lashing the crutches behind the saddle, 'but this is a hell of a good horse you've got here.'

'Damn right, sarge. You could feed a platoon for a week off 'f it!' said the corporal.

'Sure you won't come with us?' Jackrum added, standing back. 'I reckon you still must've one or two things left for the bastards to cut off, eh?'

'Thank you, sarge, it's a kind offer,' said Threeparts. 'But fast horses are going to be at a real premium soon, and I'll be in on the ground floor, as you might say. This lot'll be worth three years' pay.' He turned in the saddle and nodded at the squad. 'Best of luck, lads,' he added cheerfully. 'You'll walk with Death every day, but I've seen 'im and he's been known to wink. And remember: fill your boots with soup!' He urged the horses into a walk, and disappeared with his trophies into the gloom.

Jackrum watched him go, shook his head, and turned to the recruits. 'All right, ladies— What's funny, Private Halter?'

'Er, nothing, sarge, I just ... thought of something ...' said Tonker, almost choking.

'You ain't paid to think of things, you're paid to march. Do it!'

The squad marched away. The rain slackened to

nothing but the wind rose a little, rattling windows, blowing through the deserted houses, opening and shutting doors like someone looking for something they could have sworn they put down here only a moment ago. That was all that moved in Plotz, except for one candle flame, down near the floor in the back room of the deserted barracks.

The candle had been tilted so that it leaned against a cotton thread fastened between the legs of a stool. This meant that when the candle burned low enough, it would burn through the thread and fall all the way to the floor and into a ragged trail of straw that led to a pile of palliasses on which had been stood two ancient cans of lamp oil.

It took about an hour in the wet, dejected night, for this to happen, and then all the windows blew out.

Tomorrow dawned on Borogravia like a great big fish. A pigeon rose over the forests, banked slightly, and headed straight for the valley of the Kneck. Even from here, the black stone bulk of the keep was visible, rising above the sea of trees. The pigeon sped on, one spark of purpose in the fresh new morning—

—and squawked as darkness dropped from the sky, gripping it in talons of steel. Buzzard and pigeon tumbled for a moment, and then the buzzard gained a little height and flapped onwards.

The pigeon thought: 000000000! But had it been more capable of coherent thought, and known

something about how birds of prey catch pigeons*, it might have wondered why it was being gripped so . . . kindly. It was being held, not squeezed. As it was, all it could think was: 000000000!

The buzzard reached the valley and began to circle low over the keep. As it gyred, a tiny figure detached itself from the leather harness on its back and, with great care, inched itself around the body and down to the talons. It reached the imprisoned pigeon, knelt on it and put its arms round the bird's neck. The buzzard skimmed low over a stone balcony, reared in the air, and let the pigeon go. Bird and tiny man rolled and bounced across the flagstones in a trail of feathers, and lay still.

Eventually a voice from somewhere under the pigeon said: 'Bugger . . .'

Urgent footsteps ran across the stones and the pigeon was lifted off Corporal Buggy Swires. He was a gnome, and barely six inches tall. On the other hand, as the head and only member of Ankh-Morpork City Watch's Airborne Section, he spent most of his time so high that *everyone* looked small.

'Are you all right, Buggy?' said Commander Vimes.

'Not too bad, sir,' said Buggy, spitting out a feather. 'But it wasn't elegant, was it? I'll do better next time. Trouble is, pigeons are too stupid to be steered—'

'What've you got me?'

* And allowing for the fact that all pigeons who know how birds of prey catch are dead, and therefore capable of slightly less thought than a living pigeon.

'The *Times* sent this up from their cart, sir! I tracked it all the way!'

'Well *done*, Buggy!'

There was a flurry of wings and the buzzard landed on the battlements.

'And, er— what is his name?' Vimes added. The buzzard gave him the mad, distant look of all birds.

'She's Morag, sir. Trained by the pictsies. Wonderful bird.'

'Was she the one we paid a crate of whisky for?'

'Yes, sir, and worth every dram.'

The pigeon struggled in Vimes's hand.

'You wait there, then, Buggy, and I'll get Reg to come out with some raw rabbit,' he said, and walked into his tower.

Sergeant Angua was waiting by his desk, reading the *Living Testament of Nuggan*. 'Is that a carrier pigeon, sir?' she said, as Vimes sat down.

'No,' said Vimes. 'Hold it a minute, will you? I want to have a look inside the message capsule.'

'It does *look* like a carrier pigeon,' said Angua, putting down the book.

'Ah, but messages flying through the air are an Abomination unto Nuggan,' said Vimes. 'The prayers of the faithful bounce off them, apparently. No, I think I've found someone's lost pet and I'm looking in this little tube here to see if I can find the owner's name and address, because I am a kind man.'

'So you're not actually waylaying field reports from the *Times*, then, sir?' said Angua, grinning.

'Not as such, no. I'm just such a keen reader that I

want to see tomorrow's news today. And Mr de Worde seems to have a knack of finding things out. Angua, I want to stop these stupid people fighting so that we can all go home, and if that means allowing the occasional pigeon to have a crap on my desk, so be it.'

'Oh, sorry, sir, I didn't notice. I expect it'll wipe off.'

'Go and get Reg to find some rabbit for the buzzard, will you?'

When she'd gone Vimes carefully unscrewed the end of the tube and pulled out a roll of very thin paper. He unfolded it, smoothed it out, and read the tiny writing, smiling as he did so. Then he turned the paper over and looked at the picture.

He was still staring at it when Angua returned with Reg and half a bucket of crunchy rabbit bits.

'Anything interesting, sir?' said Angua ingenuously.

'Well, yes. You could say that. All plans are changed, all bets are off. Ha! Oh, Mr de Worde, you poor fool . . .'

He handed her the paper. She read the story carefully.

'Good for them, sir,' she said. 'Most of them look fifteen years old, and when you see the size of those dragoons, well, you've got to be impressed.'

'Yes, yes, you could say that, you could say that,' said Vimes, his face gleaming like a man with a joke to share. 'Tell me, did de Worde interview any Zlobenian high-ups when he arrived?'

'No, sir. I understand he was turned away. They don't really know what a reporter is, so I gather the adjutant threw him out and said he was a nuisance.'

'Dear me, the poor man,' said Vimes, still grinning. 'You met Prince Heinrich the other day. Describe him to me . . .'

Angua cleared her throat. 'Well, sir, he was . . . largely green, shading to blue, with overtones of *grllss* and trail of—'

'I meant describe him to me on the assumption that I'm not a werewolf who sees with his nose,' said Vimes.

'Oh, yes,' said Angua. 'Sorry, sir. Six foot two, a hundred and eighty pounds, fair hair, green-blue eyes, sabre scar on his left cheek, wears a monocle in his right eye, waxed moustache—'

'Good, well observed. And now look at "Captain Horentz" in the picture, will you?'

She looked again, and said, very quietly: 'Oh dear. They didn't know?'

'He wasn't going to tell them, was he? Would they have seen a picture?'

Angua shrugged. 'I doubt it, sir. I mean, where would they see it? There's never been a newspaper here until the *Times* carts turned up last week.'

'Some woodcut, maybe?'

'No, they're an Abomination, unless they're of the Duchess.'

'So they really didn't know. And de Worde has never seen him,' said Vimes. 'But you saw him when we arrived the other day. What did you think of him? Just between ourselves.'

'An arrogant son-of-a-bitch, sir, and I know what I'm talking about. The kind of man who thinks he knows

what a woman likes and it's himself. All very friendly right up until they say no.'

'Stupid?'

'I don't think so. But not as clever as he thinks he is.'

'Right, 'cos he didn't tell our writer friend his real name. Did you read the bit at the end?'

Angua read, at the end of the text: 'Perry, the captain, threatened and harangued me after the recruits had gone. Alas, I had no time to fish for the manacle key in the privy. Please let the Prince know where they are soonest. WDW'

'Looks like William didn't take to him, either,' she said. 'I wonder why the Prince was out with a scouting party?'

'You said he was an arrogant son-of-a-bitch,' said Vimes. 'Maybe he just wanted to pop across and see if his auntie was still breathing . . .'

His voice trailed off. Angua looked at Vimes's face, which was staring through her. She knew her boss. He thought war was simply another crime, like murder. He didn't much like people with titles, and regarded being a duke as a job description rather than a lever to greatness. He had an odd sense of humour. And he had a sense for what she thought of as harbingers, those little straws in the wind that said there was a storm coming.

'In the nuddy,' he chuckled. 'Could have slit their throats. Didn't. They took their boots away and left them to hop home in the nood.' The squad, it seemed, had found a friend.

She waited.

'I feel sorry for the Borogravians,' he said.

'Me too, sir,' said Angua.

'Oh? Why?'

'Their religion's gone bad on them. Have you seen the latest Abominations? They Abominate the smell of beets and people with red hair. In rather shaky writing, sir. And root vegetables are a staple here. Three years ago it was Abominable to grow root crops on ground which had grown grain or peas.'

Vimes looked blank, and she remembered that he was a city boy.

'It means no real crop rotation, sir,' she explained. 'The ground sours. Diseases build up. You were right when you said they were going mad. These ... commandments are *dumb*, and any farmer can see that. I imagine people go along with them as best they can, but sooner or later you either have to break them and feel guilty, or keep them and suffer. For no reason, sir. I've had a look around. They're very religious here, but their god's let them down. No wonder they mostly pray to their royal family.'

She watched him stare at the piece of pigeon post for a while. Then he said: 'How far is it to Plotz?'

'About fifty miles,' said Angua, adding, 'As the wolf runs, maybe six hours.'

'Good. Buggy'll keep an eye on you. Little Henry is going to hop home, or meet one of his patrols, or an enemy patrol ... whatever. But the midden is going to hit the windmill when everyone sees that picture. I bet de Worde would have let him out if he'd been nice and polite. *That'll* teach him to meddle with the awesome

power of a fair and free press, haha.' He sat upright and rubbed his hands together like a man who meant business. 'Now, let's get that pigeon on its way again before it gets missed, eh? Get Reg to lurch along to where the *Times* people are staying and tell them their pigeon flew in the wrong window. Again.'

That was a good time, Polly remembered.

They didn't go down to the river docks. They could see there was no boat there. They hadn't turned up and the boatman had left without them. Instead, they crossed the bridge and headed up into the forests, with Blouse leading the way on his ancient horse. Maladict went on ahead and . . . Jade brought up the rear. You didn't need a light at night when a vampire led the way, and a troll at the rear would certainly discourage hangers-on.

No one mentioned the boat. No one spoke at all. The thing was . . . the thing *was*, Polly realized, that they were no longer marching alone. They shared the Secret. That was a huge relief, and right now they didn't need to talk about it. Nevertheless, it was probably a good idea to keep up a regular output of farts, belches, nose-pickings and groin-scratchings, just in case.

Polly didn't know whether to be proud that they'd taken her for a boy. I mean, she thought, I'd worked hard to get it right, I mastered the walk, except I suppose what I really did was mistress the walk, haha, I invented the fake shaving routine and the others didn't even think of that, I haven't cleaned my

fingernails for days and I pride myself I can belch with the best of them. So, I mean, I *was* trying. It was just slightly annoying to find that she'd succeeded so well.

After a few hours of this, when true dawn was breaking, they smelled smoke. There was a faint pall of it amongst the trees. Lieutenant Blouse raised a hand for them to halt, and Jackrum joined him in whispered conversation.

Polly stepped forward. 'Permission to whisper too, sarge? I think I know what this is.'

Jackrum and Blouse stared at her. Then the sergeant said: 'All right, Perks. Go and find out if you're right, then.'

That was an aspect that hadn't occurred to Polly, but she'd left herself open. Jackrum relented when he saw her expression, nodded to Maladict, and said, 'Go with him, corporal.'

They left the squad behind and walked forward carefully, over the beds of new-fallen leaves. The smoke was heavy and fragrant and, above all, reminiscent. Polly headed to where thicker under-growth was taking advantage of the extra light of a clearing, and pushed through into an airy thicket of hazel trees. The smoke was denser here, and barely moving.

The thicket ended. A few yards away, in a wide patch of cleared ground, a mound like a small volcano was spewing flame and smoke into the air.

'Charcoal oven,' whispered Polly. 'Just clay plastered on a stack of hazel. Should sit there smouldering for days. The wind probably caught it last night and the

fire's broken out. Won't make good charcoal now, it's burning too fast.'

They edged round it, keeping to the bushes. Other clay domes were dotted about the clearing, with faint wisps of steam and smoke coming from their tops. There were a couple of ovens in the process of being built, the fresh clay stacked alongside some bundles of hazel sticks. There was a hut, and the domes, and nothing else but silence, apart from the crackle of the runaway fire.

'The charcoal-burner is dead, or nearly dead,' said Polly.

'He's dead,' said Maladict. 'There's a smell of death here.'

'You can smell it above the smoke?'

'Sure,' said Maladict. 'Some things we're good at smelling. But how did *you* know?'

'They watch the burns like hawks,' said Polly, staring at the hut. 'He wouldn't let it go out of control like that if he was alive. Is he in the hut?'

'*They* are in the hut,' said Maladict flatly. He set off across the smoky ground.

Polly ran after him. 'Man and woman?' she said. 'Their wives often live out with—'

'Can't tell, not if they're old.'

The hut was only a temporary thing, made of woven hazel and roofed with tarpaulin; the charcoal-burners moved around a lot, from coppice to coppice. It didn't have windows, but it did have a doorway, with a rag for a door. The rag had been pulled away; the doorway was dark.

I've got to be a man about this, Polly thought.

There was a woman on the bed, and a man lying on the floor. There were other details, which the eye saw but the brain did not focus on. There was a great deal of blood. The couple had been old. They would not grow older.

Back outside, Polly took frantic mouthfuls of air. 'Do you think those cavalrymen did it?' she said at last, and then realized that Maladict was shaking. 'Oh . . . the blood . . .' she said.

'I can deal with it! It's okay! I just have to get my mind right, it's okay!' He leaned against the hut, breathing heavily. 'Okay, I'm fine,' he said. 'And I can't smell horses. Why don't you use your eyes? Nice soft mud everywhere after the rain, but no hoofprints. Plenty of footprints, though. We did it.'

'Don't be silly, we were—'

The vampire had reached down and pulled something out of the fallen leaves. He rubbed the mud off it with a thumb. In thin pressed brass, it was the Flaming Cheese badge of the Ins-and-Outs.

'But . . . I thought we were the good guys,' said Polly weakly. 'If we were guys, I mean.'

'I think I need a coffee,' said the vampire.

'Deserters,' said Sergeant Jackrum, ten minutes later. 'It happens.' He tossed the badge into the fire.

'But they were on *our* side!' said Shufti.

'So? Not everyone's a nice gennelman like you, Private Manickle,' said Jackrum. 'Not after a few years of gettin' shot at and eatin' rat scubbo. On the retreat

from Khrusk I had no water for three days and then fell on my face in a puddle of horse piss, a circumstance which did nothing for my feelin's of goodwill towards my fellow man or horse. Something the matter, corporal?'

Maladict was on his knees, going through his pack with a distracted air. 'My coffee's gone, sarge.'

'Can't have packed it properly, then,' said Jackrum unsympathetically.

'I *did*, sarge! I washed out the engine and packed it up with the bean bag after supper last night. I *know* I did. I don't take coffee lightly!'

'If someone else did, they're going to wish I'd never been born,' growled Jackrum, looking round at the rest of the squad. 'Anyone else lost anything?'

'Er . . . I wasn't going to say anything, 'cos I wasn't sure,' Shufti volunteered, 'but my stuff looked as if it had been pulled about when I opened my pack just now . . .'

'Oh-ho!' said Jackrum. 'Well, well, *well*! I'll say this once, lads. Pinching from yer mates is a hanging offence, understood? Nothing breaks down morale faster'n some sneaky little sod dipping into people's packs. And if I find out someone's been at it, I'll swing on their heels!' He glared at the squad. 'I ain't gonna demand that you all empty out your packs as if you's criminals,' he said, 'but you'd better check that nothing's missing. O' course, one of you might have packed something that wasn't theirs by *accident*, okay. Packing in a rush, poor light, easy to do. In which case, you sort it out amongst yourselves,

understand? Now, I'm off to have a shave. Lieutenant Blouse is having a throw-up behind the shelter after a-viewin' of the corpses, poor chap.'

Polly rummaged desperately in her pack. She'd thrown things in any old how last night, but what she was frantically searching for was—

—not there. Despite the heat from the charcoal mounds, she shivered.

The ringlets had gone. Feverishly, she tried to remember the events of yesterday evening. They'd just dumped their packs as soon as they were in the barracks, right? And Maladict *had* made himself some coffee at suppertime. *He'd washed and dried the little machine—*

There was a thin little wail. Wazzer, the meagre contents of her pack spread around her, held up the coffee engine. It had been stamped almost flat.

'B-b-b—' she began.

Polly's mind worked faster, like a millwheel in a flood. Then everyone took their packs into the back room with all the mattresses, didn't they? So they'd still be there when the squad fought the troopers—

'Oh, Wazz,' said Shufti. 'Oh, dear . . .'

So who might have sneaked in through the back door? There was no one around except the squad and the cavalrymen. *Perhaps someone wanted to watch, and cause a little trouble on the way—*

'Strappi!' she said aloud. 'It must have been him! The little weasel ran into the cavalry and then snuck back to watch! He was dar— damn well going through our packs out the back! Oh, come on,' she

added, as they stared at her, 'can you see Wazzer stealing from anyone? Anyway, when did she have the chance?'

'Wouldn't they have taken him prisoner?' said Tonker, staring at the crushed machine in Wazzer's shaking hands.

'If he'd whipped off his shako and jacket he'd just be another stupid civilian, wouldn't he? Or he could just say he was a deserter. He could make up some story,' said Polly. 'You know how he was with Wazzer. He went through my pack, too. Stole . . . something of mine.'

'What was it?' said Shufti.

'Just something, okay? He just wanted to . . . make trouble.' She watched them thinking.

'Sounds convincing,' said Maladict, nodding abruptly. 'Little weasel. Okay, Wazz, just fish out the beans and I'll do the best I can—'

'T-there's no b-b-b—'

Maladict put a hand over his eyes. 'No beans?' he said. 'Please, has *anyone* got the beans?'

There was a general rummaging, and a general lack of a result.

'No beans,' moaned Maladict. 'He threw away the beans . . .'

'Come on, lads, we've got to get sentries posted,' said Jackrum, approaching. 'Sorted it all out, have you?'

'Yes, sarge. Ozz thinks—' Shufti began.

'It was all a bit of mis-packing, sarge!' said Polly quickly, anxious to keep away from anything

connected with missing ringlets. 'Nothing to worry about! All sorted, sarge. No problem. Nothing to worry anyone. Not . . . a . . . thing, sarge.'

Jackrum looked from the startled squad to Polly, and back, and back again. She felt his gaze boring into her, daring her to change her expression of mad, tense honesty.

'Ye-es,' he said slowly. 'Right. Sorted out, eh? Well done, Perks. Attention! Officer present!'

'Yes, yes, sergeant, thank you, but I don't think we need to be too formal,' said Blouse, who looked rather pale. 'A word with you when you have finished, if you please? And I think we should bury the, er, bodies.'

Jackrum saluted. 'Right you are, sir. Two volunteers to dig a grave for those poor souls! Goom and Tewt— what's he doing?'

Lofty was over by the blazing charcoal oven. She was holding a burning branch a foot or two from her face and turning it this way and that, watching the flames.

'I'll do it, sarge,' said Tonker, stepping beside Wazzer.

'What are you, married?' said Jackrum. '*You* are on guard, Halter. I doubt whoever did it'll come back, but if they do, you sing out, right? You and Igor come with me, and I'll show you your stations.'

'No coffee,' moaned Maladict.

'Foul muck, anyway,' said Jackrum, walking away. 'A cup of hot sweet tea is the soldier's friend.'

Polly grabbed the kettle for Blouse's shaving water, and hurried away. That was another thing you learned

in the milit'ry: look busy. Look busy and no one worried too much about what you were busy at.

Bloody, bloody Strappi! He'd got her *hair*! He'd try to use it against her if he could, that was certain. That'd be his style. What would he do now? Well, he'd want to keep away from Jackrum, that'd be another certainty. He'd wait, somewhere. She'd have to, too.

The squad had made camp upwind of the smoke. It was supposed to be a rest stop, since no one had got much sleep last night, but as Jackrum handed out tasks he reminded them: 'There is an old milit'ry saying, which is: Hard Luck For You.'

There was no question of using the woven hut, but there were a few tarpaulin-covered frames built to keep the coppiced wood dry. Those not given jobs to do lay down on the stacked piles of twigs, which were yielding and didn't smell and were in any case better than the inhabited palliasses back at the barracks.

Blouse, as an officer, had a shelter to himself. Polly had stacked bundles of twigs to make a chair that was at least springy. Now she laid out his shaving things and turned to go—

'Could *you* shave me, Perks?' said the lieutenant.

Fortunately, Polly's back was turned and he didn't see her expression.

'This damn hand is quite swollen, I'm afraid,' Blouse went on. 'I would not normally ask, but—'

'Yes, of course, sir,' said Polly, because there was no alternative. Well now, let's see . . . she'd got quite good at scraping a blunt razor across a face bare of hair, yes. Oh, and she'd shaved a few dead pigs in the kitchens

at The Duchess, but that was only because nobody likes hairy bacon. They didn't really count, did they? Panic rose, and rose faster at the sight of Jackrum approaching. She was going to cut an officer's throat in the presence of a sergeant.

Well, when in doubt, bustle. Milit'ry rule. Bustle, and hope there's a surprise attack.

'Are you not being a little strict with the men, sergeant?' said Blouse, as Polly flapped a towel round his neck.

'No, sir. Keep 'em occupied, that's the bunny. Otherwise they'll mope,' said Jackrum confidently.

'Yes, but they *have* just seen a couple of badly mutilated bodies,' said Blouse, and shuddered.

'Good practice for 'em, sir. They'll see plenty more.'

Polly turned to the shaving gear she'd laid out on another towel. Let's see . . . cut-throat razor, oh dear, the grey stone for coarse sharpening, the red stone for fine sharpening, the soap, the brush, the bowl . . . well, at least she knew how to make foam . . .

'Deserters, sergeant. Bad business,' Blouse went on.

'You always get 'em, sir. That's why the pay is always late. Walking away from three months' back pay makes a man think twice.'

'Mr de Worde the newspaper man said there had been a great many desertions, sergeant. It is very strange that so many men would desert from a winning side.'

Polly whirled the brush vigorously. Jackrum, for the first time since Maladict had joined, looked uncomfortable.

'But whose side is he on, sir?' he said.

'Sergeant, I am sure you are not a stupid man,' said Blouse, as, behind him, foam poured over the edge of the bowl and flopped on to the floor. 'There are desperate deserters abroad. Our borders appear to be sufficiently unguarded to enable enemy cavalry to operate forty miles inside "our fair country". And High Command appears to be so desperate, yes, *desperate*, sergeant, that even half a dozen untrained and, frankly, very young men must go to the front.'

The foam had a life of its own now. Polly hesitated.

'Hot towel first, please, Perks,' said Blouse.

'Yessir. Sorry, sir. Forgot, sir,' said Polly, panic rising. She had a vague recollection of walking past the barber shop in Munz. Hot towel on face. Right. She grabbed a small towel, tipped boiling water on to it, wrung it out and placed it on the lieutenant's face. He did not actually scream, as such.

'*Aaaaagh* something else worries me, sergeant.'

'Yessir?'

'The cavalry must have apprehended Corporal Strappi. I cannot see how else they found out about our men.'

'Good thinking, sir,' said the sergeant, watching Polly apply the lather across mouth and nose.

'I do hope they didn't *pff* torture the poor man,' said the lieutenant. Jackrum was silent on that issue, but meaningfully so. Polly wished he wouldn't keep glancing at her.

'But why would a deserter *pff* head straight for the *pff* front?' said Blouse.

'Makes sense, sir, for an old soldier. Especially a political.'

'Really?'

'Trust me on that, sir,' said Jackrum. Behind Blouse, Polly brushed the razor up and down the red stone. It was already as slick as ice.

'But our boys, sergeant, are not "old soldiers". It takes *pff* two weeks to turn a recruit into a "fighting man",' said the lieutenant.

'They're promising material, sir. I could do it in a couple of days, sir,' said Jackrum. '*Perks?*'

Polly nearly sliced her thumb off. 'Yes, sarge,' she quavered.

'Do you think you could kill a man today?'

Polly glanced at the razor. The edge glowed. 'I'm sorry to say I think I could, sir!'

'There you have it, sir,' said Jackrum, with a lop-sided grin. 'There's something about these lads, sir. They're quick.' He walked behind Blouse, took the razor from Polly's grateful hand without a word, and said: 'There's a few matters we ought to discuss, sir, private like. I think Perks here ought to get some rest.'

'Of course, sergeant. *Pas devant les soldats jeunes*, eh?'

'And them too, sir,' said Jackrum. 'You're dismissed, Perks.'

Polly walked away, her right hand still trembling. Behind her, she heard Blouse sigh and say: 'These are tricky times, sergeant. Command has never been so burdensome. The great General Tacticus says that in dangerous times the commander must be like the

eagle and see the whole, and yet still be like the hawk and see every detail.'

'Yessir,' said Jackrum, gliding the razor down a cheek. 'And if he acts like a common tit, sir, he can hang upside down all day and eat fat bacon.'

'Er . . . well said, sergeant.'

The charcoal-burner and his wife were buried to the accompaniment of, to Polly's lack of surprise, a small prayer from Wazzer. It asked the Duchess to intercede with the god Nuggan to give eternal rest and similar items to the departed. Polly had heard it many times before; she'd wondered how the process worked.

She'd never prayed since the day the bird burned, not even when her mother was dying. A god that burned painted birds would not save a mother. A god like that was not worth a prayer.

But Wazzer prayed for everyone. Wazzer prayed like a child, eyes screwed up and hands clenched until they were white. The reedy little voice trembled with such belief that Polly felt embarrassed, and then ashamed and, finally, after the ringing 'amen', amazed that the world appeared no different from before. For a minute or two, it had been a better place . . .

There was a cat in the hut. It cowered under the crude bed and spat at anyone who came close.

'All the food's been taken but there's carrots and parsnips in a little garden down the hill a bit,' Shufti said, as they walked away.

'It'd be s-stealing from the dead,' said Wazzer.

'Well, if they object they can hold on, can't they?' said Shufti. 'They're underground already!'

For some reason that was, at this time, funny. They'd have laughed at anything.

Now there was Jade, Lofty, Shufti and Polly. Everyone else was on guard duty. They sat by the fire, on which a small pot seethed. Lofty tended the fire. She always seemed more animated near a fire, Polly noticed.

'I'm doing horse scubbo for the rupert,' said Shufti, easily dropping into a slang learned all of twenty hours ago. 'He specifically asked for it. Got lots of dry horse jerky from Threeparts, but Tonker says she can knock over some pheasants while she's on duty.'

'I hope she spends some time watching for enemies too,' said Polly.

'She'll be careful,' said Lofty, prodding the fire with a stick.

'You know, if we're found out, we'll be beaten and sent back,' said Shufti.

'Who by?' said Polly, so suddenly she surprised herself. 'By whom? Who's going to try, out here? Who *cares* out here?'

'Well, er, wearing men's clothes *is* an Abomination unto Nuggan—'

'Why?'

'It just is,' said Shufti firmly. 'But—'

'—you're wearing them,' said Polly.

'Well, it was the only way,' said Shufti. 'And I tried them on and they didn't seem all that abominable to me.'

'Have you noticed men talk to you differently?' said Lofty shyly.

'Talk?' said Polly. 'They *listen* to you differently, too.'

'They don't keep looking at you all the time,' said Shufti. 'You know what I mean. You're just a . . . another person. If a girl walked down the street wearing a sword a man would try to take it off her.'

'Wi' trolls, we ain't allowed to carry clubs,' said Jade. 'Only large rocks. An' it ain't right for a girl to wear lichen, 'cos der boys say bald is modest. Had to rub bird doin's inna my head to grow this lot.'

That was quite a long speech for a troll.

'We didn't know that,' said Polly. 'Er . . . trolls all look the same to us, more or less.'

'I'm nat'rally craggy,' said Jade. 'I don't see why I should polish.'

'There *is* a difference,' said Shufti. 'I think it's the socks. It's like they pull you forward all the time. It's like the whole world spins around your socks.' She sighed and looked at the horsemeat, which had been boiled almost white. 'It's done,' she said. 'You'd better go and give it to the rupert, Polly . . . I mean, Ozzer. I told the sarge I could do something better but he said the lieutenant said how good it was last night—'

A small wild turkey, a brace of pheasants and a couple of rabbits, all tied together, landed in front of Shufti.

'Good job we were guarding you, eh?' said Tonker, grinning and whirring an empty sling around in one hand. 'One rock, one lunch. Maladict's staying on guard. He said he'll smell anyone before they see him

and he's too edgy to eat. What can you do with that lot?'

'Casserole of game,' said Shufti firmly. 'We've got the veg and I've still got half an onion.* I'm sure I can make an oven out of one of those—'

'On your feet! Attention!' snapped the silently moving Jackrum, behind them. He stood back with a faint smile on his face as they scrambled to their feet. 'Private Halter, I must have bleedin' amazin' eyesight,' he said, when they were approximately upright.

'Yes, sarge,' said Tonker, staring straight ahead.

'Can you guess why, Private Halter?'

'No, sarge.'

'It's because I knows you are on perimeter guard, Halter, but I can see you as clear as if you was standing right here in front of me, Halter! Can't I, Halter?'

'Yes, sarge!'

'It's just as well you *are* still on perimeter duty, Halter, because the penalty for absenting yourself from your post in time of war is *death*, Halter!'

'I only—'

'No onlys! I don't want to hear no onlys! I don't want you to think that I am a shouty man, Halter! Corporal Strappi was a shouty man, but he was a damn political! Upon my oath I am not a shouty man *but if you ain't back at your post inside of thirty seconds I'll rip yer tongue out!*'

Tonker fled. Sergeant Jackrum cleared his throat

* A woman always has half an onion left over, no matter what the size of the onion, the dish or the woman.

and continued, in a level voice: 'This, my lads, is what we call a *real* orientation lectchoor, not one of the fancy political ones like Strappi gave yer.' He cleared his throat. 'The purpose of this lectchoor is to let you know where we are. We are in the deep cack. It couldn't be worse if it was raining arseholes. Any questions?'

Since there were none from the bemused recruits, he continued, while beginning a slow stroll around the squad, 'We know enemy forces are in the area. Currently they have no boots. But there will be others with boots aplenty. Also, there may be deserters in the area. They will not be nice people! They will be impolite! Therefore Lieutenant Blouse has decreed that we will travel off the roads and by night. Yes, we have met the enemy, and we have prevailed. That was a fluke. They weren't expecting you to be rough, tough soldiers. Nor were you, so I don't want you to feel cocky about it.' He leaned forward until his face was inches from Polly's. 'Are you feeling cocky, Private Perks?'

'No, sarge!'

'Good. Good.' Jackrum stepped back. 'We are heading for the front, lads. The war. And in a nasty war, where's the best place to be? Apart from on the moon, o' course? No one?'

Slowly, Jade raised a hand.

'Go on, then,' said the sergeant.

'In the army, sarge,' said the troll. ''cos...' She began to count on her fingers. 'One, you got weapons an' armour an' dat. Two, you are surrounded by other

armed men. Er ... Many, youse gettin' paid and gettin' better grub than the people in Civilian Street. Er ... Lots, if'n you gives up, you getting taken pris'ner and dere's rules about that like Not Kicking Pris'ners Inna Head and stuff, 'cos if you kick their pris'ners inna head they'll kick your pris'ners inna head so dat's, like, you're kickin' your own head, but dere's no rule say you can't kick enemy civilians inna head. There's other stuff too, but I ran outa numbers.' She gave them a diamond grin. 'We may be slow but we ain't stoopid,' she added.

'I am impressed, private,' said Jackrum. 'And you are *right*. The only wasp in the jam is that you ain't soldiers! But I can help you there. Bein' a soldier is not hard. If it was, soldiers would not be able to do it. There is only three things you need to remember, which are, viz: one obey orders two give it to the enemy good and hard three don't die. Got that? Right! You're nearly there! Well done! I propose to assist you in the execution of all three! You are my little lads and I will look after you! In the meantime, you got duties! Shufti, get cooking! Private Perks, see to the rupert! And after that, practise your shaving! I will now visit those on guard and deliver unto them the holy word! Dismissed!'

They remained at something like attention until he was probably out of earshot, and then sagged.

'Why does he always *shout*?' said Shufti. 'I mean, he only has to ask ...'

Polly upended the horrible scubbo into a tin bowl, and almost ran to the lieutenant's shelter. He looked

up from a map and smiled at her as if she was delivering a feast.

'Ah, scubbo,' he said.

'We are actually having other stuff, sir,' Polly volunteered. 'I'm sure there's enough to go round—'

'Good heavens, no, it's been years since I've had food like this,' said Blouse, picking up the spoon. 'Of course, at school we didn't appreciate it so much.'

'You had food like this at school, sir?' said Polly.

'Yes. Most days,' said Blouse happily.

Polly couldn't quite fit this in her head. Blouse was a nob. Nobs ate nobby food, didn't they? 'Had you done something *bad*, sir?'

'I can't imagine what you mean, Perks,' said Blouse, slurping at the horrible thin gruel. 'Are the men rested?'

'Yes, sir. The dead people were a bit of a shock—'

'Yes. Bad business,' sighed the lieutenant. 'Such is war, alas. I am only sorry you had to learn so fast. Such a terrible waste all the time. I am sure things can be sorted out when we reach Kneck, though. No general can expect young men like yourselves to be instant soldiers. I shall have something to say about that.' His rabbity features looked unusually determined, as if a hamster had spotted a gap in its treadmill.

'Do you require me for anything else, sir?' said Polly.

'Er . . . do the men talk about me, Perks?'

'Not really, sir, no.'

The lieutenant looked disappointed. 'Oh. Oh, well. Thank you, Perks.'

Polly wondered if Jackrum ever slept. She did a spell of guard duty, and he stepped out from behind her with 'Guess who, Perks! You're on lookout. You should see the dreadful enemy before they see you. What're the four Ss?'

'Shape, shadow, silhouette and shine, sarge!' said Polly, snapping to attention. She'd been expecting this.

That caused a moment's pause from the sergeant before he said: 'Just *knew* that, did yer?'

'Nosir! A little bird told me when we changed guard, sir! Said you'd asked him, sir!'

'Oh, so Jackrum's little lads are gangin' up on their kindly ol' sergeant, are they?' said Jackrum.

'Nosir. Sharing information important to the squad in a vital survival situation, sarge!'

'You've got a quick mouth on you, Perks, I'll grant you that.'

'Thank you, sarge!'

'But I see you're not standing in a bleedin' shadow, Perks, nor have you done anything to change your bleedin' shape, you're silhouetted against the bleedin' light and your sabre's shining like a diamond in a chimney-sweep's bleedin' ear'ole! Explain!'

'It's because of the one C, sarge!' said Polly, still staring straight ahead.

'And that is?'

'Colour, sarge! I'm wearing bleedin' red and white in a bleedin' grey forest, sarge!'

She risked a sideways glance. In Jackrum's little piggy eyes there gleamed a gleam. It was the one you got when he was secretly pleased.

'Ashamed of your lovely, lovely uniform, Perks?' he said.

'Don't want to be seen dead in it, sarge,' said Polly.

'Hah. As you were, Perks.'

Polly smiled, straight ahead.

When she came off guard for a bowl of game casserole, Jackrum was teaching basic swordcraft to Lofty and Tonker, using hazel sticks as swords. By the time Polly had finished he was teaching Wazzer some of the finer points of using a high-performance pistol crossbow, especially the one about not turning round with it cocked and saying 'W-what is this bit for, sarge?' Wazzer handled weapons like a houseproud woman disposing of a dead mouse – at arm's length and trying not to look. But even she was better with them than Igor, who just didn't seem at home with the idea of what was, to him, randomized surgery.

Jade was dozing. Maladict was hanging by his knees under the roof of one of the sheds, with his arms folded across his chest; he must have been telling the truth when he said there were some aspects of being a vampire that were hard to give up.

Igor and Maladict . . .

She still wasn't sure about Maladict, but Igor had to be a boy, with those stitches around the head, and that

face that could only be called homely.* He was quiet, and neat, but maybe that's how Igors behaved . . .

She woke up with Shufti shaking her.

'We're moving! Better go and see to the rupert!'

'What? Huh? Oh . . . right!'

There was a bustle all around her. Polly staggered to her feet and hurried over to Lieutenant Blouse's shed, where he was standing in front of his wretched horse and holding the bridle with a lost expression.

'Ah, Perks,' he said. 'I'm not at all sure I'm doing this right . . .'

'No, sir. You've got the waffles twisted and the snoffles are upside down,' said Polly, who'd often helped in the inn's yard.

'Ah, that would be why he was so difficult last night,' said Blouse. 'I suppose I ought to know this sort of thing, but at home we had a man to do it . . .'

'Let me, sir,' said Polly. She untwisted the bridle with a few careful movements. 'What's his name, sir?'

'Thalacephalos,' said Blouse sheepishly. 'That was the legendary stallion of General Tacticus, you know.'

'I didn't know that, sir,' said Polly. She leaned back and glanced between the horse's rear legs. Wow, Blouse really *was* short-sighted, wasn't he . . .

The mare looked at her partly with its eyes, which were small and evil, but mostly with its yellowing teeth, of which it had an enormous amount. She had the impression that it was thinking about sniggering.

* And even then it was the kind of home that has a burned-out vehicle on the lawn.

'I'll hold him for you while you mount, sir,' she said.

'Thank you. He certainly moves about a bit when I try!'

'I expect he does, sir,' said Polly. She knew about difficult horses; this one had all the hallmarks of a right bastard, one of those not cowed at all by the obvious superiority of the human race.

The mare eyeballed and yellowtoothed her as Blouse mounted, but Polly had positioned herself carefully away from the uprights of the shelter. Thalacephalos wasn't the sort to buck and kick. She was the sneaky kind, Polly could see, the sort that stepped on your foot—

She moved her foot just as the hoof came down. But Thalacephalos, angry at being thwarted, turned, twisted, lowered her head, and bit Polly sharply on the rolled-up socks.

'Bad horse!' said Blouse severely. 'Sorry about that, Perks. I think he's anxious to get to the fray! Oh, my word!' he added, looking down. 'Are you all right, Perks?'

'Well, he's pulling a bit, sir—' said Polly, being dragged sideways. Blouse had gone white again.

'But he's bitten . . . he's caught you by the . . . right on the . . .'

The penny dropped. Polly looked down, and hastily remembered what she'd heard during numerous rule-free bar fights.

'Oh . . . ooo . . argh . . . blimey! Right inna fruit! Aargh!' she lamented, and then, since it seemed a

TERRY PRATCHETT

good idea at the time, brought both fists down heavily on the mare's nose. The lieutenant fainted.

It took some time to bring Blouse round, but at least it gave Polly time to think.

He opened his eyes and focused on her.

'Er, you fell off your horse, sir,' Polly volunteered.

'Perks? Are you all right? Dear boy, he had you by the—'

'Only needs a few stitches, sir!' said Polly cheerfully.

'What? From *Igor*?'

'Nosir. Just the cloth, sir,' said Polly. 'The trousers are a bit big for me, sir.'

'Ah, *right*. Too big, eh? Phew, eh? Near miss there, eh? Well, I mustn't lie around here all day—'

The squad helped him on to Thalacephalos, who was still sniggering unrepentantly. On the subject of 'too big', Polly made a mental note to do something about his jacket next time they stopped. She wasn't much good with a needle, but if Igor couldn't do something to make it look better then he wasn't the man she thought he was. And that was a sentence that begged a question.

Jackrum bellowed them into order. They were better at that now. Neater, too.

'All right, Ins-and-Outs! Tonight we—'

A set of huge yellow teeth removed his cap.

'Oh, I do apologize, sergeant!' said Blouse behind him, trying to rein back the mare.

'No bother, sir, these things happen!' said Jackrum, furiously tugging his hat back.

'I should like to address my men, sergeant.'

'Oh? Er . . . yes, sir,' said Jackrum, looking worried. 'Of course, sir. Ins-and-Outs! Attenwaitforitshun!'

Blouse coughed. 'Er . . . men,' he said. 'As you know, we must make all speed to the Kneck valley where, apparently, we are needed. Travelling by night will prevent . . . entanglements. Er . . . I . . .' He stared at them, his face contorted by some inner struggle. 'Er . . . I have to say I don't think we are . . . that is, all the evidence is . . . er . . . it doesn't seem to me that . . . er . . . I think I should tell you . . . er . . .'

'Permission to speak, sir?' said Polly. 'Are you feeling all right?'

'We just have to hope that those put in power over us are making the right decisions,' mumbled Blouse. 'But I have every confidence in you and I am sure you will do your best. Long live the Duchess! Carry on, Sergeant Jackrum.'

'*Ins-and-Outs! Form up! March!*'

And they headed into the dusk and off to war.

The order of march was as last night, with Maladict going on ahead. The clouds were holding in some heat, and were thin enough to hint at moonlight here and there. Forests by night held no problems for Polly, and this wasn't true wild forest in any case. Nor was it, in truth, a march that they were doing. It was more like a high-speed creep, in ones and twos.

She'd acquired two of the horsebows, now stuck awkwardly between the straps of her pack. They were horrible things, rather like a cross between a small

crossbow and a clock. There were mechanisms in the thick shaft, and the bow itself was barely six inches across; somehow, if you leaned your weight on it, you could cock it with enough stored energy to fire a nasty little metal arrow through an inch-thick plank. They were blued metal, sleek and evil. But there is an old milit'ry saying: better me firing it at you than you firing it at me, you bastard.

Polly eased her way along the line until she was walking alongside Igor. He nodded to her in the gloom, and then turned his attention to walking. He needed to, because his pack was twice the size of the rest of them. No one felt inclined to ask him what was in it; sometimes, you thought you could hear liquid sloshing.

Igors sometimes passed through Munz, although technically they were an Abomination in the eyes of Nuggan. It had seemed to Polly that using bits of someone who was dead to help three or four other people stay alive was a sensible idea, but in the pulpit Father Jupe had argued that Nuggan didn't want people to live, he wanted them to live *properly*. There had been general murmurs of agreement from the congregation, but Polly knew for a fact that there were a couple of people sitting there with a hand or arm or leg that was a little less tanned or a little more hairy than the other one. There were lumberjacks everywhere in the mountains. Accidents happened, fast, *sudden* accidents. And, since there were not many jobs for a one-armed lumberjack, men went off and found an Igor to do what no amount of prayer could manage.

The Igors had a motto: What goes around, comes around. You didn't have to pay them back. You had to pay them forward, and that, frankly, was the bit where people got worried. When you were dying, an Igor would mysteriously arrive on the doorstep and request that he be allowed to take away any bits urgently needed by others on his 'little litht'. He'd be quite happy to wait until the priest had gone and, it was said, when the time came he'd do very neat work. However, it happened quite often that when an Igor turned up the prospective donor took fright and turned to Nuggan, who liked *whole* people. In which case the Igor would quietly and politely leave, and never come back. He'd never come back to the whole village, or the whole lumber camp. Nor would other Igors. What goes around comes around – or stops.

As far as Polly could tell, Igors believed that the body was nothing more than a more complicated kind of clothing. Oddly enough, that's what Nugganites thought, too.

'Glad you joined, Igor?' said Polly, as they jogged along.

'Yeth, Ozz.'

'Could you take a look at the rupert's hand next time we stop, please? He's cut it badly.'

'Yeth, Ozz.'

'Can I ask you something, Igor?'

'Yeth, Ozz.'

'What're female Igors called, Igor?'

Igor stumbled and kept moving. He was silent for a while, and then said: 'All right, what did I do wrong?'

'Sometimes you forget to lisp,' said Polly. 'But mostly . . . it's just a feeling. Little things about the way you move, maybe.'

'The word you're looking for is "Igorina",' said Igorina. 'We don't lisp as much as the boys.'

They continued in more silence until Polly said, 'I thought it was bad enough cutting my hair—'

'The stitches?' said Igorina. 'I can have them out in five minuteth. They're just for show.'

Polly hesitated. But, after all, Igors *had* to be trustworthy, didn't they? 'You didn't cut your hair?'

'Actually, I just removed it,' said Igorina.

'I put mine in my pack,' Polly went on, trying not to look at the stitches around Igorina's head.

'So did I,' said Igorina. 'In a jar. It's thtill growing.'

Polly swallowed. You needed a lack of graphic imagination to talk about personal issues with an Igor. 'Mine was stolen back at the barracks. I'm sure it was Strappi,' she said.

'Oh dear.'

'I *hate* to think of him with it!'

'Why did you bring it?'

And that was the question. She'd planned, and she'd been good at planning. She'd fooled the rest of them, even. She'd been cool and sensible and she hadn't felt more than a faint pang at cutting off her hair—

—and she'd brought it with her. Why? She could have thrown it away. It wasn't *magic*. It was just hair. She could have thrown it away, just like that. Easily. But . . . but . . . ah, right, the maids could have found it. That was it. She had to get it out of the house quickly.

Right. And then she could bury it somewhere when she was a long way away. Right.

But she hadn't, had she . . .

She'd been *very busy*. Right, said the little voice in inner treachery. She had been very busy fooling everyone but herself, right?

'What could Strappi do?' said Igorina. 'Jackrum'd knock him over the moment he thaw him. He's a deserter, and a thief!'

'Yes, but he could tell someone,' said Polly.

'Okay, then say it's a lock of hair from the sweetheart you left behind you. Lots of soldiers carry a locket or something like that. You know: "Her golden hair in ringleth fair", like the song says.'

'It was *all my hair*! A locket? You couldn't hold it all in your hat!'

'Ah,' said Igorina. 'Then you could thay you loved her *very much*?'

Despite everything, Polly started to laugh, and couldn't stop herself. She bit her sleeve and tried to keep going, with her shoulders shaking.

Something that felt like a small tree prodded her in the back. 'Youse two oughta keep der noise down,' rumbled Jade.

'Sorry. Sorry,' hissed Polly.

Igorina started to hum. Polly knew the song.

> *I'm lonesome since I crossed the hill*
> *And o'er the moor and valley . . .*

And she vowed: not that one, too. One song is

enough. And I *want* to leave the girl behind me, but it seems I brought her with me . . . At which point they emerged from the trees and saw the red glow.

The rest of the squad were already gathered round, watching it. It covered quite a lot of the horizon, and brightened and faded in places as they watched.

'Is that hell?' said Wazzer.

'No, but men have made it so, I fear,' said the lieutenant. 'That is the Kneck valley.'

'It's on fire, sir?' said Polly.

'Bless you, that's just the light of cooking-fires reflected off the clouds,' said Sergeant Jackrum. 'Always looks bad by night, a battlefield. Not to worry, lads!'

'What're they cooking, elephants?' said Maladict.

'And what's that?' said Polly, pointing to a nearby hill, darker still against the night. On it, a little light was flickering on and off, very fast.

There was a whoosh and a metallic 'pop' as Blouse pulled out a small telescope and opened it up. 'It's a light clacks, the devils!' he said.

'Dere's another one over dere,' rumbled Jade, pointing to a hill a lot further away. 'Twinkle, twinkle.'

Polly stared at the redness in the sky, and then at the cold little light, winking on and off. Quiet, soft light. Harmless light. And behind it, a burning sky . . .

'It'll be in code,' said Blouse. 'Spies, I'll be bound.'

'A light clacks?' said Tonker. 'What's that?'

'An Abomination in the eyes of Nuggan,' said

Blouse. 'Unfortunately, because they'd be damn useful if we could have 'em too, eh, sergeant?'

'Yessir,' said Jackrum automatically.

'The only messages passing through the air should be the prayers of the faithful. Praise Nuggan, Praise the Duchess and so on and so forth,' said Blouse, squinting. He sighed. 'Such a shame. How far to that hill, would you say, sergeant?'

'Two miles, sir,' said Jackrum. 'Worth trying to sneak up?'

'They must know people will see them and come looking, so I expect they won't "hang around" for long' mused Blouse. 'In any case, ah, those things would be highly directional. You'd lose it once you got down in the valley.'

'Permission to speak, sir?' said Polly.

'Of course,' said Blouse.

'How do they get the light so bright, sir? It's pure white!'

'Some kind of firework thingy, I believe. Why?'

'And they send messages with light?'

'Yes, Perks. And your point is . . . ?'

'And the people who get those messages send messages back the same way?' Polly persevered.

'Yes, Perks, that is the whole idea.'

'Then . . . maybe we don't have to go all the way to *that* hill, sir? The light is being aimed towards *us*, sir.'

They all turned. The hill they were skirting loomed above them.

'Well done, Perks!' Blouse whispered. 'Let's go,

sergeant!' He swung himself off the horse, which automatically stepped sideways to make sure that he fell over when he landed.

'Right you are, sir!' said Jackrum, helping him up. 'Maladict, you take Goom and Halter and circle round to the left, the rest go round to the right – not you, Carborundum, no offence, but this has got to be *quiet*, okay? You stay here. Perks, you come with me—'

'I shall come too, sergeant,' said Blouse, and only Polly saw Jackrum grimace.

'Good idea, sir!' said the sergeant. 'I suggest you – I suggest Perks and I come with you. Everyone got that? Get to the top neat and quiet and no one, *no one* moves until you hear my signal—'

'*My* signal,' said Blouse firmly.

'That's what I meant, sir. Quick and quiet! Hit 'em hard but I want at least one left alive! Go!'

The two teams fanned out to right and left and disappeared. The sergeant gave them a minute or two's start, and then set off with unusual speed for a man of his girth, so that for a moment Polly and the lieutenant were left standing. Behind them, a dejected Jade watched them go.

The trees thinned out on the steep slope, but not enough for much underbrush to get a hold. Polly found it easier to go on all fours, grabbing at tufts and saplings to steady herself. After a while she caught a whiff of smoke, chemical and acrid. She was sure, too, that she could hear a faint clicking noise.

A tree extended a hand and pulled her into its

shadow. 'Don't you say a bleedin' word,' hissed Jackrum. 'Where's the rupert?'

'Don't know, sarge!'

'Damn! You can't let a rupert run around loose, there's no tellin' what he might take it into his little head to do, now he's got the idea he's in charge! You're 'is minder! Find 'im!'

Polly slithered back down the slope and found Blouse steadying himself against a tree, wheezing gently.

'Ah . . . Perks,' he panted. 'My asthma seems to . . . be . . . coming back . . .'

'I'll help you up, sir,' said Polly, grabbing his hand and tugging him forward. 'Could you wheeze a little more quietly, sir?'

By degrees, dragging and pushing, she bundled the man up to Jackrum's tree.

'Glad you could join us, sir!' hissed the sergeant, face contorted into an expression of maddened affability. 'If you'd care to wait here, Perks and me will crawl up the—'

'I'm coming too, sergeant,' Blouse insisted.

Jackrum hesitated. 'Yessir,' he said. 'But with respect, sir, I know about skirmishing—'

'Let's go, sergeant,' said Blouse, dropping flat and beginning to drag himself forward.

'Yessir,' muttered Jackrum darkly.

Polly eased her way forward, too. The grass here was shorter, rabbit-nibbled, with small bushes here and there. She concentrated on keeping the noise down, and aimed for the clicking. The smell of

chemical smoke grew stronger. It hung in the air around her. And, as she moved forward, she saw light, little specks of it. She raised her head.

There were three men a few feet away, silhouetted against the night. One of them was holding a large pipe, about five feet long, balanced on his shoulder at one end and on a tripod at the other. That end was aimed at the distant hill. On the other end, a foot or so behind the man's head, was a big square box. Light was leaking from joints in this; from a little stovepipe chimney on the top of it, heavy smoke poured out.

'Perks, on the count of three,' said Jackrum, on Polly's right. 'One—'

'As you were, sergeant,' said Blouse quietly, on her left.

Polly saw Jackrum's big florid face turn with an expression of astonishment. 'Sir?'

'Hold position,' said Blouse. Above them, the click-ing continued.

Milit'ry secrets, thought Polly. Spies! Enemies! And we're just watching! It was like seeing blood drain from an artery.

'Sir!' hissed Jackrum, rage smoking off him.

'Hold position, sergeant. That is an order,' said Blouse calmly.

Jackrum subsided, but only into the deceptive calm of a volcano waiting to explode. The relentless chatter of the clacks went on. It seemed to go on for ever. Beside Polly, Sergeant Jackrum seethed and fretted like a dog on a leash.

The clicking stopped. Polly heard a distant murmur of conversation.

'Sergeant Jackrum,' whispered Blouse, 'you may "get them" with all speed!'

Jackrum exploded out of the grass like a partridge. *'All right, my lads! Up boys and at 'em!'*

Polly's first thought, as she leapt up and ran, was that the distance was suddenly a lot wider than it had appeared.

All three men had turned at the sound of Jackrum's cry. The one with the clacks tube was already dropping it and reaching for a sword, but Jackrum was bearing down on him like a landslide. The man made the mistake of standing his ground. There was a brief clash of swords and then a mêlée, and Sergeant Jackrum was a sufficiently deadly mêlée all by himself.

The second man flew past Polly but she was running for the third one. He backed away from her, still reaching up to his mouth, then turned to run and found himself face to face with Maladict.

'Don't let him swallow!' Polly yelled.

Maladict's arm shot up, and lifted the struggling man aloft by his throat.

It would have been a perfect operation had not the rest of the squad arrived, having put all their effort into running and left none to spare for slowing down. There were collisions.

Maladict went down as his captive kicked him in the chest and the man tried to scramble away, cannoning into Tonker. Polly leapt over Igorina, was almost tripped by a fallen Wazzer and threw herself desperately towards

the quarry, now on his knees. He had a dagger out and waved it wildly in front of her while he grasped his throat with his other hand and made choking noises. She knocked the knife away, ran behind him and slapped him on the back as hard as she could. He fell forward. Before she could grab him a hand lifted him bodily and Jackrum's voice roared: 'Can't have the poor man chokin' to death, Perks!' His other hand punched the man in the stomach with a noise like meat hitting a slab. The man's eyes crossed and something large and white flew out of his mouth and shot over Jackrum's shoulder.

Jackrum dropped him and turned on Blouse. 'Sir, I protest, sir!' he said, quivering with anger. 'We lay there and watched these devils sending who knows what messages, sir! Spies, sir! We could've got 'em right there and then, sir!'

'And then, sergeant?' said Blouse.

'What?'

'Don't you think the people they were talking to would wonder what had happened if the messages had stopped in mid-flow?' said the lieutenant.

'Even so, sir—'

'Whereas now we have their device, sergeant, and their masters don't know we have it,' said Blouse.

'Yeah, well, but you said they was sending messages in code, sir, and—'

'Er, I think we have their cipher book as well, sarge,' said Maladict, stepping forward with the white object in his hand. 'That man tried to eat it, sarge. Rice paper. But he rushed his food, you might say.'

'And you dislodged it, sergeant, and probably saved his life. Well done!' said Blouse.

'But one of 'em got away, sir,' said Jackrum. 'He'll soon get to—'

'*Sergeant?*'

Jade was rising over the grass. As she plodded nearer they saw she was dragging a man by one foot. When she was closer it was obvious that the man was dead. Living people have more head.

'I heard the shoutin' and he come runnin' and I jumped up and he come straight into me, head first!' Jade complained. 'I didn't even get a chance to hit him!'

'Well, private, at least we can definitely say he was stopped,' said Blouse.

'Thur, thith man is dying,' said Igorina, who was kneeling by the man Sergeant Jackrum had so positively saved from choking. 'He hath been poithened!'

'Hath he? By whom?' said Blouse. 'Are you sure?'

'The green foam coming out of hith mouth ith a definite clue, thur.'

'What's funny, Private Maladict?' said Blouse.

The vampire chuckled. 'Oh, sorry, sir. They say to spies "If you're caught, eat the documents", don't they? A good way of making sure they don't give away any secrets.'

'But you've got the . . . soggy book in your hands, corporal!'

'Vampires can't be poisoned that easily, sir,' said Maladict calmly.

'It wath probably only fatal by mouth in any case, thur,' said Igorina. 'Terrible stuff. *Th*tuff. He'th dead, thur. Nothing I can do.'

'Poor fellow. Well, we have the codes, anyway,' said Blouse. 'This is a *great* discovery, men.'

'And a prisoner, sir, and a prisoner,' said Jackrum.

The one surviving man, who had been operating the clacks, groaned and tried to move.

'A bit bruised, I expect,' Jackrum added, with some satisfaction. 'When I land on someone, sir, they stay landed on.'

'Two of you, bring him with us,' said Blouse. 'Sergeant, there's a few hours to dawn, and I want to be well away from here. I want the other two buried somewhere down in the woods, and—'

'You just have to say "carry on, sergeant", sir,' said Jackrum, and it was almost a wail. 'That's how it works, sir! You tell me what you want, I give 'em the orders!'

'Times are changing, sergeant,' said Blouse.

Messages, flying across the sky. They were an Abomination unto Nuggan.

The logic sounded impeccable to Polly as she helped Wazzer to dig two graves. Prayers from the faithful ascended unto Nuggan, going upwards. A variety of unseen things, such as sanctity and grace and a list of this week's Abominations, descended from Nuggan to the faithful, going downwards. What was forbidden was messages from one human to another going, as it were, from side to side. There

could be collisions. If you believed in Nuggan, that is. If you believed in prayer.

Wazzer's real name was Alice, she confided as she dug, but it was hard to apply the name to a small stick-thin lad with a bad haircut and not much skill with a shovel, who had a habit of standing just slightly too close to you and stared just slightly to the left of your face when she talked to you. Wazzer believed in prayer. She believed in everything. That made her kind of . . . awkward to talk to, if you didn't. But Polly felt she should make the effort.

'How old are you, Wazz?' she said, shovelling dirt.

'N-n-nineteen, Polly,' said Wazzer.

'Why'd you join?'

'The Duchess told me to,' said Wazzer.

That was why people didn't talk to Wazzer much.

'Wazz, you do *know* that wearing men's clothes is an Abomination, don't you?'

'Thank you for reminding me, Polly,' said Wazzer, without a trace of irony. 'But the Duchess told me that nothing I do in pursuit of my quest will be held Abominable.'

'A quest, eh,' said Polly, trying to sound jovial. 'And what kind of quest is that?'

'I am to take command of the army,' said Wazzer.

Hairs rose on the back of Polly's neck. 'Yes?' she said.

'Yes, the Duchess stepped out of her picture when I was asleep and told me to go at once to Kneck,' said Wazzer. 'The Little Mother spoke to me, Ozz. She commanded me. She guides my steps. She led me out

191

of vile slavery. How can that be an Abomination?'

She's got a sword, thought Polly. And a shovel. This needs careful handling. 'That's nice,' she said.

'And . . . and I must tell you that . . . I . . . never in my life have I felt such love and camaraderie,' Wazzer went on earnestly. 'The last few days have been the happiest of my life. You have all shown me such kindness, such gentleness. The Little Mother guides me. She guides us all, Ozz. You believe that, too. Don't you?' The moonlight revealed the tracks of tears in the grime on Wazzer's cheeks.

'Um,' said Polly, and sought wildly for a way to avoid lying. She found it. 'Er . . . you know I want to find my brother?' she said.

'Well, that does you credit, the Duchess knows,' said Wazzer quickly.

'And, well . . . I'm also doing it for The Duchess,' said Polly, feeling wretched. 'I think about The Duchess all the time, I must admit.' Well, that was true. It just wasn't honest.

'I'm so very glad to hear that, Ozz, because I had thought you were a backslider,' said Wazzer. 'But you said that with such conviction. Perhaps this would be the time for us to get down on our knees and—'

'Wazz, you're standing in another man's grave,' said Polly. 'There's a time and place, you know? Let's get back to the others, eh?'

The happiest days of the girl's life had been spent tramping through forests, digging graves and trying to dodge soldiers on both sides? The trouble with Polly was that she had a mind that asked questions

even when she really, really didn't want to know the answers.

'So . . . the Duchess is still talking to you, is she?' she said, as they made their way among the dark trees.

'Oh, yes. When we were in Plotz, sleeping in the barracks,' said Wazzer. 'She said it was all working.'

Don't, *don't* ask another question, said part of Polly's mind, but she ignored it out of sheer horrible curiosity. Wazzer was nice – well, sort of nice, in a slightly scary way – but talking to her was like picking at a scab; you knew what was likely to be under the crust, but you picked anyway.

'So . . . what did you use to do back in the world?' she said.

Wazzer gave her a haunting smile. 'I used to be beaten.'

Tea was brewing in a small hollow near the track. Several of the squad were standing guard. No one liked the idea of men in dark clothes sneaking around.

'Mug of saloop?' said Shufti, holding them up. A few days ago they'd have called it 'sweet milky tea', but even if they couldn't walk the walk yet they were determined to talk the talk as soon as possible.

'What's happening?' said Polly.

'Dunno,' said Shufti. 'Sarge and the rupert went off over *that* way with the prisoner but no one tells us groans anything.'

'It's "grunts", I think,' said Wazzer, taking the tea.

'I've done them a couple of mugs, anyway. See what you can find out, eh?'

Polly gulped her tea down, grabbed the mugs and hurried away.

On the edge of the hollow Maladict was lounging against a tree. There was this about vampires: they could never look scruffy. Instead, they were . . . what was the word . . . *déshabillé*. It meant untidy, but with bags and bags of style. In this case Maladict's jacket was open and he'd stuck his packet of cigarettes in the band of his shako. He saluted her with his crossbow as she went past.

'Ozz?' he said.

'Yes, corp?'

'Any coffee in their packs?'

'Sorry, corp. Only tea.'

'Damn!' Maladict thumped the tree behind him. 'Hey, you went straight for the man who was swallowing the cipher. Straight for him. How come?'

'Just luck,' said Polly.

'Yeah, right. Try again. I have very good night vision.'

'Oh, all right. Well, the one on the left started to run and the one in the middle was dropping the clacks tube and reaching for his sword, but the one on the right thought that putting something into his mouth was more important even than fighting or running away. Satisfied?'

'You worked out all that in a couple of seconds? That was smart.'

'Yeah, right. Now *please* forget it, okay? I don't want

to be noticed. I don't particularly want to be here. I just want to find my brother. Okay?'

'Fine. I just thought that you'd like to know someone saw you. And you'd better get that tea to 'em before they try to kill one another.'

At least I was someone watching the enemy, Polly thought furiously as she walked away. I wasn't someone watching another soldier. Who does he think he is? Or she is?

She heard the raised voices as she pushed through a thicket.

'You can't torture an unarmed man!' That was Blouse's voice.

'Well, I'm not waiting for him to arm himself, sir! He knows stuff! And he's a spy!'

'Don't you dare kick him in the ribs again! That is an *order*, sergeant!'

'Asking nicely didn't work, did it, sir? "Pretty please with sprinkles on top" is not a recognized method of interrogation! You shouldn't be here, sir! You should say "Sergeant, find out what you can from the prisoner!" and then go somewhere and wait until I tell you what I got out of him, sir!'

'You did it again!'

'What? What?'

'You kicked him again!'

'No, I didn't!'

'Sergeant, I gave you an order!'

'*And?*'

'Tea's up!' said Polly cheerfully.

Both men turned. Their expression changed. If

they had been birds, their feathers would have gently settled back.

'Ah, Perks,' said Blouse. 'Well done.'

'Yeah . . . good lad,' said Sergeant Jackrum.

Polly's presence seemed to lower the temperature. The two men drank their tea and eyed one another warily.

'You'll have noticed, sergeant, that the men were wearing the dark-green uniform of the First Battalion the Zlobenian Fifty-ninth Bowmen. A skirmishing battalion,' said Blouse, with cold politeness. 'That is not the uniform of a spy, sergeant.'

'Yessir? But they'd let their uniforms get very dirty, then. No shine on the buttons, *sir*.'

'Patrolling behind enemy lines is not spying, sergeant. You must have done it in your time.'

'More times than you could count, sir,' said Jackrum. 'And I knew full well that if I got caught I was due a good kicking in the nadgers. But skirmishers is the worst, sir. You think you're safe in the lines, next moment it turns out that some *bastard* sitting in the bushes on a hill has been working out windage and yardage and has dropped an arrow right through your mate's head.' He picked up a strange-looking longbow. 'See these things they've got? Burleigh and Stronginthearm Number Five Recurved, made in bloody Ankh-Morpork. A real killing weapon. I say we give him a choice, sir. He can tell us what he knows, and go out easy. Or keep mum, and go out hard.'

'*No*, sergeant. He is an enemy officer taken in

battle and entitled to fair treatment.'

'No, sir. He's a sergeant, and they don't deserve no respect at all, sir. I should know. They're cunning and artful, if they're any good. I wouldn't mind if he was an officer, sir. But sergeants are *clever.*'

There was a grunt from the bound prisoner.

'Loosen his gag, Perks,' said Blouse. Instinctively, even if the instinct was only a couple of days old, Polly glanced at Jackrum. The sergeant shrugged. She pulled the rag down.

'I'll talk,' said the prisoner, spitting out cotton fluff. 'But not to that tub of lard! I'll talk to the officer. You keep that man away from me!'

'You're in no position to negotiate, soldier boy!' snarled Jackrum.

'Sergeant,' said the lieutenant, 'I'm sure you have things to see to. Please do so. Send a couple of men back here. He can't do anything against four of us.'

'But—'

'That was *another* order, sergeant,' said Blouse. He turned to the prisoner as Jackrum stumped off. 'What is your name, man?'

'Sergeant Towering, lieutenant. And if you are a sensible man, you will release me and surrender.'

'Surrender?' said Blouse, as Igorina and Wazzer ran into the clearing, armed and bewildered.

'Yep. I'll put in a good word for you when the boys catch up with us. You don't want to know how many men are looking for you. Could I have a drink, please?'

'What? Oh, yes. Of course,' said Blouse, as if caught

out in a display of bad manners. 'Perks, fetch some tea for the sergeant. Why are people looking for us, pray?'

Towering gave him a cockeyed grin. 'You don't know?'

'No,' said Blouse coldly.

'You *really* don't know?' Now Towering was laughing. He was far too relaxed for a bound man, and Blouse sounded far too much like a nice but worried man trying to appear firm and determined. To Polly, it was like watching a child bluffing in poker against a man called Doc.

'I don't wish to play games, man. Out with it!' said Blouse.

'Everyone knows about *you*, lieutenant. You're the Monstrous Regiment, you are!' he said. 'No offence meant, of course. They say you've got a troll and a vampire and an Igor and a werewolf. They say you . . .' he began to chuckle '. . . they say you overpowered Prince Heinrich and his guard and stole his boots and made him hop away in the altogether!'

In a thicket some way off, a nightingale sang. For quite a while, uninterrupted. Then Blouse said, 'Hah, no, you are in fact wrong. The man was Captain Horentz—'

'Yeah, right, like he'd tell *you* who he was with you pointing swords at him!' said Towering. 'I heard from one of my mates that one of you kicked him in the meat-and-two-veg, but I haven't seen the picture yet.'

'Someone took a picture of him getting kicked?' squeaked Polly, drenched in a sudden horror.

'Not of that, no. But there's copies all over the place of him in chains and I hear it's been sent by the clacks to Ankh-Morpork.'

'Is . . . is he annoyed?' Polly quavered, cursing Otto Chriek and his picture-making.

'Well, now, let me see,' said Towering sarcastically. 'Annoyed? No, I shouldn't think he's annoyed. "Livid" is the word, I think. Or "raging"? Yeah, I think "raging"'s the word. There's a lot of people looking for you lads now. Well done!'

Even Blouse could see Polly's distress. 'Er . . . Perks,' he said, 'it was you, wasn't it, who—'

Over and over in Polly's head the words *ogodIkickedthePrinceinthefruitandveg* were going round and round like a hamster in a runaway tread-mill until, suddenly, it ran up against something solid.

'Yessir,' she snapped. 'He was forcing himself upon a young woman, sir. If you recall?'

Blouse's frown faded, and became a grin of child-like duplicity. 'Ah, yes, indeed. He was "pressing his suit" in no small way, was he not?'

'He didn't have ironing in mind, sir!' said Polly fervently.

Towering glanced at Wazzer, grimly clutching a crossbow that Polly knew for a fact she was scared of, and Igorina, who'd much rather be holding a surgeon's knife than the sabre in her hand and looked worried sick. Polly saw his brief smile.

'And there you have it, Sergeant Towering,' said the lieutenant, turning to the prisoner. 'Of course, we all know there is some atrocious behaviour in times of

war, but it is not the sort of thing we would expect of a royal prince.* If we are to be pursued because a gallant young soldier prevented matters from becoming even more disgusting, then so be it.'

'Now I *am* impressed,' said Towering. 'A real knight errant, eh? He's a credit to you, lieutenant. Any chance of that tea?'

Blouse's skinny chest visibly swelled at the compliment. 'Yes, Perks, the tea, if you would be so good.'

Leaving the three of you with this man who's positively radiating an intention to escape, Polly thought. 'Could perhaps Private Goom go and fetch—' she began.

'A word in private, Perks?' snapped Blouse. He drew her closer, but Polly kept her eye on Sergeant Towering. He might be bound hand and foot, but she wouldn't have trusted a man who grinned like that if he'd been nailed to the ceiling.

'Perks, you are making a great contribution but I really will not have my orders continually questioned,' said Blouse. 'You are my batman, after all. I think I run a "happy ship" here, but I will be obeyed. Please?'

It was like being savaged by a goldfish, but she had to admit he had a point. 'Er . . . sorry, sir,' she said, backing away as long as possible so as not to miss the end of the tragedy. Then she turned and ran.

Jackrum was sitting by the fire, with the prisoner's bow across his huge knees, slicing some sort of black sausage with a big clasp-knife. He was chewing.

*Lieutenant Blouse read only the more technical history books.

'Where's the rest of us, sir?' said Polly, scrabbling for a mug.

'I sent 'em to scout a wide perimeter, Perks. Can't be too careful if matey-boy's got pals out there.'

. . . which was perfectly sensible. It just happened to mean that half the squad had been sent away . . .

'Sarge, you know that captain back at the barracks? That was—'

'I've got good hearing, Perks. Kicked him in the Royal Prerogative, eh? Hah! Makes it all more interestin', eh?'

'It's going to go wrong, sarge, I just *know* it,' said Polly, dragging the kettle off the hob and spilling half the water as she topped up the teapot.

'D'you chew at all, Perks?' said Jackrum.

'What, sarge?' said Polly distractedly.

The sergeant held out a small piece of sticky, black . . . stuff. 'Tobacco. Chewing tobacco,' said Jackrum. 'I favour Blackheart over Jolly Sailor, 'cos it's rum-dipped, but others say—'

'Sarge, that man's going to escape, sarge! I know he is! The lieutenant isn't in charge, *he* is. He's all friendly and everything, but I can tell by his eyes, sarge!'

'I'm sure Lieutenant Blouse knows what he's doing, Perks,' said Jackrum primly. 'You're not telling me a bound man can overcome four of you, are you?'

'Oh, *sugar*!' said Polly.

'Just down there, in the old black tin,' said Jackrum. Polly tipped some into the worst cup of tea ever made by a serving soldier and ran back to the clearing.

Amazingly, the man was still in a sitting position,

and still bound hand and foot. Her fellow Cheese-mongers were watching him dejectedly. Polly relaxed, but only a little.

'—nd there *you* have it, lieutenant,' he was saying. 'No disgrace in calling it quits, eh? He'll hunt you down soon enough, 'cos it's *personal* now. But if you were to come along with me, I'd do my best to see it goes easy with you. You don't want to get caught by the Heavy Dragoons right now. They ain't got much of a sense of humour—'

'Tea up,' said Polly.

'Oh, thank you, Perks,' said Blouse. 'I think we can at least cut Sergeant Towering's hands free, don't you?'

'Yes, sir,' said Polly, meaning 'no, sir'. The man offered his bound wrists, and Polly reached out gingerly with her knife while holding the mug like a weapon.

'Artful lad you've got here, lieutenant,' said Towering. 'He reckons I'm going to grab his knife off of him. Good lad.'

Polly sliced the rope, brought her knife hand back quickly, and then carefully proffered the mug.

'*And* he's made the tea lukewarm so's it won't hurt when I splashes it in his face,' Towering went on. He gave Polly the steady, honest gaze of the born bastard.

Polly held it, lie for lie.

'Oh, yeah. The Ankh-Morpork people've got a little printing press on a cart, over on the other side of the river,' said Towering, still watching Polly. 'For morale, they say. And they sent the picture back to the city, too, on the clacks. Don't ask me how. Oh yeah, a good

picture. "Plucky Rookies Trounce Zlobenia's Finest", they wrote. Funny thing, but it looks like the writer man didn't spot it was the Prince. But we all did!'

His voice became even more friendly. 'Now look, mates, as a foot soldier like yourselves I'm all for seeing the bloody donkey-boys made to look fools, so you come along with me and I'll see to it that at least you don't sleep in chains tomorrow. That's my best offer.' He took a sip of tea, and added, 'It's a better one than most of the Tenth got, I'll tell you. I heard your regiment got wiped out.'

Polly's expression didn't change, but she felt herself curl up into a tiny ball behind it. Look at the eyes, look at the eyes. *Liar. Liar.*

'Wiped out?' said Blouse.

Towering dropped his mug of tea. He smacked the crossbow out of Wazzer's hand with his left hand, grabbed the sabre from Igorina with his right hand, and brought the curved blade down on the rope between his legs. It happened fast, before any of them could quite focus on the change in the situation, and then the sergeant was on his feet, slapping Blouse across the face and grabbing him in an arm lock.

'And you were *right*, kiddo,' he said to Polly, over Blouse's shoulder. 'Cryin' shame you ain't an officer, eh?'

The last of the fallen tea dribbled into the soil. Polly reached slowly for her crossbow.

'Don't. One step, one move from any of you, and I'll cut him,' said the sergeant. 'Won't be the first officer I've killed, believe me—'

'*The difference between them and me is, I don't care.*'

Five heads turned. There was Jackrum, outlined against the distant firelight. He had the man's own bow, drawn taut, and aimed directly at the sergeant in complete disregard of the fact that the lieutenant's head was in the way. Blouse closed his eyes.

'You'd shoot your own officer?' said Towering.

'Yep. Won't be the first officer *I've* killed, neither,' said Jackrum. 'You ain't going anywhere, friend, except down. Easy or hard . . . I don't care.' The bow creaked.

'You're just bluffing, mister.'

'Upon my oath, I am not a bluffing man. I don't think we was ever introduced, by the way. Jackrum's the name.'

The change in the man was a whole body event. He seemed to get smaller, as if every cell had said 'oh dear' very quietly to itself. He sagged, and Blouse slumped a little.

'Can I—'

'Too late,' said Jackrum.

Polly never forgot the sound the arrow made.

There was silence, and then a thump as Towering's body finally overbalanced and hit the ground.

Jackrum laid the bow aside carefully. 'Found out who he was messing with,' he said, as if nothing much had happened. 'Shame, really. Seemed like a decent sort. Any saloop left, Perks?'

Very slowly, Lieutenant Blouse raised his hand to his ear, which the arrow had perforated en route to its

target, and then looked with strange detachment at the blood on his fingers.

'Oh, sorry about that, sir,' said Jackrum jovially. 'Just saw the one chance and I thought, well, it's the fleshy part. Get yourself a gold earring, sir, and you'll be the height of fashion! Quite a large gold earring, maybe.

'Don't you all believe that stuff about the Ins-and-Outs,' Jackrum went on. 'That was just lies. I like it when something's up. So what we do now is . . . can anyone tell me what we do now?'

'Er . . . bury the body?' hazarded Igorina.

'Yeah, but check his boots. He's got small feet and the Zlobenians have much better boots than us.'

'Steal the boots off a dead man, sarge?' said Wazzer, still in shock.

'Easier than getting 'em off a live one!' Jackrum softened his voice a little when he saw their expressions. 'Lads, this is war, understand? He was a soldier, they were soldiers, you are soldiers . . . more or less. No soldier will see scran or good boots go to waste. Bury 'em decent and say what prayers you can remember, and hope they've gone where there's no fighting.' He raised his voice back to the normal bellow. 'Perks, round up the others! Igor, cover the fire, try to make it look like we were never here! We are moving out in number ten minutes! Can make a few miles before full daylight! That's right, eh, lieutenant?'

Blouse was still transfixed, but seemed to wake up

now. 'What? Oh. Yes. Right. Yes, indeed. Er . . . yes. Carry on, sergeant.'

The fire gleamed off Jackrum's triumphal face. In the red glow his little dark eyes were like holes in space, his grinning mouth the gateway to a hell, his bulk some monster from the Abyss.

He let it happen, Polly knew. He obeyed orders. He didn't do anything wrong. But he could have sent Maladict and Jade to help us, instead of Wazzer and Igor, who aren't quick with weapons. He sent the others away. He had the bow ready. He played a game with us as pieces, and won . . .

Poor old soldier, her father and his friends had sung, while frost formed on the window panes, *poor old soldier! If ever I 'list for a soldier again . . . the devil shall be my sergeant!*

In the firelight the grin of Sergeant Jackrum was a crescent of blood, his coat the colour of a battlefield sky. 'You are my little lads,' he roared. 'And *I* will look after *you.*'

They made more than six miles before Jackrum called a halt, and already the land was changing. There were more rocks, fewer trees. The Kneck valley was rich and fertile and it was from here that the fertility had been washed; it was a landscape of ravines and thick scrub woodland, with a few small communities scratching a living from the poverty-stricken soil. It was a good place to hide. And, in here, someone had already hidden. It was a stream-carved gully, but here at the end of summer the stream was just a trickle

between the rocks. Jackrum must have found it by smell, because you couldn't see it from the track.

The ashes of the fire in the small gully were still warm. The sergeant got up, awkwardly, after inspecting them. 'Some lads like our pals from last night,' he said.

'Couldn't it just be a hunter, sarge?' said Maladict.

'It could, corporal, but it ain't,' said Jackrum. 'I brought you in here 'cos it looks like a blind gully and there's water and there's good vantage points up *there* and over *there*,' he pointed, 'and there's a decent overhang to keep the weather off and it's hard for anyone to creep up on us. Milit'ry, in other words. And someone else thought the same as me last night. So while they're out there looking for us, we'll sit snug where they've already looked. Get a couple of lads up on guard right now.'

Polly drew first watch, atop the small cliff at the edge of the gully. It *was* a good site, no doubt about it. A regiment could hide here. No one could get near without being seen, too. And she was pulling her weight like a proper member of the squad, so with any luck Blouse would find someone to shave him before she was off duty. Through a gap in the treetops below she could see a road of sorts running through the woodland. She kept an eye on it.

Eventually, Tonker relieved her with a cup of soup. On the far side of the gully, Wazzer was being replaced by Lofty.

'Where're you from, Ozz?' said Tonker, while Polly savoured the soup.

There couldn't be any harm in telling. 'Munz,' said Polly.

'Really? Someone said you worked in a bar. What was the inn called?'

Ah . . . there was the harm, right there. But she could hardly lie, now. 'The Duchess,' she said.

'That big place? Very nobby. Did they treat you okay?'

'What? Oh . . . yes. Yes. Pretty fair.'

'Hit you at all?'

'Eh? No. Never,' said Polly, nervous of where this was going.

'Work you hard?'

Polly had to consider this. In truth, she worked harder than both the maids, and they at least had an afternoon off every week.

'I was usually the first one up and the last one to bed, if that's what you mean,' she said. And to change the subject quickly, she went on: 'What about you? You know Munz?'

'We both lived there, me and Tilda— I mean Lofty,' said Tonker.

'Oh? Where?'

'The Girls' Working School,' said Tonker, and looked away.

And that's the kind of trap small talk can get you in, Polly thought. 'Not a nice place, I think,' she said, feeling stupid.

'It was not a nice place, yes. A very nasty place,' said Tonker. 'Wazzer was there, we think. We *think* it was her. Used to be sent out a lot on work hire.' Polly

nodded. Once, a girl from the school came and worked as a maid at The Duchess. She'd arrive every morning, scrubbed raw in a clean pinafore, peeling off from a line of very similar girls led by a teacher and flanked by a couple of large men with long sticks. She was skinny, polite in a dull, trained sort of way, worked very hard and never talked to anybody. She was gone in three months, and Polly never found out why.

Tonker stared into Polly's eyes, almost mocking her innocence. 'We think she was the one they used to lock up sometimes in the special room. That's the thing about the school. If you don't toughen up you go funny in the head.'

'I expect you were glad to leave,' was all Polly could think of to say.

'The basement window was unlocked,' said Tonker. 'But I promised Tilda we'd go back one day next summer.'

'Oh, so it wasn't that bad, then?' said Polly, grateful for some relief.

'No, it'll burn better,' said Tonker. 'Ever run across someone called Father Jupe?'

'Oh, yes,' said Polly, and, feeling that something more was expected of her, added, 'He used to come to dinner when my mother—he used to come to dinner. A bit pompous, but he seemed okay.'

'Yes,' said Tonker. 'He was good at seeming.'

Once again there was a dark chasm in the conversation that not even a troll could bridge, and all you could do was draw back from the edge.

'I'd better go and see to the lieu— to the rupert,' Polly said, standing up. 'Thank you very much for the soup.'

She worked her way down through the scree and birch thickets until she emerged by the little stream that ran through the gully. And there, like some awful river god, was Sergeant Jackrum.

His red coat, a tent for lesser men, was draped carefully over a bush. He himself was sitting on a rock with his shirt off and his huge braces dangling, so that only a yellowing woolly vest saved the world from a sight of the man's bare chests. For some reason, though, he'd kept his shako on. His shaving kit, with a razor like a small machete and a shaving brush you could use to hang wallpaper, was on the rock beside him.

Jackrum was bathing his feet in the stream. He glanced up when Polly approached, and nodded amiably. ' 'morning, Perks,' he said. 'Don't rush. Never rush for ruperts. Sit down for a spell. Get yer boots off. Let yer feet feel the fresh air. Look after your feet, and your feet will look after you.' He pulled out his big clasp-knife and the rope of chewing tobacco. 'Sure you won't join me?'

'No thanks, sarge.' Polly sat down on a rock on the opposite side of the stream, which was only a few feet wide, and started to tug at her boots. She felt as though she'd been given an order. Besides, right now she felt she needed the shock of clean, cold water.

'Good lad. Filthy habit. Worse'n the smokes,' said Jackrum, carving off a lump. 'Got started on it when I

was but a lad. Better'n striking a light at night, see? Don't want to give away your position. 'course, you gotta gob a bundle every so often, but gobbin' in the dark don't show up.'

Polly dabbled her feet. The icy water did indeed feel refreshing. It seemed to jolt her alive. In the trees around the gully, birds sang.

'Say it, Perks,' said Jackrum, after a while.

'Say what, sarge?'

'Oh, bleedin' hell, Perks, it's a nice day, don't muck me around. I seen the way you've been looking at me.'

'All right, sarge. You murdered that man last night.'

'Really? Prove it,' said Jackrum calmly.

'Well, I can't, can I? But you set it up. You even sent Igor and Wazzer to guard him. They're not good with weapons.'

'How good would they have to be, d'you think? Four of you against a man tied up?' said Jackrum. 'Nah. That sergeant was dead the moment we got 'im, and he knew it. It took a bloody genius like your rupert to make him think he'd got a chance. We're out in the woods, lad. What was Blouse gonna do with him? Who'd we hand him over to? Would the lieutenant cart him around with us? Or tie him to a tree and leave him to kick wolves away until he gets too tired? Much more *gentlemanly* than giving him a quiet cigarette and a swift chop where you go quick, which is what he was expecting and what I'd have given him.'

Jackrum popped the tobacco into his mouth. 'You know what most of the milit'ry training is, Perks?' he

went on. 'All that yelling from little spitbubs like Strappi? It's to turn you into a man who will, on the word of command, stick his blade into some poor sod just like him who happens to be wearing the wrong uniform. He's like you, you're like him. He doesn't really want to kill you, you don't really want to kill him. But if you don't kill him first, he'll kill you. That's the start and finish of it. It don't come easy without trainin'. Ruperts don't get that trainin', 'cos they are *gentlemen*. Well, upon my oath I am no gentleman, and I'll kill when I have to, and I said I'd keep you safe and no damn rupert's going to stop me. He gave me my discharge papers!' Jackrum added, radiating indignance. '*Me!* And expected me to thank him! Every other rupert I've served under has had the sense to write "Not posted here" or "On extended patrol" or something and shove it back in the mail, but not *him.*'

'What was it you said to Corporal Strappi that made him run away?' said Polly, before she could stop herself.

Jackrum looked at her for a while, with no expression in his eyes. Then he gave a strange little chuckle. 'Now why would a little lad like you say a little thing like that?' he said.

'Because he just vanished and suddenly some old rule means you're back on the strength, sarge,' said Polly. 'That's why I said that little thing.'

'Hah! And there's no such rule, either, not like that one,' said Jackrum, splashing his feet. 'But ruperts never read the book of rules unless they're trying to find a reason to hang you, so I was safe there.

Strappi was scared shitless, you know that.'

'Yes, but he could have slipped away later on,' said Polly. 'He wasn't *stupid*. Rushing off into the night? He must've had something real *close* to run from, right?'

'Cor, that's an evil brain you have there, Perks,' said Jackrum happily. Once again Polly had the definite feeling that the sergeant was enjoying this, just as he'd seemed pleased when she'd protested about the uniform. He wasn't a bully like Strappi – he treated Igorina and Wazzer with something approaching fatherly concern – but with Polly and Maladict and Tonker he pushed all the time, wanting you to push back.

'It does the job, sarge,' she said.

'I just had a little tate-ah-tate with him, as it were. Quiet, like. Explained all the nasty things that can happen vees-ah-vee the confusion o' war.'

'Like being found with his throat cut?' said Polly.

'Has been known to happen,' said Jackrum innocently. 'You know, lad, you're going to make a damn good sergeant one day. Any fool can use his eyes and ears, but you uses that brain to connect 'em up.'

'I'm not going to be a sergeant! I'm going to get the job done and go home!' said Polly vehemently.

'Yes, I said that once, too.' Jackrum grinned. 'Perks, I don't need no clacky thing. I don't need no newsy paper. Sergeant Jackrum knows what's going on. He talks to the men coming back, the ones that won't talk to anyone else. I know more than the rupert, for all that he gets little letters from HQ that worry him so much. Everyone talks to Sergeant Jackrum. And in his

big fat head, Sergeant Jackrum puts it all together. Sergeant Jackrum knows what's going on.'

'And what's that, sarge?' said Polly innocently.

Jackrum didn't reply immediately. Instead, he reached down with a grunt and rubbed one of his feet. The corroded shilling on a string, which had lain innocently on the woollen vest, swung forward. But there was something else. For a moment something golden slipped out of the vest's open neck. Something oval and golden, on a golden chain, flashed in the sunlight. Then he straightened up and it was dragged back out of sight.

'This is a bloody odd war, lad,' he said. 'It's true there's not just Zlobenian soldiers out there. Lads say there's uniforms they'd never seen before. We've kicked a lot of backsides over the years, so maybe they really have ganged up and it's gonna be our turn. But what I reckon is, they're stuck. They took the keep. Oh, yes, I know. But they've got to hold on to it. And winter's coming and all those lads from Ankh-Morpork and everywhere are a long way from home. We might have a chance yet. Hah, especially now the Prince is dead set on finding the young soldier that kneed him in the wedding tackle. That means he's angry. He'll make mistakes.'

'Well, sarge, I think—'

'I'm glad you do, Private Perks,' said Jackrum, suddenly becoming a sergeant again. 'And I think that after you've seen to the rupert and had a nap, you and me is going to show the lads some swordsmanship. Whatever bleedin' war this is, sooner or later young

Wazzer is going to *have* to use that blade he waggles about. Get going!'

Polly found Lieutenant Blouse sitting with his back to the cliff, eating scubbo out of a bowl. Igorina was packing away her medical kit, and Blouse's ear was bandaged.

'Everything all right, sir?' she said. 'Sorry I wasn't—'

'I quite understand, Perks, you must stand your turn like the other "lads",' said Blouse, and Polly *heard* the inverted commas clank into place. 'I had a refreshing nap and the bleeding and, indeed, the shaking has quite stopped. However . . . I do still need a shave.'

'You want me to shave you,' said Polly, her heart sinking.

'I must set an example, Perks, but I have to say you "lads" make such an effort it puts me to shame. You all seem to have faces "as smooth as a baby's bottom", I must say!'

'Yes, sir.' Polly pulled out the shaving gear and walked over to the fire, where the kettle was permanently boiling. Most of the squad was dozing, but Maladict was sitting cross-legged by the fire, doing something to his hat.

'Heard about the prisoner last night,' he said, without looking up. 'I don't think the el-tee is going to last very long, do you?'

'The who?'

'The lieutenant. From what I hear, Blouse's probably going to have a nasty accident. Jackrum thinks he's dangerous.'

'He's learning, just like us.'

'Yes, but the el-tee's supposed to know what to *do*. Do you think he does?'

'Jackrum's stuck, too,' said Polly, topping up the kettle with cold water. 'I think we just keep going.'

'If there's anything there to get to,' said Maladict. He held up the shako. 'What do you think?'

The words 'Born To Die' had been chalked on the side of the hat, next to the packet of cigarettes.

'Very . . . individual,' said Polly. 'Why do you smoke? It's not very . . . vampire, really.'

'Well, I'm not supposed to be *very* vampire,' said Maladict, lighting up with a shaking hand. 'It's the sucking. I need it. I'm on edge. I'm getting the no-coffee jitters. I'm not good with woods in any case.'

'But you're a vam—'

'Yeah, yeah, if this was crypts, no problem. But I keep thinking I'm surrounded by lots of pointy stakes. Truth is . . . I'm beginning to *hurt*. It's like going cold bat all over again! I'm getting the voices and the sweats . . .'

'Sssh,' said Polly, as Shufti grunted in her sleep. 'You can't be,' she hissed. 'You said you'd been going straight for two years!'

'Oh, *bl . . . blur . . . blood*?' said Maladict. 'Who said anything about blood? I'm talking about coffee, dammit!'

'We've got plenty of tea—' Polly began.

'You don't understand! This is about . . . craving. You never *stop* craving, you just switch it to something

that doesn't cause people to turn you into a short kebab! I *need* coffee!'

Why me? Polly thought. Do I have this little sign on me saying 'Tell me your troubles'? 'I'll see what I can do,' she said, and hastily filled the shaving mug.

Polly hurried back with the water, ushered Blouse to a rock, and stirred up some foam. She sharpened the razor, taking as long as she dared. When he coughed impatiently she took up position, raised the razor, and prayed . . .

. . . *but not to Nuggan. Never to Nuggan, since her mother died* . . .

And then Lofty was running across the ground, trying to shout a whisper. 'Movement!'

Blouse nearly lost another earlobe.

Out from nowhere came Jackrum, boots on but braces dangling. He grabbed Lofty by the shoulder and swung her round. 'Where?' he demanded.

'There's a track down there! Troopers! Carts! What do we do, sarge?'

'We keep the noise down!' muttered Jackrum. 'Are they heading up here?'

'No, they went right past, sarge!'

Jackrum turned and gave the rest of the squad a satisfied look. 'O-kay. Corporal, take Carborundum and Perks and go and have a look. The rest of you, tool up and try to be brave. Eh, lieutenant?'

Blouse bemusedly dabbed foam off his face. 'What? Oh. Yes. See to it, sergeant.'

Twenty seconds later, Polly was running after Maladict, down the slope. Here and there the bottom

of the valley could be seen through the trees, and as she glanced down she saw sunlight flash off something metal. At least the trees had coated the woodland floor with a thick layer of needles, and, contrary to received opinion, most woods aren't littered with branches that snap loudly. They reached the edge of the wood, where bushes fought one another for their place in the sun, and found a spot with a view.

There were only four troopers, in an unfamiliar uniform, riding in pairs ahead of and behind a cart. It was small, and had a canvas cover.

'What's in a little cart that four men have to protect?' said Maladict. 'It must be valuable!'

Polly pointed to the huge flag that hung limply from a pole on the wagon. 'I think it's the newspaper man,' she said. 'It's the same cart. Same flag, too.'

'Then it's a good thing they've gone right past,' hissed Maladict. 'Let's just see them out of sight and creep away like good little mice, okay?'

The party was travelling at the speed of the cart and, at this point, the two riders in the lead stopped and turned in their saddles, waiting for it to catch up. Then one of them pointed, back past the hidden watchers. There was a shout, too far away to be understood. The troopers in the rear trotted up to the cart, met with their comrades, and all four turned to look up. There was some discussion, and two riders trotted back along the road.

'Oh, darn,' said Polly. 'What have they spotted?'

The horsemen went past their hiding place. A few

moments later, they heard the horses enter the woods.

'Do we run an' get 'em?' said Jade.

'Let Jackrum do that,' said Maladict.

'But if he does, and the men don't come back—' Polly began.

'*When* they don't come back,' Maladict corrected her.

'—then those other two will get suspicious, won't they? One will probably stay here, the other will go to get help.'

'Then we'll sneak up and wait,' said Maladict. 'Look, they've dismounted. The cart's pulled in, too. If they look as though they're worried, we'll move in.'

'And do what, exactly?' said Polly.

'Threaten to shoot them,' said Maladict firmly.

'And if they don't believe us?'

'Then we'll threaten to shoot them *in a much louder voice*,' said Maladict. 'Happy? And I hope to hell they've got some coffee!'

There are three things a soldier wants to do when there's a respite on the road. One involves lighting a cigarette, one involves lighting a fire, and the other one involves no flames at all but does, generally, require a tree.*

The two troopers had a fire going and a billy-can steaming when a young man jumped down from the cart, stretched his arms, looked around, yawned, and

* Actually a tree is not, technically, required, but seems to be insisted upon for reasons of style.

sauntered a little way into the forest. He found a convenient tree and, a moment later, was apparently examining the bark at eye height with studied enthusiasm.

The tip of a steel crossbow bolt pressed against the back of his neck and a voice said: 'Raise your hands and turn around slowly!'

'What, right *now*?'

'Um . . . all right, no. You can finish what you're doing.'

'Actually I think that's going to be quite impossible. Let me just, er . . . right. Okay.' The man raised his hands again. 'You realize I just have to shout?'

'So?' said Polly. 'I just have to pull this trigger. Shall we have a race?'

The man turned round.

'See?' said Polly, stepping back. 'It's him again. De Worde. The writer man.'

'You're *them*!' he said.

'Dem who?' said Jade.

'Oh *dear*,' said Maladict.

'Look, I'd give *anything* to talk to you!' said de Worde. 'Please?'

'You're with the enemy!' hissed Polly.

'What? Them? No! They're from Lord Rust's regiment. From Ankh-Morpork! They've been sent to protect us!'

'Troops to protect you in Borogravia?' said Maladict. 'Who from?'

'You mean from whom? Er . . . well . . . you, in theory.'

Jade leaned down. '*Efficient*, aren't dey . . .'

'Look, I *must* talk to you,' said the man urgently. 'This is astounding! Everyone's looking for you! Did you kill that old couple in the woods?'

Birds sang. Far off, there was the call of the female blue-capped woodpecker.

'A patrol found the fresh graves,' said de Worde.

High above an ice heron, a winter migrant from the Hub, gave an ugly honk as it searched for lakes.

'I take it you didn't, then,' said de Worde.

'We buried them,' said Maladict coldly. 'We don't know who killed them.'

'We did take some vegetables,' said Polly. She remembered laughing about it. Admittedly it was only because it was that or start crying, but even so . . .

'You've been living off the land?' He'd tugged a notebook out of his pocket and was scribbling in it with a pencil.

'We don't have to talk to you,' said Maladict.

'No, no, you must! There's so much you need to know! You're in the . . . Ups-and-Downs, right?'

'Ins-and-Outs,' said Polly.

'And you—' the man began.

'I've had enough of this,' said Maladict, and marched away from the tree and into the clearing. The two cavalry men looked up from their fire, and there was a moment of immobility before one reached for his sword.

Maladict swung the bow quickly from one to the other, its point hypnotizing them like a swinging watch. 'I've got only one shot but there's two of you,'

he said. 'Who shall I shoot? *You* choose. Now, listen very carefully: where's your coffee? You've got coffee, haven't you? C'mon, everyone's got coffee! Spill the beans!'

They stared at the crossbow and slowly shook their heads.

'What about you, writer man?' snarled Maladict. 'Where're you hiding the coffee?'

'We only have cocoa,' said the writer, raising his hands quickly as Maladict turned on him. 'You're welcome to—'

Maladict dropped his crossbow, which fired straight up into the air*, and sat down with his head in his hands. 'We're all gonna *die*,' he said. The troopers shifted as though to stand up, and Jade raised her sapling.

'Don't even *fink* about it,' she said.

Polly turned to the writer man. 'You want us to talk to you, sir? Then *you* talk to us. Is this about . . . Prince Heinrich's . . . socks?'

Maladict stood up in one mad movement. 'I say we grease the lot of them and go home!' he said, to no one in particular. 'One, Two, Three! What We Are Fighting For!'

* And failed to hit anything, especially a duck. This is so unusual in situations like this that it should be reported under new humour regulations. If it had hit a duck, which quacked and then landed on somebody's head, this would of course have been very droll and would certainly have been reported. Instead, it drifted in the breeze a little and landed in an oak tree some thirty feet away, where it missed a squirrel.

'Socks?' said the writer, looking nervously at the vampire. 'What've socks got to do with it?'

'I just gave you an *order*, Polly,' said Maladict.

'What is it you think we don't know?' Polly insisted, glaring at de Worde.

'Well, to start with you're just about all that's left of the Ins-and-Outs—'

'*That's not true!*'

'Oh, there's prisoners and wounded, I think. But why should I lie to you? Why did he call you Polly?'

'Because I know a lot about birds,' said Polly, mentally cursing. 'How do you *know* what's been happening to the regiment?'

'Because it's my job to know things,' said the man. 'What's that bird up there?'

Polly glanced up. 'I don't have time for stupid games,' she said. 'And that's a—' She stopped. Something was wheeling high above, in the forbidden blue.

'You don't know?' said de Worde.

'Yes, of course I know,' said Polly irritably. 'It's a white-necked buzzard. But I thought they never came this far into the mountains. I only ever saw one in a book—' She raised her bow again, and tried to take control. 'Am I right, Mr It's-my-job-to-know-things?'

De Worde raised his hands again and gave her a sickly smile. 'Probably,' he said. 'I live in a city. I know sparrows from starlings. After that everything's a duck as far as I'm concerned.'

Polly glared at him.

223

'Look, please,' said the man. 'You need to listen to me. You need to know things. Before it's too late.'

Polly lowered the bow. 'If you want to talk to us, wait here,' she said. 'Corporal, we are leaving. Carborundum, pick up those troopers!'

'Hold it,' said Maladict. 'Who's the corporal in this squad?'

'You are,' said Polly. 'And you're drooling, and swaying, and your eyes look weird. So what was your point, please?'

Maladict considered this. Polly was tired and frightened and somewhere inside this was all being transmuted into anger. Hers was not an expression you wanted to see at the far end of a crossbow. An arrow couldn't kill a vampire, but that didn't mean it didn't hurt.

'Right, yeah,' he said. 'Carborundum, pick up those troopers! We are leaving!'

There was a bird whistle as Polly neared the hiding place. She identified this one as the sound of the Very Bad Bird Impersonator, and made a note to teach the girls some bird calls that at least sounded real. They were harder to do than most people thought.

The squad were in the gully, armed and at least *looking* dangerous. There was a certain amount of relaxation when they saw Jade carrying the two bound troopers. Two more were sitting disconsolately against the cliff, hands tied behind them.

Maladict walked smartly up to Blouse and saluted. 'Two prisoners, el-tee, and Perks thinks there's someone

down there you ought to talk to.' He leaned forward. 'The newspaper man, sir.'

'Then we'll jolly well keep *well* away from him,' said Blouse. 'Eh, sergeant?'

'Right, sir!' said Jackrum. 'Nothing but trouble, sir!'

Polly saluted madly. 'Please, sir! Permission to speak, sir!'

'Yes, Perks?' said Blouse.

Polly saw there was one chance, and one only. She *had* to find out about Paul. Now her mind worked as fast as it had on the hill last night, when she'd gone for the man with the code book.

'Sir, I don't know if he's worth talking to, sir, but he may be worth listening to. Even if you think he'll only tell us lies. Because sometimes, sir, the way people tell you lies, if they tell you *enough* lies, well, they sort of . . . show you what shape the truth is, sir. And we don't have to tell *him* the truth, sir. We could lie to him, too.'

'I am not by nature an untruthful man, Perks,' said Blouse coldly.

'Glad to hear it, sir. Are we winning the war, sir?'

'You stop that right now, Perks!' Jackrum roared.

'It was only a question, sarge,' said Polly reproachfully.

Around the clearing the squad waited, ears sucking up every sound. Everyone knew the answer. They waited for it to be said aloud.

'Perks, this kind of talk spreads despondency,' Blouse began, but he said it as if he didn't believe it and didn't care who knew.

'No, sir. It doesn't really. It's better than being lied to,'

said Polly. She changed her voice, gave it that edge her mother used to use on her when she was being scolded. 'It's evil to lie. No one likes a liar. Tell me the truth, please.'

Some harmonic of that tone must have found a home in an old part of Blouse's brain. As Jackrum opened his mouth to roar, the lieutenant held up a hand.

'We are not winning, Perks. But we have not lost yet.'

'I think we all know that, sir, but it's good to hear you say it,' said Polly, giving him an encouraging smile.

That seemed to work, too. 'I suppose there is no harm in at least being civil to the wretched fellow,' said Blouse, as if thinking aloud. 'He may give away valuable information under cunning questioning.'

Polly looked at Sergeant Jackrum, who was staring upwards like a man in prayer.

'Permission to be the man to interrogate the gentleman, sir,' said the sergeant.

'Permission denied, sergeant,' said Blouse. 'I'd like him to live and don't want to lose another lobe. However, you may take Perks back to the cart and drive it up here.'

Jackrum gave him the smart salute. Polly had already learned to recognize it; it meant that Jackrum had already made *plans*.

'Very good, sir,' he said. 'Come on, Perks.'

Jackrum was quiet as they walked back down over the needle-carpeted slope. Then, after a while, he said:

'D'you know why them troopers found our little nook, Perks?'

'No, sarge.'

'The lieutenant ordered Shufti to put the fire out immediately. It wasn't as if there was even any smoke. So Shufti goes and pours the kettle on it.'

Polly gave this a few seconds' thought. 'Steam, sarge?'

'Right! In a bloody great rising cloud. Not Shufti's fault. The gallopers weren't any trouble, though. Bright enough not to try to outrun half a dozen crossbows, at least. That's clever for a cavalryman.'

'Well done, sarge.'

'Don't talk to me as if I was a rupert, lad,' said Jackrum easily.

'Sorry, sarge.'

'I see you're learnin' how to steer an officer, though. You gotta make sure they gives you the right orders, see? You'll make a good sergeant, Perks.'

'Don't want to, sarge.'

'Yeah, right,' said Jackrum. It could have meant anything.

After watching the track for a minute or two they stepped out and headed towards the cart. De Worde was sitting on a stool beside it, writing in a notebook, but he stood up hurriedly when he saw them.

'It'd be a good idea to get off the track,' he said, as soon as they approached. 'There are a lot of patrols, I understand.'

'Zlobenian patrols, sir?' said Jackrum.

'Yes. In theory this' – he pointed to the flag that

hung limply from the cart – 'should keep us safe, but everyone's a bit jumpy at the moment. Aren't you Sergeant Jack Ram?'

'Jackrum, sir. And I'll thank you for not writing my name down in your little book, sir.'

'Sorry, sergeant, but that's my job,' said de Worde breezily. 'I have to write things down.'

'Well, sir, soldierin' is *my* job,' said Jackrum, climbing on to the cart and gathering up the reins. 'But you'll note how at this moment in time I am not killin' you. Let's go, eh?'

Polly climbed into the back of the cart as it lumbered off. It was full of boxes and equipment, and while it might once have been neatly organized, that organization was now but a distant memory, a clear indication that this cart was the property of a man. Next to her, half a dozen of the largest pigeons she had ever seen dozed on a perch in their wire cage, and she wondered if they were a living larder. One of them opened one eye and lazily went 'Lollollop?' which is pigeon for 'Duh?'

Most of the rest of the boxes had labels like – she leaned closer – 'Capt Horace Calumney's Patent Field Biscuits', and 'Dried Stew'. As she was musing that Shufti would have very much liked to get her hands on one or two of those boxes, a bundle of clothes hanging from the ceiling of the rocking cart moved slightly and a face appeared.

'Good mornink,' it said, upside down.

William de Worde turned round on the seat in front. 'It's only Otto, private,' he said. 'Don't be afraid.'

'Yes, I vill not bite,' said the face cheerfully. It smiled. A vampire's face does not look any better upside down, and a smile in these circumstances does nothing to improve matters. 'That is *guaranteed*.'

Polly lowered the crossbow. Jackrum would have been impressed by how quickly she had raised it. So was she, and embarrassed too. The socks were doing the thinking again.

Otto very elegantly lowered himself to the bed of the cart. 'Vhere are ve goink?' he said, steadying himself as they bounced over a rut.

'A little place I know, sir,' said Jackrum. 'Nice and quiet.'

'Good. I need to exercise the imps. Zey get fretful if zey are cooped up for too long.' Otto pushed aside a stack of paper and revealed his large picture-making box. He lifted a small hatch.

'Rise und shine, lads,' he said. There was a chorus of high-pitched voices from inside.

'I'd better just mark your card re Tiger, Mr de Worde,' said Jackrum, as the cart rolled up an old logging track.

'Tiger? Who's Tiger?'

'Oops,' said Jackrum. 'Sorry, that's what we call the lieutenant, sir, on account of him being so brave. Forget I said that, will you?'

'Brave, is he?' said de Worde.

'And clever, sir. Don't let him fool you, sir. He is one of the great milit'ry minds of his generation, sir.'

Polly's mouth dropped open. She had suggested they lied to the man, but . . . *this*?

'Really? Then why is he just a lieutenant?' said the writer.

'Ah, I can see there's no fooling you, sir,' said Jackrum, oozing knowingness. 'Yes, it's a puzzler, sir, why he calls himself a lieutenant. Still, I dare say he has his reasons, eh? Just like Heinrich calling himself a captain, right?' He tapped the side of his nose. 'I see everything, sir, and I don't say a word!'

'All I could find out was that he did some kind of desk job at your HQ, sergeant,' said de Worde. Polly saw him taking his notebook out, slowly and carefully.

'Yes, I expect that's what you would find out, sir,' said Jackrum, with a huge conspiratorial wink. 'And then, when things are at their worst, they let him out, sir. They *unleash* him, sir. Me, I don't know a thing, sir.'

'What does he do, explode?' said de Worde.

'Haha, nice one, sir!' said Jackrum. 'No, sir. What he does, sir, is *assess situations*, sir. I don't understand it myself, sir, not being a big thinker, but the proof of the pudding, sir, is in the eating of same, and last night we were jumped by eight— twenty Zlobenian troopers, sir, and the lieutenant just assessed the situation in a flash and skewered five of the buggers, sir. Like a kebab, sir. Mild as milk to look at, but rouse him and he's a whirlwind of death. Of course, you did not hear it from me, sir.'

'And he's in charge of a bunch of recruits, sergeant?' said de Worde. 'That doesn't sound very likely to me.'

'Recruits who captured some crack cavalrymen, sir,' said Jackrum, looking pained. 'That's leadership

for you. Comes the hour, comes the man, sir. I'm just a simple old soldier, sir, seen 'em come and seen 'em go. Upon my oath I am not a lying man, sir, but I look at Lieutenant Blouse in wonderment.'

'He just seemed confused, to me,' said de Worde, but there was a hint of uncertainty in his voice.

'That was a bit of concussion, sir. He took a wallop that would have felled a lesser man, and still got back on to his feet. Amazing, sir!'

'Hmm,' said de Worde, making a note.

The cart splashed across the shallow little stream and rocked into the gully. Lieutenant Blouse was sitting on a rock. He'd made an effort, but his tunic was grubby, his boots were muddy, his hand was swollen and one ear, despite Igorina's ministrations, was still inflamed. He had his sword on his knees. Jackrum carefully brought the cart to a halt by a thicket of birch trees. All four of the enemy troopers were tied up against the cliff. Apart from them, the camp appeared to be deserted.

'Where are the rest of the men, sergeant?' whispered de Worde, as he slid down off the cart.

'Oh, they're around, sir,' said Jackrum. 'Watching you. Probably not a good idea to make any sudden move, sir.'

No one else was visible . . . and then Maladict faded into view.

People never really looked at things, Polly knew. They *glanced*. And what had been a patch of scrub was now Corporal Maladict. Polly stared. He'd cut a hole in the centre of his old blanket, and the mud and grass

stains on the mildewed greyness had turned him into part of the landscape until he'd saluted. He'd also stuck leafy twigs all over his hat.

Sergeant Jackrum goggled. Polly had never really seen proper goggling before, but the sergeant had the face to do it at championship level. She could feel him drawing breath while at the same time assembling cusswords for a right royal thundering – and then he remembered he was playing Sergeant Big Jolly Fat Man, and this was not the time to segue into Sergeant Incandescent.

'Lads, eh?' he chuckled to de Worde. 'What will they think of next?'

De Worde nodded nervously, pulled a wad of newspapers from under his seat, and advanced on the lieutenant.

'Mr de Worde, isn't it?' said Blouse, standing up. 'Perks, can we manage a cup of, er, "saloop" for Mr de Worde? There's a good chap. Do take a rock, sir.'

'Good of you to see me, lieutenant,' said de Worde. 'It looks as though you've been in the wars!' he added, with an attempt at joviality.

'No, only this one,' said Blouse, looking puzzled.

'I meant that you have been wounded, sir,' said de Worde.

'These? Oh, they're nothing, sir. I'm afraid the one on my hand was self-inflicted. Sword drill, you know.'

'You're left-handed then, sir?'

'Oh, no.'

Polly, washing out a mug, heard Jackrum say out of the corner of his mouth: 'Should've seen the other two fellows, sir!'

'Are you aware of the progress of the war, lieutenant?' said de Worde.

'You tell me, sir,' said Blouse.

'All your army is bottled up in the Kneck valley. Dug in, mostly, just beyond the reach of the keep's weaponry. Your forts elsewhere along the border have been captured. The garrisons at Drerp and Glitz and Arblatt have been overwhelmed. As far as I can tell, lieutenant, your squad are the only soldiers still at large. At least,' he added, 'the only ones still fighting.'

'And my regiment?' said Blouse quietly.

'The remnant of the Tenth took part in a brave but, frankly, suicidal attempt to retake Kneck Keep a few days ago, sir. Most of the survivors are prisoners of war, and I have to tell you that almost all your high command have been captured. They were in the keep when it was taken. There are big dungeons in that fort, sir, and they're pretty full.'

'Why should I believe you?'

I do, thought Polly. So Paul is either dead, wounded or captured. And it doesn't help much by thinking of it as two chances in three that he is alive.

De Worde threw his newspapers at the lieutenant's feet. 'It's all there, sir. I didn't make it up. It's the truth. It will remain true whether you believe it or not. There are more than six countries ranged against you, including Genua and Mouldavia and Ankh-Morpork. There is no one on your side. You are alone. The only reason you're not beaten yet is because you won't admit it. I've seen your generals, sir! Great leaders,

and your men fight like demons, but they won't surrender!'

'Borogravia doesn't know the meaning of the word "surrender", Mr de Worde,' said the lieutenant.

'Can I lend you a dictionary, sir?' snapped de Worde, going red in the face. 'It's very similar to the meaning of "making some kind of peace while you've got a chance", sir! It's rather like "quitting while you've still got a head", sir! Good heavens, sir, don't you understand? The reason that there still *is* an army in the Kneck valley is that the allies haven't decided what to do with it! They're fed up with the slaughter!'

'Ah, so we still fight back!' said Blouse.

De Worde sighed. 'You don't understand, sir. They are fed up with slaughtering *you*. They've got the keep now. There's some big war engines up there. They . . . frankly, sir, some of the alliance would just as soon wipe out the remains of your army. It'd be like shooting rats in a barrel. They have you at their mercy. And yet you keep on attacking. You attack the keep! It's on sheer rock and it's got walls a hundred feet high. You make salients across the river. You're bottled up and you've got nowhere to go and the allies could simply massacre you any time they want, and you act as though you're just facing some kind of temporary setback. That's what's really happening, lieutenant! *You* are just a last little detail.'

'Have a care, please,' Blouse warned.

'Excuse me, sir, but do you know *anything* about recent history? In the past thirty years you have declared war on every single one of your neighbours

at least once. All countries fight, but *you* brawl. And then last year you invaded Zlobenia *again!*'

'They invaded us, Mr de Worde.'

'You have been misinformed, lieutenant. You invaded the Kneck province.'

'That was confirmed as Borogravian by the Treaty of Lint, more than a hundred years ago.'

'Signed at swordpoint, sir. And no one cares now, in any case. It's all got beyond your stupid little royal scuffles. Because your men tore down the Grand Trunk, you see. The clacks towers. *And* tore up the coach road. Ankh-Morpork regards that as bandit activity.'

'Have a care, I said!' said Blouse. 'I note you are displaying the Ankh-Morpork flag with evident pride on your wagon.'

'*Civis Morporkias sum*, sir. I am an Ankh-Morpork citizen. You could say that Ankh-Morpork shelters me under her wide and rather greasy wing, although I agree the metaphor could use some work.'

'Your Ankh-Morpork soldiers aren't in a position to protect you, however.'

'Sir, you are right. You could have me killed right now,' said de Worde simply. 'You know that. I know that. But you won't, for three reasons. The officers of Borogravia tend towards honour. Everyone says that. That's why they don't surrender. And I bleed most distressingly. And you don't need to, because everyone is interested in you. Suddenly, it's all changed.'

'*Interested* in us?'

'Sir, in a sense you could help a lot right now.

Apparently people back in Ankh-Morpork were amazed when . . . look, have you heard about what we call "human interest", sir?'

'No.'

De Worde tried to explain. Blouse listened with his mouth open and, at the end, said: 'Have I got this right? Although many people have been killed and wounded in this wretched war, it's not been of much "interest" to your readers? But it is now, just because of us? Because of a little skirmish in a town they've never heard of? And because of it, we're suddenly a "plucky little country" and people are telling your newspaper that your great city should be on *our* side?'

'Yes, lieutenant. We put out a second edition last night, you see. After I'd found out that "Captain Horentz" was really Prince Heinrich. Did you know this at the time, sir?'

'Of course not!' snapped Blouse.

'And you, Private, er, Perks, would you have kicked him in the . . . would you have kicked him had you known?'

Polly dropped a mug in her nervousness, and looked at Blouse.

'You may answer, of course, Perks,' said the lieutenant.

'Well, yes, sir. I would have kicked him. Harder, probably. I was defending myself, sir,' Polly said, carefully avoiding further details. You couldn't be sure what someone like de Worde would do with them.

'Right, good, yes,' said de Worde. 'Then you might

be pleased with this. Our cartoonist Fizz drew this for the special edition. It was on the front page. We've sold a record number of copies.' He handed her a flimsy piece of paper, which by the look of the creases had been folded many times.

It was a line drawing, with lots of shading. It showed a huge figure, with a large sword, a monstrous monocle and a moustache as wide as a coathanger, menacing a much smaller figure armed with nothing more than an instrument for lifting beets – in fact there was a beet stuck on the end of it. At least, that was clearly what *had* been happening right up to the point when the smaller figure, wearing a not bad attempt at an Ins-and-Outs shako and a face that looked slightly like Polly's, had kicked the other one squarely in the groinal regions. A sort of balloon was coming out of Polly's mouth, containing the words: '*That for your Royal Prerogative, you Blaggard!*' The balloon issuing from the mouth of the ogre, who could only be Prince Heinrich, said: '*Oh my Succession! That such A Small Thing could hurt so Much!*' And in the background a fat woman in a rumpled ballgown and a huge old-fashioned helmet was clasping her hands to an unbelievably large bosom, staring at the fight with a mixture of concern and admiration, and ballooning: '*Oh my Swain! I fear our Liaison is Cut short!*'

Since no one else was saying much, but was simply staring, de Worde said, rather nervously: 'Fizz is rather, er, direct in these matters, but amazingly popular. Ahem. You see, the curious thing is that although

Ankh-Morpork is probably the biggest bully around, in a subtle kind of way, we nevertheless have a soft spot for people who stand up to bullies. Especially royal ones. We tend to be on their side, provided it doesn't cost us too much.'

Blouse cleared his throat. 'It's quite a good likeness of you, Perks,' he said hoarsely.

'I only used my knee, sir!' Polly protested. 'And that fat lady certainly wasn't there!'

'That's Morporkia,' said de Worde. 'She's a sort of representation of the city, except that in her case she's not covered in mud and soot.'

'And I have to add, for my part,' said Blouse, in his talking-to-a-meeting voice, 'that Borogravia is in fact larger than Zlobenia, although most of the country is little more than barren mountainside—'

'That doesn't actually matter,' said de Worde.

'It doesn't?' said Blouse.

'No, sir. It's just a fact. It's not politics. In politics, sir, pictures like this are powerful. Sir, even the alliance commanders are talking about you, and the Zlobenians are angry and bewildered. If you, the heroes of the hour, could make a plea for a little common sense—'

The lieutenant took a long, deep breath. 'This is a foolish war, Mr de Worde. But I am a soldier. I have "kissed the Duchess", as we say. It's an oath of loyalty. Don't tempt me to break it. I must fight for my country. We will repel all invaders. If there are deserters, we will find them and rally them again. We know the country. While we are free, Borogravia will

be free. You have "had your say". Thank you. Where is that tea, Perks?'

'What? Oh, nearly done, sir!' said Polly, turning back to the fire.

It had been a sudden strange fancy, but a stupid plan. Now, out here, all the drawbacks were visible. How would she have got Paul home? Would he have wanted to come? Could she have managed it? Even if he was still alive, how could she hope to get him out of a prison?

'So you'll be guerilla fighters, eh?' said Mr de Worde, behind her. 'Madmen, all of you.'

'No, we are not irregulars,' said Blouse. 'We kissed the Duchess. We are *soldiers*.'

'Oh, well,' said de Worde. 'Then I admire your spirit, at least. Ah, Otto . . .'

The vampire iconographer ambled up, and gave them a shy smile. 'Do not be afraid. I am a Black Ribboner just like your corporal,' he said. 'Light is my passion now.'

'Oh? Er . . . well done,' said Blouse.

'Take the pictures, Otto,' said de Worde. 'These gentlemen have a war to fight.'

'Out of interest, Mr de Worde,' Blouse interrupted, 'how did you get the pictures back to your city so quickly? Magic, I assume?'

'What?' De Worde looked momentarily off balance. 'Oh no, sir. Wizards are expensive and Commander Vimes has said that there is going to be no first use of magic in this war. We send things by pigeon to our office in the keep and then by clacks from the nearest trunk tower.'

'Oh, really?' said Blouse, showing rather more animation than Polly had seen up until now. 'Using numbers to indicate a scale of grey shades, perhaps?'

'Mein Gotts!' said Otto.

'Well, yes, as a matter of fact we do,' said de Worde. 'I'm very impressed that you—'

'I have seen the clacks towers on the far bank of the Kneck,' said Blouse, his eyes lighting up. 'Very clever idea, using big shuttered boxes rather than the old-fashioned semaphore arms. And would I be right in my surmise that the box on the top, which opens its shutters once a second, is a kind of system, er, clock that makes certain the whole clacks line keeps in step? Oh, good. I thought so. One beat a second is probably the limit of the mechanisms, so no doubt all your efforts now are concentrated on maximizing the information content per shutter operation? Yes, I imagined that would be the case. As for sending pictures, well, sooner or later all things are numbers, yes? Of course, you would use each of the two columns of four boxes to send a grey code, but it must be very slow. Have you considered a squeezing algorithm?'

De Worde and Chriek exchanged a glance. 'Are you sure you haven't been talking to anyone about this, sir?' said the writer.

'Oh, it's all very elementary,' said Blouse, smiling happily. 'I had thought about it in the context of military maps which are, of course, mostly white space. So I wondered if it would be possible to indicate a required shade on one column and, on the

other side, indicate how far along that rank that shade would persist. And a delightful bonus here is that if your map is simply in black and white, then you have even more—'

'You haven't seen inside a clacks tower, have you?' said de Worde.

'Alas, no,' said Blouse. 'This is simply "thinking aloud" based on the *de facto* existence of your picture. I believe I can see a number of other little mathematical, ahem, tricks to make the passage of information even swifter, but I am sure these have already occurred to you. Of course, a fairly minor modification could potentially double the information burden of the whole system at a stroke. And that is without using coloured filters at night, which I'm sure even with the overhead of extra mechanical effort would surely increase throughput by— I'm sorry, did I say something wrong?'

The two men both wore a glazed expression. De Worde shook himself. 'Oh . . . er, no. Nothing,' he said. 'Er . . . you seem to have got the grasp of things quite . . . quickly.'

'Oh, it was perfectly straightforward once I started thinking about it,' said Blouse. 'It was exactly the same when I had to redesign the department's filing system, you see. People build something that works. Then circumstances change, and they have to tinker with it to make it continue to work, and they are so busy tinkering that they cannot see that a much better idea would be to build a whole new system to deal with the new circumstances. But to an outsider, the idea is obvious.'

'In politics as well as, er, filing systems and clackses, do you think?' said de Worde.

Blouse's brow wrinkled. 'I'm sorry, I don't think I follow . . .' he said.

'Would you agree that sometimes a country's system is so out of date that it's only the outsiders that can see the need for wholesale change?' said de Worde. He smiled. Lieutenant Blouse did not.

'Just a point to ponder, maybe,' said de Worde. 'Er . . . since you wish to tell the world of your defiance, would you object if my colleague takes your picture?'

Blouse shrugged. 'If it gives you any satisfaction,' he said. 'It's an Abomination, of course, but these days it's hard to find something that isn't. You must tell the world, Mr de Worde, that Borogravia won't lie down. We will not give in. We will fight on. Write that down in your little notebook, please. While we can stand, we will kick!'

'Yes, but once again may I implore you to—'

'Mr de Worde, you have I am sure heard the saying that the pen is mightier than the sword?'

De Worde preened a little. 'Of course, and I—'

'Do you want to test it? Take your picture, sir, and then my men will escort you back to your road.'

Otto Chriek stood up and bowed to Blouse. He unslung his picture box.

'This vill only take vun minute,' he said.

It never does. Polly watched in horrified fascination as Otto took picture after picture of Lieutenant Blouse in a variety of what the lieutenant thought

were heroic poses. It is a terrible thing to see a man trying to jut out a chin he does not, in fact, have.

'Very impressive,' said de Worde. 'I just hope you live to see it in my paper, sir.'

'I shall look forward to it with the keenest anticipation,' said Blouse. 'And now, Perks, please go along with the sergeant and put these two gentlemen back on their way.'

Otto sidled up to Polly as they walked back to the cart. 'I need to tell you somezing about your vampire,' he said.

'Oh, yes?'

'You are a friend of his?' said Otto.

'Yes,' said Polly. 'Is something wrong?'

'Zere is a problem . . .'

'He's got twitchy because he has run out of coffee?'

'Alas, if only it vas that simple.' Otto looked awkward. 'You have to understand that ven a vampire forgoes . . . the b-vord, there is a process that ve call transference? Ve force ourselves to desire something *else*? For me this vas not painful. I crave the perfection of light and shade. Pictures are my life! But your friend chose . . . coffee. And now he has none.'

'Oh. I see.'

'I vunder if you do. It probably seemed so sensible to him. It is a human craving, and no one minds if you say, as it might be, "I am dying for a cup of coffee", or "I'd kill for a cup of coffee". But without coffee, he vill, I am afraid . . . revert. You understand, this is very difficult for me to talk about . . .' Otto trailed off.

'By revert you mean . . . ?'

'First vill come mild delusions, I think. A psychic susceptibility to all kinds of influences from who knows vhere, and vampires can hallucinate so stronkly zat zey can be contagious. I zink zat is happening already. He vill become . . . erratic. This may last for several days. And then his conditioning vill break and he vill be, vunce again, a true vampire. No more Mr Nice Coffee Drinker Guy.'

'Can't I do anything to help him?'

Otto reverentially laid his picture box in the back of the cart, and turned to her. 'You can find him some coffee, or . . . you can keep a vooden stake and a big knife ready. You vould be doink him a favour, believe me.'

'I can't do that!'

Otto shrugged. 'Find someone who vill.'

'He is amazing!' said de Worde, as the cart rocked back down through the trees. 'I know the clacks is against your religion, but he seems to understand all about it.'

'Like I said, sir, he *assesses* stuff,' said Jackrum, beaming. 'Mind like a razor.'

'He was talking about clacks algorithms that the companies are only just now investigating,' said de Worde. 'That department he was talking about—'

'Ah, I can see nothing gets past you, sir,' said Jackrum. 'Very hush-hush. Can't talk about it.'

'To be frank, sergeant, I'd always assumed that Borogravia was, well . . . backward.'

Jackrum's smile was waxy and bright. 'If we seem to

be a long way back, sir, it's only so's we can get a good run-up.'

'You know, sergeant, it's a great shame to see a mind like that wasted,' said de Worde, as the cart lurched in a rut. 'This is not an age of heroes and famous last stands and death-or-glory charges. Do your men a favour and try to tell him that, will you?'

'Wouldn't dream of it, sir,' said Jackrum. 'Here is your road, sir. Where will you be heading now?'

'To the Kneck valley, sergeant. This is a good story, sergeant. Thank you. Allow me to shake you by the hand.'

'Glad to hear you think that, sir,' said Jackrum, extending his hand. Polly heard the faint clink of coins in their passage from palm to palm. De Worde took the reins.

'But I must tell you, sergeant, that we'll probably send off our stuff by pigeon within the hour,' he said. 'We will have to say you have prisoners.'

'Don't worry about that, sir,' said Jackrum. 'By the time their mates come out here to rescue those gallopers, we'll be halfway back to the mountains. Our mountains.'

They parted. Jackrum watched them out of sight, and turned to Polly.

'Him with his airs and graces,' he said. 'Did you see that? He insulted me by giving me a tip!' He glanced at his palm. 'Hmm, five Morpork dollars? Well, at least he's a man who knows how to insult you hand-somely,' he added, and the coins disappeared into his jacket with remarkable speed.

'I think he wants to help us, sarge,' said Polly.

Jackrum ignored that. 'I hate bloody Ankh-Morpork,' he said. 'Who're they to tell us what to do? Who cares what they think?'

'Do you think we can really join up with deserters, sarge?'

'Nope. They deserted once, what's to stop 'em a second time? They spat on the Duchess when they deserted, they can't kiss and make up now. You get one kiss, that's all.'

'But Lieutenant Blouse—'

'The rupert should stick to sums. He thinks he's a soldier. Never walked on a battlefield in his life. All that rubbish he gave your man was death-or-glory stuff. And I'll tell you, Perks, I've seen Death more often than I care to remember, but I've never clapped eyes on Glory. I'm all for sending the fools to look for us where we ain't, though.'

'He's not *my* man, sarge,' said Polly.

'Yeah, well, you're at home with the writin' and readin',' grumbled Jackrum. 'You can't trust the people who do that stuff. They mess around with the world, and it turns out everything you know is wrong.'

They reached the gully again. The squad had come back from their various hiding places, and most were clustered around one of the newspapers. For the first time, Polly saw the Picture.

It was actually quite good, especially of Shufti and Wazzer. *She* was mostly hidden by the bulk of Jackrum. But you could see the sullen cavalrymen

behind them, and their expressions were a picture in themselves.

'It's a good one of Tonker,' said Igorina, who didn't lisp so much when there were no officers to hear.

'Do you think having a picture like this is an Abomination in the Eyes of Nuggan?' said Shufti nervously.

'Probably,' said Polly absent-mindedly. 'Most things are.' She ran her eye down the text next to the picture. It was full of phrases like 'plucky farm boys' and 'humiliation of some of Zlobenia's best troops' and 'sting in the tail'. She could see why it had caused trouble.

She rustled through the other pages. They were crammed with strange stories about places she'd never heard of, and pictures of people she didn't recognize. But one page was a mass of grey text, under a line of much bigger printing which read:

Why This Mad State Must Be Stopped

Bewildered, her eye picked up phrases from the sea of letters: 'disgraceful invasions of neighbouring states', 'deluded worshippers of a mad god', 'a strutting bully', 'outrage after outrage', 'flying in the face of international opinion' . . .

'Don't you lads read that rubbish, you don't know where it's been,' said Sergeant Jackrum jovially, arriving behind them. 'It'll all be lies. We are leaving right— Corporal Maladict!'

Maladict, emerging from the trees, gave a lazy salute. He was still wearing his blanket.

'What *are* you doing out of uniform?'

'I'm in uniform underneath, sarge. We don't want to be seen, right? Like this, we become part of the jungle.'

'It's a forest, corporal! And without bloody uniforms, how the hell will we know our friends from our enemies?'

Maladict lit a cigarette before he replied. 'The way I see it, sarge,' he said, 'the enemy is everyone but us.'

'Just one moment, sergeant,' said Blouse, who had looked up from a newspaper and had been watching the apparition with considerable interest. 'There are precedents in antiquity, you know. General Song Sung Lo moved his army disguised as a field of sunflowers, and General Tacticus once commanded a battalion to dress as spruces.'

'*Sunflowers?*' said Jackrum, his voice oozing with disdain.

'Both actions were successful, sergeant.'

'No uniforms? No badges? No *stripes*, sir?'

'Possibly you could be an extra large bloom?' said Blouse, and his face betrayed no hint of amusement. 'And you have surely carried out actions at night, when all markings are invisible?'

'Yessir, but night is night, sir, while sunflowers is . . . is *sunflowers*, sir! I've worn this uniform for more'n fift— all my life, sir, and sneaking around without a uniform is downright dishonourable! It's for spies, sir!' Jackrum's face had gone beyond red into crimson,

and Polly was amazed to see tears in the corners of his eyes.

'How can we be spies, sergeant, in our own country?' said Blouse calmly.

'The el-tee's got a point, sarge,' said Maladict.

Jackrum turned like a bull at bay, and then to Polly's amazement he sagged. But she wasn't amazed for long. She knew the man. She didn't know why, but there was something about Jackrum that she could read. It was in the eyes. He could lie with eyes as honest and tranquil as those of an angel. And if he appeared to be backing away, it was indeed only to get a run-up later on.

'All right, all right,' the sergeant said. 'Upon my oath, I am not a man to disobey orders.' And the eyes twinkled.

'Well done, sergeant,' said Blouse.

Jackrum pulled himself together. 'I don't want to be a sunflower, though,' he said.

'Happily there are only fir trees in this area, sergeant.'

'Point well made, sir.' Jackrum turned to the awed squad. 'All right, Last Detail,' he bellowed. 'You heard the man! Spruce up!'

It was an hour later. As far as Polly could tell, they'd started out for the mountains but had travelled in a wide semi-circle so that they ended up facing back the way they had come, but a few miles away. Was Blouse leading, or had he left it to Jackrum? Neither man was complaining.

The lieutenant called a halt in a thicket of birch, thus doubling the size of the thicket. You could say that the camouflage effects were effective, because bright red and white shows up against greens and greys. Beyond that, though, language tended to run out.

Jade had scraped off her paint, and was green and grey anyway. Igorina looked like a walking brush. Wazzer quivered like an aspen all the time, so her leaves rustled permanently. The others had made more or less reasonable attempts, and Polly was pretty proud of her own efforts. Jackrum was about as tree-like as a big red rubber ball; Polly suspected that he'd surreptitiously shined up his brasswork, too. Every tree held a mug of tea in limb or hand. After all, they'd stopped for five minutes.

'Men,' said Blouse, as if he'd only just reached that conclusion. 'You may have gathered that we are heading back towards the mountains to raise a deserters' army there. This story is, in fact, a *ruse* for the benefit of Mr de Worde!' He paused, as if expecting some reaction. They stared at him. He went on: 'We are, in fact, continuing our journey to the Kneck valley. This is the last thing the enemy will be expecting.'

Polly glanced at the sergeant. He was grinning.

'It is an established fact that a small, light force can get into places that a battalion cannot penetrate,' Blouse went on. 'Men, we will be that force! Is that not right, Sergeant Jackrum?'

'Yessir!'

'We will come down like a hammer on those forces smaller than us,' said Blouse happily.

'Yessir!'

'And from those that outnumber us, we will merge silently into the forest—'

'Yessir!'

'We will slip past their sentries—'

'That's right, sir,' said Jackrum.

'—and take Kneck Keep from under their noses!'

Jackrum's tea sprayed across the clearing.

'I dare say our enemy feels impregnable just because he commands a heavily armed fort on a rocky crag with walls a hundred feet high and twenty feet thick,' Blouse continued, as if half the trees weren't now dripping tea. 'But he is in for a surprise!'

'You all right, sarge?' whispered Polly. Jackrum was making strange little noises in his throat.

'Does anyone have any questions?' said Blouse.

Igorina raised a branch. 'How will we get in, sir?' she said.

'Ah. Good question,' said Blouse. 'And all will become apparent in due time.'

'Aerial cavalry,' said Maladict.

'Pardon, corporal?'

'Flying machines, sir!' said Maladict. 'They won't know where to expect us. We touch down in a handy LZ, take them out, and then dust off.'

Blouse's clear brow wrinkled a little. 'Flying machines?' he said.

'I saw a picture of one by someone called Leonard

of Quirm. A sort of . . . flying windmill. It's just like a big screw up in the sky—'

'I don't think we need one of those, although the advice is welcomed,' said Blouse.

'Not when we've got a big screw-up down here, sir!' Jackrum managed. 'Sir, this is just a bunch of recruits, sir! All that stuff about honour and freedom and that, that was just for the writer man, right? Good idea, sir! Yeah, let's get to the Kneck valley, and let's sneak in and join the rest of the lads. That's where we ought to be, sir. You can't be serious about taking the *keep*, sir! I wouldn't try that with a thousand men.'

'I might try it with half a dozen, sergeant.'

Jackrum's eyes bulged. 'Really, sir? What'll Private Goom do? Tremble at them? Young Igor will stitch 'em up, will he? Private Halter will give 'em a nasty look? They're promising lads, sir, but they're not *men*.'

'General Tacticus said the fate of a battle may depend upon the actions of one man in the right place, sergeant,' said Blouse calmly.

'*And* having a lot more soldiers than the other bugger, sir,' Jackrum insisted. 'Sir, we should get to the rest of the army. Maybe it's trapped, maybe it isn't. All that stuff about them not wanting to slaughter us, sir, that makes no sense. The idea is to win, sir. If the rest of 'em have stopped attacking, it's because they're frightened of us. We should be down there. That's the place for young recruits, sir, where they can *learn*. The enemy is looking for 'em, sir!'

'If General Froc is among those captured, the keep will be where he is held,' said Blouse. 'I believe he was

the first officer you served under as sergeant, am I right?'

Jackrum hesitated. 'That's right, sir,' he said eventually. 'And he was the dumbest lieutenant I've ever met, bar one.'

'I am positive there is a secret entrance into the keep, sergeant.'

Polly's memory nudged her. If Paul was alive, he was in the keep. She caught Shufti's eye. The girl nodded. She'd been thinking along the same lines. She didn't talk much about her ... fiancé, and Polly wondered how official the arrangement was.

'Permission to speak, sarge?' she said.

'Okay, Perks.'

'I'd like to try to find a way into the keep, sarge.'

'Perks, are you *volunteering* to attack the biggest, strongest castle within five hundred miles? Single-handed?'

'I'll go, too,' said Shufti.

'Oh, *two* of you?' said Jackrum. 'Oh, well, *that's* all right then.'

'I'll go,' said Wazzer. 'The Duchess has told me that I should.'

Jackrum looked down at Wazzer's thin little face and watery eyes, and sighed. He turned back to Blouse. 'Let's get a move on, sir, shall we? We can talk about this later. At least we're headed to Kneck, first stop on the road to hell. Perks and Igor, you take point. Maladict?'

'Yo!'

'Er ... you scout on ahead.'

'I hear you!'

'Good.'

As the vampire walked past Polly the world, just for a moment, changed; the forest became greener, the sky greyer, and she heard a noise overhead, like 'whopwhopwhop'. And then it was gone.

Vampire hallucinations are contagious, she thought. What's going on in his head? She hurried forward with Igorina, and they set off again through the forest.

Birds sang. The effect was peaceful, if you didn't know about birdsong, but Polly could recognize the alarm calls close by and the territorial threats far off and, everywhere, the preoccupation with sex. That took the edge off the pleasure.*

'Polly?' said Igorina.

'Hmm?'

'Could you kill someone if you had to?'

Polly came right back to the here and now. 'What sort of question is that to ask anyone?'

'I think it's the sort you'd ask a tholdier,' said Igorina.

'I don't know. If they were attacking me, I suppose. Hurt them hard enough to keep them lying down, anyway. And you?'

'We have a great respect for life, Polly,' said Igorina

* It's hard to be an ornithologist and walk through a wood when all around you the world is shouting: 'Bugger off, this is my bush! Aargh, the nest thief! Have sex with me, I can make my chest big and red!'

solemnly. 'It's easy to kill thomeone, and almost impossible to bring them back again.'

'Almost?'

'Well, if you don't have a really good lightning rod. And even if you have, they're never quite the same. Cutlery tends to stick to them.'

'Igorina, why are you *here*?'

'The clan isn't very . . . keen on girls getting too involved in the Great Work,' said Igorina, looking downcast. '"Stick to your needlework", my mother keeps saying. Well, that's all very fine, but I know I'm good at the actual incisions as well. Especially the fiddly bits. And I think a woman on the slab would feel a lot better about things if she knew there was a female hand on the we-belong-dead switch. Tho I thought some battlefield experience would convince my father. Soldiers aren't choosy about who saves their lives.'

'I suppose men are the same the world over,' said Polly.

'On the inside, certainly.'

'And . . . er . . . you really can put your hair back?' Polly had seen it in its jar when they'd been breaking camp; it had spun gently in its bottle of green liquid, like some fine, rare seaweed.

'Oh, yes. Scalp transplants are easy. It stings a bit for a couple of minutes, that's all—'

There was movement between the trees, and then the blur resolved itself into Maladict. He held a finger to his lips as he drew closer, and whispered urgently: 'Charlie's tracking us!'

Polly and Igorina looked at one another. '*Who's Charlie?*'

Maladict stared at them, and then rubbed his face distractedly. 'I'm ... sorry, er ... sorry, it's ... look, we're being followed! I know it!'

The sun was setting. Polly peered over the rocky ledge, back the way they had come. She could make out the track, golden and red in the late afternoon light. Nothing was moving. The outcrop was near the top of another rounded hill; the rear of it became the floor of a little enclosed space, surrounded by bushes. It made a good lookout for people who wanted to see without being seen, and it had done so in the recent past, by the look of the old fires.

Maladict was sitting with his head in his hands, with Jackrum and Blouse on either side of him. They were trying to understand, and not making much progress.

'So you can't *hear* anything?' said Blouse.

'No.'

'And you didn't see anything and can't smell anything?' said Jackrum.

'*No!* I *told* you! But there is something after us. Watching us!'

'But if you can't—' Blouse began.

'Look, I'm a vampire,' panted Maladict. 'Just *trust* me, okay?'

'I thould, tharge,' said Igorina, from behind Jackrum. 'We Igorth often therve vampireth. In timeth of strethth their perthonal thpace can

extend ath much ath ten mileth from their body.'

There was the usual pause that follows an extended lisp. People need time to think.

'Streth-th?' said Blouse.

'You know how you can feel that someone's looking at you?' mumbled Maladict. 'Well, it's like that, times a thousand. And it's not a . . . a feeling, it's something I *know*.'

'Lots of people are looking for us, corporal,' said Blouse, patting him kindly on the shoulder. 'It doesn't mean that they'll find us.'

Polly, looking down on the gold-lit woodland, opened her mouth to speak. It was dry. Nothing came out.

Maladict shook the lieutenant's hand away. 'This . . . person isn't looking for us! They know where we are!'

Polly forced saliva into her mouth, and tried again. 'Movement!'

And then it wasn't there any more. She'd have sworn there had been something on the path, something that merged with the light, revealing itself only by the changing, wavering pattern of shadows as it moved.

'Er . . . perhaps not,' she muttered.

'Look, we've all lost sleep and we're all a little "strung out", said Blouse. 'Let's just keep things down, shall we?'

'I *need* coffee!' moaned Maladict, rocking back and forth.

Polly squinted at the distant pathway. The breeze

was shaking the trees, and red-gold leaves were drifting down. For a moment there was just a *suggestion* ... She got to her feet. Stare at shadows and waving branches for long enough and you could see anything. It was like looking at pictures in the flames.

'O-kay,' said Shufti, who'd been working over the fire. 'This might do it. It smells like coffee, anyway. Well ... quite like coffee. Well ... quite like coffee if coffee was made from acorns, anyway.'

She'd roasted some acorns. At least the woods had plenty of them at this time of year, and everybody knew that roasted, ground acorns could be substituted for coffee, didn't they? Polly had agreed that it was a worth a try, but as far as she could recall no one had ever, given the choice, said 'No, I will not touch horrible coffee any more! It's a Long Black ground-acorn substitute for me, with extra floating gritty bits!'

She took the mug from Shufti and carried it over to the vampire. As she bent down ... the world changed.

... *whopwhopwhop* ...

The sky was a haze of dust, turning the sun into a blood-red disc. For a moment Polly saw *them* in the sky, giant fat screws spinning in the air, *hovering* in the air but drifting slowly towards her—

'He's having flashsides,' whispered Igorina, at her elbow.

'Flashsides?'

'Like ... someone else's flashbackth. We don't know anything about them. They could come from *anywhere*. A vampire at this stage is open

to all sorts of influences! Give him the coffee, please!'

Maladict grabbed the mug and tried to down the contents so quickly that they spilled over his chin. They watched him swallow.

'Tastes like mud,' he said, putting down the mug.

'Yes, but is it working?'

Maladict looked up and blinked his eyes. 'Ye gods, that stuff is *gruesome*.'

'Are we in a forest or a jungle? Any flying screws?' Igorina demanded. 'How many fingers am I holding up?'

'You know, that's something an Igor should *never* say,' said Maladict, grimacing. 'But . . . the . . . feelings aren't so strong. I can suck it down! I can gut it out.'

Polly looked at Igorina, who shrugged and said, 'That's nice,' and motioned to Polly to join her a little way off.

'He, or possibly she, is right on the edge,' she said.

'Well, we all are,' said Polly. 'We're hardly getting any sleep.'

'You know what I mean. I've, er . . . taken the liberty of, er . . . being prepared.' Wordlessly, Igorina let her jacket fall open, just for a moment. Polly saw a knife, a wooden stake and a hammer, in neatly stitched little pockets.

'It's not going to come to that, is it?'

'I hope not,' said Igorina. 'But if it does, I'm the only one who can reliably find the heart. People always think it's more to the left than—'

'It's *not* going to come to that,' said Polly firmly.

* * *

The sky was red. The war was a day away.

Polly crept along just below the ridge with the tea can. It was tea that kept the army on its feet. Remember what's real . . . well, that took some doing. Tonker and Lofty, for example. It didn't matter which of them was on guard, the other one would be there as well. And there they were, sitting side by side on a fallen tree, staring down the slope. They were holding hands. They always held hands, when they thought they were alone. But it seemed to Polly that they didn't hold hands like people who were, well, friends. They held hands tightly, as someone who has slipped over a cliff would hold hands with a rescuer, fearing that to let go would be to fall away.

'Tea up!' she quavered.

The girls turned, and she dipped a couple of mugs into the scalding tea.

'You know,' she said quietly, 'no one would hate you if you ran away tonight.'

'What do you mean, Ozz?' said Lofty.

'Well, what's there in Kneck for you? You got away from the school. You could go anywhere. I bet the two of you could sneak—'

'We're staying,' said Tonker severely. 'We talked about it. Where else would we go? Anyway, supposing something *is* following us?'

'Probably just an animal,' said Polly, who didn't believe it herself.

'Animals don't do that,' said Tonker. 'And I don't think Maladict would get so excited. It's probably more spies. Well, we'll *get* them.'

'Nobody is going to take us back,' said Lofty.

'Oh. Er . . . good,' said Polly, backing away. 'Well, must get on, no one likes cold tea, eh?'

She hurried round the hill. Whenever Lofty and Tonker were together, she felt like a trespasser.

Wazzer was on guard in a small dell, watching the land below with her usual expression of slightly worrying intensity. She turned as Polly approached.

'Oh, Polly,' said Wazzer. 'Good news!'

'Oh, good,' said Polly weakly. 'I like good news.'

'She says it will be all right for us not to wear our dimity scarves,' said Wazzer.

'What? Oh. Good,' said Polly.

'But only because we are serving a Higher Purpose,' said Wazzer. And, just as Blouse could invert commas, Wazzer could drop capital letters into a spoken sentence.

'That's good, then,' said Polly.

'You know, Polly,' said Wazzer, 'I think the world would be a lot better if it was run by women. There wouldn't be any wars. Of course, the Book would consider such an idea a Dire Abomination unto Nuggan. It may be in error. I shall consult the Duchess. Bless this cup that I may drink of it,' she added.

'Er, yes,' said Polly, and wondered what she should dread more: Maladict suddenly turning into a ravening monster, or Wazzer reaching the end of whatever mental journey she was taking. She'd been a kitchen maid and now she was subjecting the Book to critical analysis and talking to a religious icon. That sort of thing led to friction. The presence of those seeking the

truth is infinitely to be preferred to those who think they've found it.

Besides, she thought as she watched Wazzer drink, you only thought the world would be better if it was run by women if you didn't actually know many women. Or old women, at least. Take the whole thing about the dimity scarves. Women had to cover their hair on Fridays, but there was nothing about this in the Book, which was pretty dar— pretty *damn* rigorous about most things. It was just a custom. It was done because it was always done. And if you forgot, or didn't want to, the old women *got* you. They had eyes like hawks. They could practically see through walls. And the men took notice, because no man wanted to cross the crones in case they started watching *him*, so half-hearted punishment would be dealt out. Whenever there was an execution, and especially when there was a whipping, you always found the grannies in the front row, sucking peppermints.

Polly had forgotten her dimity scarf. She did wear it at home on Fridays, for no other reason than that it was easier than not doing so. She vowed that, if ever she got back, she'd never do it again . . .

'Er . . . Wazz?' she said.

'Yes, Polly?'

'You've got a direct line to the Duchess, have you?'

'We talk about things,' said Wazzer dreamily.

'You, er, couldn't raise the question of coffee, could you?' said Polly wretchedly.

'The Duchess can only move very, very small things,' said Wazzer.

'A few beans, perhaps? Wazz, we really *need* some coffee! I don't think the acorns are that much of a substitute.'

'I will pray,' said Wazzer.

'Good. You do that,' said Polly. And, strangely enough, she felt a little more hopeful. Maladict had hallucinations, but Wazzer had a certainty you could bend steel round. It was the *opposite* of a hallucination, somehow. It was as if she could see what was real and you couldn't.

'Polly?' said Wazzer.

'Yes?'

'You don't believe in the Duchess, do you? I mean the real Duchess, not your inn.'

Polly looked into the small, pinched, intense face. 'Well, I mean, they say she's dead, and I prayed to her when I was small, but since you ask I don't exactly, um, *believe* as—' she gabbled.

'She is standing just behind you. Just behind your right shoulder.'

In the silence of the wood, Polly turned. 'I can't see her,' she said.

'I am happy for you,' said Wazzer, handing her the empty mug.

'But I didn't see anything,' said Polly.

'No,' said Wazzer. 'But you turned round . . .'

Polly had never asked too many questions about the Girls' Working School. She was, by definition, a Good Girl. Her father was an influential man in the community, and she worked hard, she didn't have much to do with men and, most importantly, she was

. . . well, smart. She was bright enough to do what a lot of other people did in the chronic, reason-free insanity that was everyday life in Munz. She knew what to see and what to ignore, when to obey and when to merely present the face of obedience, when to speak and when to keep her thoughts to herself. She learned the ways of the survivor. Most people did. But if you rebelled, or were merely dangerously honest, or had the wrong kind of illness, or were not wanted, or were a girl who liked boys more than the old women thought you should and, worse, were not good at counting . . . then the school was your destination.

She didn't know much about what went on in there, but imagination rushed to fill the gap. And she wondered what happened to you in that hellish pressure cooker. If you were tough, like Tonker, it boiled you hard and gave you a shell. Lofty . . . it was hard to know. She was quiet and shy until you saw firelight reflected in her eyes, and sometimes the flames were there in the absence of any fire to reflect. But if you were Wazzer, dealt a poor hand to start with, and locked up, and starved, and beaten, and mistreated Nuggan knew how (and yes, Polly thought, Nuggan probably *did* know how) and pushed deeper and deeper into yourself, what would you find down there? And then you'd look up from those depths into the only smile you ever saw.

The last man on guard duty was Jackrum, because Shufti was cooking. He was sitting on a mossy rock, crossbow in one hand, staring at something in his

hand. He spun round as she approached, and Polly caught the gleam of gold as something was shoved back in his jacket.

The sergeant lowered the bow. 'You make enough noise for an elephant, Perks,' he said.

'Sorry, sarge,' said Polly, who knew she hadn't. He took the tea mug, and turned to point downhill.

'See that bush down there, Perks?' he said. 'Just to the right of that fallen log?'

Polly squinted. 'Yes, sarge,' she said.

'Notice anything about it?'

Polly stared again. There must *be* something wrong about it, she decided, otherwise he wouldn't have asked her. She concentrated. 'The shadow's wrong,' she decided at last.

'Good lad. The reason bein', our chum is behind the bush. He's been a-watching of me, and I've been a-watching of him. Nothing else for it. He'll have it away on his toes as soon as he sees anyone move, and he's too far away to drop an arrow on him.'

'An enemy?'

'I don't think so.'

'A *friend*?'

'Cocky devil, at any rate. He doesn't care that I know he's there. You go on back up the hill, lad, and bring down that big bow we got off of the— There he goes!'

The shadow had vanished. Polly stared into the wood, but the long light was getting crimson and dusk was unfolding between the trees.

'It's a wolf,' said Jackrum.

'A werewolf?' said Polly.

'Now, what makes you think that?'

'Because Sergeant Towering said we'd got a werewolf in the squad. I'm sure we haven't. I mean, we'd have found out by now, wouldn't we? But I wondered if they'd seen one.'

'Can't do anything about it, anyway,' said Jackrum. 'A silver arrow would do the job, but we've got none.'

'What about our shilling, sarge?'

'Oh, you think you can kill a werewolf with an IOU?'

'Oh, yeah.' Then Polly added: '*You've* got a real shilling, sarge. Around your neck with that gold medallion.'

If you could have twisted steel round Wazzer's conviction, you could have heated it with Jackrum's glare.

'What's round my neck is no business of yours, Perks, and the only thing worse than a werewolf is me if anyone tries to take my shilling off me, understand?'

He softened as he saw Polly's terrified expression. 'We'll move on after we've eaten,' he said. 'Find a better place for a rest. Somewhere easier to defend.'

'We're all pretty tired, sarge.'

'So I want us all to be upright and armed if our friend comes back with his chums,' said Jackrum.

He followed her gaze. The gold locket had slipped out of his jacket, and dangled guiltily on its chain. He deftly tucked it away.

'She was just a . . . girl I knew,' he said. 'That's all, right? It was a long time ago.'

'I didn't *ask* you, sarge,' said Polly, backing away.

Jackrum's shoulders settled. 'That's right, lad, you didn't. And I ain't asking *you* about anything, neither. But I reckon we'd better find the corporal some coffee, eh?'

'Amen to that, sarge!'

'And our rupert's dreaming of laurel wreaths all round his head, Perks. We've got ourselves a goddamn hero here. Can't think, can't fight, no bloody use at all except for a famous last stand and a medal sent to his ol' mum. And I've been in a few famous last stands, lad, and they're butcher shops. That's what Blouse's leading you into, mark my words. What'll you lot do then, eh? We've had a few scuffles, but that's not war. Think you'll be man enough to stand, when the metal meets the meat?'

'You did, sarge,' said Polly. 'You said you were in a few last stands.'

'Yeah, lad. But I was holding the metal.'

Polly walked back up the slope. All this, she thought, and we haven't even got there. Sarge is thinking about the girl he left behind . . . well, that's normal. And Tonker and Lofty only think about one another, but I suppose after you've been in that school . . . and as for Wazzer . . .

She wondered how she'd have survived the school. Would she have grown hard, like Tonker? Would she have just folded up inside, like the maids who came and went and worked hard and never had a name? Or perhaps *she* would have become like Wazzer, and

found some door in her own head . . . *I may be lowly, but I talk to gods.*

. . . Wazzer had said 'not your inn'. Had she ever *told* Wazzer about The Duchess? Surely not. Surely she . . . but, no, she had told Tonker, hadn't she? That was it, then. All explained. Tonker must have mentioned it to Wazzer at some point. Nothing weird about it at all, even if practically no one ever had a conversation with Wazz. It was so hard. She was so intense, so coiled up. But that had to be the only explanation. Yes. She wasn't going to let there be any other.

Polly shivered, and was aware that someone was walking beside her. She looked up and groaned.

'You're a hallucination, right?'

OH, YES. YOU ARE ALL IN A STATE OF HEIGHTENED SENSIBILITY CAUSED BY MENTAL CONTAGION AND LACK OF SLEEP.

'If you're a hallucination, how do *you* know that?'

I KNOW IT BECAUSE YOU KNOW IT. I AM SIMPLY BETTER AT ARTICULATING IT.

'I'm not going to die, am I? I mean, right now?'

NO. BUT YOU WERE TOLD THAT YOU WOULD WALK WITH DEATH EVERY DAY.

'Oh . . . yes. Corporal Scallot said that.'

HE IS AN OLD FRIEND. YOU MIGHT SAY HE IS ON THE INSTALMENT PLAN.

'Do you mind walking a bit more . . . invisibly?'

OF COURSE. HOW'S THIS?

'And quietly, too?'

There was silence, which was presumably the answer.

'And polish yourself up a bit,' said Polly to the empty air. 'And that robe needs a wash.'

There was no reply, but she felt better for saying it.

Shufti had cooked beef stew with dumplings and herbs. It was magnificent. It was also a mystery.

'I don't recall us passing a cow, private,' said Blouse, as he handed his tin plate along for a second helping.

'Er . . . no, sir.'

'And yet you have acquired beef?'

'Er . . . yes, sir. Er . . . when that writer man came up in his cart, well, when you were talking, er, I crept round and took a look inside . . .'

'There's a name for someone who does that sort of thing, private,' said Blouse severely.

'Yeah, it's quartermaster, Shufti. Well done,' said Jackrum. 'If that writer man gets hungry, he can always eat his words, eh, lieutenant?'

'Er . . . yes,' said Blouse carefully. 'Yes. Of course. Good initiative, private.'

'Oh, I didn't think it up, sir,' said Shufti brightly. 'Sarge told me to.'

Polly stopped, spoon halfway to her mouth, and swivelled her eyes from sergeant to lieutenant.

'You teach looting, sergeant?' said Blouse. There was a joint gasp from the squad. If this was the bar back at The Duchess, the regulars would have been hurrying out of the doors and Polly would have been helping her father get the bottles off the shelf.

'Not looting, sir, not looting,' said Jackrum, calmly licking his spoon. 'Under Duchess's Regulations, Rule

611, Section 1 [c], Paragraph i, sir, it would be plundering, said cart being the property of bloody Ankh-Morpork, sir, which is aiding and abetting the enemy. Plundering is *allowed*, sir.'

The two men held eye contact for a moment, and then Blouse reached behind him and into his pack. Polly saw him draw out a small yet thick book.

'Rule 611,' he murmured. Blouse glanced up at the sergeant, and thumbed through the thin, shiny pages. '611. Pillaging, Plundering and Looting. Ah, yes. And ... let me see ... you are with us, Sergeant Jackrum, owing to Rule 796, I think you reminded me at the time ...'

There was another silence broken only by the riffle of the pages. There's no Rule 796, Polly remembered. Are they going to *fight* over this?

'796, 796,' said Blouse softly. 'Ah ...' He stared at the page, and Jackrum stared at him.

Blouse closed the book with a leathery *flwap*. 'Absolutely correct, sergeant!' he said brightly. 'I commend you on your encyclopaedic knowledge of the regulations!'

Jackrum looked thunderous. 'What?'

'You were practically word perfect, sergeant!' said Blouse. And there was a gleam in his eye. Polly remembered Blouse looking at the captured cavalry captain. This was that same look, the look which said: *now* I have the upper hand.

Jackrum's chins wobbled.

'You had something to add, sergeant?' said Blouse.

'Er, no ... sir,' said Jackrum, his face an open declaration of war.

'We'll leave at moonrise,' said Blouse. 'I suggest we all get some rest until then. And then ... may we prevail.' He nodded to the group, and walked over to where Polly had spread his blanket in the lee of the bushes. After a few moments there were some snores, which Polly refused to believe. Jackrum certainly didn't. He got up and strode out of the firelight. Polly hurried after him.

'Did you hear that?' snarled the sergeant, staring out at the darkening hills. 'The little yoyo! What right has he got, checking up in the book o' words?'

'Well, you did quote chapter and verse, sarge,' said Polly.

'So? Officers are s'posed to believe what they're told. And then he *smiled*! Did you see? Caught me out and smiled at me! Thinks he's got one over on me, just because he caught me out!'

'You did lie, sarge.'

'*I did not, Perks!* It's not lying when you do it to officers! It's presentin' them with the world the way they think it ought to be! You can't let 'em start checkin' up for themselves. They get the wrong ideas. I told you, he'll be the death of all of us. Invading the bloody keep? The man's wrong in the head!'

'Sarge!' said Polly urgently.

'Yes, what?'

'We're being signalled, sarge!'

On a distant hilltop, twinkling like an early evening star, a white light was flashing.

* * *

Blouse lowered his telescope. 'They're repeating "CQ", he said. 'And I believe those longer pauses are when they're aiming their tube in different directions. They're looking for their spies. "Seek You", see? Private Igor?'

'Thur?'

'You know how that tube works, don't you?'

'Oh, yeth, thur. You jutht light a flare in the box, and then it'th just point and click.'

'You're not going to *answer* it, are you, sir?' said Jackrum, horrified.

'I am indeed, sergeant,' said Blouse briskly. 'Private Carborundum, please assemble the tube. Manickle, please bring the lantern. I shall need to read the code book.'

'But that'll give away our position!' said Jackrum.

'No, sergeant, because although this term may be unfamiliar to you I intend to what we call "lie",' said Blouse. 'Igor, I'm sure you have some scissors, although I'd rather you didn't attempt to repeat the word.'

'I have thome of the appliantheth you mention, thur,' said Igorina stiffly.

'Good.' Blouse looked round. 'It's almost pitch dark now. Ideal. Take my blanket and cut, oh, a three-inch circle out of it, then tie the blanket over the front of the tube.'

'That will cut off motht of the light, thur!'

'Indeed it will. My plan depends upon it,' said Blouse proudly.

'Sir, they will see the light, they'll know we're here,' said Jackrum, as though repeating things to a child.

'I explained, sergeant. I will lie,' said Blouse.

'You *can't* lie when—'

'Thank you for your input, sergeant, that will be all for now,' said Blouse. 'Are we ready, Igor?'

'Jutht about, thur,' said Igorina, tying the blanket across the end of the tube. 'Okay, thur. I'll light the flare when you thay.'

Blouse unfolded the little book. 'Ready, private?' he said.

'Yup,' said Jade.

'On the word "long" you will hold the trigger for the count of two, and then let go. On the word "short" you will hold it down for the count of one, and likewise let go. Got that?'

'Yup, el-tee. Could hold it down for lots, if you like,' said Jade. 'One, two, many, lots. I'm good at countin'. High as you like. Jus' say der word.'

'Two will suffice,' said Blouse. 'And you, Private Goom, I want you to take my telescope and look for long and short flashes from that light over there, understand?'

Polly saw Wazzer's face and said quickly: 'I'll do that, sir!'

A small white hand was laid on her arm. In the miserly glimmer of the dark lantern, Wazzer's eyes glowed with the light of certainty. 'The Duchess guides our footsteps now,' she said, and took the telescope from the lieutenant. 'What we are doing is her work, sir.'

'Is it? Oh. Well . . . that's good,' said Blouse.

'She will bless this instrument of far seeing that I may use it,' said Wazzer.

'Indeed?' said Blouse nervously. 'Well done. Now . . . are we ready? Send as follows . . . long . . . long . . . short . . .'

The shutter in the tube clicked and rattled as the message flashed out across the sky. When the troll lowered the tube, there was half a minute of darkness. And then: 'Short . . . long . . .' Wazzer began.

Blouse held the code book up to his face, his lips moving as he read by the pinpoints of light escaping from the loins of the box. 'W . . . R . . . U,' he said. 'And M . . . S . . . G . . . P . . . R . . .'

'That's not a message!' said Jackrum.

'On the contrary, they want to know where we are, because they're having trouble seeing our light,' said Blouse. 'Send as follows . . . short . . .'

'I protest, sir!'

Blouse lowered the book. 'Sergeant, I am about to tell our spy that we are seven miles further away than we really are, do you understand? And I am certain they will believe us because I have artificially reduced the light output from our device, do you understand? And I will tell them that their spies have encountered a very large party of recruits and deserters heading for the mountains and are in pursuit, do you understand? I am making us *invisible*, do you understand? *Do you understand*, Sergeant Jackrum?'

The squad held their breath.

Jackrum drew himself stiffly to attention. 'Fully understood, sir!' he said.

'Very well!'

Jackrum continued at attention as the messages were exchanged, like a naughty pupil forced to stand by the teacher's desk.

Messages flashed across the sky, from hilltop to hilltop. Lights flickered. The clacks tube rattled. Wazzer called out the longs and shorts. Blouse scribbled in the book. 'S ... P ... P ... 2,' he said aloud. 'Hah. That's an order to remain where we are.'

'More flashes, sir,' said Wazzer.

'T ... Y ... E ... 3 ...' said Blouse, still making notes. 'That's "be ready to give aid". N ... V ... A ... S ... N ... That's ...'

'That's not a code, sir!' said Polly.

'Private, send as follows right now!' Blouse croaked. 'Long ... long ...'

The message went. They watched, while the dew fell and, overhead, the stars came out and twinkled messages no one ever tried to read.

The clacks went silent.

'Now we leave as soon as possible,' said Blouse. He gave a little cough. 'I believe the phrase is "Let us get the heck out of here".'

'Close, sir,' said Polly. 'Quite ... close.'

There was an old, *very* old Borogravian song with more Zs and Vs in it than any lowlander could pronounce. It was called 'Plogviehze!' It meant 'The Sun Has Risen! Let's Make War!' You needed

a special kind of history to get all that in one word.

Sam Vimes sighed. The little countries here fought because of the river, because of idiot treaties, because of royal rows, but mostly they fought because they had always fought. They made war, in fact, because the sun came up.

This war had tied itself in a knot.

Downriver, the valley narrowed to a canyon before the Kneck plunged over a waterfall a quarter of a mile high. Anyone trying to get up through the jagged mountains there would find themselves in a world of gorges, knife-edged ridges, permanent ice and even more permanent death. Anyone trying to cross the Kneck into Zlobenia now would be butchered on the shore. The only way out of the valley was back along the Kneck, which would put an army under the shadow of the keep. That had been fine when the keep was in Borogravian hands. Now that it had been captured, they'd be passing in range of their own weapons.

. . . And such weapons! Vimes had seen catapults that would throw a stone ball three miles. When it landed it would crack into needle-sharp shards. Or there was the other machine that sent six-foot steel discs skimming through the air. Once they'd hit the ground and leapt up again they were unreliable as hell, but that only made them more terrifying. Vimes had been told that the edged disc would probably keep going for several hundred yards, no matter how many men or horses it encountered on the way. And they were only the latest ideas. There were plenty of

conventional weapons, if by that you meant giant bows, catapults and mangonels that hurled balls of Ephebian fire, which clung while it burned.

From up here, in his draughty tower, he could see the fires of the dug-in army all across the plain. They couldn't retreat, and the alliance, if that's what you could call the petulier hubbub, didn't dare head up the valley into the heart of the country with that army at their back, yet didn't have enough men to hold the keep *and* corral the enemy.

And in a few weeks it would start to snow. The passes would fill up. Nothing would be able to get through. And every day, thousands of men and horses would need feeding. Of course, the men could, eventually, eat the horses, thus settling two feeding problems at a stroke. After that there would have to be the good ol' leg rota, which Vimes understood from one of the friendlier Zlobenians was a common feature of winter warfare up here. Since he was Captain 'Hopalong' Splatzer, Vimes believed him.

And then it would rain, and then the rain and the snowmelt together would turn the damn river into a flood. But before that the alliance would have bickered itself apart and gone home. All the Borogravians had to do, in fact, was hold their ground to score a draw.

He swore under his breath. Prince Heinrich had inherited the throne in a country where the chief export was a kind of hand-painted wooden clog, but in ten years, he vowed, his capital city of Rigour would be 'the Ankh-Morpork of the mountains'! For some

reason, he thought Ankh-Morpork would be pleased about this.

He was anxious, he said, to learn the Ankh-Morpork way of doing things, the kind of innocent ambition that could well lead an aspiring ruler to . . . well, find out the Ankh-Morpork way of doing things. Heinrich had a reputation locally for cunning, but Ankh-Morpork had overtaken cunning a thousand years ago, had sped past devious, had left artful far behind and had now, by a roundabout route, arrived at straightforward.

Vimes leafed through the papers on his desk, and looked up when he heard a shrill, harsh cry outside. A buzzard came in a long, shallow swoop through the open window and alighted on a makeshift perch at the far end of the room. Vimes strolled over as the little figure on the bird's back raised his flying goggles.

'How's it going, Buggy?' he said.

'They're getting suspicious, Mister Vimes. And Sergeant Angua says it's getting a bit risky now they're so close.'

'Tell her to come on in, then.'

'Right, sir. And they still need coffee.'

'Oh, damn! Haven't they found *any*?'

'No, sir, and it's getting tricky with the vampire.'

'Well, if they're suspicious now then they'll be *certain* if we drop a flask of coffee on them!'

'Sergeant Angua says we'll probably get away with it, sir. She didn't say why.' The gnome looked expectantly at Vimes. So did his buzzard. 'They've

come a long way, sir. For a bunch of girls. Well ...
mostly girls.'

Vimes reached out absent-mindedly to pet the
bird.

'Don't, sir! She'll have your thumb off!' Buggy
yelled.

There was a knock on the door, and Reg came in
with a tray of raw meat. 'Saw Buggy overhead, so I
thought I'd nip down to the kitchens, sir.'

'Well done, Reg. Don't they ask why you want raw
meat?'

'Yes, sir. I tell them you eat it, sir.'

Vimes paused before answering. Reg meant well,
after all.

'Well, it probably can't do my reputation any harm,'
he said. 'By the way, what was going down in the
crypt?'

'Oh, they're not what I'd call proper zombies, sir,'
said Reg, selecting a piece of meat and dangling it in
front of Morag. 'More like dead men walking.'

'Er ... yes?' said Vimes.

'I mean there's no real thinking going on,' the
zombie continued, picking up another lump of raw
rabbit. 'No embracing the opportunities of a life
beyond the grave, sir. They're just a lot of old
memories on legs. That sort of thing gives zombies a
bad name, Mister Vimes. It makes me so *angry*!'
Morag tried to snap at another lump of bloody rabbit
fur that Reg, oblivious for the moment, was waving
aimlessly.

'Er ... Reg?' said Buggy.

'How hard can it be, sir, to move with the times? Now take me, for example. One day I woke up dead. Did I—'

'Reg!' Vimes warned, as Morag's head bobbed back and forth.

'—take it lying down? No! And I didn't—'

'Reg, be careful! She's just had two of your fingers off!'

'What? Oh.' Reg held up a denuded hand and stared at it. 'Oh, now, will you look at that?' He peered down at the floor, with a hope that was quickly dashed. 'Blast. Any chance we can make her throw up?'

'Only by sticking your fingers down her throat, Reg. Sorry. Buggy, do the best you can, please. And you, Reg, go back downstairs and see if they've got any coffee, will you?'

'Oh dear,' murmured Shufti.

'It's big,' said Tonker.

Blouse said nothing.

'Not seen it before, sir?' said Jackrum cheerfully, as they stared at the distant keep from where they lay in some bushes half a mile away.

If there is a fairy-tale scale for castles, where the top end is occupied by those white, spire-encrusted castles with the blue pointy roofs, then Kneck Keep was low, black and clung to its outcrop like a storm cloud. A bed of the Kneck ran round it; along the peninsula on which it was built the approach road was wide and bereft of cover and an ideal stroll for those who were tired of life. Blouse took all this in.

'Er, no, sergeant,' he said. 'I've seen pictures, of course, but . . . they don't do it justice.'

'Any of them books you read tell you what to do, sir?' said Jackrum. They were lying in some bushes half a mile away.

'Possibly, sergeant. In *The Craft of War*, Song Sung Lo said: to win without fighting is the greatest victory. The enemy wishes us to attack where he is strongest. Therefore, we will disappoint him. A way will present itself, sergeant.'

'Well, it's never presented itself to me, and I've been here dozens of times,' said Jackrum, still grinning. 'Hah, even the rats'd have to disguise themselves as washerwomen to get in *that* place! Even if you get up that road, you've got narrow entrances, holes in the ceiling to pour hot oil through, gates everywhere that a troll couldn't smash through, coupla mazes, a hundred little ways you can be shot at. Oh, it's a wonderful place to attack.'

'I wonder how the alliance got in?' said Blouse.

'Treachery, probably, sir. The world's full of traitors. Or perhaps they discovered the secret entrance, sir. You know, sir? The one you're sure is there. Or p'raps you've forgotten? It's the sort of thing that can slip your mind when you're busy, I expect.'

'We shall reconnoitre, sergeant,' said Blouse coldly, as they crawled out of the bushes. He brushed leaves off his uniform. Thalacephalos or, as Blouse referred to her, 'the faithful steed' had been turned loose miles back. You couldn't sneak on horseback and, as Jackrum had pointed out, the creature was too skinny

for anyone to want to eat and too vicious for anyone to want to ride.

'Right, sir, yes, we might as well do that, sir,' said Jackrum now, all gloating helpfulness. 'Where would you like us to reconnoitre, sir?'

'There must *be* a secret entrance, sergeant. No one would build a place like that with only one entrance. Agreed?'

'Yessir. Only, perhaps they kept it a secret, sir. Only trying to help, sir.'

They turned at the sound of urgent praying. Wazzer had fallen to her knees, hands clasped together. The rest of the squad edged away slowly. Piety is a wonderful thing.

'What is he doing, sergeant?' said Blouse.

'Praying, sir,' said Jackrum.

'I've noticed he does it a lot. Is that, er, within regulations, sergeant?' the lieutenant whispered.

'Always a difficult one, sir, that one,' said Jackrum. 'I have, myself, prayed many times on the field of battle. Many times have I said the Soldier's Prayer, sir, and I don't mind admitting it.'

'Er . . . I don't think I know that one,' said Blouse.

'Oh, I reckon the words'll come to you soon enough, sir, once you're up against the foe. Gen'rally, though, they're on the lines of "O god, let me kill this bastard before he kills me".' Jackrum grinned at Blouse's expression. 'That's what I call the Authorized Version, sir.'

'Yes, sergeant, but where would we be if we all prayed all the time?' said the lieutenant.

'In heaven, sir, sitting at Nuggan's right hand,' said Jackrum promptly. 'That's what I was taught as a little nipper, sir. Of course, it'd be a bit crowded, so it's just as well we don't.'

At which point, Wazzer stopped praying and stood up, brushing dust off her knees. She gave the squad her bright, worrying smile. 'The Duchess will guide our steps,' she said.

'Oh. Good,' said Blouse weakly.

'She will show us the way.'

'Wonderful. Er . . . did she mention a map reference at all?' said the lieutenant.

'She will give us eyes that we might see.'

'Ah? Good. Well, jolly good,' said Blouse. 'I definitely feel a lot better for knowing that. Don't you, sergeant?'

'Yessir,' said Jackrum. ''cos before this, sir, we didn't *have* a prayer.'

They scouted in threes, while the rest of the squad lay up in a deep hollow among the bushes. There were enemy patrols, but it's not hard to avoid half a dozen men who stick to the tracks and aren't being careful not to make a noise. The troops were Zlobenian, and acted as though they owned the place.

For some reason Polly ended up patrolling with Maladict and Wazzer or, to put it another way, a vampire on the edge and a girl who was possibly so far over it that she'd found a new edge out beyond the horizon. She was changing every day, that was a fact. On the day they'd all joined up, a

lifetime ago, she'd been this shivering little waif who flinched at shadows. Now, sometimes, she seemed taller, full of some ethereal certainty, and shadows fled before her. Well, not in actual fact, Polly would admit. But she walked as if they should.

And then there had been the Miracle of the Turkey. That was hard to explain.

The three of them had been moving along the cliffs. They'd circled a couple of Zlobenian lookout posts, forewarned by the smell of cooking-fires but, alas, not by the smell of any coffee. Maladict seemed to be mostly in control, except for a tendency to mutter to himself in letters and numbers, but Polly had stopped that by threatening to hit him with a stick the very next time he did it.

They'd reached a cliff edge that gave yet another view of the keep, and once again Polly raised the telescope and scanned the sheer walls and jumbled rocks for any sign of another entrance.

'Look down at the river,' said Wazzer.

The circle of view blurred upwards as Polly shifted the scope; when it stopped moving she saw whiteness. She had to lower the instrument to see what she'd been looking at.

'Oh my,' she said.

'Makes sense, though,' said Maladict. 'And there's a path all along the river, see? There's a couple more women on it.'

'Tiny gateway, though,' said Polly. 'And it'd be so easy to search people for weapons.'

'Soldiers couldn't get through, them,' said the vampire.

'We could,' said Polly. 'And *we're* soldiers. Aren't we?'

There was a pause before Maladict said: 'Soldiers need *weapons*. Swords and crossbows get noticed.'

'There will be weapons inside,' said Wazzer. 'The Duchess has told me. The castle is *full* of weapons.'

'Did she tell you how to make the enemy let go of them?' said Maladict.

'All right, all right,' said Polly quickly. 'We ought to tell the rupert as soon as possible, okay? Let's get back.'

'Hold on, I'm the corporal,' said Maladict.

'Well?' said Polly. 'And?'

'Let's get back?' said Maladict.

'Good idea.'

She should have listened to the birdsong, she realized later. The shrill calls in the distance would have told her the news, if only she'd been calm enough to listen.

They hadn't gone more than thirty yards before they saw the soldier.

Someone in the Zlobenian army was dangerously clever. He'd realized that the way to spot interlopers was not to march noisily along the beaten paths, but to sneak quietly between the trees.

The soldier had a crossbow; it was sheer luck ... *probably* sheer luck that he was looking the other way when Polly came round a holly bush. She flung herself behind a tree and gestured madly at Maladict further

down the path, who had the sense to take cover.

Polly drew her sword and held it clutched to her chest in both hands. She could hear the man. He was some way away, but he was moving towards her. Probably the little lookout they had just found was a regular point on the patrol route. After all, she thought bitterly, it was just the sort of thing some untrained idiots might come across; maybe a quiet patrol could even surprise them there . . .

She shut her eyes and tried to breathe normally. This was it *this was it* this was it! This was where she found out.

What to remember *what to remember* what to remember . . . when the metal meets the meat . . . be holding the metal.

She could *taste* metal in her mouth.

The man would walk right past her. He'd be alert, but not *that* alert. A slash would be better than a stab. Yes, a good swipe at head height would kill . . .

. . . *some mother's son, some sister's brother, some lad who'd followed the drum for a shilling and his first new suit. If only she'd been trained, if only she'd had a few weeks stabbing straw men until she could believe that all men were made of straw . . .*

She froze. Down the angle of the path, still as a tree, head bowed, stood Wazzer. As soon as the scout reached Polly's tree, she'd be seen.

She'd have to do it now. Perhaps that's why men did it. You didn't do it to save duchesses, or countries. You killed the enemy to stop him killing

your mates, that they in turn might save you . . .

She could hear the cautious tread close to the tree. She raised the sabre, saw the light flash along its edge—

A wild turkey rose from the scrub on the other side of the path in one rocketing tower of wings and feathers and echoing noise. Half flying, half running, it bounded off into the woods. There was the thud of a bow and a last squawk.

'Oh, good shot, Woody,' said a voice near by. 'Looks like a big 'un!'

'Did you see *that*?' said another voice. 'Another step and I'd have tripped over it!'

Behind her tree, Polly breathed out.

A third voice, some way off, called out: 'Let's head back, eh, corp? The way that went off, the Tiger's probably run a mile!'

'Yeah, and I'm so scared,' said the closest voice. 'The Tiger's behind every tree, right?'

'Okay, let's call it a day. My wife'll cook him a treat—'

Gradually, the voices of the soldiers got lost amongst the trees. Polly lowered the sword. She saw Maladict peer out of his bush and stare at her. She raised a finger to her lips. He nodded. She waited until the birdsong had settled down a little before stepping out. Wazzer seemed to be lost in thought; Polly took her very carefully by the hand. Quietly, dodging from tree to tree, they headed back to the hollow. Most particularly, Polly and Maladict didn't talk. But they looked one another in the eye once or twice.

Of course a turkey would lie low until a hunter almost trod on it. Of course that one must've been there all the time, and only lost its bird nerve when the scout crept up. It had been an unusually large bird, one that no hungry soldier could resist, but . . . well?

Because the brain treacherously does not stop thinking just because you want it to, Polly's added: she said the Duchess could move small things. How small is a thought in the mind of a bird?

Only Jade and Igorina were waiting for them in the hollow. The others had found a better base a mile away, they said.

'We found the secret entrance,' said Polly quietly, as they headed away.

'Can we get in?' said Igorina.

'It's the washerwomen's entrance,' said Maladict. 'It's right down by the river. But there's a path.'

'Washerwomen?' said Igorina. 'But this is a *war*!'

'Clothes still get dirty, I suppose,' said Polly.

'Dirtier, I should think,' said Maladict.

'But . . . our countrywomen? Washing clothes for the enemy?' said Igorina, looking shocked.

'If it's that or starve, yes,' said Polly. 'I saw a woman come out carrying a basket of loaves. They say the keep is full of granaries. Anyway, you sewed up an enemy officer, didn't you?'

'That's different,' said Igorina. 'We are duty bound to thave our fellow ma— person. Nothing has ever been said about his— their underwear.'

'We could get in,' said Polly, 'if we disguised ourselves as women.'

Silence greeted this. Then: 'Disguised?' said Igorina.

'You know what I mean!' said Polly.

'*As washerwomen?*' said Igorina. 'These are *thurgeon's* hands!'

'Really? Where did you get them?' said Maladict. Igorina stuck out her tongue at him.

'Anyway, I don't intend that we should do any washing,' said Polly.

'Then what *do* you intend?' said Igorina.

Polly hesitated. 'I want to get my brother out if he's in there,' she said. 'And if we could stop the invasion that would be a good idea.'

'That might take extra starch,' said Maladict. 'I don't want to, you know, spoil the spirit of the moment, but that is a really awful idea. The el-tee won't agree to something as wild as that.'

'No, he won't,' said Polly. 'But he'll suggest it.'

'Hmm,' said Blouse, a little later. 'Washerwomen? Is that *usual*, Sergeant Jackrum?'

'Oh, yes, sir. I expect the women in the villages round here do it, just like they did when we held the keep,' said Jackrum.

'You mean they give aid and comfort to the enemy? Why?'

'Better than starving, sir. Fact of life. It doesn't always stop at washing, neither.'

'Sergeant, there are young men here!' snapped Blouse, blushing.

'They'll have to find out about ironing and darning sooner or later, sir,' said Jackrum, grinning.

Blouse opened his mouth. Blouse shut his mouth.

'Tea's up, sir,' said Polly. Tea was an amazingly useful thing. It gave you an excuse to talk to anyone.

They were in what remained of a half-ruined farmhouse. By the look of it, not even patrols bothered to come here – there were no signs of former fires or even the most temporary occupation. It stank of decay and half the roof was gone.

'Do the women just come and go, Perks?' said the lieutenant.

'Yes, sir,' said Polly. 'And I had an idea, sir. Permission to tell you my idea, sir?' She saw Jackrum raise an eyebrow. She was laying it on thick, she had to admit, but time was pressing.

'Please do, Perks,' said Blouse. 'Else I fear you may explode.'

'They could be spies for us, sir! We could even get them to open the gates for us!'

'Well done, private!' said Blouse. 'I do like a soldier to think.'

'Yeah, right,' growled Jackrum. 'Any sharper an' he'll cut hisself. Sir, they're *washerwomen*, sir, basically. No offence to young Perks, keen lad that he is, but your average guard pays attention when Old Mother Riley tries to open the gates. There's not just a pair of gates, neither. There's *six* pairs, and nice little courtyards between 'em for the guards to have a squint at you to see if you's a wrong 'un, and drawbridges, and spiky ceilings that drop down if someone doesn't like

the look of you. Try opening *that* lot with soapy hands!'

'I'm afraid the sergeant has a point, Perks,' said Blouse sadly.

'Well, supposing a couple of women managed to knock out a few guards, sir, they could let us in through their little door,' said Polly. 'We might even be able to capture the commander of the fort, sir! I bet there's plenty of women in the keep, sir. In the kitchens and so on. They could . . . open doors for us!'

'Oh, come on, Perks—' Jackrum began.

'No, sergeant. Wait,' said Blouse. 'Astonishingly enough, Perks, in your boyish enthusiasm you have, although you haven't realized it, given me a very interesting idea . . .'

'Have I, sir?' said Polly, who in her boyish enthusiasm had considered trying to tattoo the idea on Blouse's head. For someone so clever, he really was slow.

'Indeed you have, Perks,' said Blouse. 'Because, of course, we only need one "washerwoman" to get us inside, do we not?'

The inverted commas sounded promising. 'Well, yes, sir,' said Polly.

'And, if one as it were thinks "outside the box", the "woman" does not in fact *need* to be a woman!'

Blouse beamed. Polly allowed her brow to wrinkle in honest puzzlement.

'Doesn't she, sir?' she said. 'I don't think I quite understand, sir. I am perplexed, sir.'

' "She" could be a man, Perks!' said Blouse, almost

exploding with delight. 'One of us! In disguise!'

Polly breathed a sigh of relief. Sergeant Jackrum laughed.

'Lord bless you, sir, dressing up as washerwomen is for gettin' *out* of places! Milit'ry rules!'

'If a man gets inside, he could disable any guards near the door, spy out the situation from a military perspective, and let the rest of the troops in!' said Blouse. 'If this was done at night, men, we could be holding key positions by the morning!'

'But these aren't men, sir,' said Jackrum. Polly turned. The sergeant was looking right at her, right *through* her. *Oh darn, I mean damn . . . he knows . . .*

'I beg your pardon?'

'They are . . . my little lads, sir,' Jackrum went on, winking at Polly. 'Keen lads, full of mustard, but they ain't ones for cuttin' throats and stabbin' hearts. They signed up to be pikemen in the press, sir, in a proper army. You are my little lads, I says to 'em when I signed 'em up, and I *will* look after you. I can't stand by and let you take 'em to certain death!'

'It's my decision to make, sergeant,' said Blouse. 'We are at "the hinge of destiny". Who, in the pinch, is not ready to lay down his life for his country?'

'In a proper stand-up fight, sir, not getting beaten over the head by a bunch of nasty men for creeping around their fort. You know I've never been one for spies an' hidin' your colours, sir, never.'

'Sergeant, we have no choice. We must take advantage of the "tide of fortune".'

'I know about tides, sir. They leave little fish

gaspin".' The sergeant stood up, fists clenching.

'Your concern for your men does you credit, sergeant, but it falls to us—'

'A famous last stand, sir?' said Jackrum. He spat expertly into the fire in the tumbledown hearth. 'To hell with them, sir. That's just a way of dyin' famous!'

'Sergeant, your insubordination is getting—'

'I'll go,' said Polly quietly.

Both men stopped, turned and stared.

'I'll go,' Polly repeated, louder. 'Someone ought to.'

'Don't be daft, Perks!' snapped Jackrum. 'You don't know what's in there, you don't know what guards are waitin' just inside the door, you don't know—'

'I'll find out, then, sarge, won't I,' said Polly, smiling desperately. 'Maybe I can get to somewhere where you can see and send signals, or——'

'On this issue, at least, the sergeant and I are of one mind, Perks,' said Blouse. 'Really, private, it would simply not work. Oh, you're brave, certainly, but what makes *you* think you stand a chance of passing yourself off as a woman?'

'Well, sir . . . *what*?'

'Your keenness will not go unrecorded, Perks,' said Blouse, smiling. 'But, y'know, a good officer keeps an eye on his men and I have to say that I've noticed in you, in *all* of you, little . . . habits, perfectly normal, nothing to worry about, like the occasional deep exploration of a nostril maybe, and a tendency to grin after passing wind, a natural boyish inclination to, ahem, scratch your . . . selves in public . . . that sort of thing. These are the kind of little details that'd give

you away in a trice and tell any observer that you were a man in women's clothing, believe me.'

'I'm sure I could pull it off, sir,' said Polly weakly. She could sense Jackrum's eyes on her. *You bloomi— you bloody well know, don't you! How long have you known?*

Blouse shook his head. 'No, they would see through you in a flash. You are a fine bunch of lads, but there is only one man here who'd stand a chance of getting away with it. Manickle?'

'Yessir?' said Shufti, rigid with instant panic.

'Can you find me a dress, do you think?'

Maladict was the first to break the silence. 'Sir, are you telling us . . . *you're* going to try to get in dressed as a woman?'

'Well, I'm clearly the only one who's had any practice,' said Blouse, rubbing his hands together. 'At my old school, we were in and out of skirts all the time.' He looked around at the circle of absolutely expressionless faces. 'Theatricals, you see?' he said brightly. 'No gels at our boarding school, of course. But we didn't let *that* stop us. Why, my Lady Spritely in *A Comedy of Cuckolds* is still talked about, I understand, and as for my Yumyum— Is Sergeant Jackrum all right?'

The sergeant had folded up, but with his face level with his knees he managed to croak: 'Old war wound, sir. Come upon me sudden, like.'

'Please help him, Private Igor. Where was I . . . I can see you all look puzzled, but there's nothing *strange* about this. Fine old tradition, men dressing up as gels.

In the sixth form, the chaps used to do it for a jape all the time.' He paused for a moment, and added thoughtfully, 'Especially Wrigglesworth, for some reason . . .' He shook his head as if dislodging a thought and went on: 'Anyway, I have some experience in this field, d'ye see?'

'And . . . what would you do if— I mean *when* you got in, sir?' said Polly. 'You won't just have to fool the guards. There'll be other women in there.'

'That will not present a problem, Perks,' said Blouse. 'I shall act in a feminine way and I have this stage trick, d'ye see, where I make my voice sound *quite high-pitched, like this*.' The falsetto could have scratched glass. 'See?' he said. 'No, if we need a woman, I'm your man.'

'Amazing, sir,' said Maladict. 'For a moment I could have sworn there was a woman in the room.'

'And I could certainly find out if there are any other badly guarded entrances,' Blouse went on. 'Who knows, I might even be able to procure a key off one of the guards by means of feminine wiles! In any case, if things are all clear I shall send a signal. A towel hanging from a window, perhaps. Something clearly unusual, anyway.'

There was some more silence. Several of the squad were staring at the ceiling.

'Ye-es,' said Polly. 'I can see you've thought this out carefully, sir.'

Blouse sighed. 'If only Wrigglesworth were here,' he said.

'Why, sir?'

'Amazingly clever chap at layin' his hands on a dress, young Wrigglesworth,' said the lieutenant.

Polly caught Maladict's eye. The vampire made a face and shrugged.

'Um . . .' said Shufti.

'Yes, Manickle?'

'I do have a petticoat in my pack, sir.'

'Good heavens! Why?'

Shufti went red. She hadn't worked out an answer.

'Bandageth, thur,' Igorina cut in smoothly.

'Yes! Yes! That's right!' said Shufti. 'I . . . found it in the inn, back in Plün . . .'

'I athked the lads to acquire any thuitable linen they might find, thur. Jutht in cathe.'

'Very sound thinking, that man!' said Blouse. 'Anyone else got anything?'

'I wouldn't be at all thurprithed, thur,' said Igorina, staring round the room.

Glances were exchanged. Packs were unslung. Everyone except Polly and Maladict had *something*, produced with downcast eyes. A shift, a petticoat and, in most cases, a dimity scarf, carried out of some sort of residual, unexplainable need.

'You obviously must've thought we'd take serious damage,' said Blouse.

'Can't be too careful, thur,' said Igorina. She grinned at Polly.

'Of course, I have rather short hair at present . . .' Blouse mused.

Polly thought of her ringlets, now lost and

probably stroked by Strappi. But desperation spooled through her memory.

'They looked like older women, mostly,' she said quickly. 'They wore headscarves and wimples. I'm sure Igori— sure Igor can make up something, sir.'

'We Igorth are very rethortheful, thur,' Igorina agreed. She pulled a black leather wallet out of her jacket. 'Ten minuteth with a needle, thur, that'th all I need.'

'Oh, I can do *old* women wonderfully well,' said Blouse. With a speed that made Lofty jump, he suddenly thrust out both hands twisted like claws, contorted his face into an expression of mad imbecility and screeched, 'Oh deary me! My poor old feet! Things today aren't what they used to be! Lawks!'

Behind him, Sergeant Jackrum put his head in his hands.

'Amazing, sir,' said Maladict. 'I've never seen a transformation like it!'

'Perhaps just a wee bit less old, sir?' Polly suggested, although in truth Blouse had reminded her of her Auntie Hattie two-thirds of the way through a glass of sherry.

'You think so?' said Blouse. 'Oh, well, if you're really sure.'

'And, er, if you *do* meet a guard, er, old women don't usually try to, try to—'

'—canoodle—' whispered Maladict, whose mind had clearly been hurtling down the same horrible slope.

'—canoodle with them,' Polly finished, blushing, and then after a second's thought added, 'Unless she's had a glass of sherry, anyway.'

'And I do thuggetht you go and have a thhave, thur . . .'

'Thhave?' said Blouse.

'Shave, sir,' said Polly. 'I'll lay out the kit, sir.'

'Ooh, yes. Of course. Don't see many old women with beards, eh? Except my Auntie Parthenope, as I recall. And . . . er . . . no one's got a couple of balloons, have they?'

'Er, why, sir?' said Tonker.

'A big bosom always gets a laugh,' said Blouse. He looked round the row of faces. 'Not a good idea, perhaps? I got a huge round of applause as the Widow Trembler in *'Tis Pity She's A Tree*. No?'

'I think Igor could sew something a bit more, er, realistic, sir,' said Polly.

'Really? Oh, well, if you really think so . . .' said Blouse dejectedly. 'I'll just go and get myself into character.'

He disappeared into the building's only other room. After a few seconds, the rest of them heard him reciting 'Lawks, my poor feet!' in varying tones of fingernail screech.

The squad went into a huddle.

'What was all *that* about?' said Tonker.

'He was talking about the theatre,' said Maladict.

'What's that?'

'An Abomination unto Nuggan, of course,' said the vampire. 'It'd take too long to explain, dear child.

People pretending to be other people to tell a story in a huge room where the world is a different place. Other people sitting and watching them and eating chocolate. Very, very abominable.'

'I saw a Punch and Judy show in the town once,' said Shufti. 'Then they dragged the man away and it became an Abomination.'

'I remember that,' said Polly. Crocodiles should not be seen to eat figures of authority, apparently, although until the puppet show no one in the town knew what a crocodile was. The bit where the clown had beaten his wife had also constituted an Abomination, because he'd used a stick thicker than the regulation one inch.

'The lieutenant won't last a minute, you know,' she said.

'Yes, but he won't lithten, will he?' said Igorina. 'I'll do my betht with my scissorth and needle to make a woman of him, but—'

'Igorina, when it's *you* talking about this sort of thing some very strange pictures turn up in my head,' said Maladict.

'Sorry,' said Igorina

'Can you pray for him, Wazzer?' said Polly. 'I think we're going to need a miracle here.'

Wazzer obediently closed her eyes and folded her hands for a moment and then said shyly: 'I'm afraid she says it will take more than a turkey.'

'Wazz?' said Polly. 'Do you really—' Then she stopped, with the bright little face watching her.

'Yes, I do,' said Wazzer. 'I really talk to the Duchess.'

'Yeah, well, I used to, too,' snapped Tonker. 'I used to beg her, once. That stupid face just stared and did nothing. She never *stopped* anything. All that stuff, all that stupid—' The girl stopped, too many words blocking her brain. 'Anyway, why should she talk to *you*?'

'Because I listen,' said Wazzer quietly.

'And what does she say?'

'Sometimes she just cries.'

'*She* cries?'

'Because there are so many things that people want, and she can't give them anything.' Wazzer gave them all one of her smiles that lit up the room. 'But everything will be fine when I am in the right place,' she said.

'Well, that's all right, then—' Polly began, in that cloud of deep embarrassment that Wazzer called up within her.

'Yeah, right,' said Tonker. 'But I'm not praying to anyone, okay? Ever again. I don't like this, Wazz. You're a decent kid, but I don't like the way you smile—' She stopped. 'Oh, no . . .'

Polly stared at Wazzer. Her face was thin and all angles, and the Duchess in the painting had looked, well, like an overfed turbot, but now the smile, the actual *smile* . . .

'I'm not putting up with that!' Tonker snarled. 'You stop that right now! I mean it! You're giving me the creeps! Ozz, you stop her— him smiling like that!'

'Just calm down, all of you—' Polly began.

'Bleedin' well shut up!' said Jackrum. 'A man can't hear himself chew. Look, you're all edgy. That happens. And Wazzer here's just got a bit of religion before the fight. That happens, too. And what you do is, you save it all up for the enemy. Quieten down. That is what we in the milit'ry call an order, okay?'

'Perks?' It was Blouse.

'You'd better hurry,' said Maladict. 'His corset probably wants lacing . . .'

In fact Blouse was sitting on what remained of a chair.

'Ah, Perks. A shave, please,' he said.

'Oh, I thought your hand was better, sir . . .'

'Er . . . yes.' Blouse looked awkward. 'The problem, Perks, is . . . I have never actually shaved myself at all, to be honest. I had a man to do it for me at school, and then of course in the army I shared a batman with Blitherskite and, er, those attempts I made on my own behalf have been somewhat bloody. I never really thought about it until I got to Plotz and, er . . . suddenly it was embarrassing . . .'

'Sorry about that, sir,' said Polly. It was a strange old world.

'Later on perhaps you could give me a few tips,' Blouse went on. 'You keep yourself beautifully shaven, I can't help noticing. General Froc would be pleased. He's very anti-whiskers, they say.'

'If you like, sir,' said Polly. There was no getting out of it. She made a show of sharpening the razor. Perhaps she could manage it with only a few small cuts . . .

'Do you think I should have a reddened nose?' said Blouse.

'Probably, sir,' said Polly. *Sarge knows about me, I'm sure,* she thought. *I know he does. Why's he keeping quiet?*

'Probably, Perks?'

'What? Oh. No . . . why a red nose, sir?' said Polly, applying the lather with vigour.

'It would look more *pff* amusing, perhaps.'

'Not sure that's the purpose of the exercise, sir. Now, if you'd just, er, lie back, sir—'

'*There's something you should know about young Perks, sir.*'

Polly actually yelped. Walking as silently as only a sergeant can, Jackrum had stolen into the room.

'*pff* Sergeant?' said Blouse.

'Perks doesn't know how to shave a man, sir,' said Jackrum. 'Give me the razor, Perks.'

'Doesn't know how to shave?' said Blouse.

'Nosir. Perks lied to us, right, Perks?'

'All right, sarge, no need to drag it out,' sighed Polly. 'Lieutenant, I'm—'

'—under age,' said Jackrum. 'Right, Perks? Only fourteen, aren't you?' He looked at Polly over the top of the lieutenant's head, and winked.

'Er . . . I told a lie to get enlisted, sir, yes,' said Polly.

'I don't think a lad like that ought to be dragged into the keep, however game he is,' said Jackrum. 'And I don't think he's the only one. Right, Perks?'

Oh, so that's the game. Blackmail, Polly thought.

'Yes, sarge,' she said wearily.

'Can't have a massacre of little lads, sir, now can we?' said Jackrum.

'I see your *pff* point, sergeant,' said the lieutenant, as Jackrum gently drove the blade down his cheek. 'That is a tricky one.'

'Best to call it a day, then?' said Jackrum.

'On the other hand, sergeant, I do know that you *pff* yourself joined up as a child,' said Blouse. The blade stopped moving.

'Well, it was all different in those—' Jackrum began.

'You were five years old, apparently,' the lieutenant went on. 'You see, when I heard that I would be meeting you, a legend in the army, of course I had a look at our files so that I could, perhaps, make a few timely jokes in presenting you with your honourable discharge. You know, humorous little reminiscences about times gone by? Imagine how puzzled I was, therefore, to find that you appear to have been drawing actual wages for, well, it was a little hard to be certain, but possibly as much as sixty years.'

Polly had put a keen edge on the razor. It rested against the lieutenant's cheek. Polly thought about the murder – oh, all right, the killing of an escaping prisoner – in the wood. *It won't be the first officer I've killed* . . .

'Probably one of them clerical errors, sir,' said Jackrum coldly. In the gloomy room, with moss now colonizing the walls, the sergeant loomed large.

An owl, perched on the chimney, gave a screech. It echoed down into the room.

'In fact no, sergeant,' said Blouse, apparently oblivious of the razor. 'Your package, sergeant, had been tampered with. On numerous occasions. Once, even by General Froc. He deducted ten years from your age and signed the change. And he wasn't the only one. Frankly, sergeant, I'm forced to only one conclusion.'

'And what's that, sir?' The razor halted again, still pressed against Blouse's neck. The silence seemed to last for some time, sharp and drawn out.

'That there was some other man called Jackrum,' said Blouse slowly, 'whose records have . . . got mixed up with yours and . . . every attempt to sort it out by officers who were, er, not entirely at home with figures only made it more confusing.'

The razor started to move again, with silky smoothness. 'I think you've put your finger right on it, sir,' said Jackrum.

'I am going to write an explanatory note and add it to the packet,' Blouse went on. 'It seems to me the sensible thing to do would be to ask you here and now how old you are. How old *are* you, sergeant?'

'Forty-three, sir,' said Jackrum instantly. Polly looked up, expecting the generic thunderclap that ought to accompany such a universe-sized untruth.

'Are you sure?' said Blouse.

'Forty-five, sir. The hardships of a soldier's life show up onna face, sir.'

'Even so—'

'Ah, I recall a couple of extra birthdays what had slipped my memory, sir. I'm forty-seven, sir.'

Still no rumble of celestial disapproval, Polly noticed.

'Er . . . yes. Very well. After all, you should know, eh, sergeant? I shall amend it.'

'Thank you, sir.'

'Just like General Froc did. And Major Galosh. And Colonel Legin, sergeant.'

'Yessir. Clerical error has followed me around all the days of my life, sir. I've been a martyr to it.' Jackrum stood back. 'There we are, sir. Face as smooth as a baby's bum. Smooth is how things should be, eh, sir? I've always liked things smooth.'

They watched Lieutenant Blouse walk down through the trees to the path. They watched him join the erratic, straggling line of women on their way to the door. They listened for screams, and heard none.

'D-does *any* woman sway that much?' said Wazzer, peering through the bushes.

'Not legally, I think,' said Polly, scanning the keep with the lieutenant's telescope. 'Well, we'll just have to wait for some sort of signal that he's okay.'

Somewhere overhead, a buzzard screamed.

'No, they'll have got him the moment he walked through the door,' said Maladict. 'Bet on it.'

They left Jade on watch. With her paint scraped off, a troll could settle into rocky scenery so well that no one was likely to notice her before they walked into her, and by the time they'd walked into her it was too late.

They made their way back through the woods, and

had almost reached the ruined farmhouse when *it* happened.

'You are holding up well, Mal,' said Polly. 'Maybe those acorns did the trick? You haven't mentioned coffee at all—'

Maladict stopped, and turned slowly. To Polly's horror, his face was suddenly shiny with sweat. 'You had to bring it up, didn't you?' he said hoarsely. 'Oh, please, no! I was holding on so tight! I was doing so well!' He fell forward, but managed to get on to his hands and knees. Then he raised his head, and his eyes were glowing red. 'Fetch . . . Igorina,' he muttered, gasping. 'I *know* she's ready for this . . .'

. . . *whopwhopwhop* . . .

Wazzer was praying furiously. Maladict tried to stand up again, fell back on to his knees, and raised his arms imploringly to the sky.

'Get out of here while you can,' he mumbled, as his teeth visibly lengthened. 'I'll—'

There was a shadow, a sense of movement, and the vampire slumped forward, stunned by an eight-ounce sack of coffee beans that had dropped out of a clear sky.

Polly arrived at the farmhouse carrying Maladict on her shoulder. She made him as comfortable as possible on some ancient straw, and the squad consulted.

'Do you think we ought to try to take the sack out of his mouth?' said Shufti nervously.

'I tried, but he fights,' said Polly.

'But he's unconscious!'

'He still won't let go of it! He's *sucking* it. I'd swear he was out cold, but he just sort of reached out and grabbed it and bit! It dropped out of a clear sky!'

Tonker stared at Wazzer. 'The Duchess does room service?' she said.

'No! She says she d-didn't!'

'You get freak rainth of fish,' said Igorina, kneeling down by Maladict. 'I suppose it's possible that a whirlwind tore through a coffee plantation, and then possibly a lightning discharge in the upper ether—'

'At what point did it blow through a factory making small coffee sacks?' said Tonker. 'Ones with a jolly turbaned man printed on them apparently saying "Klatchian Rare Roasted! When a Pickaxe is Not Enough!"'

'Well, if you're going to put it like that, it does theem a little far-fetched . . .' Igorina stood up, adding, 'I think he'll be fine when he wakes up. Possibly a little talkative, though.'

'Okay, lads, get some rest,' said Jackrum, coming in. 'Let's give the rupert a couple of hours to muck things up, and then we can nip around the valley and slip down and join the rest of the army. Good grub and proper blankets to sleep on, hey? That's the ticket!'

'We don't know he's going to mess up, sarge,' said Polly.

'Oh, yeah, right, maybe he'll have married the commander of the garrison by now, eh? Stranger things have happened, although I can't remember

when. Perks and Manickle, you're on watch. The rest of you, get some shut-eye.'

A Zlobenian patrol went past in the distance. Polly watched it out of sight. It was turning into a fine day, warm with a bit of wind. Good drying weather. A good day to be a washerwoman. And maybe Blouse would succeed. Maybe all the guards were blind.

'Pol?' Shufti whispered.

'Yes, Shuf . . . Look, what was your name back in the world?'

'Betty. It's Betty. Er . . . most of the Ins-and-Outs are in the keep, right?'

'Apparently.'

'So that's where I'm most likely to find my fiancé, yes?'

We've talked about that, Polly thought. 'Could be.'

'Might be quite hard if there's a lot of men . . .' said Betty, a woman with something on her mind.

'Well, *if* we get as far as the prisoners and ask around they'll be bound to know his name. What is it?'

'Johnny,' whispered Betty.

'Just Johnny?' said Polly.

'Er . . . yes . . .'

Ah, Polly thought. I think I know how this goes . . .

'He's got fair hair and blue eyes, and I think he had one gold earring, and . . . and a funny-shaped . . . what d'you call it? Oh, yes . . . sort of carbuncle on his, his . . . bottom.'

'Right. Right.'

'Um . . . now I come to tell someone, it doesn't sound very helpful, I suppose.'

Not unless we're in a position to have a very unusual identity parade, Polly thought, and I can't imagine what position that would be.

'Not as such,' she said.

'He said everyone in the regiment knows him,' Betty went on.

'Right? Oh, good,' said Polly. 'All we need to do is ask.'

'And, er, we were going to break a sixpence in half, you know, like they do, so that if he had to be away for years we'd be sure we'd got the right person 'cos the two halves would match . . .'

'Oh, that would be a bit of a help, I expect.'

'Well, yes, except, well, I gave him the sixpence, and he said he'd get the blacksmith to break it in his vice, and he went off and, er, I think he got called away . . .' Betty's voice trailed off.

Well, that was about what I expected, Polly thought.

'I expect you think I'm a silly girl,' mumbled Betty after a while.

'A foolish woman, perhaps,' said Polly, turning to watch the landscape intently.

'It was, you know, a whirlwind romance . . .'

'Sounds more like a hurricane to me,' said Polly, and Betty grinned.

'Yes, it was a bit like that,' she said.

Polly matched smile for smile. 'Betty, it's daft to talk about silly and foolish at a time like this,' she said.

'Where are we going to look for wisdom? To a god who hates jigsaws and the colour blue? A fossil government led by a picture? An army that thinks stubbornness is the same as courage? Compared to all that, all *you've* got wrong is timing!'

'I don't want to end up in the school, though,' said Betty. 'They took away a girl from our village and she was kicking and screaming—'

'Then fight them!' said Polly. 'You've got a sword now, haven't you? Fight back!' She saw the look of horror on Betty's face, and remembered that this wasn't Tonker she was talking to. 'Look, if we get out of this alive we'll talk to the colonel. He might be able to help.' After all, perhaps your boy really *was* called Johnny, she thought, perhaps he really *was* called away suddenly. Hope is a wonderful thing. She went on: 'If we get out of this there's going to be no school and no beatings. Not for you or any of us. Not if we've got brains. Not if we're smart.'

Betty was almost in tears, but she managed another smile. 'And Wazzer's talking to the Duchess, too. She'll fix things!'

Polly stared out at the bright, unchanging land-scape, empty except for a buzzard making wide circles in the forbidden blue. 'I'm not sure about that,' she said. 'But *someone* up there likes us.'

Twilight was brief at this time of year. There had been no sign from Blouse.

'I watched until I couldn't see,' said Jade, as they sat and watched Shufti make stew. 'Some of der women

dat came out was ones I saw goin' in dis mornin', too.'

'Are you sure?' said Jackrum.

'We might be fick, sarge,' said Jade, looking hurt, 'but trolls have great . . . er . . . vis-you-all ack-you-it-tee. More women was going in dis evenin', too.'

'Night shift,' said Tonker.

'Oh well, he tried,' said Jackrum. 'With any luck he's in a nice warm cell and they've found him a pair of long pants. Get your kit together, lads. We'll creep around and into our lines and you'll be snug in bed by midnight.'

Polly remembered what she'd said, hours ago, about fighting. You had to start somewhere. 'I want to try the keep again,' she said.

'You do, Perks, do you?' said Jackrum, with mock interest.

'My brother's in there.'

'Nice safe place for him, then.'

'He might be injured. I vote for the keep.'

'Vote?' said Jackrum. 'My word, that's a new one. Voting in the army? Who wants to get killed, lads, let's have a show of hands? Knock it off, Perks.'

'I'm going to try it, sarge!'

'You are not!'

'*Try and stop me!*' The words came out before she could stop them. And that's it, she thought, the shout heard round the world. No going back after *this*. I've run off the edge of the cliff and it's all downhill from here.

Jackrum's expression stayed blank for a second or two, and then he said, 'Anyone else *voting* for the keep?'

Polly looked at Shufti, who blushed.

But: 'We are,' said Tonker. Beside her, Lofty struck a match, and held it so that it flared. That was pretty much a speech from Lofty.

'Why, pray?' said Jackrum.

'We don't want to sit around in a swamp,' said Tonker. 'And we don't like being ordered around.'

'Should have thought of that before you joined an army, lad!'

'We aren't lads, sarge.'

'You are if I says you are!'

Well, it's not as though I wasn't expecting it, Polly thought. I've played this out enough times in my head. Here goes . . . 'All right, sarge,' she said. 'It's time to have it out, here and now.'

'Ooo, er,' said Jackrum theatrically, fishing his screwed-up paper of tobacco out of his pocket.

'What?'

Jackrum sat down on the remains of a wall. 'Just injecting a little sauciness into the conversation,' he said. 'Carry on, Perks. Have your say. I thought it'd come to this.'

'You know I'm a woman, sarge,' said Polly.

'Yup. I wouldn't trust you to shave cheese.'

The squad stared. Jackrum opened his big knife and examined the chewing tobacco as though it was the most interesting thing present.

'So . . . er . . . what are you going to do about it?' said Polly, feeling derailed.

'Dunno. Can't do anything, can I? You were born like it.'

'You didn't tell Blouse!' said Polly.

'Nope.'

Polly wanted to knock the wretched tobacco out of the sergeant's hand. Now that she had got over the surprise, there was something *offensive* about this lack of reaction. It was like someone opening a door just before your battering ram hit it; suddenly you were running through the building and not certain how to stop.

'Well, we're *all* women, sarge,' said Tonker. 'How about that?'

Jackrum sawed at the tobacco.

'So?' he said, still paying attention to the job in hand.

'What?' said Polly.

'Think no one else ever tried it? Think you're the only ones? Think your ol' sarge is deaf, blind and stupid? You could fool one another and anyone can fool a rupert, but you can't fool Jackrum. Weren't sure about Maladict and still ain't, because with a vampire, who knows? And not sure about you, Carborundum, because with a troll, who cares? No offence.'

'None taken,' rumbled Jade. She caught Polly's eye and shrugged.

'Not so good at reading the signs, not knowing many trolls,' said the sergeant. 'I had *you* down pat in the first minute, Ozz. Something in the eyes, I reckon. Like . . . you were watching to see how good you were.'

Oh *hell*, Polly thought. 'Er . . . do I have a pair of socks belonging to you?'

'Yep. Well washed, I might add.'

'You'll have them back right now!' said Polly, grabbing for her belt.

'In your own time, Perks, in your own time, no rush,' said Jackrum, raising a hand. 'Well washed, please.'

'*Why*, sarge?' said Tonker. 'Why didn't you give us away? You could've given us away any time!'

Jackrum slewed his wad from cheek to cheek and sat chewing for a while, staring at nothing.

'No, you ain't the first,' he said. 'I've seen a few. Mostly by themselves, always frightened . . . and mostly they didn't last long. But one or two of them were bonny soldiers, very bonny soldiers indeed. So I looked at you lot and I thought to myself, well now, I thought, I wonder how they'll do when they find out they're not alone? You know about lions?' They nodded. 'Well, the lion is a big ol' coward, mostly. If you want trouble, you want to tangle with the lioness. They're killers, and they hunt together. It's the same everywhere. If you want big grief, look to the ladies. Even with insects, right? There's a kind of beetle where *she* bites *his* head off right while he's exercisin' his conjugals, and that's what I call serious grief. On the other hand, from what I heard he carries on regardless, so maybe it's not the same for beetles.'

He looked around at their blank expressions. 'No?' he said. 'Well, maybe I thought, a whole bunch of girls all at once, that's . . . strange. Maybe there's a reason.' Polly saw him glance briefly at Wazzer. 'Anyway, I wasn't goin' to shame you all in front of a little toad like Strappi, and then there was all that business in

Plotz, and then, well, we was gallopin', as it were, caught up in things with no time to get off. You did well, lads. Very well. Shaped up like good 'uns.'

'I'm going into the keep,' said Polly.

'Oh, don't worry about the rupert,' said Jackrum. 'Probably he's enjoying a nice bowl of scubbo right now. He went to a school for young gentlemen, so prison will be just like old times.'

'We're still going, sarge. Sorry,' said Polly.

'Oh, don't say *sorry*, Perks, you were doing well up 'til then,' said Jackrum bitterly.

Shufti stood up. 'I'm going too,' she said. 'I think my . . . fiancé is in there.'

'I have to go,' said Wazzer. 'The Duchess guides my steps.'

'I'll go, then,' said Igorina. 'I'm probably going to be needed.'

'I shouldn't fink I could get by as a washerwoman,' rumbled Jade. 'I'll stay here and watch over Mal. Hah, if he's still after blood when he wakes up he's gonna have blunt teeth!'

They looked at one another in silence, embarrassed but defiant. Then there was the sound of someone clapping, slowly.

'Oh, very nice,' said Jackrum. 'A band of brothers, eh? Sorry . . . sisters. Oh dear, oh dear. Look, Blouse was a fool. It was prob'ly all them books. He read all that stuff about it being a noble thing to die for your country, I expect. I was never that keen on readin', but I *know* the job is making some other poor devil die for his.'

He slewed his black tobacco from side to side. 'I wanted you to be safe, lads. Down in the press of men, I reckoned I could get you through this, no matter how many friends the Prince has sent after you. I look at you lads, and I think: you poor boys, you don't know nothin' about war. What you goin' to *do*? Tonker, you are a crack shot, but after one shot who's backing you up while you reload? Perks, you know a trick or two, but the blokes in the castle will maybe know a trick or five. You're a good cook, Shufti; too bad it's going to be too hot in there. Will the Duchess turn aside arrows, Wazzer?'

'*Yes. She will.*'

'I hope you are right, my lad,' said Jackrum, giving the girl a long slow look. 'Pers'nally, I've found religion in battle is as much use as a chocolate helmet. You'll need more than a prayer if Prince Heinrich catches you, I might add.'

'We're going to try it, sarge,' said Polly. 'There's nothing for us in the army.'

'Will you come with us, sarge?' said Shufti.

'No, lad. Me as a washerwoman? I doubt it. Don't seem to have a skirt anywhere about me, for a start. Er . . . just one thing, lads. How are you going to get in?'

'In the morning. When we see the women going in again,' said Polly.

'Got it all planned, general? And you'll be dressed as women?'

'Er . . . we *are* women, sarge,' said Polly.

'Yes, lad. Technical detail. But you kitted out the rupert with all your little knick-knacks, didn't you?

What're you going to do, tell the guards you opened the wrong cupboard in the dark?'

Another embarrassed silence descended. Jackrum sighed. 'This ain't proper war,' he said. 'Still, I said I'd look after you. You are my little lads, I said.' His eyes gleamed. 'And you still are, even if the world's turned upside down. I'll just have to hope, Miss Perks, that you picked up a few tricks from ol' sarge, although I reckon you can think of a few of your own. And now I'd better get you kitted up, right?'

'Perhaps we could sneak in and steal something from the villages where the servants come from?' said Tonker.

'From a bunch of poor women?' said Polly, her heart sinking. 'Anyway, there'd be soldiers everywhere.'

'Well, how do we get women's clothes on a battle-field?' said Lofty.

Jackrum laughed, stood up, stuck his thumbs in his belt and grinned. 'I *told* you, lads, you don't know *nuffin'* about war!' he said.

. . . and one of the things they hadn't known was that it has edges.

Polly wasn't certain what she'd expected. Men and horses, obviously. In her mind's eye they were engaged in mortal combat, but you couldn't go on doing that all day. So there would be tents. And that was about as far as the mind's eye had seen. It hadn't seen that an army on campaign is a sort of large, portable city. It has only one employer, and it

manufactures dead people, but like all cities it attracts
... citizens. What was unnerving was the sound of
babies crying, off in the rows of tents. She hadn't
expected that. Or the mud. Or the *crowds*. Everywhere
there were fires, and the smell of cooking. This was a
siege, after all. People had settled in.

Getting down on to the plain in the dark had been
easy. There was only Polly and Shufti trailing after the
sergeant, who'd said that more would be too many
and in any case would show up. There were patrols,
but their edge had been dulled by sheer repetitiveness.
Besides, the allies weren't expecting anyone to make
much effort to get into the valley, at least in small
groups. And men in the dark make a noise, far more
noise than a woman. They'd located a Borogravian
sentry in the gloom by the noise of him trying to suck a
morsel of dinner out of his teeth. But another one had
located them when they were a stone's throw from the
tents. He was young, so he was still keen.

'Halt! Who goes there? Friend or foe!' The light
from a cooking-fire glinted off a crossbow.

'See?' whispered Jackrum. 'This is where your
uniform is your friend. Aren't you glad you kept
it?'

He swaggered forward, and spat tobacco between
the young sentry's boots. 'My name's Jackrum,' he
said. 'That's Sergeant Jackrum. As for the other bit . . .
you choose.'

'Sergeant Jackrum?' said the boy, his mouth staying
open.

'Yes, lad.'

'What, the one who killed sixteen men at the Battle of Zop?'

'There was only ten of 'em, but good lad for knowin' it.'

'The Jackrum who carried General Froc through fourteen miles of enemy territory?'

'That's right.'

Polly saw teeth in the gloom as the sentry grinned. 'My dad told me he fought with you at Blunderberg!'

'Ah, that was a hot battle, that was!' said Jackrum.

'No, he meant in the pub afterwards. He pinched your drink and you smacked him in the mouth and he kicked you in the nadgers and you hit him in the guts and he blacked your eye and then you hit him with a table and when he came round his mates stood him beer for the evening for managing to lay nearly three punches on Sergeant Jackrum. He tells the story every year, when it's the anniversary and he's pis— reminiscing.'

Jackrum thought for a moment, and then jabbed a finger at the young man. 'Joe Hubukurk, right?' he said.

The smile broadened to the point where the top of the young man's head was in danger of falling off. 'He'll be smirking all day when I tell him you remember him, sarge! He says that where you piss grass don't grow!'

'Well, what can a modest man say to that, eh?' said Jackrum.

Then the young man frowned. 'Funny, though, he thought you were dead, sarge,' he said.

'Tell him I bet him a shilling I'm not,' said Jackrum. 'And your name, lad?'

'Lart, sarge. Lart Hubukurk.'

'Glad you joined, are you?'

'Yes, sarge,' said Lart loyally.

'We're just having a stroll, lad. Tell your dad I asked after him.'

'I will, sarge!' The boy stood to attention like a one-man guard of honour. 'This is a proud moment for me, sarge!'

'Does *everyone* know you, sarge?' whispered Polly, as they walked away.

'Aye, pretty much. On our side, anyway. I'll make so bold as to declare that most of the enemy that meets me don't know anything much afterwards.'

'I never thought it was going to be like this!' hissed Shufti.

'Like what?' said Jackrum.

'There's women and children! Shops! I can smell bread baking! It's like a . . . a city.'

'Yeah, but what we're after isn't going to be in the main streets. Follow me, lads.' Sergeant Jackrum, suddenly furtive, ducked between two big heaps of boxes and emerged beside a smithy, its forge glowing in the dusk.

Here the tents were open-sided. Armourers and saddlers worked by lantern-light, shadows flickering across the mud. Polly and Shufti had to step out of the way of a mule train, each animal carrying two casks on its back; the mules moved aside for Jackrum. *Maybe he's met them before, too,*

thought Polly, *maybe he really* does *know everyone.*

The sergeant walked like a man with the deeds to the world. He acknowledged other sergeants with a nod, lazily saluted the few officers there were around here, and ignored everybody else.

'You been here before, sarge?' said Shufti.

'No, lad.'

'But you know where you're going?'

'Correct. I ain't been *here*, but I know battlefields, especially when everyone's had a chance to dig in.' Jackrum sniffed the air. 'Ah, right. That's the stuff. Just you two wait here.'

He disappeared between two stacks of lumber. They heard a distant muttering and, after a moment or two, he reappeared holding a small bottle.

Polly grinned. 'Is that rum, sarge?'

'Well done, my little bar steward. And wouldn't it be nice if it *was* rum, upon my word. Or whisky or gin or brandy. But this don't have none of those fancy names. This is the genuine stingo, this is. Pure hangman.'

'Hangman?' said Shufti.

'One drop and you're dead,' said Polly. Jackrum beamed, as a master to a keen pupil.

'That's right, Shufti. It's rotgut. Wheresoever men are gathered together, someone will find something to ferment in a rubber boot, distil in an old kettle and flog to his mates. Made from rats, by the smell of it. Ferments well, does your average rat. Fancy a taste?'

Shufti shied away from the proffered bottle. The sergeant laughed. 'Good lad. Stick to beer,' he said.

'Don't the officers stop it?' said Polly.

'Officers? What do they know about anything?' said Jackrum. 'An' I bought this off of a sergeant, too. Anyone watching us?'

Polly peered into the gloom. 'No, sarge.'

Jackrum poured some of the liquid into one pudgy hand and splashed it on to his face. 'Ye-ouch,' he hissed. 'Stings like the blazes. And now to kill the tooth worms. Got to do the job properly.' He took a quick sip from the bottle, spat it out, and shoved the cork back in. 'Muck,' he said. 'Okay, let's go.'

'Where are we going, sarge?' said Shufti. 'You can tell us now, can't you?'

'A quiet little place where our needs will be met,' said Jackrum. 'It'll be around here somewhere.'

'You don't half smell of drink, sarge,' said Shufti. 'Will they let you in if you smell drunk?'

'Yes, Shufti, lad, they will,' said Jackrum, setting off again. 'The reason being, my pockets jingle and I smell of booze. Everyone likes a rich drunk. Ah . . . down this little valley here, that'll be our . . . yeah, I was right. This is the place. Tucked away, *delicate* like. See any clothes hanging out to dry, boys?'

There were a few washing lines strung behind the half-dozen or so drab tents in this side valley, which was little more than a wash gouged out by winter rains. If there had been anything on them it had been taken in against the heavy dew.

'Shame,' said Jackrum. 'Okay, so we'll have to do it the hard way. Remember: just act natural and listen to what I say.'

'I'm sh-shaking, sarge,' Shufti muttered.

'Good, good, very natural,' said Jackrum. 'This is our place, I think. Nice and quiet, no one watching us, nice little path up there to the top of the wash . . .' He stopped at a very large tent and tapped on the board outside with his swagger stick.

'The SoLid DoVes,' Polly read.

'Yeah, well, these ladies weren't hired for their spelling,' said Jackrum, pushing open the flap of the tent of ill repute.

Inside was a stuffy little area, a sort of canvas antechamber. A lady, lumpy and crowlike in a black bombazine dress, rose from a chair and gave the trio the most calculating look Polly had ever met. It finished off by putting a price on her boots.

The sergeant doffed his cap and in a jovial, rotund voice that peed brandy and crapped plum pudding said, 'Good evening, mad*arm*! Sergeant Smith's the name, yes indeed! An' me and my bold lads here have been so fortunate as to acquire the spoils of war, if you catch my drift, and nothing would do for it but they were clamouring, *clamouring* to go to the nearest house of good repute for to have a man made of 'em!'

Little beady eyes skewered Polly again. Shufti, ears glowing like signal beacons, was staring fixedly at the ground.

'Looks like that'd be a job and a half,' said the woman shortly.

'You never spoke a truer word, madarm!' beamed Jackrum. 'Two of your fair flowers apiece should do it, I reckon.' There was a clink as, staggering slightly,

Jackrum put several gold coins on the rickety little table.

Something about the gleam of them thawed things no end. The woman's face cracked into a smile as glutinous as slug gravy.

'Well now, we are always honoured to entertain the Ins-and-Outs, sergeant,' she said. 'If you ... gentlemen would like to step through to the, er, inner sanctum?'

Polly heard a very faint sound behind her, and turned. She hadn't noticed the man sitting on a chair just inside the door. He had to be a man, because trolls weren't pink; he made Eyebrow back in Plün look like some kind of weed. He wore leather, which was what she'd heard creaking, and he had his eyes just slightly open. When he saw her looking at him, he winked. It wasn't a friendly wink.

There are times when a plan suddenly isn't going to work. When you're in the middle of it is not the time to find this out.

'Er, sarge,' she said. The sergeant turned, saw her frantic grimace, and appeared to spot the guard for the first time.

'Oh *dear*, where's my manners?' he said, lurching back and fumbling in his pocket. He came up with a gold coin which he folded in the astonished man's hand. Then he turned round, tapping the side of his nose with an expression of idiot knowingness.

'A word of advice, lads,' he said. 'Always give the guard a tip. He keeps the riff-riff-raff out, very important. Very important man.'

He stumbled back to the lady in black, and belched hugely. 'And now, mad*arm*, if we can meet these visions of loveliness you are hiding under this here bushel?' he said.

It depended, Polly thought a few seconds later, on how and when and after drinking how much of what whether you had those visions. She *knew* about these places. Serving behind a bar can really broaden your education. There were a number of ladies back home who were, as her mother put it, 'no better than they should be', and at twelve years old Polly had got a slap for asking how good they should have been, then. They were an Abomination unto Nuggan, but men have always found space in their religion for a little sinning here and there.

The word to describe the four ladies seated in the room beyond, if you wanted to be kind, was 'tired'. If you didn't want to be kind a whole range of words were just hanging in the air.

They looked up without much interest.

'This is Faith, Prudence, Grace and Comfort,' said the lady of the house. 'The night shift has not yet come on, I'm afraid.'

'I'm sure these beauties will be a great education for my roaring boys,' said the sergeant. 'But . . . may I be so bold as to enquire about your name, mad*arm*?'

'I'm Mrs Smother, sergeant.'

'And do you have a first name, may I ask?'

'Dolores,' said Mrs Smother, 'to my . . . special friends.'

'Well now, Dolores,' said Jackrum, and there was

another jingle of coins in his pocket, 'I will come right out with it and be frank, because I can see you are a woman of the world. These frail blossoms are all very well in their way, for I know the fashion these days is for ladies with less meat on 'em than a butcher's pencil, but a gentleman such as me, who has been around the world and seen a thing or two, well, he learns the value of ... maturity.' He sighed. 'Not to mention Hope and Patience.' The coins jingled again. 'Perhaps you and I might retire to some suitable boodwah, mad*arm*, and discuss the matter over a cordial or two?'

Mrs Smother looked from the sergeant to the 'lads', glanced back in the anteroom, and looked back at Jackrum with her head on one side and a thin, calculating smile on her lips.

'Ye-es,' she said. 'You're a fine figure of a man, Sergeant Smith. Let us take a load off your ... pockets, shall we?'

She joined arm-in-arm with the sergeant, who winked roguishly at Polly and Shufti. 'We're well set, then, lads!' he chuckled. 'Now, just so's you don't get carried away, when it's time to go I'll blow my whistle and you better finish what you're doin', haha, and meet me sharpish. Duty calls! Remember the fine tradition of the Ins-and Outs!' Giggling and almost tripping up, he left the room on the arm of the proprietress.

Shufti sidled hurriedly up to Polly and whispered: 'Is sarge all right, Ozzer?'

'He's just had a bit too much to drink,' said

Polly loudly, as all four of the girls stood up.

'But he—' Shufti got a nudge in the ribs before she could say any more. One of the girls carefully laid down her knitting, took Polly's arm, flashed her finely crafted expression of interest and said, 'You're a well-set-up young man, aren't you ... what's your name, dear? I'm Gracie.'

'Oliver,' said Polly. And what the *hell* is the fine tradition of the Ins-and-Outs?

'Ever seen a woman with no clothes on before, Oliver?' The girls giggled.

Polly's brow wrinkled as, just for a moment, she was caught unawares. 'Yes,' she said. 'Of course.'

'Ooo, it looks like we've got ourselves a regular Don Joo-ann, girls,' said Gracie, stepping back. 'We may have to send out for reinforcements! Why don't you an' me and Prudence go off to a little nook I know, and your little friend will be the guest of Faith and Comfort. Comfort's very good with young men, ain't you, Comfort?'

Sergeant Jackrum had been wrong in his description of the girls. Three of them were indeed several meals short of a healthy weight, but when Comfort got up out of her large armchair you realized that it had, in fact, been quite a small armchair and had mostly been Comfort. For a large woman she had a small face, locked in a piggy-eyed scowl. There was a death's head tattoo on one arm.

'He's young,' said Gracie. 'He'll heal. Come along, Don Joo-ann ...'

In a way, Polly was relieved. She didn't take to the

girls. Oh, the profession could bring anyone down, but she'd got to know some of her town's ladies of uneasy virtue and they had an edge she couldn't find here.

'Why do you work here?' she said, as they entered a smaller, canvas-walled room. There was a rickety bed taking up most of the space.

'You know, you look a bit too young to be *that* sort of customer,' said Gracie.

'What sort?' said Polly.

'Oh, a holy joe,' said Gracie. ' "What's a girl like you doing in a place like this?" and all that stuff. Feel sorry for us, do you? At least if someone cuts up rough we've got Garry outside and after he's finished with the bloke the colonel gets told and the bastard gets bunged in clink.'

'Yeah,' said Prudence. 'From what we hear we're the safest ladies within twenty-five miles. Old Smother's not too bad. We get money to keep and we get fed and she don't beat us, which is more than can be said for husbands, and you can't wander around loose, now, can you?'

Jackrum put up with Blouse because you've got to have an officer, Polly thought. If you don't have an officer, some other officer'll take you over. And a woman by herself is missing a man, while a man by himself is his own master. Trousers. That's the secret. Trousers and a pair of socks. I never dreamed it was like this. Put on trousers and the world changes. We walk different. We act different. I see these girls and I think: idiots! Get yourself some trousers!

'Can you please get your clothes off?' she said. 'I think we'd better hurry.'

'One of the Ins-and-Outs, this one,' said Gracie, slipping her dress off her shoulders. 'Keep an eye on your cheeses, Pru!'

'Er ... why does that mean we're in the Ins-and-Outs?' said Polly. She made a show of unbuttoning her jacket, wishing that she believed in anyone there to pray to so that she could pray for the whistle.

'That's 'cos you lads always have your eye on business,' said Gracie.

And maybe there was someone listening, at that. The whistle blew.

Polly grabbed the dresses and ran out, oblivious of the yells behind her. She collided with Shufti outside, tripped over the groaning form of Garry, saw Sergeant Jackrum holding the tent flap open, and bulleted into the night.

'This way!' the sergeant hissed, grabbing her by the collar before she'd gone a few feet and swinging her round. 'You too, Shufti! Move!'

He ran up the side of the wash like a child's balloon being blown by the wind, leaving them to scramble after him. His arms were full of clothing, which snagged and danced behind him. Up above was knee-deep scrub, treacherous in the gloom. They tripped and staggered across it until they reached heavier growth, whereupon the sergeant got hold of both of them and pushed them into the bushes. The shouts and screams were fainter now.

'Now we'll just keep quiet, like,' he whispered. 'There's patrols about.'

'They'll be bound to find us,' Polly hissed, while Shufti wheezed.

'No, they won't,' said Jackrum. 'First, they'll all be running towards the shoutin', because that's natur— there they go ...' Polly heard more shouts in the distance. 'And bloody fools they are, too. They're supposed to be guarding the perimeter, and they're running towards trouble in the camp. *And* they're running straight towards lamplight, so there goes their night eyes! If I was their sergeant they'd be due a fizzer! C'mon.' He stood up, and hauled Shufti to her feet. 'Feeling all right, lad?'

'It w-was horrible, sarge! One of them put her hand ... on ... on my socks!'

'Something that doesn't often happen, I'll bet any man,' said Jackrum. 'But you did a good job. Now, we'll walk nice and quiet, and no more talking 'til I say, okay?'

They plodded on for ten minutes, skirting the camp. They heard several patrols, and saw a couple of others on the hilltops as the moon rose, but it dawned on Polly that, loud though the shouting had been, it was only part of the huge patchwork of sound that rose from the camp. The patrols this far away probably hadn't heard it, or at least were commanded by the kinds of soldiers who didn't want to get put on a fizzer.

In the dark, she heard Jackrum take a deep breath. 'Okay, that's far enough. Not a bad job

of work, lads. You're real Ins-and-Outs now!'

'That guard was out cold,' said Polly. 'Did you hit him?'

'Y'see, I'm fat,' said Jackrum. 'People don't think fat men can fight. They think fat men are funny. They think wrong. Gave 'im a chop to the windpipe.'

'Sarge!' said Shufti, horrified.

'What? What? He was coming at me with his club!' said Jackrum.

'*Why* was he doing that, sarge?' said Polly.

'Ooh, you cunning soldier, you,' said Jackrum. 'All right, I grant you that I'd just given madarm the ol' quietus, but to be fair I know when someone's just handed me a bleedin' drink full o' sleepy drops.'

'You hit a *woman*, sarge?' said Polly.

'Yeah, and maybe when she wakes up in her corsets she'll decide that next time a poor ol' drunk fat man wanders in it mightn't be such a good idea to try to roll him for his wad,' growled Jackrum. 'I'd be in a ditch wi'out my drawers on and a damned great headache if she'd had her way, and if you two was daft enough to complain to an officer she'd swear black was blue that I didn't have a penny on me when I came in and was drunk and disorderly. And the colonel wouldn't care a fig, 'cos he'd reckon a sergeant daft enough to get caught like that had it coming to him. I *know*, you see. I look after my lads.' There was a clink in the dark. 'Plus a few extra dollars won't go amiss.'

'Sarge, you didn't steal the cashbox, did you?' said Polly.

'Yeah. Got a good armful of her wardrobe, too.'

'Good!' said Shufti fervently. 'It wasn't a nice place!'

'It was mostly my money in any case,' said Jackrum. 'Business has been a bit slow today, by the feel of it.'

'But it's immoral earnings!' said Polly, and then felt a complete fool for saying it.

'No,' said Jackrum. 'It *was* immoral earnings, *now* it's the proceeds of common theft. Life's a lot easier when you learns to think straight.'

Polly was glad there was no mirror. The best that could be said for the squad's new clothing was that it covered them up. But this was a war. You seldom saw new clothes on anybody. Yet they felt awkward. And there was no sense in that at all. But they looked at one another in the chilly light of dawn and giggled in embarrassment. Wow, Polly thought, look at us: dressed as *women*!

Oddly enough, it was Igorina who really looked the part. She'd disappeared into the other tumbledown room carrying her pack. For ten minutes the squad had heard the occasional grunt or 'ouch', and then she'd returned with a full head of fair, shoulder-length hair. Her face was the right shape, missing the lumps and bumps they'd come to know. And the stitches on her forehead shrank and *disappeared* as Polly watched in astonishment.

'Doesn't that *hurt*?' she said.

'It smarts a bit for a few minutes,' said Igorina. 'You just have to have the knack. And the special ointment, of course.'

'But why's there a curved scar on your cheek now?' said Tonker. 'And *those* stitches are staying.'

Igorina looked down demurely. She'd even restyled one of the dresses into a dirndl, and looked like a fresh young maid from the beer cellar. Just to look at her was to mentally order a large pretzel.

'You've got to have *something* to show,' she said. 'Otherwise you're letting down the clan. And actually I think the stitches are rather fetching . . .'

'Well, okay,' Tonker conceded. 'But lisp a bit, will you? I know this is completely wrong, but now you look, oh, I don't know . . . weird, I suppose.'

'Okay, line up,' said Jackrum. He stood back, and gave them a look of theatrical disdain. 'Well, I've never seen such a lot of scrubb— washerwomen in all my life,' he said. 'I wish you all the luck you're bleeding well gonna need. There'll be someone watching the door for you to come out, and that's all I can promise. Private Perks, you're acting, unpaid corporal on this one. I hope you've picked up one or two little lessons on our stroll. In and out, that's what you should do. No famous last stands, please. When in doubt, kick 'em in the nadgers and scarper. Mind you, if you frighten them like you frighten me, you should have no trouble.'

'Are you sure you won't join us, sarge?' said Tonker, still trying not to laugh.

'No, lad. You won't get me in skirts. Everyone has their place, right? The place where they draw the line? Well, that's mine. I'm pretty steeped in sin, one way and another, but Jackrum always shows his colours. I'm an old soldier. I'll fight like a soldier does, in the

ranks, on the battlefield. Besides, if I went in there simpering in petticoats I'd never hear the end of it.'

'The Duchess says there is a d-different path for Sergeant Jackrum,' said Wazzer.

'And I don't know if you don't frighten me worst of all, Private Goom,' said Jackrum. He hitched up his equatorial belt. 'You're right, though. When you're inside I shall nip down, nice and quiet, and slip into our lines. If I can't raise a little diversionary attack, my name's not Sergeant Jackrum. And since it *is* Sergeant Jackrum, that proves it. Hah, there's plenty of men in this man's army that owe me a favour' – he gave a little sniff – 'or wouldn't say no to my face. And plenty of likely lads who'll want to tell their grandchildren they fought alongside Jackrum, too. Well, I'll give 'em their chance at real soldierin'.'

'Sarge, it'll be suicide to attack the main gates!' said Polly.

Jackrum slapped his belly. 'See this lot?' he said. 'It's like having yer own armour. Bloke once stuck a blade in this up to the hilt and was as surprised as hell when I nutted him. Anyway, you lads'll be making so much fuss the guards will be distracted, right? You're relying on me, I'm relying on you. That's milit'ry, that is. You give me a signal, any signal. That's all I'll need.'

'The Duchess says your path takes you further,' said Wazzer.

'Oh yeah?' said Jackrum jovially. 'And where's that, then? Somewhere with a good pub, I hope!'

'The Duchess says, um, it should lead to the town of Scritz,' said Wazzer. She said it quietly while the rest

of the squad were laughing, less at the comment than as a way of losing some of the tension. But Polly heard it.

Jackrum really, really was good, she thought. The fleeting expression of terror was gone in an instant. 'Scritz? Nothing there,' he said. 'Dull town.'

'There was a sword,' said Wazzer.

Jackrum was ready this time. There was not a flicker of expression, just the blank face that he was so good at. And that was odd, Polly thought, because there should have been something, even if it was only puzzlement.

'Handled lots of swords in my time,' he said dismissively. 'Yes, Private Halter?'

'There's one thing you didn't tell us, sarge,' said Tonker, lowering her hand. 'Why is the regiment *called* the Ins-and-Outs?'

'First into battle, last out of the fray,' said Jackrum automatically.

'So why are we nicknamed the Cheesemongers?'

'Yes,' said Shufti. 'Why, sarge? Because the way those girls were talking, it sounded like it's something we ought to know.'

Jackrum made a clicking noise of exasperation. 'Oh, Tonker, why the hell did you wait 'til you'd got your trousers off before asking me that? I'll feel embarrassed telling yer now!' And Polly thought: that's bait, right? You want to tell us. You want to get any conversation away from Scritz . . .

'Ah,' said Tonker. 'It's about sex, then, is it?'

'Not as such, no . . .'

'Well, tell me, then,' said Tonker. 'I'd like to know before I die. If it makes you feel any better I'll nudge people and go *gnher, gnher, gnher.*'

Jackrum sighed. 'There's a song,' he said. 'It starts *'Twas on a Monday morning, all in the month of May—'*

'Then it *is* about sex,' said Polly flatly. 'It's a folk song, it starts with 'twas, it takes place in May, QED it's about sex. Is a milkmaid involved? I bet there is.'

'There could be,' Jackrum conceded.

'Going for to market? For to sell her wares?' said Polly.

'Very likely.'

'O-kay. That gives us the cheese. And she meets, let's see, a soldier, a sailor, a jolly ploughboy or just possibly a man clothèd all in leather, I expect? No, since it's about us, it'll be a soldier, right? And since it's one of the Ins-and-Outs . . . oh dear, I feel a humorous double-entendre coming on. Just one question: what item of her clothing fell down or came untied?'

'Her garter,' said Jackrum. 'You've heard it before, Perks.'

'No, but I just *know* how folk songs go. We had folk singers in the lower bar for six months back hom— where I worked. In the end we had to get a man in with a ferret. But you remember stuff . . . oh, no . . .'

'Was there canoodling, sarge?' said Tonker, grinning.

'Kayaking, I expect,' said Igorina, to general sniggering.

'No, he stole the cheese, didn't he?' sighed Polly. 'As the poor girl was lying there waiting for her garter to be tied, *hem hem*, he damn well made off with her cheese, right?'

'Er . . . not damn. Not with the skirt on, Ozz,' Tonker warned.

'Then it's not Ozz, either,' said Polly. 'Fill yer hat with bread, fill yer boots with soup! And steal the cheese, eh, sarge?'

'That's right. We've always been a very practical regiment,' said Jackrum. 'An army marches on its stomach, lads. On mine, o' course, it could troop the colour!'

'It was her own fault. She should have been able to tie up her own garters,' said Lofty.

'Yeah. Probably *wanted* her cheese stolen,' said Tonker.

'Wise words,' said Jackrum. 'Off you go, then . . . cheesemongers!'

The mist was still thick as they made their way down through the woods to the path by the river. Polly's skirt kept catching in brambles. It must have done so before she'd joined up, but she'd never noticed it so much. Now it was seriously hindering her. She reached up and absent-mindedly adjusted the socks, which she'd separated to use as padding elsewhere. She was too skinny, that was the trouble. The ringlets had been useful there. They said 'girl'. In their absence, she had to rely on a scarf and a socks change.

'All right,' she whispered, as the ground levelled

out. 'Remember, no swearing. Giggle, don't snigger. No belching. No weapons, either. They can't be that stupid in there. Anyone brought a weapon?'

There was a shaking of heads.

'Did you bring a weapon, Tonk— Magda?'

'No, Polly.'

'No item of any sort with a certain weapon-like quality?' Polly insisted.

'No, Polly,' said Tonker demurely.

'Anything, perhaps, with an edge?'

'Oh, you mean this?'

'Yes, Magda.'

'Well, a woman can carry a knife, can't she?'

'It's a *sabre*, Magda. You're trying to hide it, but it's a sabre.'

'But I'm only using it like a knife, Polly.'

'It's three feet long, Magda.'

'Size isn't important, Polly.'

'No one believes that. Leave it behind a tree, please. That is an order.'

'Oh, all right!'

After a while, Shufti, who had appeared to be thinking deeply, said: 'I can't understand why she didn't just tie up her own garter . . .'

'Shuft, what the hell—' Tonker began.

'—heck,' Polly corrected her, 'and you're talking to Betty, remember.'

'What the *heck* are you talking about, Betty?' said Tonker, rolling her eyes.

'Well, the song, of course. And you don't have to lie down to tie a garter in any case. It'd be

more difficult,' said Shufti. 'It's all a bit silly.'

No one said anything for a while. It was, perhaps, easy to see why Shufti was on her quest.

'You're right,' said Polly eventually. 'It's a silly song.'

'A very silly song,' Tonker agreed.

They all agreed. It was a silly song.

They stepped out on to the river path. Ahead of them a small group of women were hurrying round the bend in the track. Automatically, the squad looked up. The keep grew out of the sheer cliff; it was hard to see where the unhewn rock ended and the ancient masonry began. They could see no windows. From here, it was just a wall extending to the sky. No way in, it said. No way out. In this wall are few doors, and they close with finality.

This close to the deep, slow river, the air was bone-chillingly cold, and grew colder the higher they looked. Around the curve they could see the little rock shelf where the back door was, and the women ahead of them talking to a guard.

'This is not going to work,' said Shufti under her breath. 'They're showing him some papers. Anyone brought theirs? No?'

The soldier had looked up and was watching the girls, with that blank official expression of someone who was not looking for excitement or adventure in his life.

'Keep moving,' murmured Polly. 'If it all gets really bad, burst into tears.'

'That's disgusting,' said Tonker.

Their treacherous feet were taking them closer all

the time. Polly kept her eyes downwards, as was proper in an unmarried woman. There would be others watching, she knew it. They'd probably be bored, they might not be expecting any trouble, but up on those walls there were eyes fixed on her.

They reached the guard. Just inside the narrow stone doorway there was another one, lounging in the shadow.

'Papers,' said the guard.

'Oh, sir, I have none,' said Polly. She'd been working out the speech on the way down through the wood. War, fears of invasion, people fleeing, no food . . . you didn't have to make things up, you just had to reassemble reality. 'I had to leave—'

'Oh, *right*,' the guard interrupted. 'No papers? No problem! If you'd just step in and see my colleague? Nice of you to join us!' He stood aside and waved a hand towards the dark entrance.

Mystified, Polly stepped inside, with the others following. Behind them, the door swung shut. Inside, she saw that they were in a long passage with many slits in the walls to rooms on either side. Lamplight shone from the slits. She could see shadows beyond them. Bowmen concealed there could turn anyone trapped in here into mince.

At the end of the corridor another door swung open. It led into a small room in which there sat, at a desk, a young man in a uniform Polly didn't recognize, although it had a captain's insignia. Standing to one side was a much, much larger man in the same uniform, or possibly two uniforms stitched together.

He had a sword. There was that about him: when this man held a sword, it was clearly being held, and held by him. The eye was drawn to it. Even Jade would have been impressed.

'Good morning, ladies,' said the captain. 'No papers, eh? Take off your scarves, please.'

And that's it, thought Polly, as the bottom of her stomach dropped away. *And we thought we were being clever.* There was nothing for it but to obey.

'Ah. You'll tell me your hair was shaved off as a punishment for fraternizing with the enemy, eh?' said the man, barely looking up. 'Except for you,' he added to Igorina. 'Didn't feel like fraternizing with any enemies? Something wrong with decent Zlobenian boys?'

'Er . . . no,' said Igorina.

Now the captain gave them a bright little smile. 'Gentlemen, let's not mess about, shall we? You walk wrong. We do *watch*, you know. You walk wrong and you stand wrong. You,' he pointed to Tonker, 'have got a bit of shaving soap under one ear. And you, sir, are either deformed or you've tried the old trick of sticking a pair of socks down your vest.'

Crimson with embarrassment and humiliation, Polly hung her head.

'Getting in or out disguised as washerwomen,' said the captain, shaking his head. 'Everyone outside this stupid country knows that one, lads, but most of them make more effort than you boys. Well, for you the war is over. This place has got big, big dungeons and I don't mind telling you you're probably going to

be better off in here than outside— Yeah, what do *you* want?'

Shufti had raised a hand. 'Can I show you something?' she said. Polly didn't turn, but watched the captain's face as, beside Polly, cloth rustled. She couldn't believe it. Shufti was raising her skirt . . .

'Oh,' said the captain, sitting back in his chair. His face went red.

There was an explosion from Tonker, but it was an explosion of tears. They came out accompanied by a long, mournful wail, as she threw herself on to the floor.

'We walked so-oo far! We lay in ditches to hide from soldiers! There's no food! We want to work! You called us boys! Why are you so-oo *cruel*?'

Polly knelt down and half picked her up, patting her on the back as Tonker's shoulders heaved with the force of her sobs.

'It's been very hard for all of us,' she said to the red-faced captain.

'*If you can take him down I can garrotte the other one with my apron string*,' whispered Tonker in her ear, between howls.

'Have you seen everything you wish to see?' said Polly to the blushing captain, every syllable tinkling with ice.

'Yes! No! Yes! Please!' said the captain, giving the guard the agonized glance of a man who knows that he's going to be the laughing stock of the whole fort inside the hour. 'Once was quite— I mean, I've seen . . . look, I'm completely satisfied. Private, go and

fetch one of the women from the laundry. I am so sorry, ladies, I . . . I have a job to do . . .'

'Do you enjoy it?' said Polly, still freezing.

'Yes!' said the captain hurriedly. 'I mean, no! No, yes! We have to be careful . . . ah . . .'

The big soldier had returned, trailing a woman. Polly stared.

'Some, er, new volunteers,' said the captain, waving vaguely towards the squad. 'I'm sure Mrs Enid will have some use for them . . . er . . .'

'Certainly, captain,' said the woman, curtsying demurely. Polly still stared.

'Off you go . . . ladies,' said the captain. 'And if you're hard workers Mrs Enid will I am sure give you a pass so's we don't have this trouble again . . . er . . .'

Shufti put both hands on his desk, leaned towards him and said 'Boo'. His chair hit the wall.

'I may not be clever,' she said to Polly. 'But I'm not *stupid*.'

But Polly was still staring at Lieutenant Blouse. He'd curtsied surprisingly well.

The soldier escorted them along a tunnel which opened on to a ledge overlooking what was either a cave or a room; it was at that level in the keep where there was not much difference. This wasn't a laundry, but clearly some hot, damp afterlife for those who required punishment with extra scrubbing. Steam rolled across the ceiling, condensed, and dripped on to a floor that was already running with water. And it went on for ever, washtub after washtub. Women

moved like ghosts through the drifting, tumbling clouds of fog.

'There you go, ladies,' he said, and slapped Blouse on the rump. 'See you tonight, then, Daphne?'

'Oh, yes!' trilled Blouse.

'Five o'clock, then,' said the soldier, and ambled off down the corridor.

'Daphne?' said Polly, when the man had gone.

'My "nom de guerre",' said Blouse. 'I still haven't found a way out of the lower areas but the guards all have keys and I shall have his key in my hand by half past five. Pardon?'

'I think Tonker – sorry, *Magda* – just bit her tongue,' said Polly.

'Her? Oh, yes. Well done for staying in character, er . . .'

'Polly,' said Polly.

'Good choice of name,' said Blouse, leading the way down some steps. 'It's a good common, maidservanty sort of name.'

'Yes, that's what I thought,' said Polly gravely.

'Er . . . Sergeant Jackrum not with you, then?' said the lieutenant, with a trace of nervousness.

'No, sir. He said he was going to lead a charge on the main gates, sir, if we sent him a signal. I hope he doesn't try without one.'

'Good heavens, the man's mad,' said Blouse. 'Splendid effort from the lads, though. Well done. You'd definitely pass for women to the casual observer.'

'Coming from you, Daphne, that is a big

compliment,' said Polly, thinking: gosh, I'm really good at keeping a straight face.

'But you didn't need to come after me,' said Blouse. 'I'm sorry I couldn't get a signal to you, but Mrs Enid allowed me to stay overnight, you see. The guards don't do so many checks at night so I made use of my time to look for ways into the upper keep. All gated or really heavily guarded, I'm afraid. However, Private Hauptfidel has taken rather a shine to me . . .'

'Well done, sir!' said Polly.

'Sorry, I want to be clear, sir,' said Tonker. '*You have a date with a guard*?'

'Yes, and I'll suggest we go somewhere dark and then when I've got what I want I shall break his neck,' said Blouse.

'Isn't that going a bit far on a first date?' said Tonker.

'Sir, did you have any trouble getting in?' said Polly. This had been nagging at her. It seemed so unfair.

'No, not at all. I just smiled and wiggled my hips and they waved me through. What about you?'

'Oh, we had a little bit,' said Polly. 'It was a bit hair— it was a bit awkward for a moment or two.'

'What did I tell you?' said Blouse triumphantly. 'It's all down to thespian ability! But you were plucky lads to try it. Come and meet Mrs Enid. A very loyal lady. The brave womenfolk of Borogravia are on our side!'

And, indeed, there was a picture of the Duchess in the alcove that served the laundry mistress for an office. Mrs Enid wasn't a particularly large woman but she had forearms like Jade, a soaking wet apron, and

the most mobile mouth Polly had ever seen. Her lips and tongue drew out every word like a big shape in the air; the laundresses, in a cavern full of hissing steam, echoes, falling water and the thud of wet clothes on stone, watched lips when ears were over-whelmed. When she was listening her mouth moved all the time, too, like someone trying to dislodge a piece of nut from a tooth. She wore her sleeves rolled up above her elbows.

She listened impassively as Blouse introduced the squad. 'I see,' she said. 'Right. You leave your lads here with me, sir. You ought to get back to the pressing room.'

When Blouse had bounced and wobbled back through the steam, Mrs Enid looked them all up and down, and then straight through.

'Lads,' she grunted. 'Hah! That's all he knows, eh? For a woman to wear the clothes of a man is an Abomination in the Eyes of Nuggan!'

'But we're dressed as *women*, Mrs Enid,' said Polly meekly.

Mrs Enid's mouth moved ferociously. Then she folded her arms. It was like a barricade going up against all that was ungodly.

'It's not right,' she said. 'I've got a son and a husband prisoner in this place and I'm working meself to the bone for the enemy just so's I can keep an eye on 'em. They're gonna invade, y'know. It's amazing what we hear down here. So what good's rescuing your men going to do 'em when we're all under the heel of the Zlobenian hand-painted clog, eh?'

'Zlobenia will not invade,' said Wazzer confidently. 'The Duchess will see to it. Be not afraid.'

Wazzer got given the sort of look she always got when someone heard her for the first time.

'Been praying, 'ave yer?' said Mrs Enid kindly.

'No, just listening,' said Wazzer.

'Nuggan talks to you, does he?'

'No. Nuggan is dead, Mrs Enid,' said Wazzer.

Polly took Wazzer's matchstick-thin arm and said: 'Excuse us a moment, Mrs Enid.' She hustled the girl behind a huge, water-driven clothes mangle. It heaved and clanked as a background to their conversation.

'Wazzer, this is getting . . .' Polly's native tongue had no word for 'freaky', but if she had known about the word she would have welcomed its inclusion '. . . strange. You're worrying people. You can't just go around saying that a god is dead.'

'Gone, then. Dwindled . . . I think,' said Wazzer, her brow furrowing. 'No longer with us . . .'

'We still get the Abominations.'

Wazzer tried to concentrate. 'No, they're not real. They're like . . . echoes. Dead voices in an ancient cave, bouncing back and forth, the words changing, making nonsense . . . like flags that were used for signals but now just flap in the wind . . .' Wazzer's eyes went unfocused and her voice altered, became more adult, more certain '. . . and they come from no god. There is no god here now.'

'So where *do* they come from?'

'From your fear . . . They come from the part that hates the Other, that will not change. They come from

the sum of all your pettiness and stupidity and dull-
ness. You fear tomorrow, and you've made your fear
your god. The Duchess knows this.'

The water-mangle creaked onwards. Around Polly
the boilers hissed, water gushed in the runnels. The
air was loaded with the smells of soap and damp
cloth.

'I don't believe in the Duchess, either,' said Polly.
'That was just trickery in the woods. Anyone'd look
round. It doesn't mean I believe in her.'

'That doesn't matter, Polly. She believes in you.'

'Really?' Polly glanced around the steaming, drip-
ping cave. 'Is she here, then? Has she graced us with
her presence?'

Wazzer had no concept of sarcasm. She nodded.
'Yes.'

Yes.

Polly looked behind her.

'Did you just say yes?' she demanded.

'Yes,' said Wazzer.

Yes.

Polly relaxed. 'Oh, it's an *echo*. This is a cave, after
all. Uh . . .'

. . . which doesn't explain why *my* voice doesn't
come bouncing back . . .

'Wazz . . . I mean, Alice?' she said thoughtfully.

'Yes, Polly?' said Wazzer.

'I think it would be a really good idea if you don't
talk too much about this to the others,' she said.
'People don't mind believing in, you know, gods and
so on, but they get very nervous if you tell them

they're showing up. Er . . . she's not *going* to show up, is she?'

'The person you don't believe in?' said Wazzer, showing a flash of spirit.

'I'm . . . not saying she doesn't exist,' said Polly weakly. 'I just don't believe in her, that's all.'

'She's very weak,' said Wazzer. 'I hear her crying in the night.'

Polly sought for further information in the pinched-up face, hoping that in some way Wazzer was making fun of her. But nothing but puzzled innocence looked back.

'Why does she cry?' she said.

'The prayers. They hurt her.'

Polly spun round when something touched her shoulder. It was Tonker.

'Mrs Enid says we're to get to work,' she said. 'She says the guards come round and check . . .'

It was women's work, and therefore monotonous, backbreaking and social. It had been a long time since Polly had got her hands in a washtub, and the ones here were long wooden troughs, where twenty women could work at once. Arms on either side of her squeezed and pummelled, wrung out garments and slapped them into the rinsing trough behind them. Polly joined in, and listened to the buzz of conversation around her.

It was gossip, but bits of information floated in it like bubbles in the washtub. A couple of guards had 'taken liberties' – that is, more than had already been taken – and had apparently been flogged for it. This

caused much comment along the tub. Apparently some big milord from Ankh-Morpork was in charge of things and had ordered it. He was some kind of wizard, said the woman opposite. They said he could see things happening everywhere, and lived on raw meat. They said he had secret eyes. Of course, everyone knew that that city was the home of Abominations. Polly, industriously rubbing a shirt on a washboard, thought about this. And thought about a lowland buzzard in this upland country, and some creature so fast and stealthy that it was only a suggestion of shadow . . .

She took a spell on the copper boilers, ramming the stewing garments under the bubbling surface, and noted that in this place without weapons of any sort she was using a heavy stick about three feet long.

She enjoyed the work, in a dumb kind of way. Her muscles did all the necessary thinking, leaving her brain free. No one knew for sure that the Duchess was dead. It more or less didn't matter. But Polly was sure of one thing. The Duchess had been a woman. Just a woman, not a goddess. Oh, people prayed to her in the hope that their pleas would be gift-wrapped and sent on to Nuggan, but that gave her no right to mess with the heads of people like Wazzer, who had enough trouble as it was. Gods could do miracles, Duchesses posed for pictures.

Out of the corner of her eye Polly saw a line of women taking large baskets from a platform at the end of the room and stepping out through another doorway. She dragged Igorina away from the wash

trough and told her to join them. 'And notice every-thing!' she added.

'Yes, corp,' said Igorina.

'Because I know one thing,' said Polly, waving at the piles of damp linen, 'and it's that this lot will need the breeze . . .'

She went back to work, occasionally joining in the chatter for the look of the thing. It wasn't hard. The washerwomen kept away from some subjects, particularly ones like 'husbands' and 'sons'. But Polly picked up clues here and there. Some were in the keep. Some were probably dead. Some were out there, somewhere. Some of the older women wore the Motherhood Medal, awarded to women whose sons had died for Borogravia. The bastard metal was corroding in the damp atmosphere, and Polly wondered if the medals had arrived in a letter from the Duchess, with her signature printed on the bottom and the son's name squeezed up tight to fit the space:

We honour and congratulate you, *Mrs L. Lapchic* of *Well Lane, Munz*, on the death of your son *Otto PiotrHanLapchic* on *June 25* at ████

The place was always censored in case it brought aid and comfort to the enemy. It astonished Polly to find that the cheap medals and thoughtless words did, in a way, bring aid and comfort to the mothers. Those in Munz who had received them wore them with a sort of fierce, indignant pride.

She wasn't sure she trusted Mrs Enid very much. She had a son and a husband up in the cells, and she'd had a chance to weigh up Blouse. She'd be asking herself: what's more likely, that he gets them all out and keeps them safe, or that there's going to be an almighty mess which might well harm us all? And Polly couldn't blame her if she went with the evidence . . .

She was aware of someone talking to her. 'Hmm?' she said.

'Look at this, will you?' said Shufti, waving a sodden pair of men's long pants at her. 'They keep putting the colours in with the whites!'

'Well? So what? These are *enemy* longjohns,' said Polly.

'Yes, but there's such a thing as doing it properly! Look, they put in this red pair and all the others are going pink!'

'And? I used to love pink when I was about seven.'*

'But pale pink? On a man?'

Polly looked at the next tub for a moment, and patted Shufti on the shoulder. 'Yes. It is *very* pale, isn't it? You'd better find a couple more red items,' she said.

'But that'd make it even worse—' Shufti began.

'That was an *order*, soldier,' Polly whispered in her ear. 'And add some starch.'

'How much?'

'All you can find.'

* It is an established fact that, despite everything society can do, girls of seven are magnetically attracted to the colour pink.

Igorina returned. Igorina had good eyes. Polly wondered if they'd ever belonged to someone else. She gave Polly a wink and held up a thumb. It was, to Polly's relief, one of her own.

In the huge ironing room, only one person was working at the long boards when Polly, taking advantage of the temporary absence of Mrs Enid, hurried in. It was 'Daphne'. All the rest of the women were gathered round, as if they were watching a demonstration. And they were.

'—the collar, d'you see,' said Lieutenant Blouse, flourishing the big, steaming, charcoal-filled iron. '*Then* the sleeve cuffs and finally the sleeves. Do one front half at a time. You should hang them immediately but, and here's a useful tip, don't iron them completely dry. It's really a matter of practice, but—'

Polly stared in fascinated wonder. She'd *hated* ironing. 'Daphne, could I have a word?' she said, during a pause.

Blouse looked up. 'Oh, P . . . Polly,' he said. 'Um, yes, of course.'

'It's amazing what Daphne knows about pleat lines,' said a girl, in awe. '*And* press cloths!'

'I *am* amazed,' said Polly.

Blouse handed the iron to the girl. 'There you are, Dympha,' he said generously. 'Remember: always iron the wrong side first, and only ever do the wrong side on dark linens. Common mistake. Coming, Polly.'

Polly kicked her heels for a while outside, and one of the girls came up with a big pile of fresh-smelling

ironing. She saw Polly, and leaned close as she went past. 'We all *know* he's a man,' she said. 'But he's having such fun and he irons like a demon!'

'Sir, how do you *know* about ironing?' said Polly, when they were back in the washing room.

'Had to do my own laundry back at HQ,' said Blouse. 'Couldn't afford a gel and the batman was a strict Nugganite and said it was girls' work. So I thought, well, it can't be hard, otherwise we wouldn't leave it to women. They really aren't very good here. You know they put the colours and the whites together?'

'Sir, you know you said you were going to steal a gate key off a guard and break his neck?' said Polly.

'Indeed.'

'Do you know *how* to break a man's neck, sir?'

'I read a book on martial arts, Perks,' said Blouse, a little severely.

'But you haven't actually *done* it, sir?'

'Well, no! I was at HQ, and you are not allowed to practise on real people, Perks.'

'You see, the person whose neck you want to break will have a weapon at that moment and you, sir, won't,' said Polly.

'I have tried out the basic principle on a rolled-up blanket,' said Blouse reproachfully. 'It seemed to work very well.'

'Was the blanket struggling and making loud gurgling noises and kicking you in the socks, sir?'

'The socks?' said Blouse, puzzled.

'In fact I think your other idea would be better, sir,' said Polly hurriedly.

'Yes . . . my, er . . . other idea . . . which one was that, exactly?'

'The one where we escape from the washhouse via the clothes-drying area, sir, after silently disabling three guards, sir. There's a kind of moving room down the corridor over there, sir, which gets winched all the way to the roof. Two guards go up there with the women, sir, and there's another guard up on the roof. Acting together, we'd take out each unsuspecting guard, which would be more certain than you against an armed man, with all due respect, sir, and that would leave us very well positioned to go anywhere in the keep via the rooftops, sir. Well done, sir!'

There was a pause. 'Did I, er, go into all that detail?' said Blouse.

'Oh, no, sir. You shouldn't have to, sir. Sergeants and corporals deal with the fine detail. Officers are there to see the big picture.'

'Oh, absolutely. And, er . . . how big was this particular picture?' said Blouse, blinking.

'Oh, very big, sir. A very big picture indeed, sir.'

'Ah,' said Blouse, and straightened up and assumed what he considered to be the expression of one with panoramic vision.

'Some of the ladies here used to work in the upper keep, sir, when it was ours,' Polly went on quickly. 'Anticipating your order, sir, I had the squad engage them in light conversation about the layout of the place, sir. Being aware of the general thrust of your strategy, sir, I think I have found a route to the dungeons.'

She paused. It had been good flannelling, she knew. It was almost worthy of Jackrum. She'd larded it with as many 'sirs' as she dared. And she was very proud of 'anticipating your order'. She hadn't heard Jackrum use it, but with a certain amount of care it was an excuse to do almost *anything*. 'General thrust' was pretty good, too.

'Dungeons,' said Blouse thoughtfully, momentarily losing sight of the big picture. 'In fact I thought I said—'

'Yessir. *Because*, sir, if we can get a lot of the lads out of the dungeons, sir, you'll be in command *inside* the enemy's citadel, sir!'

Blouse grew another inch, and then sagged again. 'Of course, there are some very senior officers here. All of them senior to me—'

'Yessir!' said Polly, well on the way to graduating from the Sergeant Jackrum School of Outright Rupert Management. 'Perhaps we'd better try to let the enlisted men out first, sir? We don't want to expose the officers to enemy fire.'

It was shameless and stupid, but now the light of battle was in Blouse's eyes. Polly decided to fan it, just in case. 'Your leadership has really been a great example to us, sir,' she said.

'Has it?'

'Oh, yes, sir.'

'No officer could have led a finer bunch of men, Perks,' said Blouse.

'Probably they have, sir,' said Polly.

'And what man could dare hope for such an

356

opportunity, eh?' said Blouse. 'Our names will go down in the history books! Well, mine will, obviously, and I shall jolly well see to it that you chaps get a mention too. And who knows? Perhaps I may win the highest accolade that a gallant officer may obtain!'

'What's that, sir?' said Polly dutifully.

'Having either a foodstuff or an item of clothing named after one,' said Blouse, his face radiant. 'General Froc got both, of course. The frock coat and Beef Froc. Of course, I could never aspire *that* high.' He looked down bashfully. 'But I have to say, Perks, that I have devised several recipes, just in case!'

'So we'll be eating a Blouse one day, sir?' said Polly. She was watching the baskets being stacked.

'Possibly, possibly, if I may dare hope,' said Blouse. 'Er . . . my favourite is a sort of pastry ring, d'you see, filled with cream and soaked in rum—'

'That's a Rum Baba, sir,' said Polly absently. Tonker and the others were watching the stacked baskets, too.

'It's been done?'

' 'fraid so, sir.'

'How about . . . er . . . a dish of liver and onions?'

'It's called liver-and-onions, sir. Sorry,' said Polly, trying not to lose concentration.

'Er, er, well, it has struck me that some dishes are named after people when really they just made a little change to a basic recipe—'

'We must go now, sir! Now or never, sir!'

'What? Oh. Right. Yes. We must go!'

It was a military manoeuvre hitherto unrecorded.

The squad, coming from different directions on Polly's signal, arrived at the baskets just ahead of the women who'd proposed to take them up, grabbed the handles and advanced. Only then did she realize that probably *no one* else wanted the job, and the women were only too happy to let idiot newcomers take the strain. The baskets were big and the wet washing was heavy. Wazzer and Igorina could barely lift one basket between them.

A couple of soldiers were waiting by the door. They looked bored, and paid little attention. It was a long walk to the 'elevator'.

Polly hadn't been able to picture it when it had been described. You had to see it. It really was just a big open box of heavy timbers, attached to a thick rope, which ran up and down in a sort of chimney in the rock. When they were aboard, one of the soldiers hauled on a much thinner rope that disappeared up into the darkness. The other one lit a couple of candles, whose only apparent role was to make the darkness more gloomy.

'No fainting now, girls!' he said. His mate chuckled.

Two of them and seven of us, Polly thought. The copper stick banged against her leg as she moved, and she knew for a fact that Tonker was limping because *she* had strapped a washing dolly under her dress. That was for *serious* washerwomen; it was a long stick with what looked like a three-legged milking stool on the end of it, the better for agitating clothes in a big cauldron of boiling water. You could probably smash a skull with it.

The stone walls dropped past as the platform rose.

'How thrilling!' trilled 'Daphne'. 'And this goes all the way up through your big castle, does it?'

'Oh, no, miss. Gotta go up through the rock first, miss. Lots of old workings and everything before we get that high.'

'Oh, I thought we were in the castle already.' Blouse gave Polly a worried look.

'No, miss. There's just the washhouse down there, 'cos of the water. Hah, it's a climb and a half even to the lower cellars. Lucky for you there's this elevator, eh?'

'Wonderful, sergeant,' said Blouse, and allowed Daphne back. 'How does it work?'

'It's corporal, miss,' said the string-puller, touching his forelock. 'It's pulled up and down by pris'ners in a treadmill, miss.'

'Oh, how horrid!'

'Oh no, miss, it's quite humane. Er . . . if you're free after work, er, I could take you up and show you the mechanism . . .'

'That would be lovely, sergeant!'

Polly put her hand over her eyes. Daphne was a disgrace to womanhood.

The elevator rumbled upwards, quite slowly. Mostly they passed raw rock but sometimes there were ancient gratings or areas of masonry, suggestive of tunnels long ago blocked—

There was a jerk, and the platform stopped moving. One of the soldiers swore under his breath,

but the corporal said, 'Don't be afraid, ladies. This often happens.'

'Why should we be afraid?' said Polly.

'Well, because we're hanging by a rope a hundred feet up the shaft and the lifting machinery's thrown a cog.'

'Again,' said the other soldier. 'Nothing works properly here.'

'Sounds like a good reason to me,' said Igorina.

'How long will it take to repair?' said Tonker.

'Hah! Last time it happened we were stuck for an hour!'

Too long, Polly thought. Too many things could happen. She looked up through the beams in the roof. The square of daylight was a long way up.

'We can't wait,' she said.

'Oh dear, who will save us?' Daphne quavered.

'We'll have to find a way to pass the time, eh?' said one of the guards. Polly sighed. That was one of those phrases, like 'Well, lookee what we have here', that meant things were only going to get a lot worse.

'We know how it is, ladies,' the guard went on. 'Your menfolk away, and all. It's as bad for us, too. I can't remember when I last kissed my wife.'

'And I can't remember when I last kissed his wife, either,' said the corporal.

Tonker jumped up, caught a beam, and chinned herself to the top of the box. The elevator shook and, somewhere, a piece of rock dislodged and crashed down the shaft.

'Hey, you can't do that!' said the corporal.

'Where does it say?' said Tonker. 'Polly, there's one of those filled-in tunnels here, only most of the stones have been knocked out. We could get in easily.'

'You can't get out! We'll get into trouble!' said the corporal.

Polly pulled his sword out of his scabbard. The space was too crowded to do much with it except threaten, but *she* had it, not him. It made a huge difference.

'You're already in trouble,' she said. 'Please don't force me to make it worse. Let's get out of here. Is that okay, Daphne?'

'Um . . . yes, of course,' said Blouse.

The other guard laid a hand on his own sword. 'Okay, girls, this has gone—' he began, and then slumped. Shufti lowered her copper stick.

'I hope I didn't hit him too hard,' she said.

'Who cares? Come on, I can give you all a hand up,' said Tonker.

'Igorina, could you have a look at him, and—' Shufti began nervously.

'He's a man, and he's groaning,' said Tonker from above. 'That's good enough for me. Come *on.*'

The lone guard watched as the others were womanhandled on to the beams.

'Er, excuse me,' he said to Polly, as she helped Blouse up.

'Yes? What?'

'Would you mind giving *me* a wallop on the back of the head?' he said, looking wretched. 'Only it looks like I didn't put up a fight against a bunch of women.'

'Why *don't* you put up a fight?' said Polly, narrowing her eyes. 'We're only a bunch of women.'

'I'm not crazy!' said the guard.

'Here, let me,' said Igorina, producing her stick. 'Blows to the head are potentially harmful and should not be undertaken lightly. Turn round, sir. Remove your helmet, please. Would twenty minutes' unconsciousness be okay?'

'Yes, thanks very mu—'

The guard folded up.

'I really hope I didn't hurt the other one,' moaned Shufti, from above.

'He's swearing,' said Polly, removing his sword. 'That sounds like he's okay.'

She handed up the candles, and then was hauled on to the trembling roof of the elevator. When she had a firm footing in the mouth of the tunnel she found a sliver of stone and stamped it hard into the space between the shaft wall and the wooden frame, which shook. It wasn't going anywhere for a while.

Tonker and Lofty were already investigating the tunnel. By candlelight, it looked like good masonry beyond the clumsy attempt at walling it up.

'It must be cellars,' said Tonker. 'I reckon they must've made the shaft not long ago and just walled up where it cut through. Could have done a better job, too.'

'Cellars are close to dungeons,' said Polly. 'Now, pinch out one candle, because that way we'll have light for twice as long, and then—'

'Perks, a word please?' said Blouse. 'Over here?'

'Yessir.'

When they were standing a little apart from the rest of the squad, Blouse lowered his voice and said: 'I don't wish to discourage initiative, Perks, but what are you doing?'

'Er . . . anticipating your orders, sir.'

'Anticipating them?'

'Yessir.'

'Ah. Right. This is still small-picture stuff, is it?'

'Exactly, sir.'

'Then my orders, Perks, are to proceed with speed and caution to release the prisoners.'

'Well done, sir. We'll go through this . . . this—'

'Crypt,' said Igorina, looking round.

The candle blew out. Somewhere ahead of them, in darkness absolute and velvet thick, stone moved on stone.

'I wonder *why* this passage was sealed up?' said the voice of Blouse.

'I think I've stopped wondering why it was sealed up in such a hurry,' said Tonker.

'I wonder who tried to open it?' said Polly.

There was a crash of, as it might be, a heavy slab falling off an ornate tomb. It could have been half a dozen other things but, somehow, that was the image that sprang to mind. The dead air moved a little.

'I don't want to worry anyone,' said Shufti, 'but I can hear the sound of sort of feet, sort of dragging.'

Polly remembered the man lighting the candles. He'd dropped the bundle of matches into the brass saucer of the candlestick, hadn't he? Moving

her hand slowly, she groped for them.

'If you didn't want to worry anyone,' came the voice of Tonker from the dry, thick darkness, 'why the hell did you just tell us that?'

Polly's fingers found a sliver of wood. She raised it to her nose, and sniffed the sulphurous smell.

'I've got one match,' she said. 'I'm going to try to light the candle again. Everyone look for a way out. Ready?'

She sidled to the invisible wall. Then she scratched the match down the stone, and yellow light filled the crypt.

Someone whimpered. Polly stared, candle forgotten. The match went out.

'O-kay,' said the subdued voice of Tonker. 'Walking dead people. So?'

'The one near the archway was the late General Puhloaver!' said Blouse. 'I have his book on *The Art of Defence!*'

'Best not to ask him to autograph it, sir,' said Polly, as the squad bunched together.

There was the whimpering again. It seemed to come from where Polly remembered Wazzer standing. She heard her praying. There were no words that she could make out, just a fierce and urgent whispering.

'Maybe these washing sticks can slow them down a bit?' Shufti quavered.

'More than being dead already?' said Igorina.

No, a voice whispered, and light filled the crypt.

It was barely brighter than a glow-worm, but a single

photon can do a lot of work in chthonic darkness. It rose above the kneeling Wazzer until it was woman height, because it was a woman. Or, at least, it was the shadow of a woman. No, Polly saw, it was the *light* of a woman, a moving web of lines and highlights in which there came and went, like pictures in a fire, a female shape.

'Soldiers of Borogravia . . . attention!' said Wazzer. And underneath her reedy little tone was a shadow voice, a whisper that filled and refilled the long room.

Soldiers of Borogravia . . . attention!

Soldiers . . .

Soldiers, attention!

Soldiers of Borogravia . . .

The lurching figures stopped. They hesitated. They shuffled backwards. With a certain amount of clattering and tongueless bickering, they formed two lines. Wazzer stood up.

'Follow me,' she said.

Follow me . . .

. . . me . . .

'Sir?' said Polly to Blouse.

'I think we go, don't you?' said the lieutenant, who seemed oblivious of Wazzer's activities now he was in the presence of the military might of the centuries. 'Oh, god . . . there's Brigadier Galosh! And Major-general the Lord Kanapay! General Annorac! I've read everything he wrote! I never thought I'd see him in the flesh!'

'*Partly* flesh, sir,' said Polly, dragging him forward.

'Every great commander of the last five hundred years was buried here, Perks!'

'I'm very pleased for you, sir. If we could just move a little faster . . .'

'It is my fondest hope that I'll spend the rest of eternity here, you know.'

'Wonderful, sir, but not starting today. Can we catch up with the rest of them, sir?'

As they passed, hand after ragged hand was raised in jerky salute. Staring eyes gleamed in hollow faces. The strange light glistened on dusty braid and stained, faded cloth. And there was a noise, harsher than the whispering, deep and guttural. It sounded like the creaking of distant doors, but individual voices rose and fell as the squad passed the dead figures . . .

Death to Zlobenia . . . get them . . . remember . . . give them hell . . . vengeance . . . remember . . . they're not human . . . avenge us . . . revenge . . .

Up ahead, Wazzer had reached some high wooden doors. They swung open at her touch. The light travelled with her, and the squad were on her heels. To be too far behind was to be in the dark.

'Couldn't I just ask Major-general—' Blouse began, dragging on Polly's hand.

'No! You can't! Don't dawdle! Come on!' Polly commanded.

They reached the doors, which Tonker and Igorina slammed behind them. Polly leaned against the wall.

'I think that was the most . . . most amazing moment of my life,' said Blouse, as the boom died away.

'I think this is mine,' said Polly, fighting for breath.

Light still glowed around Wazzer, who turned to face the squad with an expression of beatific pleasure. 'You must speak to the High Command,' she said.

You must speak to the High Command, whispered the walls.

'Be kind to this child.'

Be kind to this child . . .

. . . this child . . .

Polly caught Wazzer before she hit the ground.

'What is happening with her?' said Tonker.

'I think the Duchess really is speaking through her,' said Polly. Wazzer was unconscious, only the whites of her eyes showing. Polly laid her down gently.

'Oh, come on! The Duchess is just a painting! She's dead!'

Sometimes you give in. For Polly, that time had been the length of time it took to walk through the crypt. If you don't believe, or don't want to believe, or if you don't simply hope that there's something worth believing in, why turn round? And if you don't believe, who are you trusting to lead you out of the grip of dead men?

'Dead?' she said. 'So what? What about the old soldiers back there, who haven't faded away? What about the light? And you heard how Wazzer's voice sounded.'

'Yeah, but . . . well, that sort of thing doesn't happen to people you *know*,' said Tonker. 'It happens to . . . well, strange religious people. I mean, a few days ago she was learning how to fart loudly!'

'She?' whispered Blouse to Polly. 'She? Why is—'

Once again a part of Polly's mind overtook the sudden panic. 'Sorry, *Daphne*?' she said.

'Oh . . . yes . . . of course . . . can't be too . . . yes . . .' the lieutenant murmured.

Igorina knelt down by the girl and put a hand on her forehead. 'She's on fire,' she said.

'She used to pray all the time back at the Grey House,' said Lofty, kneeling down.

'Yeah, well, there was a lot to pray about, if you weren't strong,' growled Tonker. 'And every bloody day we had to pray to the Duchess to thank Nuggan for slops you wouldn't give to a pig! And that damn picture everywhere, that fishy stare . . . I hate it! It could drive you mad. That's what happened to Wazz, right? And now you want me to believe the fat old biddy is alive and treating our friend there like some . . . puppet or something? I don't believe that. And if it's true, it shouldn't be!'

'She's burning up, Magda,' said Lofty quietly.

'D'you know why we joined up?' said Tonker, red in the face. 'To get away! Anything was better than what we had! I've got Lofty and Lofty's got me, and we're sticking with you because there's nothing else for us. Everyone says the Zlobenians are terrible, right? But they've never done anything to *us*, they've never hurt *us*. If they want to come over here and hang a few bastards, I could give 'em a list! Everywhere there's something bad happening, everywhere the small-minded bullies are inventing new cruelties, new ways of keeping us down, that bloody face is watching! And you say it's *here*?'

'*We're* here,' said Polly. 'And you are here. And we're going to do what we came to do and get out, understand? You kissed the picture, you took the shilling!'

'I damn well didn't kiss her face! And a shilling's the least they owe me!'

'Then go!' shouted Polly. 'Desert! We won't stop you, because I'm sick of your . . . your bullshit! But you make up your mind right now, *right now*, understand? Because when we meet the enemy I don't want to think you're there to stab me in the back!'

The words flew out before she could stop them, and there was no power in the world that could snatch them back.

Tonker went pale, and a certain life drained out of her face like water from a funnel. '*What was that you said?*'

The words 'You heard me!' lined up to spring from Polly's tongue, but she hesitated. She told herself: it doesn't have to go this way. You don't have to let a pair of socks do the talking.

'Words that were stupid,' she said. 'I'm sorry. I didn't mean it.'

Tonker settled slightly. 'Well . . . all right, then,' she said grudgingly. 'Just so long as you know we're in this for the squad, okay? Not for the army and not for the bloody Duchess.'

'That was a treasonable speech, Private Halter!' said Lieutenant Blouse.

Everyone but Polly had forgotten about him, and he stood there like an easy man to forget.

'However,' he went on, 'I realize we're all

somewhat . . .' he looked down at his dress '. . . *confused* and, er, bewildered by the pace of events . . .'

Tonker tried to avoid Polly's eye. 'Sorry, sir,' she muttered, glowering.

'I must make it clear that I will not stand to hear such things repeated,' said Blouse.

'No, sir.'

'Good,' said Polly quickly. 'So let's—'

'But I will overlook it this time,' Blouse went on.

Polly could *see* Tonker snap. The head was raised slowly. 'You'll overlook it?' said Tonker. '*You* will overlook it?'

'*Careful*,' said Polly, just loud enough for Tonker to hear.

'Let me tell you something about us, lieutenant,' said Tonker, grinning horribly.

'We are here, private, *whoever* we are,' snapped Polly. 'Now let's find the cells!'

'Um . . .' said Igorina, 'we're quite close, I think. I can see a sign. Um. It's at the end of this passage. Um . . . just behind those three rather puzzled armed men with the, um . . . *efficient*-looking crossbows. Um. I think what you've just been saying was important and needed to be said. Only, um . . . not just now, perhaps? And not so loudly?'

Only two guards were watching them now, raising their bows cautiously. The other was running away down the passage, shouting.

The squad, as one man, or woman, shared the thoughts. They've got bows. We haven't. They've got

reinforcements behind them. We haven't. All we've got is a darkness full of the restless dead. We haven't even got a prayer any more.

Blouse made an effort, nevertheless. In the tones of Daphne he shrilled: 'Oh, officers . . . we seem to have got lost on the way to the ladies' room . . .'

They were not put into a dungeon, although they were marched past plenty. There were lots of bleak stone corridors, lots of heavy doors with bars and lots and lots of bolts, and lots of armed men whose job, presumably, only became interesting if all the bolts disappeared. They were put into a kitchen. It was huge, and clearly not the kind of place where people chopped herbs and stuffed mushrooms. In a gloomy, grimy, soot-encrusted hall like this, cooks had probably catered for hundreds of hungry men. Occasionally the door was opened and shadowy figures stared in at them. No one had said anything, at any time.

'They were expecting us,' muttered Shufti. The squad were sitting on the floor with their backs to a huge, ancient chopping block, except for Igorina, who was tending to the still-unconscious Wazzer.

'They couldn't have got that elevator up by now,' said Polly. 'I wedged that stone in good and hard.'

'Then maybe the washerwomen gave us away,' said Tonker. 'I didn't like the look of Mrs Enid.'

'It doesn't matter now, does it?' said Polly. 'Is that the only door?'

'There's a storeroom at the other end,' said Tonker. 'No exit, except a grille in the floor.'

'Could we get out that way?'

'Only diced.'

They stared glumly at the distant door. It had opened again, and there was some muffled conversation amongst the silhouettes beyond. Tonker had tried advancing on the open doorway, and found men with swords suddenly occupying it. Polly turned to look at Blouse, who was slumped against the wall, staring blankly upwards.

'I'd better go and tell him,' she said. Tonker shrugged.

Blouse opened his eyes and smiled wanly when Polly approached. 'Ah, Perks,' he said. 'We almost made it, eh?'

'Sorry we let you down, sir,' said Polly. 'Permission to sit, sir?'

'Treat the rather chilly flagstones as if they were your own,' said Blouse. 'And it was I that let you down, I'm afraid.'

'Oh, no, sir—' Polly protested.

'You were my first command,' said Blouse. 'Well, apart from Corporal Drebb and he was seventy and only had one arm, poor chap.' He pinched the bridge of his nose. 'All I had to do was get you to the valley. That was all. But, no, I foolishly dreamed of a world where everyone would one day wear a Blouse. Or eat one, possibly. I should have listened to Sergeant Jackrum! Oh, will I ever look my dear Emmeline in the face again?'

'I don't know, sir,' said Polly.

'That was meant to be more of a rhetorical cry

of despair than an actual question, Perks,' said Blouse.

'Sorry, sir,' said Polly. She took a deep breath, ready for the plunge into the icy depths of the truth. 'Sir, you ought to know that—'

'And I'm afraid once they realize we aren't women we'll be put in the big dungeons,' the lieutenant went on. 'Very big, and very dirty, I'm told. And very crowded.'

'Sir, we *are* women, sir,' said Polly.

'Yes, well done, Perks, but we don't have to pretend any more.'

'You don't understand, sir. We really *are* women. All of us.'

Blouse grinned nervously. 'I think you've got a little . . . confused, Perks. I seem to recall that the same thing happened to Wrigglesworth—'

'Sir—'

'—although I have to say he was very good at choosing curtains—'

'*No*, sir. I was a— I *am* a girl, and I cut my hair and pretended I was a boy and took the Duchess's shilling, sir. Take my word for it, sir, because I really don't want to have to draw you a picture. We played a trick on you, sir. Well, not a trick, really, but we, all of us, had reasons for being somewhere else, sir, or at least not being where we were. We lied.'

Blouse stared at her. 'You're sure?'

'Yes, sir. I am of the female persuasion. I check every day, sir.'

'And Private Halter?'

'Yes, sir.'

'*And* Lofty?'

'Oh, yes, sir. Both of them, sir. Don't go there, sir.'

'What about Shufti?'

'Expecting a baby, sir.'

Suddenly, Blouse looked terrified. 'Oh, *no. Here?*'

'Not for several months, sir, I believe.'

'And poor little Private Goom?'

'A girl, sir. And Igor is really an Igorina. And wherever she is, Carborundum is really Jade. We're not sure about Corporal Maladict. But the rest of us definitely have pink blankets, sir.'

'But you didn't *act* like women!'

'No, sir. We acted like men, sir. Sorry, sir. We just wanted to find our men or get away or prove a point or something. Sorry it had to happen to you, sir.'

'You're *sure* about all this, are you?'

What are you expecting me to say? Polly thought. 'Whoops, now I come to think about it, yes, we're really men after all'? She settled for saying: 'Yes, sir.'

'So . . . you're not called Oliver, then?' It seemed to Polly that the lieutenant was having a lot of difficulty with all this; he kept asking the same basic question in different ways, in the hope of getting something other than the answer he didn't want to hear.

'No, sir. I'm Polly, sir—'

'Oh? Do you know there is a song about—'

'*Yes*, sir,' said Polly firmly. 'Believe me, I'd rather you didn't even hum it.'

Blouse stared at the far wall, eyes slightly un-focused. Oh dear, Polly thought. 'You took a terrible

risk,' he said distantly. 'A battlefield is no place for women.'

'This war isn't staying on battlefields. At a time like this, a pair of trousers is a girl's best friend, sir.'

Blouse fell silent again. Suddenly, Polly felt very sorry for him. He was a bit of a fool, in that special way very clever people have of being foolish, but he wasn't a bad man. He'd been decent to the squad and he'd cared about them. He didn't deserve this.

'Sorry you had to be involved, sir,' she said.

Blouse looked up. 'Sorry?' he said, and to her amazement he was looking more cheerful than he had all day. 'Good heavens, you don't have to be *sorry*. Do you know anything about history, Polly?'

'Can we stick with Perks, sir? I'm still a soldier. No, I don't know much history, sir. At least, much that I trust.'

'Then you've never heard of the Amazon warriors of Samothrip? The most fearsome fighting force for hundreds of years. All women! Absolutely merciless in battle! They were deadly with the longbow, although in order to get maximum draw they had to cut off one of their, um . . . er . . . I say, you ladies haven't been cutting off your, um, er . . .'

'No, we haven't cut off any um ers, sir. Only hair.'

Blouse looked incredibly relieved. 'Well, and then there's the female bodyguards of King Samuel in Howandaland. All seven feet tall, I understand, and deadly with the spear. Throughout Klatch, of course, there are many stories of female warriors, often fighting alongside their men. Fearsome and fearless, I

believe. Men would desert rather than face females, Perks. Couldn't deal with 'em.'

Once again, Polly felt the slightly unbalanced feeling of having tried to jump a hurdle that turned out not to be there. She took refuge in: 'What do you think's going to happen now, sir?'

'I haven't a clue, Perks. Um . . . what's wrong with young Goom? Some kind of religious mania?'

'Could be, sir,' said Polly guardedly. 'The Duchess talks to her.'

'Oh dear,' said Blouse. 'She—'

The door opened. A dozen soldiers filed in and spread out on either side. They had a variety of uniforms – mostly Zlobenian, but several Polly recognized now as Ankh-Morporkic or whatever they called it. They were all armed, and held their weapons like men who expected to use them.

When they had lined up and were glaring at the squad, a smaller group of men stepped in. Again, there was a variety of uniforms, but they were a lot more expensive. These were worn by officers – high-ranking ones, to judge by the expressions of disdain. The tallest of them, made taller by his high, plumed cavalry helmet, stared along his nose at the women. He had pale blue eyes, and his face suggested that he did not really want to see anything at all in this room unless it had been thoroughly cleaned first.

'Who is the officer here?' he said. He sounded like a lawyer.

Blouse stood up and saluted. 'Lieutenant Blouse, sir, Tenth Infantry.'

'I see.' The man looked at his fellow officers. 'I believe we can dispense with the guard now, don't you? This matter should be handled quietly. And for heaven's sake can't we find this man a pair of trousers?'

There were a few murmurs. The man nodded to the sergeant of the guard. The armed men filed out, and the door shut behind them.

'My name is Lord Rust,' said the man. 'I head the Ankh-Morpork detachment here. At least,' and he sniffed, 'the military detachment. You have been treated well? You have not been manhandled? I see there is a . . . young lady on the floor.'

'She's in a swoon, sir,' said Polly. The blue eyes lighted upon her.

'You would be—?' he said.

'Corporal Perks, sir,' said Polly. There were some barely suppressed smiles from the officers.

'Ah. I believe you are the one seeking her brother?' said Lord Rust.

'How do you know my name?' said Polly.

'We are an, mm, efficient army,' said Rust, and treated himself to a little smile of his own. 'Your brother's name is Paul?'

'Yes!'

'We shall locate him, eventually. And I understand another lady was seeking her young man?'

Shufti curtsied nervously. 'Me, sir.'

'Again, we shall locate him, if you give us his name. Now, please listen to me carefully. You, Miss Perks, and the rest of you, will be taken from here, tonight,

entirely unharmed, and escorted back into your country as far as our patrols can take you, which, I suspect, will be quite a long way. Is that understood? You will have what you came for. Won't that be nice? And you will not return here. The troll and the vampire have been captured. The same offer applies to them.'

Polly was watching the officers. They looked nervous . . .

. . . except for one at the back. She'd thought all the guards had gone and, while this man was dressed like a guard – dressed, that is, like a badly dressed guard – he wasn't acting like one. He was leaning against the wall by the door, smoking half a cigar, and grinning. He looked like a man enjoying a show.

'Very generously,' Rust went on, 'this offer applies to you too, Lieutenant . . . Blouse, wasn't it? But in your case you would be on parole in a house in Zlobenia, very pleasant I understand, healthy walks in the countryside and all that sort of thing. This offer has not been extended to your superior officers here, I may add.'

So why make it to us? Polly thought. Are you frightened? Of a bunch of *girls*? That makes no sense . . .

Behind the officers, the man with the cigar winked at Polly. His uniform was very old-fashioned – an ancient helmet, a breastplate, some slightly rusted chain mail, and big boots. He wore it like a workman wears his overalls. Unlike the braid and brilliance in front of her, the only statement his clothes made was that he didn't intend to get hurt. They had no insignia that Polly could

see, apart from a small shield hooked on to the breastplate.

'If you will excuse me a moment,' said Blouse, 'I will consult with my men.'

'Men?' said Rust. 'They're a bunch of women, man!'

'But at this moment, sir,' said Blouse coolly, 'I would not exchange them for any six men you offered me. If you gentlemen would care to wait outside?'

Behind the group, the badly dressed man burst into silent laughter. His sense of humour was not shared by the rest of the group, however.

'You cannot possibly consider refusing this offer!' said Lord Rust.

'Nevertheless, sir,' said Blouse. 'We will take a few minutes. I think the ladies would prefer some privacy. One of them is expecting a child.'

'What, *here*?' As one man, the group drew back.

'Not yet, I believe. But if you would just step outside—'

When the officers had retreated to the masculine safety of the corridor the lieutenant turned to his squad. 'Well, men? For you, it is a very attractive offer, I have to say.'

'Not for us,' said Tonker. Lofty nodded.

'Nor me,' said Shufti.

'Why not?' said Blouse. 'You would get your husband.'

'That might be a bit difficult,' mumbled Shufti. 'Anyway, what about the invasion?'

'I'm not going to be sent home like a package,' said

Igorina. 'Anyway, that man has an objectionable bone structure.'

'Well, Private Goom can't join us right now,' sighed Blouse. 'So that leaves you, Polly.'

'Why are they doing this?' said Polly. 'Why do they want us out of the way? Why aren't they just leaving us locked up? This place must be full of cells.'

'Ah, perhaps they are sensible of the frailties of your sex,' said Blouse, and then fried in their stares. 'I didn't say *I* was,' he added quickly.

'They could just kill us,' said Tonker. 'Well, they could,' she added. 'Why not? Who'd care? I don't think we count as prisoners of war.'

'But they haven't,' said Polly. 'And they're not even threatening us. They're being very *careful*. I think they're frightened of us.'

'Oh, yeah, right,' said Tonker. 'Maybe they think we're going to chase them and give them a big wet sloppy kiss?'

'Good, then we're agreed that we're not going to accept,' said Blouse. 'Damn right ... oh, I do apologize ...'

'We all know the words, sir,' said Polly. 'I suggest we see how *much* we frighten them, sir.'

The officers were waiting with unconcealed impatience, but Rust managed a brief smile when he stepped back into the kitchen. 'Well, lieutenant?' he said.

'We have given your offer due consideration, sir,' said Blouse, 'and our reply is: stick it up your ...' He

leaned down to Polly, who whispered urgently. 'Who? Oh, yes, right. Your jumper, sir. Stick it, in fact, up your jumper. Named after Colonel Henri Jumper, I believe. A useful woollen garment akin to a lightweight sweater, sir, which if I recall correctly was named after Regimental Sergeant-Major Sweat. That, sir, is where you may stick it.'

Rust received this calmly, and Polly wondered whether it was because he hadn't understood it. The scruffy man once more leaning against the wall had understood it, though, since he was grinning.

'I see,' said Rust. 'And that is the answer from all of you? Then you leave us no choice. Good evening to you.'

His attempt to stride out was hindered by the other officers, who had less sense of the dramatic moment. The door slammed behind them, but not before the last man out turned very briefly and made a hand gesture. You would have missed it if you weren't watching him – but Polly *was* watching.

'That seemed to go well,' said Blouse, turning away.

'I hope we're not going to get into trouble for that,' said Shufti.

'Compared to what?' said Tonker.

'The last man out stuck his thumb up and winked,' said Polly. 'Did you notice him? He wasn't even wearing an officer's uniform.'

'Probably wanted a date,' said Tonker.

'In Ankh-Morpork that means "jolly good",' said Blouse. 'In Klatch, I think, it means "I hope your donkey explodes". I spotted the man. Looked like a guard sergeant to me.'

'Didn't have stripes,' said Polly. 'Why'd he want to say jolly good to us?'

'Or hate our donkey so much?' said Shufti. 'How's Wazzer?'

'Sleeping,' said Igorina. 'I think.'

'What do you mean?'

'Well, I don't think she's dead.'

'You don't *think* she is?' said Polly.

'Yes,' said Igorina. 'It's like that. I wish I could keep her warmer.'

'I thought you said she was burning up?'

'She was. Now she's freezing cold.'

Lieutenant Blouse strode over to the door, grabbed its handle and, to the surprise of all, pulled it open. Four swords were levelled at him.

'We have a sick man here!' he snapped to the astonished guards. 'We need blankets and firewood! Get them now!' He slammed the door. 'It might work,' he said.

'That door doesn't have a lock,' said Tonker. 'Useful fact, Polly.'

Polly sighed. 'Right now, I just want something to eat. This is a kitchen, after all. There could be food here.'

'This *is* a kitchen,' said Tonker. 'There could be cleavers!'

But it is always upsetting to find that the enemy is as bright as you. There was a well, but a web of bars across the top allowed for the passage of nothing bigger than a bucket. And someone with no sense of the narrative of adventure had removed from the

room anything with an edge and, for some reason, anything that could be eaten.

'Unless we want to dine on candles,' said Shufti, pulling a bundle of them out of a creaking cupboard. ' 's tallow, after all. I bet old Scallot'd make candle scubbo.'

Polly checked the chimney, which smelled as though there had not been a fire in it for a long time. It was big and wide, but six feet up a heavy grille was hung with sooty cobwebs. It looked rusted and ancient, and could probably be shifted by twenty minutes' work with a crowbar, but there's never a crowbar when you want one.

There were some couple of sacks of ancient, dry and dusty flour in the storeroom. It smelled bad. There was a thing with a funnel and a handle and some mysterious screws.* There were a couple of rolling pins, a lettuce strainer, some ladles ... and there were forks. Lots of toasting forks. Polly felt let down. It was ridiculous to expect that someone imprisoning people in some ad hoc cell would leave in all the ingredients to effect an escape but, nevertheless, she felt that some universal rule had been broken. They had nothing better than a club, really. The toasting forks might prick, the lettuce strainer might pack a punch, and the rolling pins were at least a traditional female weapon, but all you could do with

* Every long-established kitchen has one of these, and no one ever remembers why. It is generally for something that no one does any more and, even when it was done, it wasn't done with any real enthusiasm, such as celery basting, walnut shredding or, in the worst case, edible dormouse stuffing.

the thing with a funnel and a handle and mysterious screws was baffle people.

The door opened. Armed men came in to act as protection for a couple of women, carrying blankets and firewood. They scurried in with their eyes cast down, deposited their burdens, and almost ran out. Polly strode over to the guard who seemed to be in charge, and he backed away. A huge key ring jingled on his belt.

'You *knock* next time, all right?' she said.

He grinned nervously. 'Yeah, right,' he said. 'They said we weren't to talk to you . . .'

'Really?'

The jailer glanced around. 'But we reckon you're doing bloody well, for girls,' he said conspiratorially.

'So that means you won't shoot at us when we break out?' said Polly sweetly.

The grin faded. 'Don't try it,' said the jailer.

'What a big bunch of keys you have there, sir,' said Tonker, and the man's hand flew to his belt.

'You just stay in here,' he said. 'Things are bad enough already. You stay here!'

He slammed the door. A moment later they heard something heavy being pushed up against it.

'Well, now we have a fire, at least,' said Blouse.

'Er . . .' This was from Lofty. She volunteered a word so seldom that the rest turned to look at her, and she stopped in embarrassment.

'Yes, Lofty?' said Polly.

'Er . . . I know how to get the door open,' muttered Lofty. 'So it stays open, I mean.'

Had it been anyone else, someone would have laughed. But words from Lofty had obviously been turned over for some time before utterance.

'Er . . . good,' said Blouse. 'Well done.'

'I've been thinking about it,' said Lofty.

'Good.'

'It will work.'

'Just what we need, then!' said Blouse, like a man trying against all the odds to keep cheerful.

Lofty looked up at the big sooty beams that ran across the room. 'Yes,' she said.

'But there'll still be guards outside,' said Polly.

'No,' said Lofty. 'There won't.'

'There won't?'

'They'll have gone away.' Lofty stopped, with the air of one who'd said everything that needed to be said.

Tonker walked over and took her arm. 'We'll just have a little chat, shall we?' she said, and led the girl to the other side of the room. There was some whispered conversation. Lofty spent most of it staring at the floor, and then Tonker came back.

'We will need the bags of flour from the storeroom, and the rope from the well,' she said. 'And one of those . . . what are those big round things that cover dishes? With a knob on?'

'Dish covers?' said Shufti.

'And a candle,' Tonker went on. 'And a lot of barrels. And a lot of water.'

'And what will all this do?' said Blouse.

'Make a big bang,' said Tonker. 'Tilda knows a lot about fire, believe me.'

'When you say she knows a lot...' Polly began uncertainly.

'I mean every place she worked at burned down,' said Tonker.

They rolled the empty barrels to the middle of the room and filled them with water from the pump. Under Lofty's monosyllabic direction and the rope from the well, they hauled three leaking, dusty flour sacks up as high as possible, so that they twisted gently over the space between the barrels and the door.

'Ah,' said Polly, standing back. 'I think I understand. A flour mill on the other side of town blew up two years ago.'

'Yes,' said Tonker. 'That was Tilda.'

'What?'

'They'd been beating her. And worse. And the thing about Tilda is, she just watches and thinks and some-where in there it all comes together. Then it explodes.'

'But two people died!'

'The man and his wife. Yes. But I heard that other girls sent there never came back at all. Shall I tell you that Tilda was pregnant when they brought her back to the Grey House after the fire? She had it, and they took it away, and we don't know what happened to it. And then she got beaten again because she was an Abomination unto Nuggan. Does that make you feel better?' said Tonker, tying the rope to a table leg. 'There's just us, Polly. Just her and me. No in-heritance, no nice home to go back to, no relatives

that we know of. The Grey House breaks us all, some-how. Wazzer talks to the Duchess, I don't have . . . middle gears, and Tilda frightens me when she gets her hands on a box of matches. You should see her face then, though. It lights up. Of course,' Tonker smiled in her dangerous way, 'so do other things. Better get everyone into the storeroom while we light the candle.'

'Shouldn't Tilda do that?'

'She will. But we'll have to drag her away, otherwise she'll stay and watch.'

This had started like a game. She hadn't *thought* of it like a game, but it was a game called Let Polly keep The Duchess. And now . . . it didn't matter. She'd made all kinds of plans, but she was beyond plans now. They'd done bloody well, for girls . . .

A final barrel of water had been placed, after some discussion, in front of the storeroom's door. Polly looked over the top of it at Blouse and the rest of the squad.

'Okay, everybody, we're . . . er . . . about to do it,' she said. 'Are we *sure* about this, Tonker?'

'Yep.'

'And *we* won't get hurt?'

Tonker sighed. 'The dusty flour will explode. That's simple. The blast coming this way will hit the barrels full of water which'll probably last just long enough to see it rebound. The worst that should happen to us is that we get wet. That's what Tilda thinks. Would you argue? And in the other direction, there's only the door.'

'How does she work this out?'

'She doesn't. She just sees how it should go.' Tonker handed Polly the end of a rope. 'This goes over the beam and down to the dish lid. Can you hold it, lieutenant? But don't pull it until we say. I really mean that. C'mon, Polly.'

In the space between the barrels and the door, Lofty was lighting a candle. She did it slowly, as if it was a sacrament or some ancient ceremony every part of which held enormous and complex meaning. She lit a match, and held it carefully until the flame caught. She waved it back and forth on the base of the candle, which she thrust firmly on to the flagstones so that the hot wax stuck it into position. Then she applied the match to the candle wick and knelt there, watching the flame.

'Okay,' said Tonker. 'I'm just going to pick her up, and you just *carefully* lower the lid over the candle, right? C'mon, Tilda.'

She raised the girl carefully to her feet, whispering to her all the time, and then nodded to Polly, who lowered the lid with a carefulness that amounted to reverence.

Lofty walked as though asleep. Tonker stopped by the leg of the heavy kitchen table, to which she'd attached the other end of the rope holding the flour bags.

'Okay so far,' she said. 'Now, when I pull the knot we each grab an arm and we run, Polly, understand? We *run*. Ready? Got her?' She hauled on the rope. '*Run!*'

The flour sacks dropped, streaming white dust as they fell, and exploded in front of the door. Flour rose like a fog. They raced for the storeroom and fell in a heap past the barrel as Tonker screamed, 'Okay, lieutenant!' Blouse pulled the rope that raised the lid and let the candle flame reach—

The word was not *whoomph*. The *experience* was whoomph. It had a quality that overwhelmed every sense. It shook the world like a sheet, painted it white and then, surprisingly, filled it with the smell of toast. And then it was over, in a second, leaving nothing but distant screams and the rumble of collapsing masonry.

Polly uncurled, and looked up into Blouse's face. 'I think we grab things and run now, sir,' she said. 'And screaming would help.'

'I think I can manage the screaming,' muttered Shufti. 'This is *not* a very nurturing experience.'

Blouse gripped his ladle. 'I hope this isn't going to be our famous last stand,' he said.

'In fact, sir,' said Polly, 'I think it's going to be our first. Permission to yell in a bloodcurdling way, sir?'

'Permission granted, Perks!'

The floor was awash with water and bits – quite small bits – of barrel. Half the chimney had collapsed into the fireplace and the soot was blazing fiercely. Polly wondered if, down in the valley, it'd look like a signal.

The door had gone. So had a lot of wall around it. Beyond—

Smoke and dust filled the air. In it, men lay

groaning, or picked their way aimlessly across the rubble. When the squad arrived they did not simply fail to put up a fight, they failed to understand. Or hear. The women lowered their weapons. Polly spotted the sergeant, who was sitting and hitting the side of his head with the flat of his hand.

'Give me the keys!' she demanded.

He tried to focus. 'What?'

'The keys!'

'I'll have a brown one, please.'

'Are you okay?'

'What?'

Polly reached down and snatched the key ring from the unresisting man's belt, fighting down an instinct to apologize. She threw it to Blouse. 'Will you do the honours, sir? I think we'll be having a lot of visitors really soon.' She turned to the squad. 'The rest of you, get their weapons off them!'

'Some of these men are badly hurt, Polly,' said Igorina, kneeling down. 'There's one here with multiple.'

'Multiple what?' said Polly, watching the steps.

'Just . . . multiple. Multiple everything. But I know I can save his arm, because I've just found it over there. I think he must've been holding his sword and—'

'Just do what you can, okay?' said Polly.

'Hey, they're *enemies*,' said Tonker, picking up a sword.

'Thith ith an Igor thing,' said Igorina, taking off her pack. 'I'm thorry, you wouldn't underthtand.'

'I'm beginning not to.' Tonker joined Polly in her watch on the stairs. Around them, men groaned and stone creaked. 'I wonder how much damage we did? There's a lot of dust up there . . .'

'There'll be a lot of people here soon,' said Polly, more calmly than she felt. Because this is going to be it, she thought. *This* time there's going to be no turkey to save us. This is where I find out if I'm the meat or the metal . . .

She could hear Blouse unlocking doors, and the shouts from those within. 'Lieutenant Blouse, Tenth Infantry!' he was saying. 'This is a rescue, broadly speaking. Sorry about the mess.'

Probably his inner Daphne had added that last bit, Polly thought. And then the corridor was full of released men, and someone said, 'What are these women doing here! For god's sake, give me that sword, girl!'

And, right now, she wasn't inclined to argue.

Men take over. It is probably because of socks.

The squad retired to the kitchen, where Igorina was at work. She worked fast, efficiently and, on the whole, with very little blood. Her large pack was open beside her. The jars inside were blue, green and red; some of them smoked when she opened them, or gave off strange lights. Her fingers moved in a blur. It was fascinating to watch her working. At least, it was if you hadn't just eaten.

'Squad, this is Major Erick von Moldvitz! He asked to meet you.'

They turned at the sound of Blouse's voice. He'd brought a newcomer. The major was young, but much more heavily built than the lieutenant. He had a scar across his face.

'Stand easy, lads,' he said. 'Blouse here has been telling me what crackin' work you've been doing. Well done! Dressin' up as women, eh? Lucky you weren't found out!'

'Yessir,' said Polly. From outside, there came the sound of cries and fighting.

'Didn't bring your uniforms with you?' said the major.

'Could've been tricky if they were found on us,' said Polly, staring at Blouse.

'Could've been tricky anyway, eh, if you were searched?' said the major, winking.

'Yessir,' said Polly obediently. 'Lieutenant Blouse told you *all* about us, did he, sir?'

Just behind the major, Blouse was making a universal gesture. It consisted of both hands held palm up and outwards and waggled furiously with all fingers extended.

'Hah, yes. Stole some clothes from a knockin' shop, eh? Young lads like you shouldn't have gone in a place like that, eh? Those places are an Abomination, if they're run right!' said the major, wagging a finger theatrically. 'Anyway, we're doing well. Hardly any guards this deep in the keep, y'see. The whole place was built on the basis that the enemy would be on the *outside*! I say, what's that man doin' to the man on the slab?'

'Patching him up, thur,' said Igorina. 'Thewing hith arm back on.'

'He's an enemy, ain't he?'

'Code of the Igorth, thur,' said Igorina reproachfully. 'A thpare hand *where needed*, thur.'

The major sniffed. 'Oh well, can't argue with you fellows, eh? But when you've finished, we've got plenty of chaps out there who could do with your help.'

'Thertainly, thur,' said Igorina.

'Any news of my brother, sir?' said Polly. 'Paul Perks?'

'Yes, Blouse here mentioned him, Perks, but there's men locked up everywhere and it's a little tricky right now, eh?' said the major brusquely. 'As for the rest of you, we'll get you into a pair of trousers as soon as possible and you can join in the fun, eh?'

'The fun,' said Tonker, in a hollow voice.

'The fun being . . . ?' said Polly.

'We've got as far as the fourth floor already,' said von Moldvitz. 'We might not have the whole keep back, but we hold the outer courtyards and some of the towers. By morning, we'll control who comes in and goes out. We're back in the war! They won't invade now. Most of their top brass are in the inner keep.'

'Back in the war,' murmured Polly.

'And we will win!' said the major.

'Oh, *sugar*,' said Shufti.

Something was going to give, Polly knew. Tonker had that look she got before she exploded, and even Shufti was fidgeting. It would only be a matter of time

before Lofty found her box of matches, which Polly had hidden in a cupboard.

Igorina packed up her bag and smiled brightly at the major. 'Ready to go, thur,' she said.

'At least remove the wig, eh?'

'It'th my own hair, thur,' said Igorina.

'Looks a bit . . . cissy, then,' said the major. 'It would be better if—'

'I am, in fact, female, sir,' said Igorina, dropping most of the lisp. 'Trust me, I'm an Igor. We know about this sort of thing. And my needlework ith second to none.'

'A *woman*?' said the major.

Polly sighed. 'We all are, sir. Really women. Not just dressed up as women. And right now I don't want to put any trousers on because then I'd be a woman dressed up as a man dressed up as a woman dressed up as a man, and then I'd be so confused I wouldn't know how to swear. And I want to swear right now, sir, very much.'

The major turned stiffly to Blouse. 'Did you know about this, lieutenant?' he barked.

'Well . . . yes, sir. Eventually. But even so, sir, I would—'

This cell was an old guardroom. It was damp, and had two creaking bunks.

'On the whole,' said Tonker, 'I think it was better when we were locked up by the enemy.'

'There's a grille in the ceiling,' said Shufti.

'Not big enough to climb through,' said Polly.

'No, but we can hang ourselves before they do it.'

'I'm told it's a very painful way to die,' said Polly.

'Who by?' said Tonker.

Occasionally the sounds of battle filtered through the narrow window. Mostly it was yells; often it was screams. Fun was being had.

Igorina sat staring at her hands. 'What's *wrong* with these?' she said. 'Didn't I do a good job on that arm? But *no*, they're afraid I might touch their privates.'

'Perhaps you could have promised to operate only on officers,' said Tonker. No one laughed, and probably no one would have bothered to run for it if the door had swung open. It was a proud and noble thing to escape from the enemy, but if you were escaping from your own side, where would you escape to?

On one of the bunks, Wazzer slept like a hibernating bear. You had to watch her for some time to see her breathe.

'What can they do to us?' said Shufti nervously. 'You know . . . *really* do to us?'

'We were wearing men's clothes,' said Polly.

'But that's only a beating.'

'Oh, they'll find some other stuff, believe you me,' said Tonker. 'Besides, who knows we're here?'

'But we got them out of prison! Our side!'

Polly sighed. 'That's *why*, Shufti. *No one* wants to know that a bunch of girls dressed up as soldiers and broke into a big fort and let out half an army. Everyone knows females can't do that. Neither side wants us here, understand?'

'On a battlefield like this, who'll worry about a few more bodies?' said Tonker.

'Don't say that! Lieutenant Blouse spoke up for us,' said Shufti.

'What, *Daphne*?' said Tonker. 'Hah! Just another body. They've probably locked him up somewhere, just like us.'

There was a distant cheering, which went on for some time.

'Sounds like they've got the building,' said Polly.

'Hooray for us,' said Tonker, and spat.

After a while, a small hatch was opened in the door and a silent man handed through a big can of scubbo and a tray of horse-bread. It wasn't bad scubbo or, at least, not bad scubbo by the standards of bad scubbo. There was some discussion about whether being fed meant you weren't going to be executed, until someone pointed out the tradition of the Last Hearty Meal. Igorina gave it as her cultural opinion that the stew was not only hearty but lungy and livery too. But at least it was hot.

A couple of hours later a can of saloop was handed through, with some mugs. This time, the guard winked.

An hour after that, the door was unlocked. A young man in a major's uniform stepped inside.

Oh well, let's go on as we started, Polly thought. She leapt to her feet. 'Squaddd . . . tennn . . . *hut!*'

With reasonable speed, the squad at least managed to stand up straight and in a line. The major acknowledged her by tapping the peak of his cap

with a stick. It was definitely thinner than an inch.

'Stand easy . . . corporal, isn't it?' he said.

'Yessir.' That sounded promising.

'I am Major Clogston, of the Provost's office,' said the major. 'And I'd like you to tell me all about it. About everything. I will make notes, if you don't mind.'

'What's this about?' said Tonker.

'Ah, you'd be . . . Private Halter,' said Clogston. 'I've already spoken at length to Lieutenant Blouse.' He turned, nodded at the guard hovering in the doorway, and shut the door. He also closed the hatch.

'You are going to be tried,' he said, sitting down on the spare bunk. 'The politicos want you to be tried by a full Nugganatic court, but that would be tricky here, and no one wants this to go on for any longer than it has to. Besides, there has been an . . . unusual event. Someone has sent a communiqué to General Froc asking about you all by name. At least,' he added, 'by your surnames.'

'Was that Lord Rust, sir?'

'No, it was someone called William de Worde. I don't know if you've run across his newspaper thing? We're wondering how he knew you were captured.'

'Well, *we* didn't tell him!' said Polly.

'It makes things a little . . . tricky,' said Clogston. 'Although, from your point of view, a lot more hopeful. There are those members of the army who are, let us say, considering the future of Borogravia. That is, they would like there to be one. My job is to present your case to the tribunal.'

'Is that a court martial?' said Polly.

'No, they're not that stupid. Calling it a court martial would indicate that they accept that you are soldiers.'

'*You* did,' said Shufti.

'*De facto* is not *de jure*,' said Clogston. 'Now, as I said ... tell me your story, Miss Perks.'

'That's Corporal, thank you!'

'I apologize for the lapse. Now ... go on ...' Clogston opened his bag and produced a pair of half-moon spectacles, which he put on, and took out a pencil and something white and square. 'Whenever you're ready?' he added.

'Sir, are you really going to write on a jam sandwich?' said Polly.

'What?' The major looked down, and laughed. 'Oh. No. Excuse me. I really mustn't miss meals. Blood sugar, you know ...'

'Only it's oozing, sir. Don't mind us. We've eaten.'

It took an hour, with many interruptions and corrections, and two more sandwiches. The major used up quite a lot of notebook, and occasionally had to stop and stare at the ceiling.

'... and then we were thrown in here,' said Polly, sitting back.

'Pushed, really,' said Igorina. 'Nudged.'

'Mmm,' said Clogston. 'You say Corporal Strappi, as you knew him, was ... suddenly very ill at the thought of going into battle?'

'Yessir.'

'And in the tavern in Plün you really kneed Prince Heinrich in the fracas?'

'In or about the fracas, sir. And I didn't know it was him at the time, sir.'

'I see you haven't mentioned the attack on the hill-top where, according to Lieutenant Blouse, your prompt action got the enemy code book . . .'

'Not really worth mentioning, sir. We didn't do much with it.'

'Oh, I don't know. Because of you and that nice man from the newspaper the alliance has had two regiments trotting around in the mountains after some guerrilla leader called "Tiger". Prince Heinrich insisted, and is in fact in command. He is, you could say, a sore loser. Very sore, according to rumour.'

'The newspaper writer believed all that stuff?' said Polly, amazed.

'I don't know, but he certainly wrote it down. You say Lord Rust offered to let you all go home quietly?'

'Yessir.'

'And the consensus was that he could . . .'

'Stick it up his jumper, sir.'

'Oh, yes. I couldn't read my own writing. J . . . U . . . M . . .' Clogston carefully wrote the word in capital letters, and then said: 'I am not saying this, I am not here, but some . . . senior . . . people on our side are wondering if you *would* just quietly go . . .?'

The question hung in the air like a corpse from a beam.

'I'll put that down as "jumper" too, then, shall I?' said Clogston.

'Some of us have got nowhere to go *to*,' said Tonker.

'Or no one to go with,' said Shufti.

'We haven't done anything wrong,' said Polly.

'Jumper it is, then,' said the major. He folded up his little spectacles and sighed. 'They won't even tell me what charges are going to be made.'

'Being Bad Girls,' said Tonker. 'Who are we fooling, sir? The enemy wanted just to be quietly rid of us, and the general wants the same thing. That's the trouble about the good guys and the bad guys. They're all guys!'

'Would we have got a medal, sir, if we'd been men?' Shufti demanded.

'Yep. Certainly. And Blouse would have been promoted on the spot, I imagine. But right now we're at war, and this might not be the time—'

'—to thank a bunch of Abominable women?' Polly suggested.

Clogston smiled. 'I was going to say "to lose concentration". It's the political branch who are pushing for this, of course. They want to stop word getting around. And high command want this over quickly for the same reason.'

'When is all this going to start?' said Polly.

'In about half an hour.'

'This is stupid!' said Tonker. 'They're in the middle of a war and they're going to take the time to hold a trial for a few women who haven't even done anything wrong?'

'The general has insisted,' said Clogston. 'He wants this cleared out of the way.'

'And what authority has this tribunal got?' said Polly coldly.

'Thousands of men under arms,' said Clogston. 'Sorry. The trouble is, when you say to a general "You and whose army?" he just has to point out of the window. But I intend to prove that the meeting should be a court martial. You all kissed the Duchess? You took the shilling? *I* say that makes it military business.'

'And that's good, is it?'

'Well, it means there are procedures. The last Abomination from Nuggan was against jigsaw puzzles. They break the world into pieces, he says. That's making people think, at last. The army may be crazy, but at least it's crazy by numbers. It's *reliably* insane. Er, your sleeping friend . . . will you leave her here?'

'No,' said the squad, as one woman.

'She needs my constant attention,' said Igorina.

'If we leave her she might have a sudden attack of vanishing without a trace,' said Tonker.

'We stick together,' said Polly. 'We don't leave a man behind.'

The room chosen for the tribunal was a ballroom. More than half the keep had been taken back, Polly learned, but the distribution of ground was erratic. The alliance still held the central buildings, and the armoury, but were entirely surrounded by Borogravian forces. The current prize to fight for was the main gate complex, which hadn't been built to withstand attack from inside. What was happening

out there now was a brawl, a midnight bar fight but on a huge scale. And, since there were various war engines atop the towers now occupied by either side, the keep was shooting at itself, in the finest traditions of the circular firing squad.

The floor in here smelled of polish and chalk. Tables had been pushed together to make a rough semicircle. There must have been more than thirty officers, Polly thought. Then she saw the other tables behind the semicircles, and the maps, and the people scurrying in and out, and realized that this was not just about *them*. This was a war-room.

The squad were marched in, and stood at attention. Igorina had browbeaten a couple of guards to carry Wazzer on a stretcher. That circle of stitches under her eye was worth more than a colonel's pips. No soldier wanted to be on the wrong side of the Igors.

They waited. Occasionally an officer would glance at them, and go back to looking at a map, or talking. Then Polly saw some whispering going on, heads turned again, and there was a drift towards the semi-circle of seats. There was a definite sense that here was a tiresome chore that, regrettably, had to be done.

General Froc did not look directly at the squad until he had taken his seat in the centre of the group and adjusted his papers neatly. Even then, his eye passed over them quickly, as if it was afraid to stop. Polly had never seen him before. He was a handsome man, and still had a fine head of white hair. A scar down one side of his face had just missed an eye, and showed up against the wrinkles.

'Things are moving well,' he said, to the room at large. 'We have just heard that a flying column led by the remnant of the Tenth are closing on the keep and attacking the main gates from outside. Someone must have seen what is happening. The army is on the move!'

There was a certain amount of refined cheering at this, none of it from the squad. The general glanced at them again.

'Is this all of them, Clogston?' he said.

The major, who at least had a small table to himself, stood up and saluted. 'No, sir,' he said. 'We are awaiting—'

The doors opened again. Jade was brought in, chained between two much larger trolls. Maladict and Blouse trailed behind her. It seemed that in all the rush and confusion no one had found any trousers for Blouse, and Maladict looked slightly blurred. His chains jingled constantly.

'I object to the chains, sir,' said Clogston.

The general held a whispered consultation with a few of the other officers. 'Yes, we do not want undue formality,' he said, nodding at the guards. 'Remove them. You trolls can go. I just want the guards to remain on the door. Now, let us proceed. This really shouldn't take too long. Now then, you people,' he settled himself in his chair, 'this really is very simple. With the exception of Lieutenant Blouse, you will agree to be returned to your homes and placed in the charge of a responsible male, understood? And no more will be said about this matter. You have showed

considerable spirit, there is no doubt about that, but it was misplaced. We are not ungrateful, however. We understand that none of you is married and so we will present you all with suitable, indeed, with handsome dowries—'

Polly saluted. 'Permission to speak, sir?'

Froc stared at her, and then looked pointedly at Clogston.

'You'll have a chance to speak later, corporal,' said the major.

'But what exactly have we done wrong, sir?' said Polly. 'They should tell us.'

Froc looked at the far end of the row of chairs. 'Captain?' he said.

A short officer got to his feet. In Polly's face, the tide of recognition raced across the mudflats of hatred.

'Captain Strappi, political division, sir—' he began, and stopped at the groan from the squad. When it had died away he cleared his throat, and went on: 'Twenty-seven Abominations have been committed under Nugganatic law, sir. I suspect there have been many more. Under military law, sir, we have the simple fact that they posed as men in order to join up. I was there, sir, and saw it all.'

'Captain Strappi, may I congratulate you on your rapid promotion?' said Lieutenant Blouse.

'Yes, indeed, captain,' said Clogston. 'Apparently you were a humble corporal only a few days ago?'

Plaster dust drifted down again as something heavy struck the wall outside. Froc brushed it off his paperwork.

'Not one of ours, I hope,' he said, to a certain amount of laughter. 'Do go ahead, captain.'

Strappi turned to the general. 'As you know, sir, it is occasionally necessary for us in the political division to assume a lower rank in order to gain intelligence. Covered under the Regulations, sir,' he added.

The look that General Froc gave him stirred a little teacup of hope in Polly's breast. No one could like something like Strappi, not even a mother. Then the general turned back to Clogston.

'Is this germane, major?' he said testily. 'We know they disguised themselves as—'

'—women, sir,' said Clogston smoothly. 'That's all we know, sir. Apart from Captain Strappi's assertion, and I intend to suggest later that this is tainted, I haven't yet heard any evidence that they have dressed in any other way.'

'We have the evidence of our own eyes, man!'

'Yes, sir. They're wearing dresses, sir.'

'And they're practically bald!'

'Yes, sir,' said Clogston. He picked up a thick book, dripping with bookmarks. 'Book of Nuggan, sir: "It is a Beatitude unto Nuggan that An Woman shall wear her hair short, that the amorous propensities of men be not therefore inflamed."'

'I don't see a lot of bald women around!' snapped Froc.

'Yes, sir. It is one of those utterances that people find somewhat tricky, like the one about not sneezing. I should say at this point, sir, that I intend to show that Abominations are routinely committed by all of

us. We have got into the habit of ignoring them, in fact, which opens up an interesting debate. In any case, short hair is Nugganatically correct. In short, sir, and in short hair, the ladies appear to have been involved in nothing more than a little laundry, a kitchen accident and the release of your good self from the cells.'

'I saw them!' snarled Strappi. 'They looked like men and they acted like men!'

'Why were you in the recruiting party, captain?' said Major Clogston. 'I would not have thought one of those would have been a hotbed of seditious activity?'

'Is that a relevant question, major?' said the general.

'I don't know, sir,' said Clogston. 'That's why I asked. I don't think we would wish it to be said that these ladies had not been given a fair hearing?'

'Said by whom?' said Froc. 'My officers can be relied upon to be discreet.'

'Said by the ladies themselves, sir?'

'Then we must require that they do *not* speak to anyone!'

'Oh, I say!' said Blouse.

'And how will you enforce this, sir?' said Clogston. 'Against these women who, we are agreed, stole you out of the jaws of the enemy?'

There was some muttering amongst the officers.

'Major Clogston, did you have lunch?' said the general.

'No, sir.'

'Colonel Vester said you become a little . . . erratic when you miss meals . . .'

'No, sir. I become tetchy, sir. But I think a little tetchiness is called for right now. I put a question to Captain Strappi, sir.'

'Very well, captain, perhaps you will tell us why you were with that recruiting party?' said the general wearily.

'I was ... investigating a soldier, sir. A non-commissioned officer. Our attention had been drawn to irregularities in his files, sir, and where there are irregularities we generally find sedition. I hesitate to talk about this, sir, because this sergeant has been of some service to yourself—'

'Hrumph!' said the general loudly. 'This is not a matter for discussion here, I think.'

'It was just that according to the files, several officers had helped—' Strappi went on.

'Hrumph! Not matters for this court, captain! Are we agreed, gentlemen?'

'Yes, sir, it was just that the major asked me and I—' Strappi began, bewildered.

'Captain, I suggest you learn what a hrumph means!' roared Froc.

'So what were you looking for when you rummaged through our stuff?' said Polly, as Strappi shrank.

'Mmmmmy cccccoffee!' said Maladict. 'Yyyyyou ssssstole mmmmmy cccccoffee!'

'And you ran away when you were told you were going into combat, you little dog's pizzle!' said Tonker. 'Polly said you pissed your drawers!'

General Froc slammed his fist on the table, but

Polly noticed that one or two officers were trying to conceal a smile. 'These are not matters for this inquiry!' he said.

'Although, sir, one or two of them seem to me to be subjects for investigation later on,' said a colonel, further along the table. 'The personal belongings of enlisted men may only be searched in their presence, general. This may seem a trivial point, but men have mutinied over it in the past. Did you, in fact, believe the . . . men to be women when you did this, captain?'

Oh, say yes, please say yes, Polly thought, as Strappi hesitated. *Because when we talk about how those cavalrymen found us so quickly, it'll mean you set them on a bunch of Borogravian girls. Let's see how that one plays in Plün! And if you didn't know, then why were you rummaging?*

Strappi preferred the rock to the hard place. Stone clattered down in the courtyard outside, and he had to raise his voice to make himself heard.

'I was, er, generally suspicious of them, sir, because they were so keen—'

'Sir, I protest!' said Clogston. 'Keenness is not a military vice!'

'In moderation, certainly,' said Froc. 'And you found evidence of some sort, did you?'

'I did find a petticoat, sir,' said Strappi, feeling his way with care.

'Then why didn't you—' Froc began, but Strappi interrupted.

'I did serve for a while with Captain Wrigglesworth, sir,' he said.

'And?' said Froc, but the officer on his left leaned over and whispered something to him. 'Oh, *Wrigglesworth*. Ha, yes,' said Froc. 'Of course. Fine officer, Wrigglesworth. Keen on, er—'

'Amateur dramatics,' a colonel supplied, in a non-committal voice.

'Right! Right! Ver' good for morale, that sort of thing. Hrumph.'

'With respect, general, I think I can offer a way through?' said another man with a general's rank.

'Really, Bob?' said Froc. 'Oh, well . . . feel free. The record will show that I am yielding the floor to General Kzupi.'

'I'm sorry, sir, I thought these proceedings were not being recorded?' said Clogston.

'Yes, yes, of course, thank you *so* much for jogging my memory,' said Froc. 'However, if we *were* to have a record, that is what it would show. Bob?'

'Ladies,' said General Kzupi, flashing the squad a glossy smile. 'And you too, of course, Lieutenant Blouse, and you too, er . . .' he looked quizzically at Maladict, who stared straight back '. . . sir?' General Kzupi, though, was not to be derailed by an eyeballing vampire, even one that couldn't stand still. 'Firstly, may I offer on behalf of all of us, I think, our thanks for the incredible job you have done? A splendid effort. But, sadly, the world we live in has certain . . . rules, you understand? To be frank, the problem here is not that you are women. As such, that is. But you persist in *maintaining* that you are. You see? We can't have that.'

'You mean if we put on uniforms again, and swaggered around belching and saying "har har, fooled you all" that would be all right?' said Polly.

'Perhaps I could help?' said yet another voice. Froc looked along the table.

'Ah, Brigadier Stoffer. Yes?'

'This is all rather damn silly, general—'

'Hrumph!' said Froc.

'What say?' said Stoffer, looking puzzled.

'There *are* ladies present, brigadier. That is, ahah, the problem.'

'Damn right!' said Tonker.

'Understood, general. But the party was led by a man, am I right?'

'Lieutenant Blouse tells me he is a man, sir,' said Clogston. 'Since he is an officer and a gentleman, I will take his word for it.'

'Well, then, problem solved. These young ladies helped him. Smuggled him in, and so forth. *Assisted* him. Fine traditions of Borogravian womanhood and all that. Not *soldiers* at all. Give the man a big medal and make him a captain, and all this'll be forgotten.'

'Excuse me one moment, general,' said Clogston. 'I will consult with what we would call the accused if anyone would enlighten me as to the precise nature of the charges.'

He walked over to the squad and lowered his voice. 'I think this is the best offer you're going to get,' he said. 'I can probably get the money, too. How about it?'

'It's completely ridiculous!' said Blouse. 'They

410

showed tremendous courage and determination. All this would not have been possible without them.'

'Yes, Blouse, and you would be allowed to say that,' said Clogston. 'Stoffer has come up with quite a clever idea. Everyone gets what they want, but you just have to avoid any suggestion that you were in fact acting as soldiers. Brave Borogravian women going to the aid of a gallant hero, that *works*. You could take the view that these are changing times, and you are helping them change faster. Well?'

The squad exchanged glances.

'Er . . . I'd be happy about that,' Shufti ventured. 'If everyone else is.'

'So you'd have your baby without a husband?' said Polly.

'He's probably dead anyway, whoever he was,' sighed Shufti.

'The general has influence,' said Clogston. 'He might be able to—'

'No, I'm not buying into this,' said Tonker. 'It's a gooey little lie. To hell with them.'

'Lofty?' said Polly.

Lofty struck a match, and stared at it. She could find matches anywhere.

There was another *crump*, high above.

'Maladict?' said Polly.

'Llet tthe bball rroll. II ssay nno.'

'And you, lieutenant?' Clogston asked.

'It's dishonourable,' said Blouse.

'Could be problems for you if you don't accept, though. With your career.'

'I suspect I haven't got one, major, whatever happens. No, I will not live a lie. I know, now, that I'm not a hero. I'm just someone who wanted to be one.'

'Thank you, sir,' said Polly. 'Er . . . Jade?'

'One of der trolls what arrested me hit me with his club an' I frew a table at him,' said Jade, looking at the floor.

'That was mistreatment of a pris—' Blouse began, but Clogston said: 'No, lieutenant, I know something about trolls. They are very . . . physical. So . . . he's a rather attractive lad, is he, private?'

'I got a good feelin' about him,' said Jade, blushing. 'So I don't want to be sent home. Nothin' for me there, anyway.'

'Private Igor . . . ina?' said Blouse.

'I think we ought to give in,' said Igorina.

'Why?' said Polly.

'Because Wazzer's dying.' She raised a hand. 'No, *please* don't cluster round. Give her air, at least. She hasn't eaten. I can't get any water down her at all.' She looked up with red-rimmed eyes. 'I don't know what to *do*!'

'The Duchess talked to her,' said Polly. 'You all heard. And you know what we saw down in the crypt.'

'And I said I don't believe any of that!' said Tonker. 'It's her . . . mind. They made her crazy enough. And we were all so tired, we'd see *anything*. All that stuff about wanting to get to the High Command? Well, here they are, and I don't see any miracles. Do you?'

'I don't think she would have wanted us to give in,' said Polly.

No.

'Did you hear that?' said Polly, although she wasn't certain that the word had turned up in her head via her ears.

'No, I didn't!' said Tonker. 'I didn't hear it!'

'I don't think we can accept this compromise, sir,' said Polly to the major.

'Then I won't,' said Shufti promptly. 'I don't . . . this wasn't . . . I only came because . . . but . . . look, I'm staying with you. Erm . . . what can they do to us, sir?'

'Put you in a cell for a long time, probably,' said the major. 'They're being kind to you—'

'Kind?' said Polly.

'Well, they think they're being kind,' said Clogston. 'And they could be a lot worse. And there's a war on. They don't want to look bad, but Froc didn't get to be a general by being nice. I have to warn you about that. You're still turning this down?'

Blouse looked round at his men. 'I believe we are, major.'

'Good,' said Clogston, winking.

Good.

Clogston went back to his table and shuffled his papers. 'The allegedly accused, sir, regretfully turn down the offer.'

'Yes, I thought they might,' said Froc. 'In that case, they are to be returned to the cells. They will be dealt with later.' Plaster showered down as something hit the outer wall again. 'This has gone quite far enough!'

'We won't be sent to the cells!' Tonker shouted.

'Then that is mutiny, sir!' said Froc. 'And we know how to deal with that!'

'Excuse me, general, does that then mean the tribunal *does* agree that these ladies are soldiers?' said Clogston.

General Froc glared at him. 'Don't you try to tie me up with procedural nonsense, major!'

'It's hardly nonsense, sir, it's the very basis—'

Duck.

The word was the faintest, merest suggestion in Polly's head, but it also seemed to be wired to her central nervous system. And not only hers. The squad ducked, Igorina throwing herself across her patient's body.

Half the ceiling collapsed. The chandelier fell down and exploded in a kaleidoscope of splintering prisms. Mirrors shattered. And then there was, by comparison at least, silence, broken only by the thud of a few late bits of plaster and the tinkle of a tardy shard.

Now . . .

Footsteps approached the big doors at the end of the room, where the guards were just struggling to their feet. The doors swung open.

Jackrum stood there, shining like the sunset. The light glinted off his shako badge, polished to the point where it would blind the incautious with its terrible gleam. His face was red, but his jacket was redder, and his sergeant's sash was the pure quill of redness, its very essence, the red of dying stars and dying soldiers. Blood dripped off the cutlasses thrust into his belt. The guards, still shaking,

tried to lower their pikes to bar his way.

'Do not try it, lads, I beg you,' said Jackrum. 'Upon my oath I am not a violent man, but do you think Sergeant Jackrum is going to be stopped by a set of bleedin' cutlery?'

The men looked at Jackrum, steaming with barely controlled rage, and then at the astonished generals, and took an immediate decision on their own desperate initiative.

'Good lads,' said Jackrum. 'With your permission, General Froc?'

He did not wait for a reply but marched forward with parade-ground precision. He came to boot-crashing attention in front of the senior generals, still brushing plaster dust from their uniforms, and saluted with the precision of a semaphore.

'I beg to report, sir, that we now hold the main gates, sir! Took the liberty of putting together a force of the Ins-and-Outs, the Side-to-Sides and the Backwards-and-Forwards, sir, just in case, saw a big cloud o' flame and smoke over the place, and arrived at the gates just as your lads did. Got 'em coming and going, sir!'

There was a general cheer, and General Kzupi leaned towards Froc. 'In view of this pleasing development, sir, perhaps we should hurry up and close this—'

Froc waved him into silence. 'Jackrum, you old rogue,' he said, leaning back in his chair. 'I heard you were dead. How the devil are you?'

'Fightin' fit, sir!' barked Jackrum. 'Not dead at all, despite the hopes of many!'

'Glad to hear it, man. But, while your rosy face is a welcome sight at any time, we are here to—'

'Fourteen miles I carried you, sir!' Jackrum roared, sweat pouring down his face. 'Pulled that arrow out of your leg, sir. Sliced that devil of a captain who pushed an axe in your face, sir, and I'm glad to see the scar's looking well. Killed that poor sentry lad just to steal his water bottle for you, sir. Looked into his dyin' face, sir, for you. Never asked for nothing in return, sir. Right, sir?'

Froc rubbed his chin and smiled. 'Well, I seem to remember there was that little matter of fudging some details, changing a few dates—' he murmured.

'Don't give me that bleedin' slop, sir, with respect. That wasn't for me, that was for the army. For the Duchess, sir. And, yeah, I see a few other gentlemen round this table who had reason to do the same little service for me. For the Duchess, sir. And if you was to leave me one sword I'd stand and fight any man in your army, sir, be he never so young and full of mustard!'

In one movement he pulled a cutlass from his belt and brought it down on the paperwork between Froc's hands. It bit through into the wood of the table, and stayed there.

Froc didn't flinch. Instead he looked up and said calmly, 'Hero though you may be, sergeant, I fear that you have gone *too* far.'

'Have I gone the full fourteen miles yet, sir?' said Jackrum.

For a moment there was no sound but that of the

cutlass, vibrating to a halt. Froc breathed out. 'Very well,' he said. 'What is your request, sergeant?'

'I notes you have my little lads before you, sir! I'm hearing that they are in a spot of *bother*, sir!'

'The *girls*, Jackrum, are to be restrained in a place of safety. This is no place for them. And that is my order, sergeant.'

'I said to 'em when they signed up, sir, I said: if anyone drags you away they'll have to drag me away, too, sir!'

Froc nodded. 'Very loyal of you, sergeant, and very much in your character. Nevertheless—'

'And I have information vital to these here deliberations, sir! There is something I must tell you, sir!'

'Well, by all means tell us, man!' said Froc. 'You don't have to take all—'

'It requires that some of you gentlemen quit this room, sir,' said Jackrum, desperately. He was still at attention, still holding the salute.

'Now you do ask too much, Jackrum,' said Froc. 'These are loyal officers of her grace!'

'No doubt of it, sir! Upon my oath I am not a gossiping man, sir, but I will speak my piece to those I choose, sir, or speak it to the world. There's ways to do that, sir, nasty new-fangled ways. Your choice, sir!'

At last, Froc coloured. He stood up abruptly. 'Are you seriously telling me that you'd—'

'This is my famous last stand, sir!' said Jackrum, saluting again. 'Do or die, sir!'

All eyes turned to Froc. He relaxed. 'Oh, very well. It can't do any harm to listen to you, sergeant.

God knows you've earned it. But make it quick.'

'Thank you, sir.'

'But try this again and you'll be on the biggest fizzer you can imagine.'

'No worry there, sir. Never been one for fizzers. I will by your leave point to certain men . . .'

They were about half of the officers. They rose with greater or lesser protest, but rise they did, under Froc's sapphire glare, and filed out into the corridor.

'General, I protest!' said a departing colonel. 'We are being sent out of the room like naughty children while these . . . females are—'

'Yes, yes, Rodney, and if our friend the sergeant doesn't have a damn good explanation I'll personally turn him over to you for punishment detail,' said Froc. 'But he's entitled to his last wild charge if any man is. Go quietly, there's a good chap, and keep the war going until we get there. And have you finished this strange charade, sergeant?' he added, as the last of the officers left.

'All but one last thing, sir,' said Jackrum, and stamped over to the guards. They were at attention already, but nevertheless contrived to become more attentive. 'You lads go outside this door,' said the sergeant. 'No one is to come close, understand. And I know you boys won't try to eavesdrop, because of what'd happen to you if I ever found that you had done so. Off you go, hup, hup, hup!'

He shut the doors behind them and the atmosphere changed. Polly couldn't quite detect how, but perhaps it was that the click of the doors had said

'This is our secret' and everyone present was in on it.

Jackrum removed his shako and laid it gently on the table in front of the general. Then he took off his coat and handed it to Polly, saying, 'Hold this, Perks. It's the property of her grace.' He rolled up his sleeves. He relaxed his enormous red braces. And then, to Polly's horror if not to her surprise, he brought out his paper screw of foul chewing tobacco and his blackened penknife.

'Oh, I say—' a major began, before a colleague nudged him into silence. Never had a man cutting a wad of black tobacco been the subject of such rapt, horrified attention.

'Things are going well outside,' he said. 'Shame you aren't all out there, eh? Still, the truth's important too, right? And that's what this tribunal is for, no doubt about it. It must be important, the truth, else you wouldn't be here, am I right? 'course I am.'

Jackrum finished the cut, palmed the stuff into his mouth and got it comfortable in a cheek, while the sounds of battle filtered through from outside. Then he turned and walked towards the major who had just spoken. The man cringed a little in his chair.

'What've you got to say about the truth, Major Derbi?' said Jackrum conversationally. 'Nothing? Well, then, what shall *I* say? What shall I say about a captain who turned and ran sobbing when we came across a column of Zlobenians, deserting his own men? Shall I say that ol' Jackrum tripped him up and pummelled him a bit and put the fear of . . . Jackrum into him, and he went back and 'twas a famous victory he had

that day, over two enemies, one of them being in his own head. And he came to ol' Jackrum again, drunk with battle, and said more'n he ought . . .'

'You bastard,' said the major softly.

'Shall I tell the truth today . . . *Janet*?' said Jackrum. The sounds of battle were suddenly much louder. They poured into the room like the water rushing to fill a hole in the ocean floor, but all the sound in the world could not have filled that sudden, tremendous silence.

Jackrum strolled on towards another man. 'Good to see you here, Colonel Cumabund!' he said cheerfully. 'O' course, you were only Lieutenant Cumabund when I was under your command. Plucky lad you were, when you led us against that detachment of Kopelies. And then you took a nasty sword wound in the fracas, or just above, and I got you through with rum and cold water, and found that plucky you might be, but lad you weren't. Oh, how you gabbled away in your feverish delirium . . . Yes, you did. That's the truth . . . *Olga*.'

He stepped round the table and started to stroll along *behind* the officers; those he passed stared woodenly ahead, not daring to turn, not daring to make any movement that would attract attention.

'You could say I know *something* about all of yez,' he said. 'Quite a lot about some of you, just enough about most of you. A few of you, well, I could write a book.' He paused just behind Froc, who stiffened.

'Jackrum, I—' he began.

Jackrum put a hand on each of Froc's shoulders.

'Fourteen miles, sir. Two nights, 'cos we lay up by day, the patrols were that thick. Cut about pretty dreadful, you were, but you got better nursing from me than any sawbones, I'd bet.' He leaned forward until his mouth was level with the general's ear, and continued in a stage whisper: 'What is there left about you that I don't know? So . . . are you really looking for the truth . . . *Mildred*?'

The room was a museum of waxworks. Jackrum spat on the floor.

'You cannot prove anything, sergeant,' said Froc eventually, with the calm of an icefield.

'Well now, not as such. But they keep telling me this is the modern world, sir. I don't need proof, exactly. I know a man who'd have such a tale to tell, and it'd be in Ankh-Morpork in a couple of hours.'

'If you leave this room alive,' said a voice.

Jackrum smiled his evillest smile, and bore down on the source of the threat like an avalanche. 'Ah! I thought one of yez would try that, Chloe, but I note you never made it beyond major, and no wonder since you try to bluff with no bleedin' cards in your hand. Nice try, though. But, first, I could take you to the bleedin' cleaners before those guards were back in here, upon my oath, and, second, you don't know what I've writ down and who else knows. I trained all you girls at one time or another, and some of the cunning you got, some of the mustard, some of the sense . . . well, you got it from me. Didn't you? So don't any of you go thinking you can be artful about this, because when it comes to cunning I am Mister Fox.'

'Sergeant, sergeant, sergeant,' said Froc wearily, 'what is it you *want*?'

Jackrum completed his circuit of the table and finished in front of it, once again like a man before his judges.

'Well, blow me down,' he said quietly, looking along the row of faces. 'You didn't know, did you ... you didn't *know*. Is there a ... a *man* among you that knew? You thought, every one of you, that you were all alone. All alone. You poor devils. And look at you. More'n a third of the country's High Command. You made it on your own, ladies. What could you have done if you'd acted tog—'

He stopped, and took a step towards Froc, who looked down at her cloven paperwork. 'How many did *you* spot, Mildred?'

'That will be "general", sergeant. I'm still a general, sergeant. Or "sir" will do. And your answer is: one or two. One or two.'

'And you promoted them, did you, if they was as good as men?'

'Indeed not, sergeant. What do you take me for? I promoted them if they were *better* than men.'

Jackrum opened his arms wide, like a ringmaster introducing a new act. 'Then what about the lads I brought with me, sir? As cracking a bunch of lads as I've ever seen.' He cast a bloodshot eye around the table. 'And I'm good at weighing up a lad, as you all know. They'd be a credit to your army, sir!'

Froc looked at her colleagues on either side. An unspoken question harvested unsaid answers.

'Yes, well,' she said. 'All seems clear to us, in the light of new developments. When beardless lads dress up as gels, there's no doubt that people will get confused. And that's what we've got here, sergeant. Mere confusion. Mistaken identities. Much ado, in fact, about nothing. Clearly they are boys, and may return home right now with an honourable discharge.'

Jackrum chuckled and stuck out a palm, flexing the fingers upwards like a man bargaining. Once again, there was the communion of spirits.

'Very well. They can, if they wish, continue in the army,' said Froc. 'With discretion, of course.'

'No, sir!'

Polly stared at Jackrum, and then realized the words had, in fact, come from her own mouth.

Froc raised her eyebrows. 'What *is* your name again?' she said.

'Corporal Perks, sir!' said Polly, saluting.

She watched Froc's face settle into an expression of condescending benevolence. If she uses the words 'my dear' I shall *swear*, she thought.

'Well, my dear—'

'Not your dear, sir or madam,' said Polly. In the theatre of her mind The Duchess Inn burned to a cinder and her old life peeled away, black as charcoal, and she was flying, ballistic, too fast and too high and unable to stop. 'I am a soldier, general. I signed up. I kissed the Duchess. I don't think generals call their soldiers "my dear", do they?'

Froc coughed. The smile remained, but had the decency to be a bit more restrained. 'And private

soldiers don't talk like that to generals, young lady, so we'll let that pass, shall we?'

'Just here, in this room, I don't know what passes and what stays, sir,' said Polly. 'But it seems to me that if you are still a general then I'm still a corporal, sir. I can't speak for the others, but the reason I'm holding out, general, is that I kissed the Duchess and she knew what I was and she . . . didn't turn away, if you understand me.'

'Well said, Perks,' said Jackrum.

Polly plunged on. 'Sir, a day or two ago I'd have rescued my brother and gone off home and I'd have thought it a job well done. I just wanted to be safe. But now I see there's no safety while there's all this . . . this stupidity. So I think I've got to stay and be a part of it. Er . . . try to make it less stupid, I mean. And I want to be me, not Oliver. I kissed the Duchess. We all did. You can't tell us we didn't and you can't tell us it doesn't count, because it's between us and her—'

'You all kissed the Duchess,' said a voice. It had an . . . echo.

You all kissed the Duchess . . .

'Did you think that it meant nothing? That it was just a kiss?'

Did you think it meant nothing . . .

. . . just a kiss . . .

The whispered words washed against the walls like surf, and came back stronger, in harmonies.

Did you kiss meant nothing meant a kiss just think a kiss meant a kiss . . .

Wazzer was standing up. The squad stood petrified as she walked unsteadily past them. Her eyes focused on Polly.

'How good to wear a body again,' she said. 'And to breathe. Breathing is wonderful . . .'

How good . . .

To breathe wonderful a body again to breathe . . .

Something was in Wazzer's face. Her features were all there, all correct, her nose was as pointed and as red, her cheekbones as hollow . . . but there were subtle changes. She held up a hand and flexed her fingers.

'Ah,' she said. 'So . . .' There was no echo this time, but the voice was stronger and deep. No one would ever have said that Wazzer's voice had been attractive, but this one was. She turned to Jackrum, who dropped on to his fat knees and whipped off his shako.

'Sergeant Jackrum, I *know* that you know who I am. You have waded through seas of blood for me. Perhaps we should have done better things with your life, but at least your sins were soldier's sins, and not the worst of them, at that. You are hereby promoted to sergeant major, and a better candidate for the job I have never met. You are steeped in deviousness, cunning and casual criminality, Sergeant Jackrum. You should do well.'

Jackrum, eyes cast down, raised a knuckle to his forehead. '. . . not worthy, your grace,' he muttered.

'Of course you aren't.' The Duchess looked around. 'Now, where is my army . . . ah.' There was no echo at

all in the voice now, and none of Wazzer's cowering and downcast eyes. She positioned herself directly in front of Froc, who was staring with his mouth open.

'General Froc, you must do one final service for me.'

The general glared. 'Who the hell are you?'

'You need to ask? As always, Jackrum thinks faster than you. You know me. I am the Duchess Annagovia.'

'But you are—' one of the other officers began, but Froc held up a hand again.

'The voice ... is familiar,' she said, in a faraway whisper.

'Yes. You remember the ball. I remember it, too. Forty years ago. You were the youngest captain ever. We danced, stiffly in my case. I asked you how long you had been a captain, and you said—'

'Three days,' breathed Froc, with her eyes shut.

'And we ate Brandy Pillows, and a cocktail that I believe was called—'

'Angel's Tears,' said Froc. 'I kept the menu, your grace. And the dance card.'

'Yes,' said the Duchess. 'You did. And when old General Scaffer led you away, he said, "That'll be something to tell your grandchildren, my boy." But you were ... so dedicated that you never had children ... my boy ...'

... my boy ... my boy ...

'I see heroes!' said the Duchess, staring at the tableau of officers. 'All of you gave up ... much. But I demand more. Much more. Is there any amongst you

who for the sake of my memory will not die in battle?'
Wazzer's head turned and looked along the row. 'No.
I see there is not. And now I demand that you do what
the ignorant might feel is the easier thing. You must
refrain from dying in battle. Revenge is not redress.
Revenge is a wheel, and it turns backwards. The dead
are not your masters.'

'What is it you want of me, ma'am?' Froc managed.

'Call in your other officers. Make what truces are
necessary, for now. This body, this poor child, will
lead you. I am weak, but I can move small things.
Thoughts, perhaps. I will leave her . . . something, a
light in the eye, a tone in the voice. Follow her. You
must invade.'

'Certainly! But how—'

'You must invade Borogravia! In the name of
sanity, you must go home. The winter is coming, the
trusting animals are not fed, old men die of cold,
women mourn, the country corrodes. Fight Nuggan,
because he is nothing now, nothing but the poisonous
echo of all your ignorance and pettiness and
malicious stupidity. Find yourself a worthier god.
And let . . . me . . . go! All those prayers, all those
entreaties . . . to me! Too many hands clasped, that
could more gainfully answer your prayers by effort
and resolve! And what was I? Just a rather stupid
woman when I was alive. But you believed I watched
over you, and listened to you . . . and so I had to, I had
to listen, knowing that there was no help . . . I wish
people would not be so careless about what they
believe. Go. Invade the one place you've never

conquered. And these women will help. Be proud of them. And, lest you think to twist my meaning, lest you doubt . . . let me, as I leave, return to you this gift. Remember. A kiss.'

. . . a kiss . . .

. . . a kiss a kiss return to you kiss . . .

. . . remember . . .

As one woman, as one man, the crowd in the room reached up hesitantly to their left cheek. And Wazzer folded up, very gently, collapsing like a sigh.

Froc was the first to speak. 'This is . . . I think we need to . . .' She faltered into silence.

Jackrum got to his feet, brushed the dust off his shako, placed it on his head and saluted. 'Permission to speak, sir?' he said.

'Oh, good heaven, Jackrum!' said Froc distractedly. 'At a time like this? Yes, yes . . .'

'What are your orders, sir?'

'Orders?' Froc blinked, and looked around. 'Orders, orders . . . yes. Well, I *am* the commander, I *can* request a . . . yes, I can request a truce, sergeant—'

'That's sergeant major, sir,' said Jackrum. 'Right you are, sir, I'll organize a runner to go to the alliance.'

'I suppose a . . . white flag would be—'

'Good as done, sir. Leave it to me,' said Jackrum, radiating efficiency.

'Yes, of course . . . Er, before, before we go any further . . . ladies and gentlemen, I . . . er . . . some of the things said here . . . the whole issue of women joining as . . . women . . . obviously . . .' She raised her hand to her cheek again, in a kind of wonderment.

'They are welcome. I . . . salute them. But for those of us that went before, perhaps it is not . . . not yet the time. You understand?'

'What?' said Polly.

'Lips sealed, sir!' said Jackrum. 'You can leave it all to me, sir! Captain Blouse's squad, attention! You will obtain uniforms! You can't go around still dressed as washerwomen, oh dear me!'

'We *are* soldiers?' said Polly.

'O' course you are, otherwise I wouldn't be shouting at you, you 'orrible little woman! The world's turned upside down! It's a bit more important than you right now, eh? You've got what you're after, right? Now get hold of a uniform, find yourself a shako and wipe your face, at least. *You* are taking the official truce to the enemy.'

'Me, sarge?' said Polly.

'Right! Just as soon as the officers have done the official letter. Tonker, Lofty . . . see what you can find for Perks to wear. Perks, don't be cowed, and bull yourself up. The rest of you, hurry up and wait!'

'Sergeant Jac— er, sergeant major?' said Blouse.

'Yessir?'

'I'm *not* a captain, you know.'

'Are you not?' said Jackrum, grinning. 'Well, leave it to Jackrum, sir. We shall see what the day brings, eh? Minor point, sir. I should lose the dress if I was you!'

Jackrum marched off, his inflated chest as red as a robin's and twice as threatening. He shouted at orderlies, harried guards, saluted officers and, despite everything, hammered the blade of purpose out of

the red-hot steel of panic. He was a sergeant major in a roomful of confused ruperts, and he was happier than a terrier in a barrel of rats.

Stopping a battle is much harder than starting it. Starting it only requires you to shout 'Attack!' but when you want to stop it, everyone is busy.

Polly could *feel* the news spreading. *They're girls!* The orderlies scuttling in and out once more kept staring at them, as if they were some kind of strange insects. I wonder how many Jackrum missed, Polly thought. I wonder . . .

Bits of uniform turned up. Jade found some trousers that fitted by locating a clerk who was Polly's height, lifting him up and pulling them off him. A jacket was acquired. Lofty even stole a shako of the right size and polished the badge with her sleeve until it gleamed. Polly was just doing up her belt when she spotted a figure on the far side of the room. She'd completely forgotten about *him.*

She pulled the belt tight and thrust the leather through the buckle as she walked and then strode through the crowds of figures. Strappi saw her coming, but it was too late. There was no escape short of running, and captains didn't run from corporals. He stood his ground, like a rabbit hypnotized by the approaching vixen, and raised his hands as she approached.

'Now then, Perks, I'm a captain and I had a job to—' he began.

'And how long do you think you'll hold that rank,

now, *sir*?' hissed Polly. 'When I tell the general about our little fight? And how you sicked the Prince on to us? And how you bullied Wazzer? And about my hair, you sticky little miserable apology for a man! Shufti's a better man than you and she's pregnant!'

'Oh, we knew there were women getting in,' said Strappi. 'We just didn't know how far the rot went—'

'You took my hair because you thought it meant something to me,' hissed Polly. 'Well, you can keep it! I'll grow some more, and no one is going to stop me, understand? Oh, and one other thing. This is how far the rot goes!'

It was a blow rather than a slap, and it knocked him down so hard that he rolled. But he was Strappi, and staggered upright with a finger pointed for vengeance.

'She struck a superior officer!' he screamed.

A few heads turned. They looked at Strappi. They looked at Polly. Then they looked back grinning to what they had been doing.

'I should run away again, if I was you,' said Polly. She turned on her heel, feeling the heat of his impotent fury.

As she was about to rejoin Jade and Maladict, someone touched her arm. She spun round.

'What? Oh . . . sorry, Major Clogston,' she said. She felt she wouldn't be able to deal with Strappi again, not without committing murder. That would probably get her into trouble, even now.

'I should like to thank you for a most enjoyable day,' said the major. 'I did my best, but I think we were all . . . outclassed.'

'Thank you, sir,' said Polly.

'This was a pleasure, Corporal Perks,' said Clogston. 'I shall watch your future career with interest and envy. Congratulations. And since in here protocol seems to be flapping loose, I will shake you by the hand.'

They shook. 'And now, we have duties,' said Major Clogston, as Jade arrived with a white sheet on a pole. 'Oh, and by the way . . . my name is Christine. And, you know, I really don't think I could get used to wearing a dress again . . .'

Maladict and Jade were chosen to see Polly through the castle, a troll because a troll commands respect and a vampire because a vampire demands it. There were groans and cheers as they elbowed their way along the passages, because news had already got around. That was another reason for taking Jade. Trolls could push.

'Okay,' said Jackrum, bringing up the rear. 'At the bottom of these steps there's a door, and beyond that door is enemy territory. Put the white flag out *first*. Important safety tip.'

'Can't you come with us, sarge?'

'Hah, me? I dare say there's a few people out there who'd take a pot shot at me white flag or no. Don't you worry. The word's gone out.'

'What word's that, sarge?'

Jackrum leaned closer. 'They ain't gonna shoot a girl, Perks!'

'You *told* them?'

'Let's just say that news gets around fast,' said

Jackrum. 'Grab the advantage. And I'll find your brother while you're gone, upon my oath. Oh, one other thing ... look at me, Perks.' Polly turned, in the crowded, jostling corridor. Jackrum's eyes twinkled. 'I know I can trust you, Perks. I'd trust you like I'd trust myself. Best of luck. And make the most of it, lad. Kissin' don't last!'

Well, that couldn't be plainer, Polly thought, as the armed men by the door beckoned them forward.

'Stick to the walls, okay, ladies? And be quick with that rag!'

The heavy door swung open. Half a dozen arrows bounced and pinwheeled along the corridor. Another one tore through the flag. Polly waved it desperately. She heard distant shouting, and then cheers.

'Okay, go!' said a guard, pushing her forward.

She stepped out into the sudden daylight and, to make sure, waved the flag overhead a few more times. There were men in the courtyard and lining the battlements around it. There were bodies, too.

A captain, with blood soaking through his jacket, stepped across the fallen and held out his hand. 'You may give that to me, soldier,' he said.

'No, sir. I must deliver it to your commander, and wait for his reply, sir.'

'Then you give it to me, soldier, and I will bring you back the reply. You have surrendered, after all.'

'No. This is a truce. That's not the same thing. I have to hand this over personally and you aren't big enough.' A thought hit her. 'I demand to take this to Commander Vimes!'

The captain stared at her, and then looked closer. 'Aren't you one of those—'

'Yes,' said Polly.

'And you locked them in chains and threw the key away?'

'Yes,' said Polly, seeing her life start to flash past her eyes.

'And they had to hop miles with shackles on and no clothes?'

'Yes!'

'And you're just . . . *women*?'

'Yes!' said Polly, letting the 'just' go for now.

The captain leaned closer and spoke while trying not to move his lips. 'Dan gug show. Ell done. Agout time soes arragunk arsetards ere aken own a eg!' He leaned back. 'Commander Vimes it is, then. Follow me, miss.'

Polly felt hundreds of eyes on her as the squad was let into the inner keep. There were one or two wolf whistles, because there were more soldiers in there, including quite a few trolls. Jade bent down, snatched up a rock and hurled it at one of them, hitting him between the eyes.

'No one move!' shouted Maladict, waving his hands urgently as a hundred men raised their weapons. 'That was the troll version of blowing a kiss!'

And, indeed, the troll who had been hit was waving at Jade, a little unsteadily.

'Can we knock it off with the lovey-dovey, please?' said Polly to Jade. 'The soft people are likely to get the wrong idea.'

'It's stopped the whistling, though,' Maladict observed.

More people watched them as they climbed flight after flight of stone steps. No one could take this place, Polly could see that. Every flight was seen by another one higher up, every visitor would be sighted on before she'd even glimpsed a face.

A figure stepped out of the shadows as they reached the next floor. It was a young woman, in old-fashioned leather and mail armour, with a breastplate. She had long, very fair hair; for the first time in weeks, Polly felt a twinge of envy.

'Thank you, captain, I'll take over from here,' she said, and nodded to Polly. 'Good evening, Corporal Perks . . . if you would follow me, please?'

'She's a woman! And a sergeant!' Maladict whispered.

'Yes, I know,' said Polly.

'But she gave an order to that captain!'

'Maybe she's a political . . .'

'And she's *obviously* female!'

'I'm not blind, Mal,' said Polly.

'I'm not deaf, either,' said the woman, turning and smiling. 'My name is Angua. If you will wait here, I'll have some coffee sent in. There's a bit of an argument going on in there at the moment.'

They were in a sort of anteroom, not much more than a widened area of corridor with a few benches. There were big double doors at the far end, behind which voices were being raised. Angua left.

'Just like that?' said Maladict. 'What's to stop us taking over the place?'

'All those men with crossbows we passed on the way up?' said Polly. Why us? she thought, looking blankly at the wall.

'Oh, yes. Those. Yes. Er . . . Poll?'

'Yes?'

'I'm actually Maladicta.' She sat back. 'There! I've told someone!'

'Dat's nice,' said Jade.

'Oh, good,' said Polly. *I'd be going out to give the latrines their afternoon swill about now*, she thought. *This has got to be better than that, right?*

'I thought I did pretty well,' Maladicta went on. 'Now, I know what you're thinking. You're thinking: vampires have a pretty good time of it whatever sex they are, right? But it's the same everywhere. Velvet dresses, underwired nightgowns, acting crazy all the time, and don't let's even go near the whole "bathing in virgin's blood" thing. You get taken a lot more seriously if they think you're male.'

'Right,' said Polly. *All in all, it's been a long day. A bath would be nice.*

'I thought I did pretty well right up until the whole coffee thing. A necklace of the roast beans, that'd be the thing. I'll be better prepared another time.'

'Yeah,' said Polly. 'Good idea. With real soap.'

'Soap? How would soap work?'

'What? Oh . . . sorry,' said Polly.

'Did you hear *anything* I said?'

'Oh, that. Yes. Thank you for telling me.'

'Is that *it*?'

'Yes,' said Polly. 'You're you. That's good. I'm me,

whoever I am. Tonker's Tonker. It's all just . . . people. Look, a week ago the high spot of my day was reading the new graffiti in the men's latrines. I think you'd agree that a lot has happened since then. I don't think I'm going to be surprised at anything any more. The coffee-bean necklace sounds good, by the way.' She drummed her feet on the floor impatiently. 'Right now, I just wish they'd hurry up in there.'

They sat and listened, and then Polly became aware of a little column of smoke coming from behind a bench on the other side of the space. She walked over and peered over the back. A man was lying there, head on one arm, smoking a cigar. He nodded when he saw Polly's face.

'They're going to be ages yet,' he said.

'Aren't you that sergeant I saw in the old kitchen? Making faces behind Lord Rust from Ankh-Morpork?'

'I was *not* making faces, miss. That's how I *always* look when Lord Rust is talking. And I *was* a sergeant once, it's true, but, look, no stripes.'

'Make der faces once too often?' said Jade.

The man laughed. He hadn't shaved today, by the look of it. 'Something like that, yes. Come along to my office, it's warmer. I only came out here because people complain about the smoke. Don't worry about that lot in there, they can wait. I'm only down the passage.'

They followed him. The door was, indeed, only a few steps away. The man pushed it open, walked across the little room beyond, and sat down in a

chair. The table in front of it overflowed with papers.

'I think we can get enough food up here to see you through the winter,' he said, picking up a sheet of paper apparently at random. 'Grain's a bit short but we've got a handy surplus of white drumhead cabbage, keeps wonderfully, full of vitamins and minerals ... but you might want to keep your windows open, if you follow me. Don't stare. I *know* the country's a month away from starvation.'

'But I haven't even shown this letter to anyone!' Polly protested. 'You don't know what we—'

'I don't have to,' said the man. 'This is about food and mouths. Good grief, we don't *have* to fight you. Your country is going to fall over anyway. Your fields are overgrown, most of your farmers are old men, the bulk of the grub goes to the army. And armies don't do much for agriculture except marginally raise the fertility of the battlefield. The honour, the pride, the glory ... none of that matters. This war stops, or Borogravia dies. Do you understand?'

Polly remembered the gale-swept fields, the old people salvaging what they could ...

'We're just messengers,' she said. 'I can't negotiate—'

'You know your god's dead?' said the man. 'Nothing left but a voice, according to some of our priests. The last three Abominations were against rocks, ears and accordion players. Okay, I might be with him on the last one, but ... rocks? Hah! We can advise you if you're going to look for a new one, by the way. Om's very popular at the moment. Very few abominations,

no special clothing, and hymns you can sing in the bath. You won't get Offler the Crocodile God up here with your winters, and the Unorthodox Potato Church is probably a bit too uncomplicated for—'

Polly started to laugh. 'Look, sir, I'm just a . . . what *is* your name, please?'

'Sam Vimes. Special envoy, which is kind of like an ambassador but without the little gold chocolates.'

'Vimes the Butcher?' said Maladicta.

'Oh, yes. I've heard that one,' said Vimes, grinning. 'Your people haven't really mastered the fine art of propaganda. And I'm telling you because— well, have you *heard* of Om?'

They shook their heads.

'No? Well, in the *Old Book of Om* there's a story about some city full of wickedness, and Om decided to destroy it with holy fire, this being back in the old smiting days before he'd got religion. But Bishop Horn protested about this plan, and Om said he'd spare the city if the bishop could find one good man. Well, the bishop knocked on every door, and turned up empty-handed. It turned out, after the place had been reduced to a glass plain, that there were probably plenty of good people there and, being good, they weren't the sort to admit it. Death by modesty, a terrible thing. And you, ladies, are the only Borogravians I know much about, apart from the military who, frankly, aren't chatty. You don't appear to be as insane as your country's foreign policy. You're the one piece of international goodwill it has. A bunch of young boys outwitting crack cavalrymen?

Kicking the Prince in the fork? People at home liked that. And now it turns out that you're girls? They'll *love* that. Mr de Worde is going to have fun with that when he finds out.'

'But we don't have any power! We can't negotiate a—'

'What does Borogravia want? Not the country. I mean the people.'

Polly opened her mouth to reply, and then shut it again and *thought* about the answer. 'To be left alone,' she said. 'By everybody. For a while, anyway. We can change things.'

'You'll accept the food?'

'We are a proud country.'

'What are you proud of?'

It came swiftly, like a blow, and Polly realized how wars happened. You took that shock that had run through her, and let it boil.

. . . it may be corrupt, benighted and stupid, but it's ours . . .

Vimes was watching her face. 'From this desk here,' he said, 'the only thing your country has to be proud of right now is you women.'

Polly stayed silent. She was still trying to cope with the anger. It made it worse to know that he was right. *We have our pride. And that's what we're proud of. We're proud of being proud . . .*

'Very well, then, will you *buy* some food?' said Vimes, watching her carefully. 'On credit? I suppose you still have someone in your country who knows about the kind of international

affairs that don't involve edged weapons?'

'People would accept that, yes,' said Polly hoarsely.

'Good. I'll send a clacks back tonight.'

'And why would you be so generous, Mr Ankh-Morpork?'

'Because I'm from a wonderfully warm-hearted city, corporal . . . hah, no, I can't say that and keep a straight face,' said Vimes. 'Do you want to know the truth? Most people in Ankh-Morpork hadn't even heard of your country until the clacks went down. There's dozens of little countries round here selling one another hand-painted clogs or beer made from turnips. Then they knew you as the bloody mad idiots who fight everyone. Now they know you as . . . well, people who do just what they'd do. And tomorrow they'll laugh. And there're other people, people who sit and think about the future every day, who believe it's worth a little to be friends with a country like that.'

'Why?' said Maladicta suspiciously.

'Because Ankh-Morpork is a friend to all freedom-loving people everywhere!' said Vimes. 'Gods, it must be the way I tell 'em. *Ze chzy Brogocia proztfik!*' He saw their blank expressions. 'Sorry, I've been away from home too long. And frankly, I'd rather be back there.'

'But why did you say you were a cherry pancake?' said Polly.

'Didn't I say I am a citizen of Borogravia?'

'No. *Brogocia* is the cherry pancake, *Borogvia* is the country.'

'Well, I made the effort, at least. Look, we'd rather Prince Heinrich wasn't ruler of two countries. That'd

make one quite big country, much bigger than the other ones round here. So it'd probably get bigger still. He wants to be like Ankh-Morpork, you see. But what he means is he wants power, and influence. He doesn't want to earn them, he doesn't want to grow into them or learn the hard way how to use them. He just wants them.'

'That's playing politics!' said Maladicta.

'No. It's just telling the truth. Make peace with him, by all means. Just leave the road and the towers alone. You'll get the food anyway, at whatever price. Mr de Worde's article will see to that.'

'You sent the coffee,' said Polly.

'Oh, yes. That was Corporal Buggy Swires, my eye in the sky. He's a gnome.'

'And you set a werewolf on us?'

'Well, set is a bit strong. Angua followed you, just to be on the safe side. She's a werewolf, yes.'

'The girl we met? She didn't look like one!'

'Well, they don't, usually,' said Vimes. 'Right up until the moment when they do, if you see what I mean. And she was following you because I was looking for anything that'd stop thousands of people dying. And that's not politics either,' said Vimes. He stood up. 'And now, ladies, I have to go and present your document to the alliance leaders.'

'You came out for a smoke at the right time, didn't you?' said Polly, slowly and carefully. 'You *knew* we were on our way, and you made sure you'd get to us first.'

'Of course. Can't leave this to a bunch of . . . oh, yes . . . ruperts.'

'Where is my brother, Mister Vimes?' said Polly stiffly.

'You seem very sure I know . . .' said Vimes, not looking her in the face.

'I'm certain you do,' said Polly.

'Why?'

'Because no one else does!'

Vimes stubbed out his cigar. 'Angua was right about you,' he said. 'Yes, I, er, *arranged* for him to be put in what I like to call "protective custody". He's fine. Angua will take you to him now, if you like. Your brother, possibility of revenge, blackmail, who knows what . . . I thought he might be safer if I knew exactly who held the keys.'

The end of the journey, Polly thought. But it wasn't, not any more. She got the distinct impression that the man opposite was reading her thoughts.

'That's what all this was about, isn't it?' he said.

'No, sir. It's just how it started,' said Polly.

'Well, it continues like this,' said Vimes. 'This is going to be a busy day. Right now I shall take this offer of a truce into the room down the passage and present it to the very important men' – his voice went flat to say those words – 'who are discussing what to do about Borogravia. You'll get a truce, the food, and probably some other help.'

'How do you know that?' said Polly. 'They haven't discussed it!'

'Not yet. But, as I said . . . I used to be a sergeant. Angua!'

The door opened. Angua came in. As Vimes had said, you couldn't tell who was a werewolf until you found out . . .

'And now I'd better have a shave before I go to see the very important men,' said Vimes. 'People set a lot of store by shaving.'

Polly felt embarrassed walking down the steps with Sergeant Angua. How did you start a conversation? 'So you're a werewolf, then?' would be sort of idiotic. She was glad that Jade and Maladicta had been left in the waiting room.

'Yes, I am,' said Angua.

'But I didn't say it!' Polly burst out.

'No, but I'm used to situations like this. I've learned to recognize the way people don't say things. Don't worry.'

'You followed us,' said Polly.

'Yes.'

'So you must've known we weren't men.'

'Oh, yes,' said Angua. 'My sense of smell is much better than my eyesight, and I've got sharp eyes. Humans are smelly creatures. For what it's worth, though, I wouldn't have told Mister Vimes if I hadn't heard you talking to one another. Anyone could have *heard* you, you don't need to be a werewolf for that. Everyone's got secrets they don't want known. Werewolves are a bit like vampires in that way. We're tolerated . . . if we're careful.'

'*That* I can understand,' said Polly. So are we, she thought.

Angua stopped by a heavy, studded door. 'He's in here,' she said, producing a key and turning it in the lock. 'I'll go back and chat to the others. Come and find me when you're ready . . .'

Polly stepped inside, heart pounding, and there was Paul. And there was a buzzard, on a perch by the open window. And on the wall, where Paul was working so intensely that his tongue was sticking out of the corner of his mouth and he hadn't even noticed the door opening, was another buzzard, flying in the heart of the sunrise.

Right now, Polly could forgive Ankh-Morpork anything. Someone had found Paul a box of coloured chalks.

The long day got longer. She had a kind of power. They all did. People gave them space, watched them. The fighting had stopped and they were the cause and no one knew exactly why.

There were lighter moments. They might have power, but General Froc gave the orders. And General Froc might give the orders, but it was permissible to suppose that it was Sergeant-major Jackrum who anticipated them.

And perhaps that was why Shufti asked Polly and Tonker to go with her, and they were ushered into a room where a couple of guards stood on either side of a sheepish young man called Johnny who had fair hair and blue eyes and a gold earring and his trousers

round his knees in case Shufti wanted to check his other distinguishing feature.

He also had a black eye.

'This the one?' said Major Clogston, who was leaning against the wall eating an apple. 'The general has asked me to tell you that there will be a dowry of five hundred crowns, with the army's compliments.'

Johnny brightened up slightly when he heard that. Shufti gave him a long and careful look.

'No,' she said at last, turning away. 'That's not him.'

Johnny opened his mouth, and Polly snapped: 'No one asked you to speak, private!' And, such was the nature of the day, he shut up.

'I'm afraid he's the only candidate,' said Clogston. 'We've got any amount of earrings, heads of fair hair, blue eyes and Johnnies – and, surprisingly, a fair number of carbuncles. But he's the only one with everything. Are you sure?'

'Positive,' said Shufti, still staring at the boy. 'My Johnny must have been killed.'

Clogston walked over and lowered her voice. 'In that case, uh, the general did say, informally, that a marriage certificate, a ring and a widow's pension could be arranged,' she said.

'Can she do that?' whispered Polly.

'For one of you? Today? You'll be amazed what can be done,' said Clogston. 'Don't think too badly of her. She means well. She's a very *practical* man.'

'No,' said Shufti. 'I . . . it's . . . well, no. Thank you, but no.'

'Are you sure?' said Polly.

'Positive,' said Shufti, looking defiant. Since she was not naturally a defying kind of person it was not quite the look that she thought it was and it ought to have been, having overtones of haemorrhoid sufferer, but the effort was there.

Clogston stepped back. 'Well, if you're certain, private? Fair enough, then. Take that man away, sergeant.'

'Just a moment,' said Shufti. She walked over to the bewildered Johnny, stood in front of him, held out her hand and said: 'Before they take you away again I want my sixpence back, you son of a bitch!'

Polly held out her hand to Clogston, who shook it and smiled. There had been another little victory, of sorts. If the landslide is big enough, even square pebbles will roll.

Polly headed back to the rather larger cell that had been made available as the women's barracks, or at least the barracks for the official women. Men, grown men, had fallen over themselves to put cushions in there, and bring in wood for the fire. It was all very strange. Polly felt they were being treated as something dangerous and fragile, like, say, a huge and wonderful jar full of poison. She turned the corner into the big courtyard and there was de Worde with Mr Chriek. There was no escaping them. They were definitely people looking for someone.

The man gave her a look in which reproach was mingled with hope. 'Er . . . so you're women, then?' he said.

'Er, yes,' said Polly.

De Worde took out his notebook.

'This is an *amazing* story,' he said. 'You really fought your way here and got in disguised as washerwomen?'

'Well, we *were* women, and we did some washing,' said Polly. 'I suppose it was quite a cunning disguise, really. We got in by *not* being disguised, you could say.'

'General Froc and Captain Blouse say they're very proud of you,' de Worde went on.

'Oh, he *has* got promoted, then?' said Polly.

'Yes, and Froc said you did wonderfully well, for women.'

'Yes, I suppose we did,' said Polly. 'Yes. Very well, for women.'

'The general went on to say . . .' de Worde consulted his notebook, 'that you are a credit to the women of your country. I wonder if you'd care to comment?'

He looked innocent, so possibly he didn't understand the raging argument that had just broken out in Polly's head. *A credit to the women of your country. We're proud of you.* Somehow those words locked you away, put you in your place, patted you on the head and dismissed you with a sweetie. On the other hand, you had to start somewhere . . .

'That's very nice of him,' said Polly. 'But we just want to get the job done and go home. That's what soldiers want.' She thought for a moment, and then added: 'And hot sweet tea.' To her amazement, he wrote this down.

'Just one last question, miss: do you think the world would be a different place if more women were

soldiers?' de Worde asked. He was smiling again, she noted, so this was probably a joky kind of question.

'Oh, I think you'd have to ask General Froc that,' said Polly. And I'd like to watch her expression if you do . . .

'Yes, but what do you think, miss?'

'That's corporal, please.'

'Sorry, corporal . . . and?'

The pencil was hovering. Around it, the world turned. It wrote things down, and then they got everywhere. The pen might not be mightier than the sword, but maybe the printing press was heavier than the siege weapon. Just a few words can change everything . . .

'Well,' said Polly, 'I—'

There was a sudden bustling around the gates at the other end of the courtyard, and some cavalry officers arrived. They must have been expected, because Zlobenian officers were converging in a great hurry.

'Ah, I see the Prince is back,' said de Worde. 'He's probably not going to be happy about the truce. They sent some gallopers out to meet him.'

'Can he do anything about it?'

De Worde shrugged. 'He left some very senior officers here. It would be rather shocking if he did.'

The tall figure had dismounted, and was striding towards Polly, or rather, she realized, the big doorway next to her. Frantic clerks and officers trailed after him, and were brushed off. But when a white oblong was waved in front of his face by one man he grabbed

it and stopped so quickly that several other officers bumped into him.

'Um,' said de Worde. 'The edition with the cartoon, I expect. Um.'

The paper was thrown down.

'Yes, probably that was it,' said de Worde.

Heinrich advanced. Now Polly could make out his expression. It was thunderous. Beside her, de Worde turned over to a fresh page in his notebook and cleared his throat.

'You're going to *talk* to him?' said Polly. 'In *that* mood? He'll cut you down!'

'I have to,' said de Worde. And, as the Prince and his retinue reached the doorway he took a step forward and said, in a voice that cracked slightly, 'Your highness? I wonder if I could have a word?'

Heinrich turned to scowl at him, and saw Polly. For a moment, their gazes locked.

The Prince's adjutants knew their master. As the man's hand flew to his sword they closed on him in a mob, completely surrounding him, and there was some frantic whispering, in which some rather louder injections from Heinrich on the broad theme of 'What?' could be heard, followed by a toccata on 'The hell you say!'

The crowd parted again. The Prince slowly and carefully brushed some dust off his spotless jacket, glanced only briefly at Otto and de Worde and, to Polly's horror, strolled towards her . . .

. . . with one white-gloved hand extended.

Oh no, she thought. But he's cleverer than Vimes

thinks he is, and he can control his temper. And, suddenly, I'm *everyone's* mascot.

'For the good of our *great* countries,' said Heinrich, 'it is suggested that we publicly shake the hand of friendship.' He smiled again, or at least allowed the corners of his mouth to turn up.

Because she could think of no other way out, Polly took the huge hand and obediently shook it.

'Oh, ver' good,' said Otto, grasping his picture box. 'I can only take zer vun, of course, because unfortunately I shall have to use flash. Just vun moment . . .'

Polly was learning that an art form which happens in a fraction of a second nevertheless needs a long time to take place, allowing a smile to freeze into a mad grimace or, in the worst cases, a death rictus. Otto muttered to himself as he adjusted the equipment. Heinrich and Polly maintained the grip and stared at the picture box.

'So,' muttered the Prince, 'the soldier boy *isn't* a soldier boy. That is your good luck!'

Polly kept her fixed grin. 'Do you often menace frightened women?' she said.

'Oh, that was nothing! You are only a peasant girl, after all! What do you know of life? And you showed spirit!'

'Everyone say chiz!' Otto commanded. 'Vun, two, three . . . oh, bug—'

By the time the after-images had died away, Otto was back on his feet again. 'Vun day I hope to find a filter zat vorks,' he muttered. 'Thank you, everyvun.'

'That was for peace and goodwill between nations,' said Polly, smiling sweetly and letting go of the Prince's hand. She took a step back. 'And this, your highness, is for me . . .'

Actually, she didn't kick. Life was a process of finding out how far you could go, and you could probably go too far in finding out how far you could go. But a mere twitch of a leg was enough, just to see the idiot collapse in the ridiculous, knock-kneed, protective crouch.

She marched away, singing inside. This was not a fairy-tale castle and there was no such thing as a fairy-tale ending, but sometimes you could threaten to kick the handsome prince in the ham-and-eggs.

And now, there was one *other* little thing.

The sun was setting before Polly found Jackrum again, and blood-red light shone through the high windows of the keep's biggest kitchen. He was sitting alone at a long table by the fire, in full uniform, and he was eating a slab of thick bread plastered with pork dripping. A mug of beer was not far from his other hand. He looked up as she approached, and nodded companionably towards another chair. Around them, women ran to and fro.

'Pork drippin' with salt and pepper, and a mug of beer,' he said. 'That's the ticket. You can keep your *cuisine*. Want a slice?' He waved a hand at one of the kitchen girls who was dancing attendance on him.

'Not right now, sarge.'

'Sure?' said Jackrum. 'There's an old sayin': kissing

don't last, cooking do. I hope that it's one you don't have cause to reflect upon.'

Polly sat down. 'Kissing is lasting so far,' she said.

'Shufti get sorted out?' said Jackrum. He finished the beer, snapped his fingers at the serving girl, and pointed to the empty mug.

'To her own satisfaction, sarge.'

'Fair enough. You can't get fairer. So what next, Perks?'

'Dunno, sarge. I'll go with Wa— with Alice and the army and see what happens.'

'Best of luck. Look after 'em, Perks, 'cos I ain't coming,' said Jackrum.

'Sarge?' said Polly, shocked.

'Well, looks like we're going to be short by one war at present, eh? Anyway, this is it. The end of the road. I've done my bit. Can't go on now. Shot me quiver with the general, and I dare say *he* will be glad to see the back of me. Besides, old age is creepin' on. I killed five poor devils when we attacked today, and afterwards I found meself wonderin' why. Not good, that. Time to get out before I blunt me own edge.'

'You're sure, sarge?'

'Yeah. Seems to me the ol' "my country right or wrong" thing has had its day. Time to put my feet up and find out what it is we've been fighting for. Sure you won't have any dripping? It's got crunchy bits. That's what I call *style*, in dripping.'

Polly waved away the proffered slab of grease-smeared bread, and sat in silence while Jackrum engulfed it.

'Funny thing, really,' she said, at last.

'What's that, Perks?'

'Finding out that it's not about you. You think you're the hero, and it turns out you're really part of someone else's story. Wazz— Alice will be the one they remember. We just had to get her here.'

Jackrum said nothing but, as Polly would have predicted, pulled his crumpled bag of chewing tobacco out of his pocket. She slipped a hand in her own pocket and pulled out a small packet. Pockets, she thought. We've got to hang on to pockets. A soldier needs pockets.

'Try this, sarge,' she said. 'Go on, open it.'

It was a small, soft leather pouch, with a drawstring. Jackrum held it up so that it twisted this way and that.

'Well, Perks, upon my oath I am not a swearing man—' he began.

'No, you're not. I've noticed,' said Polly. 'But that grubby old paper was getting on my nerves. Why didn't you ever get a proper pouch made for yourself? One of the saddlers here sewed that up for me in half an hour.'

'Well, that's life, isn't it?' said Jackrum. 'Every day you think "ye gods, it's about time I had a new bag", but then it all gets so busy you end up using the old one. Thank you, Perks.'

'Oh, I thought, "What can I give the man who has everything?" and that was all I could afford,' said Polly. 'But you don't have everything, sarge. Sarge? You don't, do you?'

She sensed him freeze over.

'You stop right there, Perks,' he said, lowering his voice.

'I just thought you might like to show someone that locket of yours, sarge,' said Polly cheerfully. 'The one round your neck. And don't glare at me, sarge. Oh, yeah, I could walk away and I'd never be sure, really *sure*, and maybe you'd never show it to anyone else, ever, or tell them the story, and one day we'll both be dead and . . . well, what a waste, eh?'

Jackrum glared.

'Upon your oath, you are not a dishonest man,' said Polly. 'Good one, sarge. You told people every day.'

Around them, beyond the dome, the kitchen buzzed with the busyness of women. Women always seemed to be doing things with their hands – holding babies, or pans, or plates, or wool, or a brush, or a needle. Even when they were talking, busyness was happening.

'No one would believe yer,' said Jackrum, at last.

'Who would I want to tell?' said Polly. 'And you're right. No one would believe me. I'd believe *you*, though.'

Jackrum stared into his fresh mug of beer, as if trying to see the future in the foam. He seemed to reach a decision, pulled the gold chain out of his noisome vest, unfastened the locket, and gently snapped it open.

'There you go,' he said, passing it across. 'Much good may it do you.'

There was a miniature painting in each side of the

locket: a dark-haired girl, and a blond young man in the uniform of the Ins-and-Outs.

'Good one of you,' said Polly.

'Pull the other one, it's got bells on,' said Jackrum.

'No, honestly,' said Polly. 'I look at the picture, and look at you . . . I can see that face in her face. Paler, of course. Not so . . . full. And who was the boy?'

'William, his name was,' said Jackrum.

'Your sweetheart?'

'Yes.'

'And you followed him into the army . . .'

'Oh, yeah. Same old story. I was a big strong girl, and . . . well, you can see the picture. The artist did his best, but I was never an oil painting. Barely a water-colour, really. Where I came from, what a man looked for in a future wife was someone who could lift a pig under each arm. And a couple of days later I *was* lifting a pig under each arm, helping my dad, and one of my clogs came off in the muck and the ol' man was yelling at me and I thought: the hell with this, Willie never yelled. Got hold of some men's clothes, never you mind how, cut my hair right off, kissed the Duchess, and was a Chosen Man within three months.'

'What's that?'

'It's what we used to call a corporal,' said Jackrum. 'Chosen Man. Yeah, I smiled about that, too. And I was on my way. The army's a piece of piss compared to running a pig farm and looking after three lazy brothers.'

'How long ago was that, sarge?'

'Couldn't say, really. I swear I don't know how old I am, and that's the truth,' said Jackrum. 'Lied about my age so often I ended up believing me.' She began, very carefully, to transfer the chewing tobacco into the new bag.

'And your young man?' said Polly quietly.

'Oh, we had great times, great times,' said Jackrum, stopping for a moment to stare at nothing. 'He never got promoted on account of his stutter, but I had a good shouty voice and officers like that. But Willie never minded, not even when I made it to sergeant. And then he got killed at Sepple, right next to me.'

'I'm sorry.'

'You don't have to be, you didn't kill him,' said Jackrum evenly. 'But I stepped over his body and skewered the bugger that did. Wasn't his fault. Wasn't my fault. We were soldiers. And then a few months later I had a bit of a surprise, and he was called William, too, just like his father. Good job I had a bit of leave, eh? Me gran raised him for me, put him to a trade as an armourer over in Scritz. Good trade, that. No one kills a good armourer. They tell me he looks just like his dad. A captain I met once had bought a bloody good sword off him. Showed it to me, not knowin' the hist'ry, o' course. *Damn* good sword. It had scrollwork on the hilt and everything, very classy. He's married with four kids now, I heard. Got a carriage and pair, servants, big house . . . yeah, I see you're paying attention . . .'

'Wazzer – well, Wazzer and the Duchess said—'

'Yeah, yeah, they talked about Scritz, and a sword,'

said Jackrum. 'That's when I knew it wasn't just me watchin' over you lads. I knew you'd survive. The old girl needed you.'

'So you've got to go there, sarge.'

'Got to? Who says? I've served the old girl the whole of my life, and she's got no call on me now. I'm my own man, always have been.'

'Are you, sarge?' said Polly.

'Are you crying, Perks?'

'Well . . . it's a bit sad, sarge.'

'Oh, I dare say I sobbed a bit too, once in a while,' said Jackrum, still tucking the tobacco into the new pouch. 'But when all's said and done, I've had a good life. Saw the cavalry break at the Battle of Slomp. I was part of the Thin Red Line that turned aside the Heavy Brigade at Sheep's Drift, I saved the Imperial flag from four real bastards at Raladan, and I've been to a lot of foreign countries and met some very interesting people, who I mostly subsequently killed before they could do me over good and proper. Lost a lover, still got a son . . . there's many a woman who's faced worse, believe me.'

'And . . . you spotted other girls . . .'

'Hah! Became a kind of hobby, really. Most of 'em were frightened little things, running away from god knows what. They got found out soon enough. And there were plenty like Shufti, chasin' their lad. But there were a few who had what I call the *twinkle*. A bit of fire, maybe. They just needed pointing in the right direction. I gave them a leg up, you might say. A sergeant's a powerful man, sometimes. A word here, a

nod there, sometimes even doctorin' some paper-
work, a whisper in the dark—'

'—a pair of socks,' said Polly.

'Yeah, that sort of thing,' said Jackrum, grinning.
'Always a big concern to them, the whole latrine
business. Least of your worries, I used to say. In peace
no one cares, in battle everyone takes a piss the same
way, and damn quickly, too. Oh, I helped 'em. I was
their whatsit, their *eminence grease*, and grease it was,
too, slidin' them to the top. Jackrum's Little Lads, I
called 'em.'

'And they never suspected?'

'What, suspect Jolly Jack Jackrum, so full of rum
and vinegar?' said Jackrum, the old evil grin coming
back. 'Jack Jackrum, who could stop a bar fight by
belchin'? No, sir! I dare say some of 'em suspected
something, maybe, I dare say they worked out that
there was something going on somewhere, but I was
just the big fat sergeant who knew everyone and
everything and drank everything, too.'

Polly dabbed at her eyes. 'What are you going to do
now, then, if you don't go to Scritz?'

'Oh, I've got a bit put by,' said Jackrum. 'More than
a bit, in point of actual fact. Pillage, plunder, loot . . .
it all adds up, whatever you call it. I didn't piss it all up
against a wall like the other lads, right? I expect I can
remember most of the bleedin' places I buried it.
Always thought I might open an inn, or maybe a
knocking shop . . . oh, a proper high class place, you
don't have to look at me like that, nothin' like that
stinking tent. No, I'm talkin' about one with a chef

and chandeliers and a lot of red velvet, very exclusive. I'd get some nobby lady to front it and I'd be the bouncer and run the bar. Here's a tip, lad, for your future career, and it's one some of the other Little Lads learned for 'emselves: sometimes it'll help if you visits one of them naughty places, otherwise the men'll wonder about you. I always used to take a book to read and advise the young lady to get some sleep, 'cos they does a tough job.'

Polly let that pass, but said: 'You don't want to go back and see your grandchildren?'

'Wouldn't wish meself on him, lad,' said Jackrum firmly. 'Wouldn't dare. My boy's a well-respected man in the town! What've I got to offer? He'll not want some fat ol' biddy banging on his back door and gobbing baccy juice all over the place and telling him she's his mother!'

Polly looked at the fire for a moment, and felt the idea creep into her mind. 'What about a distinguished sergeant major, shiny with braid, loaded with medals, arriving at the front door in a grand coach and telling him he's his father?' she said.

Jackrum stared.

'Tides of war, and all that,' Polly went on, mind suddenly racing. 'Young love. Duty calls. Families scattered. Hopeless searching. Decades pass. Fond memories. Then . . . oh, an overheard conversation in a bar, yeah, that'd work. Hope springs. A new search. Greasing palms. The recollections of old women. At last, an address—'

'What're you *saying*, Perks?'

'You're a *liar*, sarge,' said Polly. 'Best I've ever heard. One last lie pays for all! Why not? You could show him the locket. You could tell him about the girl you left behind you . . .'

Jackrum looked away, but said: 'You're a shining bastard of a thinker, Perks. And where would I get a grand coach, anyway?'

'Oh, *sarge*! Today? There are . . . *men* in high places who'll give you anything you ask for, right now. You know that. Especially if it means they'd see the back of you. You never put the bite on them for anything much. If I was you, sarge, I'd cash in a few favours while you can. That's the Ins-and-Outs, sarge. Take the cheese while it's there, 'cos kissin' don't last.'

Jackrum took a deep, long breath. 'I'll think about it, Perks. Now you push off, all right?'

Polly stood up. 'Think hard, sarge, eh? Like you said, anyone who's got anyone left is ahead of the game right now. Four grandchildren? *I'd* be a proud kid if I had a grandad who could spit tobacco juice far enough to hit a fly on the opposite wall.'

'I'm warning you, Perks.'

'It was just a thought, sarge.'

'Yeah . . . right,' Jackrum growled.

'Thanks for getting us through it, sarge.'

Jackrum didn't turn round.

'I'll be going, then, sarge.'

'Perks!' said Jackrum, as she reached the door. Polly stepped back into the room.

'Yes, sarge?'

'I . . . expected better of 'em, really. I thought they'd

be better at it than men. Trouble was, they were better than men at being like men. They do say the army can make a man of you, eh? So . . . whatever it is you are going to do next, do it as you. Good or bad, do it as you. Too many lies and there's no truth to go back to.'

'Will do, sarge.'

'That's an order, Perks. Oh . . . and Perks?'

'Yes, sarge?'

'Thanks, Perks.'

Polly paused when she got to the door. Jackrum had turned her chair to the fire, and had settled back. Around him, the kitchen worked.

Six months passed. The world wasn't perfect, but it was still turning.

Polly had kept the newspaper articles. They weren't accurate, not in the detail, because the writer told . . . stories, not what was actually happening. They were like paintings, when *you* had been there and had seen the real thing. But it was true about the march on the castle, with Wazzer on a white horse in front, carrying the flag. And it was true about people coming out of their houses and joining the march, so that what arrived at the gates was not an army but a sort of disciplined mob, shouting and cheering. And it was true that the guards had taken one look at it and had seriously reconsidered their future, and that the gates had swung open even before the horse had clattered on to the drawbridge. There was no fighting, no fighting at all. The shoe had dropped. The country had breathed out.

Polly didn't think it was true that the painting of
the Duchess, alone on its easel in the big, empty
throne room, had smiled when Wazzer walked
towards it. Polly had been there and didn't see it
happen, but lots of people swore it had, and you
might end up wondering what the truth really was, or
whether there were lots of different kinds of truth.

Anyway, it had worked. And then . . .

. . . they went home. A lot of soldiers did, under the
fragile truce. The first snows were already falling and,
if people had wanted a war, then the winter had given
them one. It came with lances of ice and arrows of
hunger, it filled the passes with snow, it made the
world as distant as the moon . . .

That was when the old dwarf mines had opened up,
and pony after pony emerged. It had always been said
there were dwarf tunnels everywhere, and not just
tunnels; secret canals under the mountains, docks,
flights of locks that could lift a barge a mile high in
busy darkness, far below the gales on the mountain
tops.

They brought, indeed, cabbage and potatoes and
roots and apples and barrels of fat, things that *kept*.
And winter was defeated, and the snowmelt roared
down the valleys, and the Kneck scrawled its random
wiggles across the flat silt of the valley.

They'd gone home, and Polly wondered if they'd
ever really been away. Were we soldiers? she
wondered. They'd been cheered on the road to
P r i n c e M a r m a d u k e P i o t r e A l b e r t H a n s
JosephBernhardtWilhelmsberg, and had been much

463

better treated than their rank deserved, and even had
a special uniform designed for them. But the vision of
Gummy Abbens kept rising in her mind . . .

We weren't soldiers, she decided. We were girls in
uniform. We were like a lucky charm. We *were*
mascots. We weren't real, we were always a symbol of
something. We'd done very well, for women. And we
were temporary.

Tonker and Lofty were never going to be dragged
back to the school now, and they'd gone their own
way. Wazzer had joined the general's household, and
had a room of her own, and quietness, and made her-
self useful and was never beaten. She'd written Polly a
letter, in tiny spiky handwriting. She seemed happy; a
world without beatings was heaven. Jade and her beau
had wandered off to do something more interesting,
as trolls very sensibly did. Shufti . . . had been on a
timetable of her own. Maladicta had disappeared.
And Igorina had set up by herself in the capital, deal-
ing with women's problems, or at least those women's
problems that weren't men. And senior officers had
given them medals, and watched them go with fixed,
faint smiles. Kisses don't last.

And, now, it wasn't that good things were happen-
ing, it was just that bad things had stopped. The old
women still grumbled, but they were left to grumble.
No one had any directions, no one had a map, no one
was quite certain who was in charge. There were argu-
ments and debates on every street corner. It was
frightening and exhilarating. Every day was an
exploration. Polly had worn a pair of Paul's old

trousers to clean the floor of the big bar, and had got barely a 'hurrumph' from anyone. Oh, and the Girls' Working School had burned down, and on the same day two slim masked figures had robbed a bank. Polly had grinned when she heard that. Shufti had moved into The Duchess. Her baby was called Jack. Paul doted on it. And now . . .

Someone had been drawing in the gents' privy again. Polly couldn't wash it off, so she contented herself with correcting the anatomy. Then she swooshed the place clean – at least, clean by pub urinal standards – with a couple of buckets and ticked off the chore, just as she did every morning. When she arrived back in the bar there were a group of worried men there, talking to her father. They looked mildly frightened when she strode in.

'What's happening?' she said.

Her father nodded to Gummy Abbens, and everyone stepped back a little. What with the spittle and the bad breath, you never wanted a conversation with Gummy to be particularly intimate.

'The swede-eatersh is at it again!' he said. 'They're gonna invade 'cos the Prince saysh we belong to him now!'

'It's all down to him being the Duchess's distant cousin,' said Polly's father.

'But I heard it still wasn't settled!' said Polly. 'Anyway, there's still a truce!'

'Sheems like he's shettling it,' said Gummy.

The rest of the day passed at an accelerated pace. There were groups of people talking urgently in the

streets, and a crowd around the gates to the town hall. Every so often a clerk would come out and nail another communiqué on the gates; the crowd would close over it like a hand, open again like a flower. Polly elbowed her way to the front, ignoring the mutterings around her, and scanned the sheets.

The same old stuff. They were recruiting again. The same old words. The same old croakings of long dead soldiers, inviting the living to join them. General Froc might be female, but he was also, as Blouse would have said, 'a bit of an old woman'. Either that or the heaviness of those epaulettes had weighed her down.

Kissing don't last. Oh, the Duchess had come alive before them and turned the world upside down for a space and maybe they had all decided to be better people, and out of certain oblivion had come a space to breathe.

But then ... had it really happened? Even Polly sometimes wondered, and she *had* been there. Was it just a voice in their heads, some kind of hallucination? Weren't soldiers in desperate straits famous for seeing visions of gods and angels? And somewhere in the course of the long winter the miracle had faded, and people had said 'yes, but we've got to be practical'.

All we were given was a chance, thought Polly. No miracle, no rescue, no magic. Just a chance.

She walked back to the inn, her mind buzzing. When she got there, a package was waiting. It was quite long, and heavy.

'It came all the way from Scritz on the cart,' said Shufti excitedly. She'd been working in the kitchen. It

had become, now, *her* kitchen. 'I wonder what it can be?' she said pointedly.

Polly levered the lid off the rough wooden crate, and found that it was full of straw with an envelope lying on top of it. She opened it.

Inside was an iconograph. It looked expensively done, a stiff family group with curtains and a potted palm in the background to give everything a bit of style. On the left was a middle-aged man looking proud; on the right was a woman of about the same age, looking rather puzzled but nevertheless pleased because her husband was happy; and here and there, staring at the viewer with variations of smile and squint, and expressions extending from interest to a sudden recollection that they should have gone to the toilet before posing, were children ranging from tall and gangly to small and smugly sweet.

And sitting on a chair in the middle, the focus of it all, was Sergeant-major Jackrum, shining like the sun.

Polly stared, and then turned the picture over. On the back was written, in big black letters: 'SM Jackrum's Last Stand!' and, underneath, 'Don't need these.'

She smiled, and pulled aside the straw. In the middle of the box, wrapped in cloth, were a couple of cutlasses.

'Is that old Jackrum?' said Shufti, picking up the picture.

'Yes. He's found his son,' said Polly, unwinding a blade. Shufti shuddered when she saw it.

'Evil things,' she said.

467

'Things, anyway,' said Polly. She laid both the cutlasses on the table, and was about to lift the box out of the way when she saw something small in the straw at the bottom. It was oblong, and wrapped in thin leather.

It was a notebook, with a cheap binding and musty yellowing pages.

'What's that?' said Shufti.

'I think ... yes, it's his address book,' said Polly, flicking through the pages.

This is it, she thought. It's all here. Generals and majors and captains, oh my. There must be ... hundreds. Maybe a thousand! Names, *real* names, promotions, dates ... everything ...

She pulled out a white pasteboard oblong that had been inserted like a bookmark. It showed a rather florid coat of arms and bore the printed legend:

William De Worde

EDITOR, THE TIMES OF ANKH-MORPORK

'The Truth Shall Make Ye Frep'

Gleam Street, Ankh-Morpork
c-mail: WDW@Times.AM

Someone had crossed out the 'p' in 'frep' and pencilled in an 'e' above it.

It was a sudden strange fancy ...

How many ways can you fight a war? Polly wondered. We have the clacks now. I know a man who writes things down. The world turns. Plucky little countries seeking self-determination . . . could be useful to big countries with plans of their own.

Time to grab the cheese.

Polly's expression as she stared at the wall would have frightened a number of important people. They would have been even more concerned at the fact that she spent the next several hours writing things down, because it occurred to Polly that General Froc had not got where she was today by being stupid and therefore she could profit from following her example. She copied out the entire notebook, and sealed it in an old jam jar which she hid in the roof of the stables. She wrote a few letters. And she got her uniform out of the wardrobe and inspected it critically.

The uniforms that had been made for them had a special, additional quality that could only be called . . . girlie. They had more braid, they were better tailored, and they had a long skirt with a bum roll rather than trousers. The shakos had plumes, too. *Her* tunic had a sergeant's stripes. It had been a *joke*. A sergeant of women. The world had been turned upside down, after all.

They'd been mascots, good-luck charms . . . And, perhaps, on the march to PrinceMarmadukePiotreAlbertHansJosephBernhardt Wilhelmsberg a joke was what everyone needed. But, maybe, when the world turns upside down, you can turn a joke upside down too. Thank you, Gummy,

even though you didn't know what it was you were teaching me. When they're laughing at you, their guard is down. When their guard is down, you can kick them in the fracas.

She examined herself in the mirror. Her hair, now, was just long enough to be a nuisance without being long enough to be attractive, so she brushed it and left it at that. She put the uniform on, but with the skirt over her trousers, and tried to put aside the nagging feeling that she was dressing up as a woman.

There. She looked completely harmless. She looked slightly less harmless with both cutlasses and one of the horsebows on her back, especially if you knew that the inn's dartboards now had deep holes in the bullseyes from all the practising.

She crept along the hall to the window that over-looked the inn yard. Paul was up a ladder, repainting the sign. Her father was steadying the ladder and calling out instructions in his normal way, which was to call out the instruction just a second or two after you'd already started doing it. And Shufti, although Polly was the only one in The Duchess who still called her that and knew why, was watching them, holding Jack. It made a lovely picture. For a moment, she wished she had a locket.

The Duchess was smaller than she'd thought. But if you had to protect it by standing in the doorway with a sword, you were too late. Caring for small things had to start with caring for big things, and maybe the world wasn't big enough.

The note she left on her dressing table read: 'Shufti,

I hope you and Jack are happy here. Paul, you look after her. Dad, I've never taken any wages, but I need a horse. I'll try to have it sent back. I love you all. If I don't come back, burn this letter and look in the roof of the stables.'

She dropped out of the window, saddled up a horse in the stables, and let herself out of the back gate. She didn't mount up until she was out of earshot, and then rode down to the river.

Spring was pouring through the country. Sap was rising. In the woods, a ton of timber was growing every minute. Everywhere, birds were singing.

There was a guard on the ferry. He eyed her nervously as she led the horse aboard, and then grinned.' 'Morning, miss!' he said cheerfully.

Oh, well . . . time to start. Polly marched in front of the puzzled man.

'Are you trying to be *smart*?' she demanded, inches from his face.

'No, miss—'

'That's sergeant, mister!' said Polly. 'Let's try *again*, shall we? I said, are you trying to be smart?'

'No, sergeant!'

Polly leaned until her nose was an inch from his. '*Why not?*'

The grin faded. This was not a soldier on the fast track to promotion. 'Huh?' he managed.

'If you are not trying to be smart, mister, you're happy to be stupid!' shouted Polly. 'And I'm up to here with stupid, understand?'

'Yeah, but—'

'But *what*, soldier?'

'Yeah, but . . . well . . . but . . . nothing, sergeant,' said the soldier.

'That's good.' Polly nodded at the ferrymen. 'Time to go?' she suggested, but in the tones of an order.

'Couple of people just coming down the road, sergeant,' said one of them, a faster man with an uptake.

They waited. There were, in fact, three people. One of them was Maladicta, in full uniform.

Polly said nothing until the ferry was out in midstream. The vampire gave her the kind of smile only a vampire can give. It would have been sheepish, if sheep had different teeth.

'Thought I'd try again,' she said.

'We'll find Blouse,' said Polly.

'He's a major now,' said Maladicta. 'And happy as a flea because they've named a kind of fingerless glove after him, I heard. What do we want him for?'

'He knows about the clacks. He knows about other ways war can be fought. And I know . . . people,' said Polly.

'Ah. Do you mean the "Upon my oath, I am not a lying man, but I know people" kind of people?'

'Those were the kind of people I had in mind, yes.' The river slapped against the side of the ferry.

'Good,' said Maladicta.

'I don't know where it's going to lead, though,' said Polly.

'Ah. Even better.'

At which point, Polly decided that she knew

enough of the truth to be going on with. The enemy wasn't men, or women, or the old, or even the dead. It was just bleedin' stupid people, who came in all varieties. And no one had the right to be stupid.

She looked at the other two passengers who'd sidled aboard. They were country lads in ragged, ill-fitting clothes, keeping away from her and staring intently at the deck. But one glance was enough. The world turned upside down, and history repeated. For some reason, that suddenly made her feel very happy.

'Going to join up, lads?' she said, cheerily.

There was some mumbling on the theme of 'yes'.

'Good. Then stand up straight,' said Polly. 'Let's have a look at you. Chins up. Ah. Well done. Shame you didn't practise walking in trousers, and I notice you didn't bring an extra pair of socks.'

They stared, mouths open.

'What are your names?' said Polly. 'Your *real* names, please?'

'Er . . . Rosemary,' one of them began.

'I'm Mary,' said the other. 'I heard girls were joining, but everyone laughed, so I thought I'd better pretend to—'

'Oh, you can join as men if you want,' said Polly. 'We need a few good men.'

The girls looked at one another.

'You get better swear words,' said Polly. 'And the trousers are useful. But it's your choice.'

'A choice?' said Rosemary.

'Certainly,' said Polly. She put a hand on a shoulder of each girl, winked at Maladicta and added: 'You are

my little lads – or not, as the case may be – and *I* will
look after . . . *you.*'

And the new day was a great big fish.

THE END

SOUL MUSIC
Terry Pratchett

'Classic English humour, with all the slapstick,
twists and dry observations you could hope for'
The Times

*'Be careful what you wish for. You never know who
might be listening.'*

THERE'S no getting away from it. From whichever
angle, Death is a horrible, inescapable business. But
someone's got to do it. So if Death decides to take a
well-earned moment to uncover the meaning of life and
discover himself in the process, then there is going to be
a void of specific dimensions that needs to be occupied,
particularly so when there is trouble brewing in
Discworld. There aren't too many who are qualified to
fill Death's footsteps and it certainly doesn't help the
imminent cataclysm that the one person poised
between the mortal and the immortal is only sixteen
years old...

'Very clever madcap satire which has universal
appeal. If you haven't tried him, this is a fun one
to start with'
Today

'Pratchett lures classical themes and popular
mythologies into the dark corners of his
imagination, gets them drunk and makes them
do things you wouldn't dream of doing with
an Oxford don'
Daily Mail

9780552153195

INTERESTING TIMES

Terry Pratchett

'Funny, delightfully inventive and refuses to lie
down in its genre'
Observer

'A foot in the neck is nine points of the law.'

THERE are many who say that the art of diplomacy is
an intricate and complex dance between two
informed partners, determined by an elaborate set of
elegant and unwritten rules. There are others who
maintain that it's merely a matter of who carries the
biggest stick. Like when a large, heavily fortified and
armoured empire makes a faintly menacing request of a
much smaller, infinitely more cowardly neighbour. It
would be churlish, if not extremely dangerous, not to
comply – particularly if all they want is a wizard, and
they don't specify whether competence is an issue...

'Imagine a collision between Jonathan Swift at his
most scatological and J.R.R. Tolkien on speed...
This is the joyous outcome'
Daily Telegraph

'Like Dickens, much of Pratchett's appeal lies in his
humanism, both in a sentimental regard for his
characters' good fortune, and in that his writing is
generous-spirited and inclusive'
Guardian

9780552153218

MASKERADE
Terry Pratchett

'As funny as Wodehouse and as witty as Waugh'
Independent

'I thought: opera, how hard can it be? Songs. Pretty girls dancing. Nice scenery. Lots of people handing over cash. Got to be better than the cut-throat world of yoghurt, I thought. Now everywhere I go there's…'

DEATH, to be precise. And plenty of it. In unpleasant variations. This isn't real life. This isn't even cheesemongering. It's opera. Where the music matters and where an opera house is being terrorised by a man in evening dress with a white mask, lurking in the shadows, occasionally killing people, and most worryingly, sending little notes, writing maniacal laughter with five exclamation marks. Opera can do that to a man. In such circumstances, life has obviously reached that desperate point where the wrong thing to do **has** to be the right thing to do…

'Cracking dialogue, compelling illogic and unchained whimsy…Pratchett has a subject and a style that is very much his own'
Sunday Times

'Entertaining and gloriously funny'
Chicago Tribune

9780552153232

FEET OF CLAY
Terry Pratchett

'The work of a prolific humorist at his best'
Observer

'Sorry?' said Carrot. 'If it's just a thing, how can it commit murder? A sword is a thing' – he drew out his own sword; it made an almost silken sound – 'and of course you can't blame a sword if someone thrust it at you, sir.'

FOR members of the City Watch, life consists of troubling times, linked together by periods of torpid inactivity. Now is one such troubling time. People are being murdered, but there's no trace of anything alive having been at the crime scene. Is there ever a circumstance in which you can blame the weapon not the murderer? Such philosophical questions are not the usual domain of the city's police, but they're going to have to start learning fast...

'Like most true originals, Pratchett defies categorization... Deliciously and amiably dotty... Driven by Swiftian logic and equally intellectually inventive'
The Times

'Fantastical, inventive and finally serious... It's enjoyable as crime fiction, but the real attraction is the laughter waiting to be uncovered on every page'
Observer

'An explosion of imaginative lunacy'
Daily Express

9780552153256

JINGO
Terry Pratchett

'Generous, amusing and the ideal boarding point for
those who have never visited Discworld'
Sunday Telegraph

*'Neighbours…hah. People'd live for ages side by side,
nodding at one another amicably on their way to work,
and then some trivial thing would happen and someone
would be having a garden fork removed from their ear.'*

THROUGHOUT history, there's always been a perfectly
good reason to start a war. Never more so if it is over
a 'strategic' piece of old rock in the middle of nowhere.
It is after all every citizen's right to bear arms to defend
what they consider to be their own. Even if it isn't. And
in such pressing circumstances, you really shouldn't let
small details like the absence of an army or indeed the
money to finance one get in the way of a righteous fight
with all the attendant benefits of out-and-out
nationalism…

'Pratchett's writing is a constant delight. No one mixes
the fantastical and the mundane to better comic effect
or offers sharper insights into the absurdities of
human endeavour'
Daily Mail

'One of those very rare writers who appeals to
everyone…He satisfies the need for fast-moving,
breathtaking plots with entirely satisfying endings, and
the equally primitive desire for an alternative world, full
of thrills but benign, into which one can step for pleasure
and enlivenment'
Daily Express

'Vintage Pratchett…Perennially funny…A sharp satire
on the futility of war'
Metro

9780552154161

Visit

www.**terrypratchett**.co.uk

to discover everything you need to know
about Terry Pratchett and his writing, plus all
manner of other things you may find interesting, such as
videos, competitions, character profiles and games.